THE END OF THE WORLD

The wall shivered and quaked, then fell toward her with a horrible, slow-motion grace. She flung her arms up, staring in terror at the mass of brick and burning debris hurtling straight down upon her.

"Lou. *Louise!*"

Not the Fire Man's voice. Whitaker's voice.

The door. Someone was at the door. She tried to get up but only managed to roll onto the floor. Black oblivion hovered at the edges of her mind. She could feel the coolness of the tile floor under her hands, see the door vibrate from the force of Whitaker's pounding. Scrabbling along the floor, she forced her hands up the door, her fingers around the knob. She felt the click of the lock, then a wash of cool air as Whitaker hauled her out, onto the grass.

Whitaker kept talking to her, his voice her only lifeline in a world that had suddenly turned into a whirling mess of lights and screaming sirens. Someone fitted something over her mouth and nose.

Whitaker held her hands. "It's okay, Lou. It's oxygen."

Darkness swooped toward her, roaring. With her mouth and nose covered, she could only wail silently as she fell into darkness.

NOWHERE TO RUN . . . NOWHERE TO HIDE . . . ZEBRA'S SUSPENSE WILL *GET* YOU — AND WILL MAKE YOU BEG FOR MORE!

WENDY HALEY

DEAD HEAT

ZEBRA BOOKS
KENSINGTON PUBLISHING CORP.

To my good friend Linda Brazie, who dared the fire walk and preceded me into freedom. Special thanks to Lynette Potter, George Grey, Dr. Games, and all the firefighters who risk their lives to keep us safe.

ZEBRA BOOKS are published by

Kensington Publishing Corp.
475 Park Avenue South
New York, NY 10016

Zebra and the Z logo Reg. U.S. Pat & TM Off.

First Printing: February, 1994

Printed in the United States of America

Dead Heat

Portsmouth, Virginia

He used a crowbar to pop the lock on the rear door of the old warehouse. The moment he stepped inside, he knew it was perfect.

Setting the gas can down on the floor beside him, he put his hands on his hips and surveyed his domain. A ribbon manufacturer had once occupied the building, and had left a ton of stuff behind when he went out of business. Boxes, spools, broken crates, fabric—and all combustible. It should go up nicely.

He piled a double armload of refuse against a tinder-dry inner wall. Excitement rode him hard as he opened the gas can and emptied it onto the pile. He dribbled a trail of gasoline after him as he walked toward the door.

Turning, he tossed the can back inside and lit a match. For a moment, just a single, precious moment, he felt like God.

"Let there be light," he said, tossing the match onto the still-wet trail of gasoline.

Blue-tipped flame raced along the path, hot and hungry, to meet the soaked refuse. Fire exploded upward and outward, consuming the gasoline vapors in one incandescent flash.

"Yeah," he breathed.

He watched the yellow and orange flames lick up the wall, watched the wood blacken and char. He felt heat against his skin, running through his veins, sinking deep, deep inside to turn his heart into a raging coal in his chest.

A small, scurrying shape dashed between his feet and outside, followed by another and another. Rats, he thought. They always managed to get out. And the cockroaches. Scuttling ahead of the smoke and flames to safety and another six million years of evolution.

He could have watched forever, but prudence drew him away, down the alley to the opposite street. Even in a neighborhood like this, someone was bound to report the fire sooner or later. He ducked into the lee of a storefront and waited for the action to start.

It took twenty minutes for the first fire truck to arrive. By that time the warehouse was fully ablaze, flames shooting out every window. The fire fighters moved with swift efficiency, hooking their hoses to the hydrants, playing the powerful streams of water into the inferno.

The fire roared back at them, dwarfing their voices, defying their puny efforts. He smiled. Tonight, fire reigned supreme, and nothing was going to keep it from consuming the meal it had been given.

The firemen knew; they'd given up trying to save the warehouse, and had turned their efforts to keeping the fire from spreading to adjacent buildings. A crowd had gathered, the same jabbering, pointing throng of humanity that collected at fires everywhere.

He watched them, understanding the avid look on their faces. Ruddy fire-glints shone in their eyes, the swift flash of their teeth when they spoke. It had been like this from the beginning; emotion tucked into the innermost recesses of the species, a memory of the first man who'd seen fire, touched it perhaps, and who had been fascinated by its beauty and awed by its power.

The warehouse roof groaned like a mortally wounded animal. Then, with exquisite slowness, it broke apart and fell in. Freed, the fire burst through in a red-orange tower, sending sparks and chunks of burning wood showering down all around. A collective moan, part fear, part admiration, went up from the crowd.

The figures of the firefighters were silhouetted against the lurid glare, their hats and boots making them look like capering devils dancing in the fires of hell. He wanted to join them, to scoop up handfuls of flame. To cast it away, all around, and set the world afire.

Sweat beaded on his forehead, ran in rivulets down his cheeks. The walls of the burning building hulked dark against the fire's glow, like blackened hands cupping molten lava. Smoke rose up in a tremendous, spark-filled column that seemed to fill the entire night sky. Maybe, he thought, blackening heaven itself. He drew in a breath that was almost a sob.

Lucifer had the right of it. The power to destroy was *much* headier than the power to create.

One

The shipyard dwarfed people.

Sight, smell and sound, it seemed impossibly huge, a world of behemoths. Men scurried among the hulking shapes of machinery, crawled like ants across scaffoldings that embraced the massive hulls of the ships. Human voices were lost in the roar of machinery. The fishy smell of the Elizabeth River lay heavy as oil on the air, and the breeze carried a dusting of grit from sandblasting.

Lou stood on the flying bridge of the dry dock, her feet spread for balance against the wind as she looked out over the yard. Wisps of terra-cotta hair, fugitives from beneath her hard hat, fanned in front of her face. She took a deep, appreciative breath, grit and all. For this was her world. Tough on men, even tougher on the women who dared enter it.

A seagull kited toward her, its wings tilting effortlessly to keep it in place before her.

"You're early," she told it. "Lunch doesn't start for ten minutes."

She could have sworn she saw disappointment in those beady black eyes. The bird hovered for a moment longer as though hoping she were wrong, then angled off toward the snack bar.

Movement below caught her eye. She looked down between her feet to see George Fagan, ship supervisor for the freighter *Santana,* waving up at her. "Come down" he mouthed.

With a sigh, she headed toward the stairway. Between her feet, she could see George following her path. Their shadows mingled and merged—foreshortened by the noonday sun.

A thin layer of grit blast coated the metal stairs of the wing wall. Her boots slithered a bit on the slippery stuff, and she made a mental note to have someone hose it down.

George waited for her at the bottom of the stairs, the wariness in his eyes belying his smile. Time and sun had turned the man into leather strung on wires, and etched a fan of creases around his washed-out blue eyes. A thinning mop of blond hair hung lank beneath his hard hat.

"I heard there's a problem with the repairs on my ship," he said without preamble.

"There's lamination in that weld in the forward hold."

"Shit! That's going to set us back days! Damn it, Lou, you know how important this job is to us."

"I got that memo, too," she said, and began quoting from memory. "In these days of military cuts, the only way our shipyard can expect to survive is to develop commercial markets. Thus, any job for Enterprise Shipping will be a priority." She spread her hands. "It's still a lousy weld, and it doesn't pass."

"It'll hold."

"Yes," she agreed, "When it's redone."

He swore under his breath. "This is killing me."

10

She spread her hands, knowing that despite the squawking, Fagan was as fanatical about quality as she. Those repairs would get done, and done right. "You wanted a heads-up, George, so I gave it to you."

"That's not a heads-up. That's a kick in the balls."

It was a cheap shot to a woman who'd been called ball-buster more often than she'd been called Ms. Malotti, and just for doing her job. She hadn't expected it of Fagan.

"Maybe so," she said. "But I'm not going to have that ship go down somewhere in the North Atlantic because I ignored a lousy weld."

"Hey, don't get mad. I didn't mean it the way it sounded. It's just that all this work is gettin' to everyone. First they lay off a fifth of our people, then they load the rest of us up with work. Guys are making mistakes they shouldn't be making, probably because their boss keeps hangin' over their shoulders crying, 'Hurry up, you've got three more welds to do before you go home, or else!'"

Truce offered.

"Tell me about it." Truce accepted. "We've been run ragged trying to keep up with it all, and no one's said boo to the brass about it."

"Miss your shop foreman?"

"You bet. Deveraux had the guts to squawk when things weren't right, and the stroke to make some of it stick."

"What's the new assistant foreman doing?"

"Getting the job done as best he can." She shrugged. "Steggans isn't a bad fella. He's just new, and not feeling comfortable enough to go upstairs and start beating on people's desks. But we're all hanging on by our fingernails and hoping Deveraux gets back early."

"Uh-uh, Malotti. Don't get your hopes up. My uncle

11

had the same back surgery Deveraux's getting, and he was out four months."

"That's not what Deveraux told me," Lou said, alarmed by the prospect of it. "He said six weeks."

Fagan shook his head, holding out four fingers for emphasis. "Wanna bet? Twenty says you won't see him until September."

Anxiety rolled her stomach into a hard knot. Harry Deveraux was the best quality assurance foreman she'd ever known, and the fairest. He always backed his inspectors. She didn't think she could count on Steggans.

Swift shadows darted across the asphalt floor of the dry dock, distorting as they passed over the rippled surface. Lou glanced at her watch. Twelve o'clock on the dot. The seagulls arrowed toward the snack bar in a voracious swoop that was mirrored on the ground by hungry shipyard employees.

"It never ceases to amaze," she said. "How do they know?"

Fagan squinted up at the gulls. "Who, the birds?" He snorted. "Let me buy you a sandwich to make up for the ball-busting remark."

"It's okay, George. But I don't have time for lunch; we're humping today."

She turned away. Fagan fell into step beside her, his feet as sure as her own amid the scatter of cables, wiring and tools.

"What do you think of Steggans?" he asked.

"I hardly know the man."

"Come on, Lou. He's been here nearly five months. You've got to have *some* opinion. From what I hear, he's not only a lousy manager, but he's a real prick to boot."

Lou raised her brows. "Where did you hear that?"

"Shit, Dave told me. He's had nothing but trouble

with the guy since he walked into the assistant QA foreman job courtesy of his cousin, the owner. That job should have been yours. You've busted your ass for years trying to move up."

Long ago, Lou had learned not to gossip with people who named names when telling where they'd gotten *their* gossip. So she merely shrugged and said, "I like what I do." It was the truth, if not all of it.

"Steggans isn't gonna be happy about the *Santana* not being able to sail out of here tomorrow. And that opinion's going to reflect the party line."

"That weld still doesn't pass," Lou said.

Fagan's expression mirrored her thought: *You're going to be hung out to dry.* To give him credit, he didn't seem to be happy about it.

She met his gaze levelly for a moment, then turned away. "Let me know when you've got the weld fixed so I can reinspect and get that ship out of here."

"Yes, ma'am."

Lou walked around the wet slip and headed toward the offices. As she rounded the corner of the pipe shop, she noticed three men standing near the wall. Two wolfed messy snack-bar hamburgers; the third was smoking, apparently oblivious to the fact that he happened to be standing three feet from the chain-link enclosure in which the welding tanks were stored.

"Of all the stupid . . ." Lou muttered. She veered toward him, expertly dodging a pair of forklifts.

She stopped in front of the smoker. He couldn't have been older than twenty, and looked achingly young and raw. *Younger than my son,* she thought, feeling a sudden weight of years settling on her shoulders. Wordlessly, she pointed to the tanks. The young man stared at her for a moment, smoke dribbling out his nostrils, then dropped the cigarette and ground it beneath his boot.

"There's a reason for that No Smoking sign over your head," she said.

"Sorry."

He wasn't, but he would be if she caught him doing it again. "There've been a couple of fires in trash barrels lately," she said. "You wouldn't know anything about it, would you?"

"No, ma'am."

"Do you know what would have happened to you if your foreman had caught you here?"

"Yes, ma'am."

"Find a better place to smoke next time, okay?"

She turned on her heel and walked away, feeling older than God. "Kids," she muttered. "It's a wonder they live long enough to get reduced rates on their car insurance."

She nodded as she passed a group of men standing outside the machine shop. A long, low wolf whistle followed her. It might have cheered her if she hadn't recognized it as an attempt to intimidate rather than to flirt. Who in his right mind would flirt with a full-figured, forty-three-year-old woman in overalls and steel-toed boots? She chose to ignore it.

"Hey, Lucretia!" one of the men called.

That stopped her. Some of the men called her Lucretia—as in Borgia. Quality Assurance inspectors were never welcome in the shipyard, female ones even less so. Fortunately, she had a good memory for voices; hear someone speak once or twice, and she could usually pick the voice out in a crowd.

She turned to face the men. "Hey, Dellwood."

"I . . ."

"It's okay, Dellwood. I *like* Lucretia Borgia. She had a real way with men, don't you think?"

The look on his face was downright comical. Lou smiled at him before continuing on her way. A moment later, she brushed the scene from her mind. After twenty-three years of working in a shipyard, it took a hell of a lot more than that to bother her.

Like her foreman being out on sick leave at the worst possible time.

Her anxiety soured into indigestion. She took the ever-present roll of antacids out of her pocket and popped two into her mouth. They tasted as chalky as her mood. Trouble hung in the air; she could feel it in the hair-lifting unease that crawled up her spine and settled at the back of her neck.

"Take it easy, Louise," she said. "Whatever happens, you're a survivor. Always have been."

Still, she found herself wishing again she'd somehow found the time to get a degree. But she'd been a single mother trying to be a good one, and hadn't wanted to spend her evenings away from Wade as well as her days. Besides, she'd loved the shipyard work, loved the challenge despite the unrelenting flak she'd had to endure. And that was before they'd even *thought* of harassment suits.

Her boots grated on the metal stairs as she jogged up the three flights to her office. This was her one concession to fitness, and a grudging one. Once upstairs, she made her way through the warren of partitioned cubicles to the section that housed Quality Assurance.

QA was empty but for Mason Bostwich, the environmental specialist, and the secretary, Sandy Harrison, who brought in a portable TV every day to watch her favorite soap at lunchtime.

Noting the half-mast position of Mason's eyelids, Lou called, "What's the matter, Mace? All that toxic waste get to you at last?"

"It was the barbecue sandwich," he groaned.

"That's what I said. Toxic waste."

His eyelids lifted marginally. "Go away."

"All right, I'll take pity on you." Smiling, she tossed the roll of antacids into his lap. "Don't eat them all at once. With the chemical composition of that barbecue, I'm afraid you might explode."

He muttered something that she prudently ignored. As she moved past Sandy's desk, she noticed that the TV was tuned to the news instead of the usual program.

"Hey, what's going on?" Lou asked. "Must be something really important to get you to switch from Larry and Lorna."

"It's Linc and Paula," Sandy corrected without looking up from the screen. "Look at this, Lou. There's been another fire set by that same guy."

"Another one?" Lou moved so that she could see the screen. "He's been busy lately, hasn't he?"

"Yeah."

Lou leaned forward to peer more closely at the TV as the camera panned the arson site. The arsonist had been thorough; only a shell of blackened brick remained. Scorch marks on nearby buildings showed how close the fire had come to taking out the whole block.

The reporter stepped into view, her smooth blond good looks a striking contrast to the destruction behind her. "Authorities believe the person who set this fire is responsible for several other arsons in the area. The question is: Where and when will he strike again. He's struck in Virginia Beach, Norfolk, and now at an

16

empty Portsmouth building that once housed the Premier Ribbon Factory."

"Hey, that's only a mile or so from here," Lou said.

"They're calling him the Wednesday Night Firebug," Sandy said. "There've been five fires in the past two months, and every one of them on a Wednesday."

"Makes you wonder, doesn't it?" Lou pulled her hardhat off and ran her fingers through her hair. "Maybe Wednesday is his wife's night out with the girls, and he just doesn't have anything else to do."

"I wish you wouldn't joke about it," Sandy said. "He's got to be really sick. And one of these days, he might pick a place that isn't empty. Then someone's going to get killed. If you ask me, they . . . Damn that phone!" Sandy reached to answer it, her tone smoothing as she said, "Quality Assurance. Yes, sir. Yes, I will."

Lou started to move away, but stopped when the other woman held up her hand.

"That was Mr. Steggans," Sandy said. "And he wants to see you as soon as you get in."

"Damn," Lou muttered.

"What'd you do?"

Lou pulled her hardhat off and tossed it over the left-hand partition with a practiced movement. It landed with a clunk that told her she'd hit her target. "Walked slower than a telephone call, apparently," she said.

"Huh?"

"Never mind." With a sigh, Lou turned away.

She found Steggans sitting in his office, flipping through a computer printout. It wasn't a spacious room—those went to production superintendents and even higher-ups, but it had a window, and a door that could be closed against the hoi polloi.

Lou paused in the doorway. "You wanted to see me?"

He looked up. His expression was shuttered, his eyes bland. "Come on in, Lou. Have a seat." He pointed to the pair of black plastic chairs in front of his desk.

Lou slid into the nearest chair. She met his gaze, arranging her arguments in her mind as she prepared for battle.

"Do you want a Coke?" he asked.

The offer surprised her. "Sure. Thanks."

He opened a nearby cabinet, extracted two cans of Coke, and held one out to her.

Lou accepted it. As she drank, she looked him over, trying to gauge his mood. Steggans was a big man, just starting to go to fat. He had a blunt sort of face, snub-nosed and square-jawed, and his ears stuck out just enough to be noticeable. He'd been in the Navy for twenty years before coming to Carmichael's, but she couldn't remember his ship or rank. He'd walked into his position due to the fact that his second cousin was the new owner of the shipyard. Lou tried assess his talents objectively. He wasn't a stupid man, or even a slow learner; in a couple of years, he might even be a good assistant shop foreman. Right now, however, he was a liability.

As always, Lou chose to meet the situation head-on. "You heard about the *Santana,*" she said.

"Bad news travels fast, yes. But that's not what this meeting is about. After all, a bad weld is a bad weld. And bad welds get fixed, right?"

Lou stared at him speculatively. It was a statement worthy of Harry Deveraux. So worthy, in fact, that it had to have been taken directly from the Deveraux lexicon. She set her Coke down and waited for the other shoe to fall.

Steggans propped his clasped hands on the desk. "The *Santana* weld was done on third shift. In fact, we've had other mistakes made on that shift, enough to convince me that we need to have a second QA Inspector to keep an handle on things."

So it wasn't going to be confrontation, just a subtle use—abuse—of power. "And that's me."

He nodded.

"I thought it was customary to put the person with the least seniority in the lousy jobs," she said.

"You're our most experienced QA inspector, Lou. I need you on that shift."

"I'm a morning person."

"Not any more."

Lou opened her mouth to protest, then closed it again. Without Deveraux's backing, this fight couldn't be won. She had a son in college, a mortgage, and twenty years of sweat invested in this job. So she swallowed what she wanted to say. It was a big, uncomfortable lump, but she got it down.

She pushed her chair back and rose to her feet. "When do I start?"

"Monday." His eyes looked like cracked blue glass, flat and hard. "Think of it as a three-day weekend."

Struggling even harder with her temper, Lou turned and walked out. It took all her wavering self-control to keep from slamming the door behind her.

It was going to be a long, hard summer.

Two

"You should've quit," Fagan told her.

Lou suppressed a yawn. Ten days of late shift had wrung her out, squeezed her dry, and shredded what was left. She'd been skeptical about the notion of bio-rhythms, but if they existed, hers were definitely shot. But she had enough energy to appreciate the view across the river, where the lights of the Norfolk skyline looked like diamond dust sprinkled across the indigo velvet of a cloudy night sky.

"Quit?" she echoed, reluctantly turning away from the view. "And do what, starve?"

"Eating is nice," Fagan said. "But sometimes I think it'd be easier to work at 7-Eleven."

"Not with a kid in college."

"Tell me about it. I've got two coming up through high school, and my ex is already asking for college money. But hey, you could take the traditional path for a change; find yourself a rich husband, kick back and relax for a while, and let someone else do the worry-ing. And the paying."

For a moment, Lou wondered if he might be pushing her button. But no, she'd never told anyone about her failed marriage, the husband who'd walked out on her and Wade, left the country and left her penniless.

"I'll do it on my own, thanks," she said.

"Suit yourself. Maybe *I'll* find a rich husband."

She couldn't help but laugh. "You'd better, with two in college at the same time."

"Yeah."

"How did the reinspect go on the *Santana?*"

"She went out today, free and clear."

Lou frowned; she always liked to make her own reinspections. "I thought there were two, three days of work left on her."

"Nope. I pulled a couple of guys off another job. It put me behind on those, but at least we got the priority work done." He pushed his hardhat up and scratched his forehead. "I wish we could take a breather, but we've got two more Enterprise ships coming in tomorrow."

"At least we'll all have jobs a while longer."

"It's *too* much work. I've been here twelve hours straight, and it's not going to get better. With the big push to kiss Enterprise's ass, every damn thing is a priority."

She smiled. "This, too, shall pass."

"That what your crystal ball says?"

"No," she said with less humor than she expected. "Just twenty years of outwaiting and outliving this stuff. Hey, I even outlived old Carmichael himself."

"You and Steggans getting along okay?"

"We don't have any problems," she said. "One thing you can say for the guy—he's working as hard as the rest of us."

"I guess you're right."

It seemed a grudging sort of admission, but Lou had learned how closed the ranks of the shipyard could be.

She'd never breached it completely, never would. Steggans would have an easier time of it, being burdened by the single handicap of being management.

"I've got to go," Lou said. "Time to get back to work."

She waved once over her shoulder, then walked along the finger pier toward the main shipyard. Puddles dotted the asphalt surface, left behind by the afternoon's rain.

A couple of sailors walked toward her, headed for the living barge moored beside their ship. Slick plastic visitors' passes glistened on the breast of their uniforms. They'd been out on the town, judging from the smell of beer and stale cigarette smoke that wafted ahead of them. Lou sighed; ten years ago, the Navy hadn't looked quite so young.

"Hi," one of them said, looking her over.

"I'm old enough to be your mother," she said.

"My mother don't look anything like *you*. How about partying with us awhile?"

Lou kept walking. "Go sleep it off, sailor."

His reply got lost in the shipyard noise, probably to his good fortune. She couldn't help but smile. God, these boys were raw! And they looked younger every year.

She swung left, past one of the Quonset huts that served as storage sheds. Material had overflowed the capacity of the building; in true Carmichael fashion, the excess had been enclosed in a chain-link fence beside the structure. Empty fifty-gallon drums, awaiting disposal, lined the far wall of the fence.

A breeze wafted into her face, bringing the smell of acetone. Lou stiffened. The shipyard was incredibly noisy and smelly, but she knew every sound, every odor in the place. This didn't belong, not here. She veered toward the Quonset to investigate.

A sliver of blackness at the front caught her eye, and she drew in a sharp, startled breath when she realized that the door was slightly ajar. Her skin prickled at the wrongness of it; the Quonsets were kept locked except when someone had to get something in or out of it.

"What's going on here?" she muttered.

Something moved furtively in the wedge of shadow cast by the stacked drums. Lou stopped, her heart kicking into trip-hammer high gear. She looked around for help, but this wasn't a highly traveled area of the shipyard, even when the full day crew was working.

There might be a couple of hundred people a short distance away, but here, in this shuttered little corner, she was alone with whoever hid in that wedge of darkness. She could feel, actually feel, the lurker watching her.

"Who's there?" she called.

Fear crawled through her like a fat black spider, winding its frigid arms around her chest. She could make out a vague shape against the side of the building, a man-shaped piece of blackness just a shade denser than the shadows around it. Menace hung in the air like hot acid, and for a moment she could taste the sourness of her own terror. The thought brought her chin up defiantly; fear had never ruled Lou Malotti.

"You're not supposed to be in there, whoever you are," she called. "Come on out."

Then she saw the smoke. Black and oily, it dribbled out from the doorway of the Quonset hut and rose into the sky.

"Good God!" she whispered.

Her terror submerged in an adrenaline rush, she pelted toward the nearest cluster of shops. The rigger shop was dark—no one working tonight. She slammed her palm against the closed door in frustration, then headed for the pipe shop. Relief flooded through her when she heard the hiss of acetylene torches.

She raced inside, automatically dodging the sparks that skittered across the concrete floor like angry fireflies. The men glanced up at her, torch-glare reflecting in the eyepieces of their safety glasses.

"Call Fire Control!" she yelled. "There's a fire in storage shed five!"

A clatter of movement answered her. Lou grabbed the nearest fire extinguisher and slammed back outside. Shouts and running footsteps pursued her back to the Quonset.

Smoke poured out of the doorway, chugging upward as though spewed from an engine. She took a deep breath of air, drawing the thick taste of heat into her lungs, and ran closer. Fire licked upward along the metal walls of the Quonset, and she caught a glimpse of something pale lying just inside the door. She snatched a pile of rags from a nearby trash barrel.

"What are you doing?" The voice was deep and male, and belonged to six-foot-five, three-hundred-and-twenty-pound Tyrene Bell.

"Trying to close the door," she gasped. "If we can cut off the air—"

"Gimme those."

She obeyed, moving up behind him with the extinguisher. Smoke bellied out of the doorway as though in counterattack. Then something popped with the sound of tearing metal. Tyrene reeled backward as a searing orange-red sheet of flame shot outward.

"Look out, Malotti!" he shouted.

Lou raised the extinguisher and sent a stream of chemical foam into the flames. More men arrived, with more extinguishers. They beat the fire back somewhat, but the smoke only got worse, enveloping them in a noxious, choking cloud.

"Christ, what's in there?" someone shouted.

Lou drew in a breath, coughed it out. The smoke seemed to settle on her like a hot black hand, constricting her throat and bringing tears streaming down her cheeks.

"Get back!" someone yelled.

Tyrene came looming out of the smoke. Looping one huge, hard arm around Lou's waist as he ran past, he scooped her up and bore her backward. She got a glimpse of a billow of incandescent flame blasting toward her before the soul-shaking *whomph* of an explosion knocked Tyrene off his feet.

She landed hard. For a moment the world reeled around her, filled with heat and flame and the echoes of the blast echoing painfully in her ears. Then someone hauled her up and carried her to a cooler spot. She sat down the moment he let go of her, not noticing the water that soaked the seat of her jeans.

"Here," a man said, holding a mask over her face.

She breathed in greedily, sucking cool oxygen deep into her burning lungs. Her vision started to clear, and she saw her rescuers, wearing the bright yellow hardhat of Fire Control, bending over her.

"You okay?" he asked.

Unable to speak yet, Lou gave him a thumbs-up.

"Stay here," he said.

He trotted back into the roiling smoke. A moment later he came back, supporting a limping Tyrene. He eased the welder down beside Lou, then returned to the fire.

Lou offered her mask to the big man. He took it, draining a couple of huge lungfuls in before handing it back.

"You okay?" she asked.

"Yeah. Scared enough to turn white, but okay."

She started to laugh, but it turned into a cough. "Now I know how a basketball feels. Man, did I hit hard."

"I know. You landed on me."

"I just kept you from getting toasted," she said, holding up a lock of frizzled hair. "By the way . . . thanks, Tyrene."

"Hey, I was just copping a last feel before heading for the Pearly Gates."

The joke fell flat. Maybe tomorrow Lou could laugh at the notion of dying. Not tonight. It had been too close; had they been a few feet nearer to the building, they'd have caught that blast head-on. She started to shiver with reaction. To hide it, she drew her knees up and hugged them. The fire was reflected in every puddle of water, a beaded necklace of flickering yellow jewels against the dark asphalt. She didn't find it beautiful.

"Looks like they're getting a handle on it," Tyrene said. "Man, I could really use a beer!"

With a groan, Lou struggled to her feet. "I'll buy you one later."

She walked toward the burning Quonset, ignoring Tyrene's protests. Stopping the first Fire Control man she saw, she asked, "Who's boss tonight?"

"Boris," the man said. Turning, he pointed toward a shadowy form half-hidden in the smoke. "Over there."

The foreman turned as Lou approached, his blocky form silhouetted against the light. Boris was Herman

Boecshten, who'd immigrated from Hamburg twelve years ago. The portly German proved himself to be smart, fair and as tough as rawhide. By the look on his face, he didn't like this fire one bit.

He shouldn't, she thought. And she was about to give him a reality that was worse than what he was probably imagining.

"I've got to talk to you," she called.

The foreman motioned her closer. "You found this fire?"

"Yeah. It was set, Herman. I saw someone sneaking around the back of the hut."

"Who?"

"I couldn't see his face."

The lines of his broad face turned downward, and for a moment his brown eyes seemed bleached of color. "There's an ambulance coming. You go get checked out, then come back here. The arson investigator will want to talk to you."

"I can help—"

"Take Tyrene with you. Go."

Lou would have bucked Arnold Schwarzenegger sooner than she'd have defied the fat little German just now. Meekly, she walked back to the spot where Tyrene waited.

"We've been kicked out," she said.

"Praise Jesus, and watch my dust as I go."

She held out her hand to help him to his feet. "Don't get excited. We've got to come back—"

"Damn. It's been a hell of a long night, Lucretia baby."

"—but not until after we get that beer."

He grinned, hitching up his pants with his thumbs. "The Lord does work in mysterious ways!"

And so do men, she thought. So do men.

27

Lou stepped out of the elevator into chaos. The office swarmed with people, most of whom were talking. She recognized the production superintendent, two vice-presidents, the managers of both Safety and Security, and Dwayne Steggans.

She sighed, wishing she could step right back into the elevator and leave. But Steggans had already spotted her, and was striding toward her.

"Where have you been?" he demanded. "You left the hospital an hour ago."

"I stopped to get something to eat."

"Damn it, the arson investigator has been waiting to see you!"

She ran her hand through her hair, feeling the roughness of the burned ends against her palms. "Look, after almost being blown up tonight, I think I deserved time to eat a hamburger and fries."

"Sorry, Lou," he said. "You're right. I'm just a little upset by what happened—we all are." He pointed toward his office. "Lieutenant Whitaker's in there."

Lou tapped softly at the office door. When there was no response, she opened the door a crack and peered in. Whitaker had tipped the chair back so that its back rested against the wall, propped his feet on the desk, and was in the process of inspecting the insides of his eyelids. A gentle snore rose in the quiet room.

"Ahem," she said.

Without opening his eyes, he said, "Miss Malotti? Come on in. I'm Whitaker."

"Don't mind me," she said, suppressing a grin. "I respect a man who can snooze in the middle of an arson investigation."

That got his eyes open. They were battleship grey,

matching the hair at his temples. She liked his face; square, almost too rugged, with a bit of I've-been-around-and-seen-some-hard-times cynicism for seasoning. Dimples on each side of his mouth had become creases, and lines radiated from the outer corners of his eyes. He wasn't wearing a suit, as she expected, but a pair of jeans and a Redskins sweatshirt.

He waved her to a chair in front of him. "I assume you checked out all right?"

"Minor smoke inhalation, that's all. I feel pretty lucky, all in all."

"You were. Lucky, that is," he added. "I understand you were first on the scene."

"Other than the arsonist, yes."

"Why do you think someone set the fire?"

"Because he was hiding in the fenced-in area behind the Quonset."

"That's on the opposite end from the door, right?"

"Right."

"Do you know what was stored in that building?" he asked.

"Are you asking if I know what exploded?"

He smiled. "Yes."

"I don't have the vaguest idea. All fuels and flammables are taken directly to Hazardous Waste. Everything's logged; you can get with our environmental specialist about it tomorrow."

"Mason Bostwich," he said.

Lou stared at him, feeling stirrings of exasperation. "You're obviously way ahead of me on this."

"I've had a couple of hours to do my homework."

"You were snoring."

"It's a ploy I use to throw people off track." He rose to his feet and held out his hand to her. "Come on.

Walk out to the shed with me and show me where everything was."

Lou tipped her head back to look at him, a little surprised by his size. He wasn't quite as tall or wide as Tyrene, but then, nobody was. Still, he topped her five-eight by a good six inches, and every inch of it looked solid. Even if she hadn't been sore from head to toe, she would have taken his hand and let him lift her to her feet. Independent she might be, but foolish, no.

He led her toward the elevator, politely but firmly refusing to allow the Carmichael brass to accompany them. Lou grabbed a pair of hardhats from a table near the door and tossed one to Whitaker.

"Are you feeling okay?" Whitaker asked as the elevator started down.

Lou stretched, wincing at the resulting twinges. "Other than feeling like a secondhand punching bag, I'm fine."

"You ought to go home after we're done. Take a hot bath—"

"You've got to be kidding. I'm already hours into my shift and getting behinder every minute."

He looked her over appraisingly. "Are you that indispensable?"

"No. That's why I need to get some work done."

Lou looked away, feeling as though he could see straight through her while keeping everything of himself hidden behind those smoky grey eyes. She fell silent, withdrawing.

Once outside, they headed toward the storage shed. Lou's first glimpse of the site astonished her. Blackened, dented drums littered the ground amid the twisted remnants of equipment that had been in the shed. The only thing left of the Quonset was the concrete ramp and a still-smoking pile of wood and metal fragments.

"Damn," Lou murmured.

"Where was the person hiding?"

She pointed to the bent poles that marked the boundary of the fenced area. "He was there, against the side of the building."

"Did you recognize him?"

"Couldn't. He was in the shadows."

"How do you know it was a man, then?"

Lou stared at him in surprise, then cast back into her memory. Her picture of that moment was clear and precise, graven into her mind with fear. That lurking shape, blacker than the darkness that concealed it . . . No, she couldn't have been mistaken.

"It was the way he held himself, the way he moved. The slope of the shoulders, the angle of the head was masculine." She met Whitaker's cool grey gaze levelly. "At no point did I think of him as anything but male."

He nodded, but his face didn't show whether he accepted it or not. "Then you walked around to the front—"

"No. I smelled smoke, then went around. And I ran, not walked. The door was slightly ajar, and I could see smoke coming out."

"You didn't see or hear this man coming out of the enclosure during this time?"

She shook her head. "I headed for the shops to get the alarm out. Getting the fire put out was my main concern, not him. He had plenty of time to get away."

"Had the lock been forced?"

Something nagged at the edges of her mind, but slipped away when she tried to pin it down. "I . . . don't know."

"Is something bothering you?"

31

She glanced up at him, grateful for his perception. "It's just that I have a very good visual memory, and I don't remember the door being damaged in any way. But I may have been so focused on the smoke that I just didn't *see* the damage."

"How would you go about getting a key to the shed?"

Lou crossed her arms over her chest. "I can't believe you haven't checked that out already."

"Okay, I have." He grinned. "Just being thorough."

"In case you're wondering about me, if I were going to burn the place down, I'd have done a better job of it."

"That, I believe." He conjured a business card from somewhere and handed it to her. "If you think of anything else, anything at all, give me a call."

She slipped the card into her back pocket. "Sure."

He walked away from her, leaving shiny footprints in the soot.

Suddenly feeling very alone, Lou looked out over the blasted remains of the Quonset. She'd come closer to dying than she liked to think about. Too close. The memory of it brought her gaze up to scan the buildings around her, to probe the depths of every shadow large enough to hide a man.

"Easy, girl, don't spook yourself," she muttered. "It's over. Life is good. And you've got a hell of a lot to do tonight."

Tilting her hardhat at a jaunty angle, she went to work.

Three

"Jeez, Louise!"

Lou, juggling two bags of groceries as well as her purse, keys and briefcase, nearly dropped the whole load in surprise. "Where the hell did you learn that?" she demanded, closing the door behind her with her foot.

Green flashed as her two Amazonian parrots jockeyed for position on the perch. The cage took up nearly the whole dining room; six feet tall, with a four-foot circumference, it was made of steel bars, probably the only thing an Amazonian couldn't gnaw through. She'd built it herself nine years ago when Elihu, the male, had come into her life.

"Jeez, Louise!" Elihu cried again.

"Wade, you sneaky . . ." Almost losing her hold on the groceries, Lou dropped the purse and briefcase to compensate. "I'm going to strangle that son of mine! He's here one weekend a month, eats my food, monopolizes my washing machine, and then has the nerve to corrupt my birds."

"Ooooooh, baby. Ooooooh, BABY!"

"I'm going to kill him," Lou muttered.

Elihu and Emily skated from one end of the perch

to the other, cackling a weird, parrot imitation of Wade's boisterous laughter. *"Haw, haw, haw! Haw, haw, haw!"*

"Ah, shut up." Lou couldn't help but laugh with them, stupid as it was. With a sigh that felt as though it came from the soles of her feet, she dropped into the nearest chair, groceries and all. "God, I'm beat!"

Her bruises had begun to turn colors in the four days since the fire, but her abused muscles still protested every movement—which meant she didn't move more than what was absolutely necessary. Housework didn't fall into that category; her usually immaculate town house was a wreck. Books and magazines lay in piles on the coffee table, video tapes overflowed their storage cases, and a layer of dust coated every other horizontal surface. She didn't want to *think* about laundry.

"You two don't help much," she said, glaring at the parrots. "Why don't you try sleeping during the day for a while? A dead woman couldn't sleep through the racket you make."

Silence.

"And don't try to make me feel guilty for not playing with you all day. There are two of you. An arrangement made, if you recall, so that you could keep each other company."

Continued silence.

"And," she began to wither under the double black-beady stare, "I leave the TV on so you can watch 'Days of Our Lives.' "

A spreading cold from the grocery bags got her out of her chair and she headed for the kitchen. As she put the frozen food away, she heard Elihu crooning to Emily.

"You ain't nothin' but a hound dog . . ."

She shook her head. Wade had taught the parrots to

34

sing—sort of. Elvis and Sinatra. She'd tried to raise her son to be a normal human being, but something had definitely gone askew.

"You haven't lived," she muttered, "until you've heard a parrot singing 'I Did It My Way.' "

"Ooooh, BABY!"

Yesterday's newspaper still lay unopened on the kitchen table. Whistling under her breath, she slipped the rubber band off and spread it open.

WEDNESDAY NIGHT FIREBUG STRIKES AGAIN! the headline screamed.

Lou sat down to read the cover story. The arsonist had struck in Western Branch this time, completely destroying a house that was under construction. Icy fingers of unease danced up her spine as she stared at the picture that accompanied the headline; that house was only a couple of miles from her own.

The Wednesday Night Firebug. The headline gave him substance somehow; made him real, put a date and time to his destruction. And after the fire in the shipyard, she no longer had a that's-too-bad-but-it's-not-really-my-problem illusion of safety.

Something still nagged at her, something she should be remembering about that night. But the more she tried to find it, the more elusive it became.

"Apple! Apple!" Emily shrieked.

A welcome interruption. Lou pushed the newspaper aside, glad to do her parrot's bidding.

"I'm out of apples," she called, peering into the crisper drawer. "How about a pear?"

"You ain't—"

"Nothin' but a hound dog," she finished for Elihu. "Pear it is."

She chopped the pear into beak-sized pieces, piling them on a blue plastic plate that bore the scars of pre-

35

vious feedings. As she carried the fruit into the living room, she could hear the rasp of the parrots' talons as they sidled along their perch.

"Do you want to come out for a while?" Lou asked.

"Ooooh, baby!" Elihu leaned forward and spread his wings.

"I'll take that as a yes," Lou said. "You know, if you weren't such slobs, you'd get to spend more time out of the cage."

Balancing the plate in one hand, she opened the cage with the other. Emily hurtled toward the opening, seeming to fill the cage with a swirling green blur. Startled, Lou stepped back.

Elihu came after her, wings churning, powerful beak agape. Reflexively, Lou swung the plate up between them. The parrot bit down on the top rim of it, taking a chunk out of the thick plastic.

"Hey!" Lou flung the plate away.

The parrot swung around in an impossibly tight mid-air turn and swooped at her again. Lou couldn't believe this was happening. But that was her mind; her body reacted instantly to the threat, taking her into a knee-burning slide across the carpet to avoid the bird's attack.

"Elihu!" she shouted. "Stop it!"

Emily shrieked somewhere at Lou's back, and a cold tide of terror rushed through her. She couldn't protect herself against them both. She scrambled up. Her left foot slid across the slick surface of the plate, sending her stumbling against the cage. Emily, still inside, beat her wings against the bars in a frenzy of fear.

Lou reeled away from the cage as Elihu attacked her again. Time seemed suspended, a surrealistic moment in which she could almost count each feather in his outspread wings, almost see her reflection in the black beads of his eyes as he came at her. She flung up her arm to protect her face. Pain lanced up her arm as his talons raked bloody grooves in her skin from elbow to wrist.

Lou flung herself forward, toward the open door of the kitchen. The moment her shoes hit the tile floor, she whirled and slammed the door closed.

Panting, she stood with her cheek pressed to the cool, hard wood. It wouldn't have surprised her to hear Elihu chopping at the other side; reality had been replaced by a Hitchcockian nightmare. But silence had fallen in the other room, eerie after the frenzy a moment ago.

Lou closed her eyes, struggling to bring her breathing under control. Her heart beat so hard it felt as though it were about to come right through her ribcage.

Then, absurdly, she heard Elihu crooning. Sinatra this time. Lou turned and leaned her back against the door, then slowly sank to a sitting position.

"Ooooh, baby!"

She drew her knees up and rested her forehead on them. Hot tears leaked out of the corners of her eyes, tears she hadn't shed after coming so near to dying a few nights ago. But this was different. This *hurt*. Elihu had been her friend for nine years. She loved him, loved his quirky bird habits, even loved the way he sang those stupid songs Wade taught him.

And now . . . And now she was going to have to do something about him. What if her mother had come in, frail as she was, and had been attacked?

She reached up and pulled the phone off the counter. With shaking fingers, she dialed the vet's number.

"Dr. Seagrave's office," the receptionist intoned.

"This is Lou Malotti. I need to speak to him."

"I'm sorry, but he's with—"

"I need to talk to him *now!*"

Apparently there was enough hysteria in her voice to overcome the receptionist's protective instincts, for a moment later the vet came on the line.

"Seagrave here. What's the matter, Ms. Malotti?"

"Elihu attacked me," she said, trying not to babble. "I opened the cage to give them some fruit, and he just flew out at me. It was right out of *The Birds.*"

"Are you all right?"

She took a deep breath. "I think so. Just scratched a little, and shook up a lot. What's wrong with him? Should I call Animal Control?"

"Ah . . . I don't think he's dangerous, Ms. Malotti. What I think you experienced was aggression typical of breeding behavior. Usually it's confined to the cage, but if you're in the habit of letting him out, and he happened to be unusually excited—"

"Breeding behavior?" she yelped.

"This is the time of year for it. And Emily is now sexually mature, you know."

"Oh." Lou felt the tension run out of her shoulders. "I was between him and the cage during most of the attack."

"There you go."

The world fell back into place. Excitement flooded through her with the realization of what Elihu's behavior really meant. "I'm going to have babies," she said.

Seagrave chuckled. "Well, I'm not sure I would say it quite that way, but—"

"How long?"

"Gestation is twenty-four days. If you'll drop by the office, I'll see that you get some literature on breeding so you'll know what to expect. You'll have to provide them with nesting material, and make sure the house stays warm—"

"Before we go that far, Doctor, how about telling me how I'm supposed to deal with a parrot who's out of his cage and feeling territorial about *my* dining room?"

"You'll just have to limit his territory. In other words, put him back in his cage and keep him there. You could wait until dark, when his activity level decreases."

"No can do," she said. "He's between me and the bathroom. I guess I'll just have to figure something out."

"I'm sure you'll do fine. Call if you have any trouble, of course. Now if you'll excuse me, I'm wanted in surgery . . ."

"Okay," she said. "Thanks."

She sat for a moment after hanging up, assessing the throb in her arm. The scratches were shallow but long, and hurt like hell. Good. Nothing like a bit of pain to stiffen a person's backbone.

With a sigh, she levered herself to her feet. She took a cookie sheet out of the cabinet and held it before her like a shield as she pushed the kitchen door open a crack.

Elihu perched on top of the cage, watching his ladylove through the bars as she ate a piece of pear he'd apparently brought to her. Conquering hero, Lou thought.

Lou edged into the room, keeping the cookie sheet ready. She wasn't going to hurt him, but she'd damn well knock him silly if he tried attacking her again. He tracked her movements, his neck feathers ruffling.

"Don't mess with me, Elihu," she said. "Remember, you've already done your bit for continuation of the species."

Obviously unimpressed by her bravado, he swiveled

his head to look at her with the opposite eye. But at least he stayed put. Lou edged slowly toward the cage, swiveling to keep her face—and the cookie sheet—to the parrots.

"Now, take it easy," she murmured. "Don't get excited."

Elihu spread his wings. The sunlight lay heavy across the cage, gilding the brass bars and turning the bird's plumage into a glory of bright color. He'd never looked more beautiful.

The doorbell rang, startling Elihu into flight. After a moment, he settled onto the TV. Oh, God, Lou thought. There goes the living room.

Lou saw the silhouette of a man in the long rectangle of frosted glass beside the door. "Go away," she hissed through clenched teeth. "Go *away!*"

The doorbell rang again. Elihu launched back into flight, finally coming to rest on the back of the chair nearest the door. Lou sighed; there was no way she could even get to the door, let alone open it.

"Who is it?" Lou shouted.

"Whitaker. From Arson, remember? I'd like to talk to you a moment, if you don't mind."

She blinked in surprise. "I don't mind, but could you come around back? My parrot's out. I'm afraid if I open this door, he'll get outside."

"On my way."

"There's a gate at the back fence. It's unlocked."

Lou eased her way back into the kitchen under Elihu's vigilant gaze, opening the door just as Whitaker reached the back porch. He stepped inside and closed the door behind him, moving quickly and silently for such a big man. He wore business attire—sort of— navy dress pants, a blue and maroon striped tie, and a short-sleeved shirt that showed big, hairy forearms.

40

Lou smoothed her hair, deciding that she liked big, hairy forearms. "Sorry about that," she said. "I couldn't—"

"What happened to your arm?" he asked.

"My parrot did it."

His eyebrows went up. "You have a killer parrot?"

"Breeding parrot. They get aggressive."

"Ah. That explains the cookie sheet."

Laughter turned his eyes smoky and deepened the dimple-creases bracketing his mouth. Lou's internal temperature went up several degrees.

"Want some help?" he asked.

She shook her head. "Parrots don't like strangers at the best of times."

"What difference does it make? Right now, he doesn't seem to like you, either."

"Okay," she said, capitulating. "Get yourself a cookie sheet."

"How about a net?"

"Don't have one."

"A sheet, tablecloth—"

She spread her hands. "Upstairs in the linen closet."

"There's one hanging on your neighbor's line. I'll get it."

Lou thought about protesting, then shrugged. Desperate times required desperate measures. She led the way back into the living room, unconscionably glad for the large male presence behind her. Elihu hissed at them from his perch atop the cage.

"I thought you said he was a parrot," Whitaker whispered in Lou's ear.

"He is."

"Sounds like a snake to me."

"My son has been teaching him things."

"Ah." Whitaker spread the sheet between his hands.

41

"Okay, walk toward him. I'll trap him when he goes for you."

Slowly, she turned her head to look at him over her shoulder. "My hero."

"I'll trade, but remember, the guy who grabs him has to get him back in the cage."

"Rationalization," she said.

"Logic."

"Humph. Well, here goes." She walked forward, cookie sheet at the ready. "Careful of that beak," she said. "It can bend a doorknob—or take your finger right off."

Elihu spread his wings in warning as Lou moved closer to the cage. She spoke to him, babbled nonsense, really, more concerned with keeping her tone soothing than what she was saying. His head swiveled from side to side, tracking her with first one eye then the other.

She caught a flash of blue out of the corner of her eye as Whitaker moved. Before either she or Elihu could react, the lieutenant scooped the parrot up into the folds of the sheet and popped him back into the cage.

Whitaker closed and latched the barred door before Elihu could recover enough to be indignant. But once he got going, he set up a howl of shrieks, hissings and *Jeez Louises* that sounded as though it came from twenty parrots. After a moment, though, he settled down and snuggled up to Emily.

Lou turned to Whitaker, who'd folded the sheet into a neat square. "You work fast, I'll give you that."

"Reflexes. I've got hamsters."

"Hamsters?" she echoed, bewildered.

"And a dog. *And* four kids."

"Four!"

42

"Want to meet them?"

Lou searched frantically for anchorage in the chaos of the conversation. "Huh?"

"I'll take that as a yes. This weekend?"

"You *do* work fast."

"I'm a man of action."

Beginning to get a handle on things, Lou said, "Since you've invited me to meet your kids, I'm assuming you're not married."

"Widowed. You're divorced."

"How did you know?"

"I'm a good interrogator. Your secretary told me everything except your shoe size. By the way, my first name's Bob. My friends, though, call me Whitaker."

"What does everybody else call you, then?" she countered.

"Mr. Whitaker. Or Lieutenant."

Lou wavered between exasperation and beguilement. Whichever, this was too good to pass up. "I'm free Sunday."

"Good." He glanced at his watch. "Do you have time to answer a few questions?"

"Business or personal?"

"Business, I'm afraid."

"How about a cup of coffee?"

He gave her a smile that would have turned the head of a stronger woman than she. "I'd love one. But first, let me do something with that arm."

He took care of her wounds with the expertise and the ruthlessness of long practice. Afterward, he made her sit down while he made the coffee. Lou was impressed.

She stirred sugar into her coffee, then took a sip. Not bad. Strong enough to make the taste buds stand at attention, but not bad. "Do you think that Wednes-

43

day Night Firebug guy had anything to do with the shipyard fire? I know it was on a Monday, but couldn't he change days once in a while?"

"I'm not discounting any possibilities," he said, sliding into the opposite seat. "But he's not the only person setting fires around here. The other day we had a guy who burned down a house with his three kids in it. Why? Because he and his live-in had a fight, and he wanted to get back at her. A two-year-old girl died in that fire, and all the man could say was that he 'didn't mean any harm.' "

A hardness came into his eyes, and a cold, clear anger. This was the arson investigator, a man who lived with fire and the ugliness of the people who set them. A week ago, she wouldn't have understood. But now she did. Arson was a particularly uncaring crime; throw the match and walk away, and let the fire do the rest. If someone dies, well, it was the fire's fault.

"And then we have the people who use the arsonist as a cover for their own fires," he continued. "It's a good excuse to get rid of property that has become a white elephant."

"Lovely," Lou said.

"Can you think of anyone who had a grudge against the company? Someone who'd been fired, or written up for violations, that sort of thing."

"There are probably a couple of dozen who fall into that category. Remember, we've got twenty-two hundred people working there. Your best bet is to talk to the individual shop foremen. They'd know better than anyone."

"That's what I've been doing. Mr. Steggans suggested I talk to you, said you've been there long enough to know the troublemakers and the problem spots. And everyone who's come through QA."

44

"I suppose I do." She turned the mug between her palms. "We've been a pretty tight crew over the years, but there were a couple of guys who didn't work out. Milt Greenfield quit after two years. I think it was September . . . no, October 1987. He couldn't take the stress. Then there was Steven Havlichek. He was fired after passing a faulty boiler weld that blew a couple of months later. Steve was lucky, though; he'd have gone to jail if someone had died aboard that ship."

"He would?" Whitaker's surprise was obvious.

"Sure. We're held personally responsible—involuntary manslaughter or negligence that causes death."

"Can you think of any other reason why someone would set fire to that storage shed?"

She shook her head. "Actually, if someone really wanted to strike back at the shipyard, he would have done better to set fire to the offices, or maybe the hazardous-waste storage shed. Burning the Quonset just seems so . . . frivolous."

"Frivolous?"

"Yeah. If *I* were going to hurt Carmichael's, I'd have done a much better job of it."

"You don't think this guy was very smart?"

"He was smart enough to get the job done," she said. "Has anyone found anything missing, like personnel records?"

Whitaker smiled. "You have echoes of a criminal mind, Ms. Malotti."

"Doesn't everybody?"

"Unfortunately." He glanced at his watch, then drained his mug and stood up. "I've got to get going. How's 2:00 P.M. on Sunday?"

"Fine," she said.

"I'll pick you up."

She shook her head. "I'll drive myself."

"So you can leave on your own if things turn out grim?"

"Whitaker, I've been single for over twenty years, and learned all the lessons I need to learn."

He didn't seem upset, which raised his stock still higher. He merely wrote his address down on the back of his business card and handed it to her. "Don't dress up," he said. "This is family backyard barbecue stuff."

Lou accompanied him to the front door, ignoring Elihu's strident hiss.

"Do you think you can find the guy who set that fire?" she asked.

"If I put all the puzzle pieces together the right way, I'll find him." He paused at the door, turning to look down at her. "You cut your hair."

She reached up to touch the freshly-trimmed ends that just brushed the curve of her jaw. "I got a little singed the other day."

"I like it."

With that, he was gone. Lou closed the door after him, feeling as though she'd just gotten off a roller-coaster ride.

"Jeez Louise!" Elihu cried.

She smiled. "You said it, bud."

Four

Slowly, he reached out and crumpled the newspaper in his fist. Firebug, they'd called him. The story in Thursday's paper had been bad enough. But today they'd run a feature on him, and made him out to be some slavering maniac. It was time to set the record straight.

He picked up the phone and stabbed out the number for the *Virginian-Pilot/Ledger Star.* "I want to talk to the reporter who wrote the feature story on the arsonist," he said to the woman who answered.

"It's Sunday, sir, and Mr. MacLaren—"

"Is he there, or not?"

"Yes, but—"

"Get him on the phone. Tell him I'm handing him another headline."

She put him on hold. He filled the silence by humming what he could remember of *Bolero.* Finally, a man's voice came on the line.

"MacLaren." The voice was a bit on the raspy side. A smoker perhaps.

He couldn't help but smile. "Mr. MacLaren, I object to being called a firebug."

"I . . ." The reporter's tone changed abruptly. "Who is this?"

"Who do you think?"

He could almost hear the gears shifting in the reporter's head. "What's the matter with firebug?" MacLaren asked a moment later.

"It's demeaning. You could use it to describe some kid setting fires in dumpsters, but not me."

"You consider yourself on a . . . grander scale?"

"Absolutely."

"Tell me something," MacLaren said. "Why Wednesdays?"

He considered hanging up, then decided, why not? It would make tomorrow's headlines much more interesting. "Wednesday is a good day for me."

"Why do you set fires?"

He could feel the reporter's excitement, hear it in his voice. Well, so he should be; this interview was probably going to make the guy famous. He smiled, feeling the creamy surge of power.

"I do it because . . ." he paused for effect, "I like to watch things burn. The power to destroy is very compelling, Mr. MacLaren—"

"Kevin."

"Kevin. I want you to understand something before you write another story about me. I'm not some raving maniac running through the streets shooting women and children. I *think* about what I'm doing."

"You plan each fire?"

"Always. I pick my sites very carefully."

"Have you picked your next one?"

"Yes."

"Will you strike on a Wednesday again?"

"It's a good day for me," he said again.

"This Wednesday?"

"Sure, why not?" He could sense the man's revulsion, even through the phone. It should have angered him. But MacLaren was also afraid, obviously afraid. That fear tempered his revulsion, made it palatable.

The reporter's breath rasped over the line. "Aren't you afraid of telling the authorities too much?"

"Oh, no," he said, smiling. "There's no protection against someone like me, and they know it. They can't watch every building in the area. And don't forget, I'm not limited to Southside; the new tunnel has made Hampton and Newport News *very* accessible."

"Shit," MacLaren muttered. "Look, this thing you have with setting fires . . . Could you stop if you wanted to?"

Closing his eyes, he thought about it. The memory of the ribbon factory bloomed in his mind. Flames shooting up into the night sky, sparks raining down all around, and best of all, the avid fascination of the watching human beings. *They* recognized the fire's beauty and power. And he'd given it to them.

"Why would I want to stop?" he asked after a moment.

"Aren't you afraid of getting caught?"

"Why should I be?"

The reporter paused as though weighing the chances of angering him into ending the interview, then said, "Bob Whitaker, the Arson Investigator, has the rep of being *very* good."

"So am I," he replied. "Too good to be caught."

"That sounds like a challenge."

He shrugged. "Just fact. Now, I've been thinking about this firebug thing—"

"I can't keep calling you 'the arsonist' in every headline and every article."

"Call me Fire Man."

"Fireman?" MacLaren echoed. "Isn't that a contradiction in terms?"

"No. Not fireman, but Fire Man. Two words."

"Fire Man."

He could hear the capitals in the reporter's voice. Yes. It was going to look good in print. "Use it, Kevin. It's catchy enough to sell lots of newspapers."

"Okay, okay. I'll see what I can do. But I've got to talk to my editor, and it's bound to take a couple of days—"

"I'll be watching for it," he said. "Bye."

"Wait! Don't hang up," MacLaren gabbled. "You can't just disappear like this. People are going to want to know more about you."

He intended to disconnect. But the reporter's words touched something in him, holding his finger poised above the button. A burning factory flared in his memory, and the picture of ruddy flames reflecting in the eyes of the watching people. His public. In a way, they were as fascinated with the fire maker as with the fire, for he'd done what they only contemplated deep in the secrecy of their own thoughts. He ignored the rules that governed the rest of mankind.

He dared destroy. Openly. Gloriously.

"When can I talk to you again?" MarLaren asked.

"What are you going to call me in your next story?"

"Fire Man."

"I'll call you Thursday morning," he said. "After the next fire. You can tell me again how good the arson investigator is."

Satisfied, he hung up.

Sun glinted off the water below as Lou reached the end of the West Norfolk bridge and turned onto Mount Vernon.

"One-oh-six," she muttered, peering out the window at the houses. "One-oh-eight . . . Ah, there it is."

The Whitaker domain was a smallish Victorian house nestled comfortably within the spreading branches of grand old oak trees. Although the house was fairly well kept, it had the air of a fading, genteel lady—keeping up appearances, but gently giving in to age. There was no driveway at the front; in these turn-of-the-century homes, the garages were accessed by an alleyway in the back.

Lou parked at the curb and strode up a sidewalk that had long ago given in to the demands of the tree roots below. But it had been freshly swept, and someone had planted bright yellow pansies along the border.

Evidently Whitaker had been watching for her, for the door opened as she mounted the three steps onto the porch. His clothes were casual, but not his eyes. "Hi," he said. "You're right on time."

"I'm always on time," she said.

"You look good. No, let me rephrase that—you look *good.*"

"I'll take that as a compliment, although considering that the only other times you saw me I was wearing overalls and steel-toed boots, and had been almost blown up and almost ripped to shreds by a parrot—"

"Just say thank you."

"Thank you."

He took her by the arm, his grasp warm and almost possessive. "Come on, the kids are out back."

The interior of the house had aged as genteelly as the outside. The bland, modern furniture didn't do it justice. Lou imagined her grandmother's furniture here—big, sprawly things that wouldn't be dwarfed by the ten-foot ceilings.

"This is a beautiful old house," she said. "Look at those moldings!"

"We're under permanent reconstruction, I'm afraid. I can't remember a time when I wasn't breathing plaster dust. Nearly twenty years now. The neighborhood's changed, we've changed, but the work never seems to."

He led her into a kitchen that had been modern some forty years ago. But despite that, the room was big and spacious, and the light pouring through the pair of south-facing windows was enough to send Van Gogh running for his paintbrushes. Lou found herself mentally tearing out the cheap fifties-laminate cabinets and replacing them with buttery oak, pulling up the spotted linoleum and laying down ceramic . . .

"I know that look," Whitaker said.

She laughed. "I couldn't help myself."

"Me, either. That's why I stayed here after . . ." His voice checked. Then he went on so smoothly it hardly seemed like an interruption. "But this room is going to have to wait until I get Blaire through college."

"I know what you mean," she said. "My son's just finishing his third year, and it's been a real struggle to pay for it all. And I'm not off the hook yet—he wants to go to law school."

"At least he'll make a decent living when he's out. He can take care of his dear old mother for a change."

"Dear old mother my . . . foot. He wants to be a cop."

"That lets out the decent living." Whitaker opened the refrigerator and rummaged around inside. "Coke or Seven-Up?" he asked from the depths.

"Seven-Up, thanks."

A door slammed somewhere close. "Dad! Daaaad!" The voice was girlish, the volume was not.

"In the kitchen, Kelsey," Whitaker called.

The far door swung open, and a whirlwind of long legs and curly brown hair shot into the room. "Hey, Dad, what's this word?"

The whirlwind resolved into a tall, thinnish girl who looked nine or ten years old. She held a well-worn paperback in her hands.

"Lou, meet Kelsey, my youngest," Whitaker said with obvious pride.

"Hi, Kelsey," Lou said. "It's nice to meet you."

"Hi."

No encouragement there, Lou thought. The girl had her father's eyes, clear and grey and intelligent. Her gentle, heart-shaped face must have come from her mother. And the cautious, closed look came from a child's wariness toward a father's lady friend.

The door swung open again with enough force to send it thumping into the wall behind. Lou got a single, startled glimpse of an enormous four-legged shape and a pink lolling tongue before Whitaker stepped in front of her.

"Down!" he said. "Sit! Mind your manners."

Oh, Lou thought. It's a *dog*. She stepped out from behind Whitaker's sheltering back. "I'm not scared of dogs," she said. "You can let her . . . Wow!" Her eyes widened as she got her first good look at this one.

Whitaker turned to face her, his hand resting on the animal's massive, grey-furred head. The dog's back reached his belt buckle. "This is Shamu. She's an Irish Wolfhound."

"She's beautiful," Lou said, extending her hand to be sniffed. "And big!"

"Last time we had her weighed, she was a hundred and twenty-eight pounds."

Lou stroked the dog's head and neck, feeling the bristly hair rasp pleasantly across her palm. "You're a

53

sweetheart, aren't you?" she asked. "If I'd known you were here, I'd have brought you a nice, juicy bone. You can let her go, Whitaker. She doesn't bother me."

"She will."

"Oh, come on. What are you going to do, sit on her all afternoon? Give her a chance to get used to me."

Shamu wagged her heavy whip of a tail frantically, glancing up at her master with eyes that would have softened Vlad the Impaler's heart. Whitaker, being merely human, capitulated. "Okay, Shamu," he said. "You can have her."

His phrasing did give Lou the briefest stab of alarm. She stood still while the dog sniffed her fore and aft. Enthusiastically. And very thoroughly. Then, the inspection over, the wolfhound gently butted her in the stomach in a less-than-subtle bid for attention. Lou stroked her ears, grinning up at Whitaker.

"How many women have you run off this way?" she asked, stroking the dog's massive grey head.

"Only the prissy ones."

He returned to the refrigerator, coming up a moment later with two cans of soda in his hands. Lou took hers and allowed the dog to lick the condensation off the can.

"She likes you," Kelsey said.

Lou smiled at the child's apparent surprise. "Oh, I'm not so bad once you get to know me."

"Most people are scared of Shamu."

"That's just 'cause she's so big." Lou scratched behind Shamu's ears, and the dog closed her eyes in pleasure. "But my grandpa had a farm out in Suffolk, and I grew up around animals. And anyone who'd think that this dog was vicious has got a screw loose somewhere."

Kelsey stared at her for a moment, her small face

54

inscrutable. Then she thrust her book out. "What's this word?"

"Which? This one?" Lou peered at the page. "Accountable. In this sentence, it means, ah, being held responsible."

"Oh. Thanks." Carefully, the child marked her page. "Come on outside and I'll show you the yard."

"You two go on," Whitaker said. "I'm going to pull the steaks out of the fridge."

Lou followed the child toward the door. Glancing back once, she caught Whitaker watching her with warm approval in his eyes. Evidently she'd passed the Shamu test.

The back yard was pure heaven. Shaded by the huge, overhanging oaks, the grass was overgrown enough to be comfortable. Azaleas grew tall against the back fence, their branches heavy with lavender blooms. The smell of hot charcoal hung in the air, warring with the fragrance of flowers.

Two boys—young men, really—stopped playing Frisbee and came to meet Lou. Kelsey introduced them. Sixteen-year-old Mike had his dad's grey eyes and broad-shouldered build. When his acne cleared up in a couple of years, he'd be a real heart-stopper. Keefe, at thirteen, had an athlete's grace, dark auburn hair and the most gorgeous blue eyes God had ever put in a human face.

"Dad said you work in a shipyard," Keefe said, cutting right to the chase.

"That's right. I'm a quality assurance inspector. I'm the guy who looks over the other guys' shoulders to make sure the repairs are done properly."

"Does it bother them?"

"Sometimes," she said, then corrected herself. "No, most of the time."

"Do you get to go on the ships?"

She smiled. "Every day."

The screen door slammed behind her. Lou turned, expecting Whitaker. But instead of the lieutenant, she saw a girl about eighteen or so, clasping a large cardboard box in her arms.

"Hi," she said, setting the box on the ground. "I'm Blaire, the oldest." All the good looks the boys were growing into had crystallized in her fresh young face. Thick brown hair, the same gorgeous blue eyes as her brother Keefe—Blaire was absolutely stunning.

Shamu came galloping around the side of the house, tongue lolling in a delighted dog smile. Blaire gently upended the box and swung the end flap open. A clot of small, brown, furry bodies tumbled out.

Hamsters! Lou thought. Then, they're *not* going to feed them to the dog, not while I'm here. She started forward as Shamu bent her great head.

But the wolfhound merely nosed the hamsters, who seemed not to mind at all. Then the little beasts set off across the yard. The dog herded them solicitously, nudging any stragglers back into the pack. When the hamsters neared the azaleas, she expertly turned them back toward the house. Apparently it wasn't an unusual sight in the Whitaker yard; the boys returned to their game of Frisbee, and Kelsey retired to a nearby lawn chair and began to read.

Lou said the first thing that came into her mind. "This isn't normal."

"You're right," Blaire replied. "She's not a herding breed."

"I wasn't talking about the dog."

Blaire laughed. "I am, though. Shamu spent so much time keeping us in line that she became addicted

56

to it. Now that we're growing up, she's turned her attentions to the hamsters."

Slowly, Lou turned to look at the girl beside her. "You're telling me the dog took care of you?"

"Oh, we had our share of babysitters when Dad had to work, but it takes a parent or a dog to take proper care of four extra-active kids."

Oddly enough, it made sense. And who was to say whether or not a dog could do as good a job raising people as puppies?

"I understand you've got a breeding pair of parrots," Blaire said.

"Elihu and Emily," Lou agreed. "And I found out about the breeding the hard way."

The girl nodded. "Dad told me about it. Would you mind if I dropped by sometimes to monitor the process? You don't come across many breeding parrots."

"Sure," Lou said. "Come by anytime." An impetuous offer, born of her instinctive liking for the girl.

"Blaire plans to be a vet," Whitaker said.

Lou turned to see him standing at the edge of the patio, balancing a tray of steaks with a waiter's flourish. A disaster waiting to happen, she thought, watching the meat slither toward the edge of the plate.

"Stop showing off before our dinner ends up in the dirt," Blaire said.

"Why don't you cook, hon, and let me tend to my date."

"Sure, Dad." Blaire shot Lou a smile over her shoulder as she went to take the tray from her father. "At least now we can have our steaks some other way than charred. Lou, how 'bout you? Rare, medium or well done?"

"Medium."

"Picky, picky," Whitaker said. As he walked toward

Lou, he scooped up two lawn chairs. "Here you go. Relax and enjoy the breeze."

Lou settled into the nearest chair. He put his chair beside hers, close enough so that their forearms touched. She enjoyed the contact.

"Are you having a good time?" he asked.

"I've been duly indoctrinated."

"Some people think the hamster herding is weird."

"Of course it's weird," she said. "But then, I have a parrot who sings Sinatra and the King."

She glanced at him from the corner of her eye. He sipped his drink, watching the boys play.

"My wife died in an accident four years ago," he said without turning toward Lou. "For a while, I was worried I couldn't care for the kids properly. I'm still not sure I did so well, but they seem to have turned out okay."

"Yes, they have. You did a good job raising them. And so did the dog."

He grimaced. "Blaire's been at it again. Sometimes she treats me like an idiot child."

"Let her. She needs to know she carried the torch, too."

Lou watched his eyes change as he realized what she meant. "You've spent a long time alone," he said.

"Mine was by choice."

"What happened?"

"Sam walked out when Wade was three months old, said he had to 'find himself.' We never saw him again. I heard he moved to Australia or New Zealand."

"Do you think he found himself?"

"People like Sam aren't looking for themselves, but for someone else."

"What did you do?"

She lifted her shoulders in feigned indifference; she

didn't like to think about those tough, early years. "What I had to."

"Come on, Lou. Give."

His eyes had turned dark with something that looked like compassion. And here, with the sun warm on her shoulders and the aroma of steaks cooking on the grill, she felt something blossom within her. It might have been the beginning of trust.

"Thousands of women have been in my shoes, Whitaker. Since my ex had left for parts unknown, I had to do it all alone. I interviewed for several of the jobs women are supposed to do, but none of them paid enough to keep me and Wade. One day I happened to see an ad for an apprentice welding program at the shipyard. Old man Carmichael, who owned the place, was a renegade from the word go, liked to shake things up. So he hired me."

"You must have impressed him."

"Yeah." She laughed, truly amused. "I asked him once why he took a chance on me. Know what he said? He said, 'Malotti, I just wanted to see if you were going to be able to weld with those nice, big tits of yours.' "

Whitaker drew his breath in sharply. "I can't imagine you letting that pass without comment."

"You're right. I said, Mr. Carmichael, I weld with a *torch,* not tits. And then I went back to work. Even if there'd been such a thing as harassment suits back then, I wouldn't have said anything different, not with a child to support."

"But you moved up."

"Yes, I moved up. I took every transfer that offered a chance of promotion, and I busted my tail to learn everything I could. It was good for me, Whitaker. I got tough."

59

"Too tough to remarry?"

"Too independent. Men don't like independent women."

"Who told you that?" he asked.

"A man."

He shook his head. "Uh-uh. He may have looked like a man, but he'd obviously never grown up."

Lou stared at him for a moment, trying to delve behind those clear grey eyes. Then she realized he meant it. Something warm went through her, something she hadn't felt in so long she'd almost forgotten it existed.

"Steaks are done," Blaire called. "Mike, Keefe, Kelsey—inside! Get the rest of the stuff out and onto the table."

"General Blaire," Whitaker murmured, rising. "Remind me to get her a whip for her next birthday." He held his hand out to Lou. "Welcome to the Whitakers. If you dare."

Smiling, she took his hand. She'd had worse offers.

Five

"I'm going to pop," Lou said as Blaire set a strawberry shortcake on the table.

"Does that mean you don't want dessert?" Blaire asked.

"Of course not. Do I look like the kind of person who goes around avoiding strawberry shortcake?"

"No," Whitaker said. "You've got sense."

The phone shrilled, loud even through the kitchen door. "I hope that's Tony," Blaire said, rushing to answer it.

Lou leaned back and surveyed Whitaker's domain; the airy dining room with its fourteen-inch moldings and sun-filled windows, the mismatched dishes paired with dainty silverware that only a woman could have chosen, and the tableful of healthy kids who were putting shortcake away like locusts.

"This is a nice way to live," she murmured.

She'd been talking more to herself than to Whitaker, but he stopped eating to look down the table just as she had. "It's pretty decent, isn't it?" he asked.

"Yes. It makes me realize just how lonely it is with Wade gone. Homes tend to echo without kids."

The boys scraped the last of the whipping cream off

their plates and got up. "Nice to meet you, Lou," Mike mumbled through a mouthful of shortcake. He swallowed, then spoke more clearly. "Dad, can I use Mom's car? Me and Keefe have soccer practice."

"Sure," Whitaker said.

"But Blaire was supposed to drive me to Shannon's at five!" Kelsey protested.

"Sorry, squirt," Mike said. "Dad's already given us the car."

"Well, *you* drive me, then."

"No can do. Soccer practice starts in twenty minutes."

Kelsey drew herself up, her dark, winged brows contracting in a scowl. "This is more important. We're working on the *science* project."

"Welcome to the real world," Whitaker murmured to Lou, under the cover of the burgeoning argument.

Blaire came back into the dining room, disappointment in her eyes and a cordless phone in her hand. "Quiet, you guys. We'll work this out somehow. Dad, this is for you. Some newspaper guy named MacLaren. I told him you weren't giving interviews, but he said it's really important . . ."

"That's okay, hon. I'll talk to him."

He took the phone from her. Apparently the reporter had a lot to say, for Whitaker remained silent for an appreciably long time. Lou watched his eyes change from clear grey to the chill colorlessness of a winter sky.

One by one, the kids fell silent, watching the cold rage spread across their father's face. "He said that?" Whitaker shouted. "He told you Wednesday? That goddamn . . ." Taking a deep breath, he lowered his voice. "He's going to call you again. Whatever you do, don't antagonize him into hanging up. Promise him your sister if you have to, but give me time to get a tap on that line."

He clicked the phone off and sat for a moment, visibly struggling with his temper. Finally he rose and said, "Mike, you and Keefe get to soccer practice in your mother's car. Blaire, you take my car and get your sister to her science project, then come back here and get these dishes done and the animals in. Lou, you can drop me off at the station on your way home."

The kids melted away. For a moment it seemed as though every door in the house slammed, then silence fell. Lou could actually hear the clock ticking while she watched the tendons flex in Whitaker's big hands.

"Ooh," she said at last. "I just *love* masterful men!"

He exhaled sharply, and some of the icy rage drained from his eyes. "Was I that bad?"

"You cleared the room."

"I didn't see *you* running."

"I never run," she said. "At least not from a man who has a hamster herd in his back yard."

He raked his hand through his hair. "Something very urgent has come up. I've got to deal with it. Sorry, Lou."

"Don't worry about it. Find my purse for me, will you? I'll drive you down."

"You don't mind?" he asked.

"Mind? How could I mind? I've been *designated.*"

She chose not to hear what he muttered under his breath as he vanished into the kitchen. He emerged a moment later with her purse.

"Here," he said, dropping it into her outstretched hands. "Let's go."

He seemed to fill the passenger seat of her Corolla, partly because of his size, partly because of the simmering rage that made him seem even larger than he was.

"It's the Effingham Street station," he said.

"I know the way." Lou turned onto Broad Street and headed downtown. "Do you want to talk about it?"

63

With a sigh, he stretched his long legs as far as he could. "The arsonist called the newspaper. Told them that the Wednesday Night Firebug isn't to his taste. He wants to be called Fire Man. Two words, not one."

"That sounds awful weird, even for an arsonist."

"Yeah. I think we've got a real, died-in-the-wool nut case here."

She glanced at him. The setting sun shot ruddy sparks in his silver-streaked hair and set a flaming highlight across his eyes. A shiver went through her. Not because of Whitaker. No, it was the image of fire that seemed to have claimed him.

"Tell me the rest," she said, although she wasn't sure she wanted to know.

"He said he'd already picked the place and time of his next strike."

"Wednesday?"

"This Wednesday."

Dread settled heavily in the pit of her stomach. "It sounds like a challenge."

"It is. There's not a damn thing I can do to stop him, and he knows it. Even if I could put a man in every building in the area, I couldn't stop him. A little gasoline, a match . . . It only takes a second."

Out of the corner of her eye, she saw that his hands were flexing and relaxing, flexing and relaxing. "Are you supposed to take this personally?"

"No."

"Then why are you?"

"Because he's on my turf. Because he's telling me I can't stop him, and he's doing it in a public forum."

"Can't you muzzle the newspaper?"

He shook his head. "Oh, they'll work with us. But now that this guy's had a taste of notoriety, I doubt he's going to want to fade back off stage. If we don't give him at least some of the attention he wants, he might try bigger and better things in order to get it."

"Scary," she said. It was an inadequate word to describe what she felt. But somehow, she didn't want to say anything stronger. Didn't want to *think* anything stronger lest it give him substance somehow. And yes, lest it expose the dark little corners of her mind, reveal the fears, the vulnerabilities, all those things she'd kept to herself all these years.

"Here we are," Whitaker said. "Turn right here and pull into the parking lot."

The area was all but deserted; everyone must be at Sunday dinner. The sun had sunk below the level of the buildings, painting alternating bars of light and shadow across the road and turning the yellow brick of the firehouse ochre. Lou eased past a hook and ladder parked just outside the door and pulled up to the curb.

Whitaker slung the door open the moment she stopped the car. "Thanks for the ride," he said, levering himself out.

With that, he turned and trotted away. Lou shook her head. So much for romance. And so much for worrying about revealing too much about herself; Whitaker wouldn't have noticed if she'd painted a sign on her forehead.

Something moved at the fringes of her vision. Startled, she turned to stare down the street, where a clot of town houses blocked the sun. Shadows pooled thickly at their bases. Windows seemed to stare back at her like blind, blank eyes.

She caught movement again, just there at the corner. A furtive sort of movement. Her breath held suspended, she strained to hear any sound other than the staccato beat of her own heart. Memory swept through her, black and visceral, of another lurker in the shadows. Was he watching her, unseen in the darkness?

She could feel the fading warmth of the sun on her shoulder and arm. Like sitting in a spotlight, she thought. He *had* to be able to see her. Was he squatting in his little wedge of shadow, watching every move she made, committing her face to memory? The hairs at the back of her neck lifted in involuntary horror.

Fire Man.

It might not be him. Then again . . . Lou glanced over her shoulder, wondering if she should get Whitaker. Wishing she could get Whitaker.

"No time," she muttered under her breath.

She eased the Corolla into gear. Then, with a suddenness that made the tires squeal, she made a sharp U-turn and headed for the spot where she'd seen the movement.

Nothing. Not even a stray cat. Lou began to doubt her own perceptions. Had she actually seen movement, or had her imagination been working overtime?

She cruised slowly down the block, peering into every doorway, every crack and cranny where a man might hide. Nothing.

"I'm starting to hope there *is* some maniac arsonist lurking around . . . just so I know I'm not crazy," she muttered.

She eased the car around the corner. The town houses were now on her right, blocking what little was left of the sunset. To her left, the street was bordered by the blank wall of a Sunday-empty business. Only the faintest glimmer of daylight reached here.

Lou kept her headlights off, for they'd blind her to her surroundings. Smooth, violet dusk seemed to wrap her up and suck her in. Instinct told her to get the hell out, but she suppressed it. So many times she'd seen

66

disaster happen because someone couldn't stay on the scene, make decisions, and cope with the situation. If she could just get a look at this guy, or find out where he was hiding to watch the station . . .

Something moved in the tiny rectangle of her side-view mirror. Something large. Coming toward her and coming fast. Time clicked into slow motion, freeze-frames of terror as her pulse screamed a tattoo in her brain.

He's behind you!

Her window was open, her door unlocked. No chance to do anything about it; she could hear his footsteps grating on the surface of the road. The dark shape filled the mirror now, swooping at her like some great, black bird of prey.

Lou stomped the accelerator, hard. The Corolla leapt forward, leaving a trail of hot rubber behind. The rear end shimmied and tried to stew around, but she wrestled the car back under control. Taking a screaming right at the corner, she accelerated out of the turn and ran the red light onto Effingham Street.

She could see the station house in her rearview mirror. But even if the front door happened to be open, twenty-odd feet separated the front door from the curb, and that was twenty feet too far. The parking lot was out; too empty, too hidden from view. Just the thought of running across it made her skin crawl. So she drove home, her gaze more on her rearview mirror than on the road ahead.

Her hands didn't start to shake until she was safe inside, the door closed and locked behind her. Safe. She sank to her knees as the trembling spread to the rest of her body.

"Jeez, Louise!" Elihu cried.

Lou took a deep breath, then another. Thank God

67

the living-room lamps were on a timer, and the room was flooded with light. It reassured her, gave her the chance to calm her body's reaction.

Her mouth twisted in a cynical smile. Tough Lou Malotti. It was a good thing none of her co-workers had seen her like this, a damn good thing. The thought got her to her feet, and put her brain back in gear.

Emily's claws rasped on the perch as she skated from one end to the other. *"Apple, apple!"*

"Keep your shorts on," she said. "I've got a phone call to make."

"Looove me tender . . ." Elihu warbled.

With a sigh, she headed for the kitchen. "Sometimes, Wade, I'd like to strangle you."

She dialed Whitaker's work number, then tucked the phone between her shoulder and chin while she cut up an apple for the parrots.

Three rings, four. Finally, someone answered, a deep male voice that fairly radiated impatience. "Portsmouth Fire Department, arson investigator's office. Rutherford here."

"May I speak to Lieutenant Whitaker? This is Lou Malotti."

"He's out of the office. Can I have him call you back?"

"Do you have any idea when?"

"Sorry, no."

Disappointment shafted through her. *What did you expect—that he'd rush over here to hold your hand?* Kind of, actually. "Just give him a message for me, then. Tell him I noticed some guy watching the station house from across the street."

"I'll tell him."

He hung up, cutting off her thanks. "Wow, reacted all over that one, didn't you?" she asked the silent phone.

With a shrug, she carried the fruit to the living room and fed it through the bars a piece at a time. Elihu cocked first one beady eye at her, then the other.

"Forget it," she said. "No way am I opening that cage door."

The big picture window framed the night. Lou stared out into the darkness, starting at every movement, every swirl of discarded paper. She jerked the curtains closed, unable to overcome the need to shut the darkness out.

"You're really spooked," she muttered.

She whipped her annoyance into anger, using it to hold her unease at bay. She'd learned long ago that fear could be controlled. *Had* to be controlled. Anyone who'd ever climbed seventy feet down a metal ladder into the echoing hold of a ship knew that. Anyone who'd been cornered by a couple of grinning yahoos out to bust the uppity female inspector knew that.

The firebug was Whitaker's enemy. Not hers. She'd blundered into him, and managed to blunder back out. And she was too damned old to start complaining about her tendency to take action and worry about danger later; if she hadn't been a risk taker, she'd still be working as a secretary somewhere.

She'd done what needed to be done, informed Whitaker, and now it was finished. Over. Like she'd done innumerable times in the past twenty years, she took her fear and laid it aside, almost as though she were folding laundry.

Paying the bills, keeping Wade in college, socking enough away in her IRA to make sure her son wouldn't have to support her in her old age—those were *real* worries. And she wasn't about to let her home become a prison because she couldn't find the courage to walk out the door.

"So, take yourself to a movie," she said. "Something mindless and violent."

It took some willpower to open the door. But she did it. And found everything normal, the stars and moon in their proper places, the cars parked in their assigned spaces, her neighbor's kids playing last-minute hopscotch beneath the streetlight. She sighed; content that her world had fallen back into place.

He picked himself up off the pavement and swiped at his scraped knees. That woman . . .

"You bitch," he snarled under his breath.

Shit, most people wouldn't have noticed him, and damn few would have thought of following him. He'd hardly paid attention to her; Whitaker was the one he'd been waiting for. Then she'd come after him, tires squealing, and he'd panicked. Someone else would have had sense enough to be afraid. But she kept coming, following him into the side street as though they'd been roped together.

He didn't think she realized just how close she'd come to dying tonight.

At least he'd managed to stay between her and the light; there was no way she could have seen anything but a silhouette as he ran toward her.

"Screw with me again, bitch, and you'll be sorry," he muttered.

He eased back around the corner and took up his position in the shadows again. A white car pulled up in front of the station. His lip curled. Although the vehicle was unmarked, the cops might as well have had the siren on. Then Whitaker came out and got in. Now *that* was interesting; the reporter must have contacted the powers that be. That meant the phone at the *Pilot* was going to be bugged.

He watched Whitaker's profile as the car pulled away. The lieutenant's features looked as though they'd been rough-carved in stone. Grim. Unyielding.

"I'm not afraid of you," he said. "Are you afraid of me?"

Maybe not. Whitaker didn't look as though much scared him. Ah, a man who had a handle on the world. A man who set things right.

The lieutenant might not agree, but *he* thought they had a lot in common.

Echoes of screams picked at his memory. Times past. That had been another wrong set right. At a cost. *He'd* learned the cost. Whitaker hadn't yet; he was living in the artificial world of civilization's rules. It tended to insulate, to protect.

"Now you've walked into *my* world," the Fire Man said. "The rules are gone, and the ante is much higher."

Pushing the memories away, he walked around to the back of the station house, where the bulky shape of a dumpster squatted. Night had leached the color from it, turning it from brick red to grey. He took a flask from his pocket and poured its contents into the opening.

Then he lit a match. He stood for a moment, enjoying the yellow bloom of flame against the darkness, then tossed it into the dumpster.

His calling card, addressed to Whitaker. "Just so you know I mean business," he said.

Six

The overhead lights turned the rain into a silver-flecked sheet as Lou ran along the pier toward the office. Mist had already begun to rise along the edges of the river, and was bound to become full-fledged fog by morning.

The office windows shone lemon-yellow, a tantalizing offering of light and dryness. Lou headed for them, shivering as water sluiced off her hardhat and trickled beneath her collar.

"What a night!" she muttered.

She splashed through the rapidly spreading pond in front of the door, cursing under her breath as her boots slithered on the mud. The wind followed her in, bringing a spray of rain with it.

"Ease up, will you?" she said, slamming the door against the rain.

Her boots squelched as she made her way upstairs. She wished she had something dry to change into; there was nothing as clammy and uncomfortable as cold jeans. Thank God she'd thought to make coffee before going out into the shipyard.

She fed quarters into the snack machine and got a pack of peanut-butter crackers and a bag of popcorn.

Her reflection, a distorted, fun-house image in the glass front, seemed to stare back accusingly.

"What?" she demanded. "It's got no more calories than a sandwich and fries from the snack bar, and there's less chance of having to get my stomach pumped."

"Talking to yourself is the first sign of old age."

Lou turned to see Dwayne Steggans watching her from the next office, his elbows propped on the top of the partition. He looked as though he'd just come in; his hair was wet, his blue jacket dark with water.

"Are you still here?" she asked in surprise.

"Nope. Just got back. If you hadn't been talking to yourself, you'd have heard the elevator. Thanks," he said as Lou tossed him a paper towel. He wiped the beaded water off his face. "I figured the rain was balling things up and dropped in to see if I could help."

She studied him, surprised but pleased. "It's not too bad, actually. Some of the people on outside jobs had to take a break; you can hardly see your hand in front of your face out there. Hopefully it will slack off soon."

"I hope so." He straightened. "I'll take a walk around, see what's going on."

"Watch your step," she said. "It's as slick as glass out there."

"Hey, watching me fall on my can might improve morale."

Again he surprised her; she hadn't thought he possessed a sense of humor. "Hey, would you happen to know if Jay finished that reinspect on the *Gabriella?* I left a copy of my report on his desk Friday night."

Steggans rubbed his jaw with the back of his hand. "Ah, I had to fire Jay today."

"What?" she yelped. "Why?"

"I caught him drinking."

"Oh, man. I'd heard he was having some problems at home, but Jay's always been a pretty steady guy—"

"Well, he was loaded today. An hour after he cleared out his stuff, security found him passed out in the back of his car."

Lou shook her head. Jay had been in QA for three years now. A quiet man, he kept mostly to himself. Stayed out of office politics and did nothing to get himself into the gossip mill. He'd been good at his job—not spectacular, but good enough. She glanced up at Steggans, found him frowning.

"You're sure you put that report on Jay's desk?" he asked.

"Positive."

"We went through his stuff pretty thoroughly, and I don't remember seeing it. You'd better come give it a look."

Lou followed him to the cubicle that had once been Jay Nesmith's. All his things were gone, the grotesque papier-mâché pencil box his daughter had made him a few years ago, the plastic cube containing pictures of his family, the Far Side mug. The desk had become an impersonal stretch of metal, the computer a blank grey eye. Steggans pointed to a box of papers that sat on the floor beside the chair.

"Everything that was in his desk is in there," he said.

Lou squatted and began to sift through the contents of the box. After going through it twice, she straightened. "It's not here. But don't worry about it; I logged that job into my computer like I always do."

"Why don't you print it out for me while I'm outside? I should be back in a half hour or so." Steggans picked up a hardhat from the top of Jay's file cabinet and put it on, then turned away.

Lou headed back to her office. Damn, she felt bad for Jay. Not that she condoned what he'd done; too much rode on QA inspections—and inspectors—to allow for that kind of slip-up. But the man had a wife and three kids to support, and after being fired for drunkenness on the job, had as much chance of becoming Pope as of getting hired into a QA spot again. She made a mental note to take up a collection in the department; it might help put food on the table for a while.

And speaking of food, the shine had gone off the crackers and popcorn. She set them aside. Just as she reached to turn her computer on, however, the phone rang.

Ignore it, she told herself. At twelve-fifteen at night, it could only mean more work. Four rings, five. Six. It *might* be Wade. An accident maybe, but more likely an emergency request for money. With a sigh, she picked the receiver up.

"Quality Assurance," she said.

"Lou?"

Her pulse speeded up. "Hi, Whitaker. What are you doing up so late on a lousy Monday night?"

"Returning your phone call."

Cradling the phone between her chin and shoulder, she reached to turn her computer on. "Oh, yeah."

"Don't sound so enthusiastic."

"I'm thrilled, take my word for it. I'm just up to my eyeballs in work just now."

"I'll keep it short, then. You left a message saying you saw somebody watching the station house yesterday?"

"Yeah. I saw him sneaking around down by those town houses and followed him." Lou tapped out the access code for the QA database program. The screen filled with numbers. Numbers that didn't mean anything to her. "I didn't ask for that," she muttered. "Whatever the hell it is."

"What did he look like?"

She frowned, scrolling through the file. "Who?"

"The man you followed," Whitaker growled. "Christ, Lou, will you talk to me?"

"Oh, that guy. I never got a look at his face."

"Come on, you can do better than that. Was he tall or short, thin or fat?"

Lou tapped her personal access code into the computer. The screen blinked, then filled with more meaningless data. A little of this, a little of that, sometimes recognizable, sometimes not.

"Lou!"

"He was a shadow, that's all," she said, her attention still on the computer screen. "What can you learn from some guy's shadow, other than it was dark and sneaky and scared the pants off me? Look, I just gave you all the information I have. And I've got to go."

"Just a minute—"

"Whitaker, I've got *big* problems here. I'll call you later."

She hung up. When the phone started to ring again a moment later, she switched it to the answering machine. Turning back to the computer, she tried another database file. Again, she found it skewed. Occasionally she saw a page of coherent material, but then it would repeat itself over and over, completely filling up the rest of the file.

"Jeez, Louise," she muttered, fumbling in her drawer for a roll of antacids. They tasted worse than ever. She washed the residue down with lukewarm coffee, grimaced, then went to Mason Bostwich's desk and switched on his computer.

"Please be a hardware problem," she said.

The same thing happened on Mason's computer. The problem was with the main database program, not hardware.

The silence seemed to wrap around her, as though the air itself realized the enormity of the loss. How could this have happened? A ton of safeguards had been built into the system; it would take a deliberate, informed act to touch the main program.

And who had the technical knowledge? Jay Nesmith, the computer enthusiast. Who had the motive? Jay Nesmith, the guy who'd just been fired. Did he have the opportunity? Sure. If he'd built in some kind of back-door access code for himself, he could have tapped into the program from just about anywhere.

She leaned her elbows on the desk, feeling as though someone had punched her in the stomach. All that work, gone. They were so far behind already that it would have taken a minor miracle to get them caught up. Now, it had passed beyond the sublime: Carmichael's was in deep doo-doo.

The elevator snicked open and a moment later Dwayne Steggans strode into view, considerably wetter than he'd been before.

"Did you . . ." His eyes narrowed. "What's the matter?"

"There's a problem with the main database program," she said. The words felt grim in her mouth, big, hard boulders destined to sink a man.

"Huh?"

"I can't access it."

"Could be your terminal—"

"I couldn't access it on Mason's, either."

With a hiss of indrawn breath, he strode to the nearest computer. "Damn him! He told me I'd be sorry, but I thought he was just blowing off steam. But oh, Nellie,

77

did he pull off a good one!" He smacked his fist into his palm, over and over. Lou knew he'd rather it had been Jay's face. "That sorry bastard. If he thinks he's got problems now, wait until Van Allen hears about this."

Oh, brother, Lou thought. Arthur Van Allen, Carmichael's new owner, was a cold, cold man. With his tight-fisted control on the company and cold-bloodedness when handing out pink slips, he'd earned himself the nickname Eichmann.

She raked her hand through her hair. "You had Jay escorted off the yard, right?"

"Right. You know the security procedures as well as I do. If he accessed that program, it wasn't from here."

"I just don't know." The notion didn't sit well. Lou rolled her shoulders as though trying to make a too-small jacket fit.

"Well, I do," Steggans said. "We're going to have to look into this real hard, especially on the tail of that fire. Who knows, maybe he had something to do with that. If he'd been stealing material and hiding it in the Quonset—"

"Then he'd have absolutely no reason to burn it down, would he?" Lou pointed out.

"Whatever. All I can say is that he's got a lot of tough questions to answer."

Turning on his heel, Steggans strode toward his office. To call Eichmann at home, no doubt, and tell him the news. Lou shook her head sadly.

Lou drove straight home after her shift, wanting nothing more than a long, hot shower to erase the clammy chill of the night. The rain had stopped, but the fog had rolled in thick and grey. Her headlights hardly made a dent in it. She got home by instinct, and by keeping her right wheels on the white line at the shoulder. Traffic remained light, fortunately, but the coming rush hour was bound to be a nightmare.

Never a timid driver, she was nonetheless glad to get home. That is, until she saw a car occupying her private parking space. The driver got out as she drove up. Tall, broad shoulders, dark hair frosted with moisture.

"Whitaker," she muttered. She was too tired to be glad to see him. And she was much too tired to argue with him, if that was what he had in mind.

She parked a few yards down and walked back. He leaned against the car, watching her come with an indefinable expression on his face.

"Whitaker—" she began.

"Hi, Lou." It was a female voice, and familiar.

Lou peered around Whitaker's broad back and spotted Blaire sitting in the car. "Hi, Blaire."

"We came to see your parrots; Dad said this was the only time during the day we'd be sure to catch you awake."

"I'm not sure you've caught me awake now," Lou replied, shooting Whitaker a glance from beneath her brows.

"I hope you don't mind," the girl said. "It's not his fault; I waited until he was too tired to fight me, then bugged him until he gave in."

Lou smiled in spite of her fatigue. "You've got a great future ahead of you, kid."

"My condolences to her husband, whoever that unfortunate soul turns out to be," Whitaker added. "Let us in, Lou. It's cruddy out here."

"Don't tell me," she said. "I've been tromping around in it all night." She swung the door open and stepped back. "Enter my humble abode. The male, by the way, is Elihu, the female, Emily. I've got to warn you, they don't like strangers."

At this distance, the parrots looked like beautiful enameled statues. But the moment Elihu spotted the visitors, he seemed to swell with indignation. Blaire stayed well back from the cage, talking softly to the birds. Lou peeled her soggy jacket off and dropped it on the square yard of tile that served as a pseudofoyer.

"Let's leave her alone," Whitaker said, retrieving the jacket and hanging it neatly on the doorknob.

"Not until I'm sure she's not going to open the cage."

"She knows better than that. After all—"

"She's studying to be a vet," Lou finished for him.

He took hold of her arm just above the elbow, his grip gentle, but firm enough to indicate that he hadn't forgiven her for hanging up on him.

Lou let him draw her into the kitchen, willing to lose that battle as long as she won the war.

"You look like hell," he said, startling her.

"Gee, thanks." She pulled her arm out of his grasp. "Look, Whitaker, I know I didn't return your calls last night. But I had a real crisis on my hands, and quite frankly, that took precedence over *your* problem. I'm wet and cold, and I'm so tired my bones ache. You want a fight, pick another day."

"I don't want a fight." He opened her refrigerator and peered inside. "Sit down. Want some orange juice while I make breakfast?"

"Yes." With a sigh, she slid into the nearest chair. "Hey! Who said you could make breakfast in my kitchen?"

"Those bags under your eyes."

"Do you have any other charming compliments to offer?"

"Well, I like that shirt."

Surprised, Lou glanced down. She'd grabbed one of Wade's South Carolina T-shirts out of the clean-but-unfolded laundry that had been sitting on top of the washer for a couple of weeks.

"You've got to be kidding," she said.

He laughed. "Sure. It's been a while since I saw one quite so well . . . packed."

"You must like big women, then."

"Small girls tend to get lost when a guy my size hugs them."

Lou turned away hastily. *I'm not going to ask, I'm not going to ask . . .*

"You're not going to ask, are you?"

Astonished, she swiveled around to face him. Did the man read minds?

Smiling, he pulled her up out of the chair and reeled her in. He was big and solid and felt wonderful, and she let herself lean into him. After a moment, he set her back in her chair, then went to lay bacon in the frying pan.

Lou felt a bit grim despite the delicious aroma of cooking bacon. That hug had been a brotherly sort of embrace. Not at all the sort of hug a man gave when he was interested in a woman.

Hell, she thought. Call a spade a spade; the wolfhound had shown more interest.

"Tell me something," he said without turning around. "How come you followed that guy on your own?"

"In the time it took for me to walk upstairs and get you, he might have been gone. I figured I had a chance of getting a look at him, and decided to go for it."

"Kind of dangerous, don't you think?"

Alarm bells went off all through Lou's mind as she compared the stiffness of his shoulders with the mild reasonableness of his tone. She decided against telling him anything that had occurred in that dark street. "I never even got out of the car," she said. Truth—not all of it, but enough, hopefully, to get him off her back.

"You keep saying 'he.' If it was a shadow, how do you know it was a man?"

"Didn't we have this conversation once before?"

"Yes, we did. And you were as forthcoming then as now."

"Well, shoot. Do you want me to tell you something that isn't true?"

His shoulders hunched. "Christ, Lou, this isn't a courtroom. All I want are your impressions, no matter how wild they sound. I'm getting desperate with this guy. Give me *something.*"

"Okay." She closed her eyes, letting her mind bring up that memory. She could see the buildings that lined the street, the sharp-edged transitions from light to shadow and back again . . . and there in the silver-bordered side-view mirror, the dark, swooping shape. "I'm sure it was a man by the way he moved. Quick and aggressive. He looked big, but you've got to remember that I saw him in the side-view mirror, and was surprised to boot, so my perceptions—"

"Don't analyze it," he said.

"Whatever you say."

"At last," he muttered.

She chose to ignore that one. "He seemed big. Tall, wide shoulders, although that could have been his jacket."

He looked at her over his shoulder. "Jacket?"

"I think so," she said, surprised by the depth of her own memory. "Jacket or coat. I registered the shadow as kind of . . . swooping toward me. Now, thinking back on it, he must have been wearing a coat or jacket and that it flapped around him as he ran."

82

"Good," he said. "Real good. Anything else?"

Lou searched through her memory files, wishing she could find something useful to him. Finally, however, she shook her head. "Sorry. I guess I wasn't much help."

He turned back to the stove. "A man was spotted around the ribbon factory just before the fire, and the citizen who described him said he was wearing some kind of coat, like a trench coat."

"Coincidence?"

"Maybe," he said. "Or maybe not. Someone set fire to the dumpster behind the station."

"Do you carry a gun?"

"No. I've never needed one. Never liked them, actually."

"I suggest you start."

He didn't answer. Lou watched his quick, efficient movements as he slid the bacon out of the pan and broke a half-dozen eggs into the hot grease. Subject closed, apparently.

"Those aren't all for me, I hope," she said.

"Nope. You're feeding me and Blaire, too. I got a call from your boss last night."

"Deveraux?"

He glanced at her over his shoulder. "Steggans."

"I suppose he told you about Jay Nesmith."

"In excruciating detail. He thinks it's possible the man had been stealing and set the fire to cover up for it."

"Hmm."

"You don't agree?"

She lifted one shoulder, then let it drop. "I wouldn't have pegged Jay for it, no. But I wouldn't have pegged him to get drunk on the job, either. Hasn't anyone talked to him?"

"He's missing."

"What?"

"His wife said he never came home last night. She filed a report with the police early this morning."

Lou clasped her hands, then unclasped them and tucked them between her knees. The taste of dread soured the back of her throat. "Did he go bar-hopping with the guys, or maybe just buy a bottle to drown his sorrows somewhere?"

"I hope so," Whitaker said. "There are a lot of people who want to talk to that guy. Sunnyside up?"

"Over easy. What are you going to do if he doesn't show up?"

"It's not my bailiwick, Lou. He's police business now." He divided the eggs among three plates. "Unless, of course, he burns something down."

"You don't think . . ."

"Wednesday nights his wife takes the kids and visits her mother in Virginia Beach."

Lou frowned. "How convenient. But he's been living here for a number of years, and we haven't seen these arsons until recently. Did he maybe catch pyromania like the flu?"

"No. But maybe he'd been fighting it, and it just finally got too strong for him to ignore."

Again, Lou got that doesn't-quite-fit feeling of unease. It didn't smell right, not at all. But then Blaire stepped into the room, dispelling the gathering gloominess.

"Hey, something really smells good," she said. "Hurry up, Dad. Not only am I starving, but Lou looks like she's about to fall out of her chair."

"We'll be out of here in a couple of minutes," Whitaker said, brandishing the spatula. "Ungrateful child."

Blaire grinned at her father, then turned back to Lou. "Your parrots are gorgeous. And Elihu isn't at all the demon Dad made him out to be."

"You should have seen him the other day," Whitaker said.

Blaire's gaze didn't waver from Lou's face. "What are you going to do with the fledglings?"

"I haven't thought about it," Lou said. "I don't have room for them, or the energy. Elihu and Emily are quite enough. Hey, I know! Why don't you take them?"

"No," Whitaker said.

"Yes," Blaire said. "I'd love them."

"No!"

"Oh, let her have them," Lou said. "With that zoo you have over there, what difference will a few more animals make?"

He brought the plates to the table, then sat down in the chair opposite Lou's. Laughter danced in his eyes. Lou realized that despite his protests, he didn't mind adding the birds to his menagerie.

The others' voices faded as her thoughts turned back to Jay Nesmith. She tried to imagine quiet, unassuming Jay as the maniac arsonist, and as the threatening dark shape that had swooped at her in that shadowed street. No go. It just didn't fit.

Something nagged at her, tilting at the edges of her memory. But the more she tried to grasp, the more elusive it became. If she could only . . .

"Dig in, Lou," Whitaker said. "There's nothing worse than cold eggs."

His voice shattered her train of thought. With a sigh, she picked up her fork and began to eat. God, she wished she could have pinned that nagging bit of memory down. She had the feeling it was important.

Seven

Lou's watch read eight o'clock as she ran downstairs to answer the door. A glance in the peephole showed Blaire, right on time as she'd promised.

"Hi," Lou said, swinging the door wide. "Come on in. I feel awful saying hi and bye—"

"I told you I don't mind," Blaire said. "The parrots and I will do just fine."

"Okay, but I don't know why you want to spend an evening with a couple of birds."

"I like birds," Blaire said. "Besides, both the boys are home, and they've got friends over—"

"And the house is full of boys in the throes of puberty." Lou said it *poo-berty,* like her mother always did. "You can't walk, talk or breathe without a fascinated audience, most of whom are seriously in lust with you."

"You've been there."

Lou looked the younger woman up and down, then patted her own generous hip. "Not quite, honey. Even twenty years ago, I didn't have your firepower."

Blaire laughed. "Get out. Seriously, though; you'll have to come out when the boys *and* Dad are there. It's an interesting sociological phenomenon. They stare, and he swells up like a great big toad."

"Being fatherly?"

"Being male, and territorial."

"Ah, yes," Lou said, thinking that she wouldn't mind if Whitaker acted a little male and territorial around her. "Well, I've got to run. Don't let any strangers in, and lock up when you leave."

"Don't worry."

"Oooooh, baby," Elihu exclaimed.

"Did you teach him that?" Blaire asked.

"My son. Lovely boy that he is." Lou slipped her jacket on and headed for the door. "There are some apples in the fridge, if you want to give them a treat," she called over her shoulder. "Cut it small enough to push through the bars. And be careful of Elihu. He's a tricky little b—devil."

"Yes, Mommy dearest."

Lou stopped in her tracks. "Gawd, was I that bad?"

"You sounded just like Dad. Is it age, you think, or something that happens to the brain due to parenthood?"

"Parenthood," Lou said, walking out.

What a great kid, she thought as she got into the Corolla. How many teenagers would take time to pursue a friendship with some woman her father had brought around? One with an independent mind. Was that a Whitaker trait, or a wolfhound one?

"Oh, Wade, have I got a surprise for you," she said.

She headed to work, swinging onto the new 164 interchange. It still felt strange, all these new highways and byways, and not entirely welcome. Progress had come to Western Branch with a vengeance. Town houses, gas stations, the new Chesapeake Square Mall—and traffic lights. Many traffic lights.

As the road curved southeast to meet the West Norfolk bridge, she noticed a sullen red stain in the dark-

87

ness ahead. One swift, encompassing thought shot through her mind: Wednesday night. The arsonist had promised a fire, and he'd kept that promise. Smack in the middle of downtown. The sheer audacity of it was sobering; that, and the thought of what could have happened if he'd decided to strike during the day when those office buildings were full of people.

Instead of turning toward the shipyard, she took a right on Broad Street and headed toward downtown. Inevitability settled in the pit of her stomach. Every passing block brought the fire into clearer focus. The glow resolved into a close-packed cluster of flame, against which the silhouettes of buildings cut an orange-limned skyline.

She could have avoided it. Should have avoided it. But the fire drew her powerfully, it and the awareness that its creator had touched her life, however briefly. The Fire Man.

"Wednesday night," she whispered. "Right on schedule."

Police and firefighters had blocked the area to traffic, so she parked the car and walked in as far as she could. She wasn't alone; a swiftly growing crowd had gathered, thrill-seekers, the merely curious, people with video cameras, and one guy, honest-to-God, with a sketchbook. Incendiary art? Lou wondered, boggled by the idea.

The fire had been set in an aging, five-story office building that was being renovated. A dark webbing of steel scaffolding hugged the walls, glowing cherry-red in places where the flames had punched through plywood-covered windows. Smoke belched from every opening and billowed up into the sky in a massive black column. Firemen struggled to bring the blaze under control, aiming powerful streams of water into the building. Roaring defiance, the fire fought back, retreating in one place only to break out with renewed violence somewhere else.

Even at this distance, Lou could feel the heat on her face like a dry desert hand, pulling her skin taut over cheekbones and chin, sucking the moisture out of her lips.

"Holy shit," a nearby man said, awe in his voice.

Lou nodded agreement. But not because of the fire, impressive as it was. She tilted her head back, watching as the flames leaped higher, punching through the roiling cloud of smoke.

The Fire Man's challenge, written upon the sky itself.

The flames looked like hungry beasts, devouring everything they touched. A poetic notion, but inaccurate. Animals ate to survive, killed to survive; fire, like man, destroyed until it was stopped or until there was nothing left to consume.

Despite the sweat beading on her forehead and upper lip, Lou began to shiver. She understood. Finally and completely, she understood.

The firebug liked it. The destruction, the roaring power of the fire, amoral and uncaring—he liked it. And because he'd set it, the fire's power became his. So seductive, so very compelling. Light a match, screw the world.

He had to be here. Laughing at the people scurrying. gawking, watching their fascination, enjoying their fear. No wonder Whitaker wanted him so badly.

Her throat tightened around the sudden taste of terror. He could be anyone. The man standing beside her, or the one over there. Or behind her, maybe. She felt naked, exposed, her back a vast, unprotected expanse just begging for the strike.

He knows what I look like.

She could feel him. It was almost as though a cord connected them, a strange sort of bond forged in that shadowy street a few days ago. His malice beat at her, a dark, primeval sweep of terror that defied all logic, all civilized convention. This was the Fire Man's world. His creation, his destruction.

He knows what I look like.

She glanced around at the crowd, finding herself awash in a sea of fire-lit eyes. The roar of the fire, the shrieking of sirens, the amorphous crowd noise all merged into a clamoring whole. Lou took a deep breath, but it was like sucking an empty tank. Claustrophobia clawed at her throat, sent jagged black patches shredding across her vision.

Every ounce of instinct screamed *run!* But she resisted it, forcing herself to move slowly through the crowd and watch for anyone who might be following her. Someone bumped her, hard enough to startle, and she had to bite down on her lip to keep from crying out.

Once clear, she ran back to her car and got in, locking all the doors. Her hands shook so badly that it took her three tries to get the key in the ignition.

"Take it easy, Malotti," she muttered.

With an effort of will, she brought her trembling under control and got the car started at last. The engine revved as fast as her heart, and she forced herself to ease up on the gas pedal. With the street ahead blocked, she backed out and around the corner.

Everything smelled like smoke—her clothes, her hair, even her skin. The Fire Man's calling card. She caught sight of herself in the rearview mirror, and grimaced at the echoes of fear haunting her eyes.

Tough Lou Malotti. She'd prided herself on the fact that she never ran from anything.

Hah.

That bitch.

He watched her face in the lurid light of the fire, saw the watchfulness, the fear, the awareness that he was somewhere close.

If she only knew.

She looked younger in this light, but no more vulnerable. Even afraid, she had an air of self-reliance that rasped along his nerves like jagged iron filings. Bitch. She kept turning up in places she wasn't supposed to be. Bothering him. Looking for him. And like now, *feeling* him. She'd become a problem, both because of her perception and because he couldn't trust her to run away if she spotted him. Bitch. Pushy bitch; most men would have thought twice about coming after him, even in a car.

He stayed back in the shadows, away from the crowd, and tried to watch the blaze. His gaze kept straying from the fire to her face, from her face to the fire. Rage blossomed in him, as hot as the blaze outside. She had no right. This was his time, when all the world belonged to him.

Get out!

He wanted to keep the contest between himself and Whitaker clean, without outside entanglements.

Get out!

He wanted to be left alone to enjoy his handiwork without looking over his shoulder to see if she'd stumbled onto him again. Why her, of all the people in the world? Somehow, fate had appointed her as his personal affliction. Fate; those bitch-goddesses who couldn't seem to keep their noses out of people's business. He'd slipped through their hands too often, and now they'd picked one of their own to dog his path.

For a moment, fire roared in the recesses of his mind. A big fire, big enough to put him in the history books. He'd create that one some day.

His vision cleared abruptly, and he realized *she* had vanished from sight. Heart thumping, he scanned the crowd. He wouldn't he surprised to find her searching for him, gazing into face after face until she found him.

"Damn you," he hissed between clenched teeth. "Damn you."

Then he spotted her, walking quickly back toward her car. He took a step toward her. Then, out of the corner of his eye, he saw Whitaker stride up to the barricade.

He hesitated, glancing from the lieutenant to the woman. Which required his attention? Which was more dangerous?

Whitaker. The bitch. Whitaker, the bitch.

Eenie, meenie, minie, moe . . . Instinct made the decision for him. Turning, he followed the woman.

She'd already reached her car, however. Too late. He stopped, fists clenched, to watched the Corolla until it turned the corner. God, he wished he had X-ray vision like Superman's, something that could take that car and make it crash. Something nice and hot, an exploding gas tank, maybe.

"Later, doll," he said, turning back to Whitaker and the fire.

Lou walked out to the end of the finger pier and sat down to eat her lunch—if this 2:00 A.M. meal could be called lunch. She kept her back to the city behind her, not wanting to know if the fire's glow still stained the sky.

The breeze swirled off the river, heavy with the smell of fish and diesel. A working river, the Elizabeth. But the night erased some of what man had done to her, and sprinkled stardust and moon-glow over the muddy water. Lou sighed, glad for the sight of something that couldn't be touched by fire.

"Here's to you, old girl."

She raised her Coke in a salute—then froze as she caught movement out of the corner of her eye. Heart pumping madly, she turned to face it.

And she heaved a sigh of relief, seeing that it was only Tyrene Bell. Although, she amended, "only" couldn't be used to describe Tyrene in any shape, form or manner. The big man moved with a sureness that showed he knew just how much of the world he occupied, and liked it. Indestructible Tyrene, who could lift loads of pipe a forklift might envy. Of course, he never got in fights; who'd be crazy enough to roust a fella his size?

"Hi, Tyrene." Noticing the small cooler he carried, she added, "Pull up a chair and spread your tablecloth out."

He sat down beside her. "Ahh, fine dining," he said, flipping the cooler open. "Damn. Tuna salad again. What you got in there?"

"Ham and cheese."

"Want to trade?"

"Uh-uh. There's enough fish in the air to suit me." She leaned over to peer into the cooler. "But I'll swap a chocolate-chip cookie for one of those brownies."

"Those are my wife's double-chocolate-and-walnut brownies, famous all over Portsmouth."

"Okay, *two* cookies."

93

He grinned, a flash of white in his dark face. "You drive a hard bargain, Lucretia lady."

They ate in companionable silence. Lulled by the gentle lapping of the water against the pier, Lou found herself fighting to keep her eyes open.

"Not used to workin' nights yet?" Tyrene asked.

"I don't think I'm ever going to be," she said.

He chuckled. "You ain't got it so hard. Think about me; I got six kids, two under three years old, and I got to try and sleep during the day."

"My condolences," she said, with complete sincerity.

Tyrene pulled an almost-empty pack of cigarettes out of his pocket and shook one out. He lit it, cupping his hand around the lighter flame to protect it from the breeze off the river.

"Smoking's bad for your health," Lou said.

He drew in deeply. "So's six kids."

"I know a dog that babysits. Herds hamsters, too. Want me to find out how much she charges?"

"Huh?"

"You heard me."

"Oh, man. You been drinking?"

She laughed. "It's true. I know four kids who swear their wolfhound raised them."

He leaned his elbows on his knees and stared out over the river. Lou followed his gaze. A fish broke the surface briefly, leaving a swirl of moonlight-silvered bubbles on the dark water.

"I love this time of year," Lou murmured.

"Don't get used to it. Weatherman said it's going to turn cool again. Lows in the forties, if I remember him right."

"Oh, brother. And I thought I could turn the furnace off for good."

"Yeah." He sighed, taking a deep drag on his cigarette. Smoke dribbled from his nostrils. "You know, I never thought I'd say it, but I miss that old bastard Carmichael."

"Everyone hated him when he was here."

"Hey, Carmichael's heart may have been black as Satan's, but at least he had one. That Eichmann, now, is one cold mother."

"Better get in the habit of calling him Van Allen, Tyrene. You might slip up around the wrong person."

He shrugged. "He's not gonna bother with us blue-collar folk. As long as we do our jobs and keep making money for him, he ain't about to notice us until it's time to hand out our pink slips."

Too true, Lou thought. And not limited to the blue-collar folks. Van Allen had made it clear early on that profit was his goal, and that employees were as replaceable as bolts.

Cupping his palm around the cigarette, Tyrene took a last drag and then flicked the butt toward the river. It flew in a glowing orange arc, then winked out of existence as the water closed around it.

"See that moon?" he asked. "My grandmamma would have called that a hangin' moon."

Lou looked up. The moon hovered sharp as a scimitar overhead, surrounded by the hard-edged glitter of stars. A hanging moon. Not a comforting thought. Unconsciously, she rubbed her forearms.

"Lou, I got a problem," he said.

She turned to look at him. "What's the matter?"

"You know the *Gabriella?*"

"She went out today, didn't she?"

"Yeah." He rubbed his hand across his jaw, a fretful gesture. "The night before last, I was supposed to redo that weld in the boiler room. But then I got pulled off that to do somethin' else. Thing is, I don't know if anybody else was put on the redo."

"What?"

"Now, look. You got to be cool about this. They sure don't tell me everything everybody does. Maybe somebody on the morning shift did it fast and nasty and they reinspected it right afterward. But that's cutting it mighty close."

Something cold and hard settled in Lou's chest, and it felt like trouble. "Especially since I heard that Van Allen came into the yard with some Enterprise brass to watch the *Gabriella* go out all painted and pretty."

"Oh, man." Tyrene drew in his breath with a hiss. "Forget what I told you..Forget everything."

"I can't."

"I got a bad feeling about this," he said. "Real bad."

"Me too." Retrieving her trash, she thrust it back into the paper lunch bag and stood up. "You're out of this now, Tyrene. As far as I'm concerned, I don't remember who told me."

"Let it go," he said.

She shook her head. "I'll be quiet checking it out, believe me. But if I find out that ship went out of here with a failed weld, I'm going to raise holy hell. That was a boiler valve, man. Big, big problems."

"You got twenty years here. You start messin' with this, you're gonna find yourself on the street."

His words brought her insecurities rising up in a gut-clenching wave: Wade's college expenses, her mortgage, her car payment, the too-slim IRA. She shrugged them away. "There's right and wrong, Tyrene. And this is dead wrong."

"Oh, man."

"I'm going back to the office. You'd better stick around here for a while so no one ties us together."

"You be careful."

To her surprise, she didn't have to force a smile. "You can bet on that."

She headed for the office, her strides lengthening the closer she got. God, she hated working nights! This wouldn't have happened if she'd been working days; between her and Deveraux, they'd pretty much kept track of everything that went on.

Things started clicking into place in her mind, and every one rang an alarm bell: Deveraux out on sick leave, the QA database screwed up, the funny business with the *Gabriella*. And the senior inspector assigned to nights, where she'd be cut off from the lifeline of the department.

Lou felt as though she'd stepped into quicksand; the ground quaking all around her, ready to suck her in, and nobody there to throw her a line. Who'd set her up? Steggans? Not necessarily, and not because he put her on nights. Actually, his inexperience at the yard was his best defense. This smelled like someone who knew exactly how things worked, and knew what to do to make them work *his* way.

She took the elevator up to the office instead of the back stairs; late at night like this, she found the silent emptiness of the building oppressive.

First, she checked the log to see if anyone had done a reinspect on the *Gabriella*. No one had. Or rather, no one had written it down; with the computer off limits until the repair tech could find the problem, QA business had returned to the stone age of pencil and paper.

She moved to the scheduling file. Eddy Simmon had been scheduled for the *Gabriella* first thing Wednesday morning, but no entry had been made as to whether the inspection had been completed or not.

The phone shrilled, startling her. She picked it up hastily. "QA, Malotti here."

"Lou, this is Sam down at the machine shop. I'm going over the specs for a valve for the helicopter transport, and they don't look right. I know you worked with something similar a couple of months ago—"

"I remember the job," she said. "I'll pull those records and come right down."

"Thanks."

With a sigh, she tossed the receiver back into the cradle. Her search was going to have to wait. She swiveled her chair around to the file cabinet behind her.

"If you were smart," she muttered as she flipped through the files, "you'd take Tyrene's advice and leave this thing alone."

But she wasn't. And she couldn't.

The rest of the night passed in a blur of work. Everything seemed to take twice as long without the computer, and exhaustion set in long before her shift was over.

Bleary-eyed, Lou stood at the window and watched the dawn spread out across the river in a wash of pink and gold. It seemed like a benediction, and she took it personally. "Thank you, God," she murmured.

Steggans came in a half hour early, and looked as tired as she felt. She gave him enough time to get a cup of coffee and sit down before going to his office.

"Can we talk?" she asked, pausing in the open doorway.

"I've got a ton of things to do—"

"It'll only take a minute."

"All right," he said. "But make it quick."

He waved her to a chair, then folded his hands on the desk and waited for her to begin.

"I'd like to know who did the reinspect on the *Gabriella*."

His eyebrows went up. "Jay Nesmith."

"Jay?" She stared at him in astonishment. "But you fired him for drunkenness the day he was supposed to do that!"

"I fired him that afternoon. Apparently he did the reinspect that morning." Opening his center drawer, he pulled out a folder and spun it across the desk to Lou. "We found this late yesterday afternoon; it had fallen behind his desk."

Lou went through the report carefully, ignoring Steggans's impatiently drumming fingers. Everything seemed to be there. But despite the accurate figures, the neatly written evaluation, alarm bells kept ringing in the back of her brain. *Walk away,* whispered a small, cautious voice in her mind. Remember those twenty years, remember the mortgage, your retirement, that seven-hundred-dollar-a-month house payment.

She almost managed it. But then, rising like a big white bird out of the murk of her thoughts, came the old bugaboo of do-the-right-thing-and-damn-the-consequences. Ethics. The old right and wrong. They'd haunted her all her life.

"I can't accept this report." she said.

"Why not? Look, Lou . . ." He rubbed his chin, a fretful gesture. "I didn't make the decision to let the *Gabriella* sail out of here. Van Allen did. I showed him the report, explained the situation with Jay, and left it up to him."

"He doesn't know diddly about ships," Lou said.

Steggans's lips twitched, and for a moment she thought he might be about to laugh. "There might be some, ah, truth in that. But he let three QA people check the report, and all three of them thought it looked fine."

"Sure, it *looks* fine," Lou protested. "But this guy was fired for drunkenness that same day."

"In the afternoon. The time on that report reads nine-fifteen. Lou, it's been checked and rechecked and checked again. Everyone is satisfied."

It made sense. Anyone would accept it.

It was logical, reasonable. And safe. She lined all those nice, logical facts up in her mind and looked at them. They still made sense. Two plus two equals four—clean, neat and easy to see. Math had always been her best subject.

But another thought hovered at the edge of that tidy picture, and she just couldn't shake it. The timing of this was just too convenient. *Ask and ye shall receive. Van Allen wants to bring Enterprise brass down to the yard, and* voilà! *here's Jay's lost report!*

And the QA database just happened to be inaccessible. How convenient. To get the Enterprise contracts, the shipyard had bid very, very close, leaving no fat to absorb mistakes.

Lou watched Steggans's expression closely, but couldn't find the slightest flicker or alarm or guilt on his face. In a way, she felt sorry for him; it couldn't be easy walking a tightrope between Van Allen and the rest of the shipyard, especially with the complication of blood-ties. She didn't think Van Allen was any warmer to his cousin than he was to anybody else.

"A penny for your thoughts," he said.

Lou sighed. "I just wish Jay would show up so we could ask him some questions."

"Like he'd tell us."

"Yeah." She closed the report with a snap. "What does the tech say about the computer?"

"He's says he's working on it. Today, he suggested we just reformat—"

"And lose everything?" Lou yelped.

"That was my reaction." He did smile this time. "Don't we have a copy of the data somewhere else?"

Lou nodded. "Sure. Deveraux has a copy."

"That's *great*—"

"But he's been out," Lou interjected. "What . . . three and a half weeks now? Has anyone been keeping copies of the latest entries?"

Steggans's face fell. "No. We've been running so crazy, no one thought of it."

Deveraux would have. Lou didn't say it aloud, of course.

"You can reformat and slide the data from Deveraux's copy back in," she said. "But then you'll lose the files from the past three weeks For sure."

"Well, three weeks lost is better than all of it."

"Is it?"

His eyes narrowed. "What do you mean?"

"I'd like to take a look at those recent files," she said. "With Jay drinking on the job, I think all his recent inspections should be looked at."

"You've got to be kidding."

"No, I'm not."

"No way can I authorize that. Mr. Van Allen would have a stroke."

Lou studied him, looking for guilt in the cracked-glass gaze. There was none; but then, she didn't see innocence, either. "Just do me a favor, okay? Delay reformatting that database until we're sure we've looked at every possible way of retrieving what we've lost."

"We?" he repeated.

"Okay, me. *I* want to look into it."

101

He leaned back in his chair, regarding her from beneath his lashes. "I don't see why we can't do that. At least for a few days."

His acquiescence surprised her. Maybe, just maybe, he wasn't quite as accepting of those neat facts as he'd seemed to be. And maybe, just maybe, he'd back her up if she found something. He didn't offer out loud, however, and she didn't ask. Obviously, he wasn't about to put his neck on the block without a very good reason.

Okay, fine. Neither was she.

He took the report from her, closed it, and dropped it back into his drawer. "Go on, get out of here and get some sleep. You look like a raccoon."

"Yes, *sir!*"

"And tell me if you find anything," he called after her.

"You bet."

It wasn't until Lou reached the parking lot that she realized Steggans's new-found cooperation hadn't extended to putting her back on day shift.

Oh, well, some days—or nights—you took what you could get.

Eight

Fire chased Lou through a dreamscape city. She ran down one empty street after another. Alone. No one to help her, no one even to hear her cries for help. Buildings lined every street, their blank, empty windows staring down upon her as she ran. Uncaring witnesses to her terror.

He stalked her down one street and the next, a flaming man-shape that laughed as it set the world afire. The buildings burst into flame as she ran between them, turning the street into a tunnel through hell. Gobbets of fire dripped down all around her, like tiny fire demons dancing wildly upon the asphalt. She whirled around, among, between the capering flames in a dance as mad as theirs.

Glancing over her shoulder, she saw that her pursuer had closed the gap between them, following so close now that she could feel the heat of him on her skin.

His mouth opened. He had no tongue, only a blood-red lash of flame.

"Lou," he rasped. "Come to me. Let me touch you. Hold you."

"No!" Cornering like a rabbit, she darted down a nearby alley.

Still he gained on her. She could feel his heat, his hatred. Her breath came in quick rasps now, from exertion and from fear. "Lou!" he called. "Louise. Loouise!"

"Ooooooh, baby!"

She sat bolt upright, out of the dream and into reality. And Elihu, who'd rescued her, crooning an absurd parody of "You Ain't Nothin' but a Hound Dog" into his ladylove's feathered ear.

Late afternoon sunlight streamed through the living room window, laying a bright golden bar across the sofa where she'd fallen asleep. She could feel its warmth on her skin.

"There's the heat," she said, using logic to banish the last shreds of her nightmare. Glancing up at the parrot's cage, she added, "And there's the guy who was *really* calling my name."

Elihu cocked one eye at her, then the other. *"Jeez, Louise! Jeeez, Louuise!"*

"You know, for once I'm glad it was you," she muttered, pushing up from the sofa.

The parrot herded his mate along the perch, away from Lou. "Don't get your shorts in a knot," she said. "I'm just going over there to plug the phone back in."

He glared at her, obviously skeptical.

"Why don't you do something useful, like crack your sweetie one of those nice peanuts Blaire left for you? Or is that considered woman's work?"

He made a noise that sounded an awful lot like a raspberry. Giving one back, Lou turned and went into the kitchen. Led by her stomach, of course. Dinnertime. Was it going to be a baked potato and salad, or a nice, big slice of the lasagna she'd put in the freezer last week?

"Lasagna," she said without missing a beat. *"And*

the salad. If I didn't have hopes of getting another one of those hugs from Loo-tenant Whitaker, I'd by God have garlic bread, too."

Three bright yellow Post-its flagged the door of the refrigerator. Lou scanned them quickly, noting that Blaire's handwriting was as neat and precise as the girl herself. "Wade called. Said he'd call back sometime this evening," the first said. "Don't forget to keep track of the weather. A cold front is coming in during the next few days, and you'll have to turn on the furnace. You can't let Emily get a chill," said the second. "Suggest you build or buy a nesting box. Getting the nest ready will help Emily's egg production, you know."

"Eek," Lou said. "I've gathered a monster to my bosom! I wonder if she does this to Papa Whitaker?"

Whistling under her breath, she shoved the lasagna into the microwave and programmed the automatic defrost. Something turned over in her brain, something that should have been obvious before but somehow wasn't. She stood for a moment, staring stupidly at the flashing LDC readout, then picked up the phone and dialed Whitaker's work number.

"Come on," she muttered. "Be there."

By some miracle, he was.

"Has Jay Nesmith ever turned up?" she asked.

"What happened to hello?"

"Hello. Has Jay turned up?"

"Funny you should ask. He called some friend of his at the shipyard this afternoon. Seems he's been on one hell of a bender, found himself in Fresno when he finally sobered up."

"Fresno! Why would he go to Fresno? Vegas, I could understand. And why didn't he call his wife instead of some guy at the shipyard?"

"I can't guess about Fresno, but if I'd run off on a

bender like that, I'd call *anybody* but my wife until she had a chance to cool off."

"I'd never cool off," Lou said. "And if that remark is an indication of character—"

"Damn it, Lou, it was an off-the-wall comment. Even if I were a drinking man, I've never had the time to go on a bender. Not that it hasn't occurred to me, with four kids to raise. And why did you want to know about Jay?"

"Huh?" Lou asked, still on issues of character and benders.

"Why did you want to know if Jay had shown up?"

"Well . . . I have to talk to his wife, and wanted to know if I should congratulate her or commiserate with her."

Lou almost told him about the *Gabriella*. The words were right there, ready to be said. But she didn't say them. This was an already complicated situation, and she didn't need it getting any murkier. Besides, with this Fire Man thing going on, he had plenty of other things to worry about. "I saw the fire last night," she said. "Actually, I was *at* the fire last night. It was right on my way to work."

Whitaker drew his breath in with a hiss. "Have you seen today's paper?"

"Not yet. Is he featured?"

"In spades. And in caps: FIRE MAN CHALLENGES AUTHORITIES. CATCH ME IF YOU CAN, DARES ARSONIST.

"Oh, brother."

"And he's promised to set another fire next Wednesday."

She nodded. *Of course.* The memory of a fiery dream plucked at the corners of her mind, coiling a hard knot of dread deep in her stomach.

"He scares me," she said, more to herself than to Whitaker.

"He scares me, too," he replied, almost as softly. "I've got to get him, Lou."

"Yes, you do."

"What's my first name?"

Startled, Lou dredged through her memory files. "Uh . . ."

"It's Bob."

"You know, talking to you is kind of like going through a revolving door," she said in exasperation. "Is there a specific purpose to this topic of conversation?"

"I *knew* you didn't remember my name."

"I've got a lot on my mind, you know, and there are only so many bytes available. I remember the essential stuff and dump the rest. You tell me to call you Whitaker, I call you Whitaker."

"Want to get together Saturday night?"

Oh, she thought, a suspicious warmth blossoming in her chest. "Shall I wear jeans, for hamster herding?"

"Hamster herding is retained as essential information?"

Lou considered several replies, discarding each as counterproductive. "Saturday will be fine."

"For your information, no hamsters and no kids. I'm taking you somewhere nice. Six o'clock okay?"

"Six is fine."

"Good. I've got to run; got a Fire Man to catch."

He hung up before she had a chance to say goodbye. Shaking her head, she dropped the receiver back into the cradle. "This is the weirdest relationship I've ever had," she muttered. "If it *can* be considered a relationship."

The microwave pinged. Ah well, there was always lasagna.

Jay Nesmith's family lived in a good-sized colonial a few blocks down from Coleman's nursery. Nice house, nice yard, everything kept up with meticulous care. Lou assessed it mentally, found it in line with a QA inspector's salary—if his wife worked.

Stepping up onto the porch, she rang the bell. Jay Nesmith's wife had obviously been waiting; she opened the door before the last bong sounded.

"Mrs. Nesmith, I'm Lou Malotti. I spoke to you on the phone earlier—"

"Come on in." Mrs. Nesmith had Lou's general proportions on a five-foot-two frame. Her plump face should have been good humored, but showed little but fatigue just now.

They might be having troubles, Lou thought, but she still loves him. "I'm sorry to bother you at a time like this, Mrs. Nesmith. I know you want to get Jay home and settled in—"

"Call me Kathy. And don't worry about intruding. You said something about wanting to see his computer?"

Lou nodded, following Kathy toward the back of the house. The furnishings were typical suburban-family; some new, some obviously well used, nothing out of the ordinary.

"Jay never talked much at work," she said. "But I think I remember him saying something about you being a teacher . . . ?"

"Bank teller. I work at Nationsbank, in Churchland. Here we are," Kathy said, opening a door to the right of the hallway.

Jay's study was a pleasant room, with its chocolate brown carpeting and the walls painted a deep apricot. An Indian blanket hung over the hide-a-bed and added dash to the color scheme. On the far wall, a Macintosh sat on a computer table.

"May I?" Lou asked.

"Can you use a Mac?"

Lou nodded. "I've got one at home," she said, sitting down in Jay's battered chair and switching the computer on.

"I don't know what you expect to find. Three people from Carmichael's security department came out yesterday and went through everything pretty carefully."

"Did they find anything?"

Kathy shook her head. "They wanted to take the disk drive with them, but I wouldn't let them."

"I'm surprised you let them in at all."

"It didn't occur to me to refuse. I just thought it was some horrible mistake, and once they saw that there was nothing here, they'd leave Jay alone. But they acted like he was some kind of criminal, and one of them even threatened to bring the police into it." Her chin went up. "I kicked them out in a hurry, believe me."

"Why did you let me come?" Lou asked.

"Because you asked nicely, and because Jay always said you were a straight-up person."

Lou stared at her in surprise. "He never said much more than hello to me."

"That didn't mean he was blind. He knew who was a jerk and who was all right. If there's something in his files that can help you with your problem, then you're welcome to it."

The rewards of living right, Lou thought, watching

109

as Kathy opened a cabinet and pulled out a floppy-disk storage box.

"Here," she said. "These are Jay's backups."

"You didn't show these to the security guys?"

"No."

"If the shipyard decides to press charges, they'll get a warrant."

Kathy's mouth compressed into a thin line. "Fine. But until they do, these belong to Jay. And if I were you, I'd use the disks rather than the hard drive. I don't trust those guys not to have messed with something."

Lou grimaced. Kathy was probably more right than she thought. At this point, almost anyone at Carmichael's was suspect. *Except me, Deveraux, Tyrene— and maybe Steggans.*

She flipped through the box, found the program she wanted, and booted up the computer.

"The information on the disks should be current," Kathy said. "Jay is a real fuddy-duddy about keeping everything just so. But I doubt you'll find anything unusual there, just a bunch of computer games and correspondence, family budgets and stuff like that."

"It's worth a try," Lou said. "If he happened to have put some notes in here on that inspection we shared, it would save me about two weeks' work."

"Well, Jay rarely brought work home. Why should he?" she added with stinging bitterness. "He spent twelve hours a day at that place as it was."

Lou glanced at the other woman. "So do the rest of us. Goes with the territory, I guess."

"He liked his job. But he was never one to make friends at work. Well, except for Harry Deveraux. He likes Harry a lot."

"Everyone likes Harry," Lou said, watching the

other woman's hands clasp and unclasp nervously. "What's the matter, Kathy?"

They didn't know each other, but something sparked between them. Maybe it was sympathy, one woman's response to another's pain. Maybe it was just stress, and Lou happened to be the handiest shoulder to cry on. Whichever, words began to spill out of Kathy in a flood.

"He's never been one to get drunk," she said. "Oh, he'll have a beer or two sometimes, but never at work." Tears began to run down her face. She accepted the tissue Lou held out, wiping ineffectually at the flow. "We . . . had some problems lately. The usual things, I guess. But for him to get himself fired, then run off to God-knows-where—"

"Fresno," Lou said.

"Why Fresno?"

Lou got up and put her arm around the other woman's shoulders. "Maybe it was just the place he ended up. He's been under a lot of stress lately. Maybe when he got fired, something just snapped. It happens."

"Now that I know he's okay, I want to *kill* him!"

Kathy's face changed as the words sunk in. She and Lou exchanged a glance, then broke into smiles.

"Men are just like kids sometimes," Lou said.

"Tell me about it."

"I'm glad he's okay. Have you talked to him?"

"No. He sent a message through some guy at the shipyard, said for us not to worry, and he'd be back as soon as he gets a few things straightened out." She flushed suddenly, as though just now realizing that she'd revealed a good chunk of her private life to a stranger. She stepped backward, out of Lou's embrace. "God, look at the time! I've got to get dinner started;

111

the boys are going to be coming in from baseball practice soon, ravenous as always. Go on, take your time."

"Thanks."

With the kitchen sounds as company, Lou went through Jay's data files. A methodical man, indeed; everything was labeled, sorted, and alphabetized. She grimaced, thinking about the ragtag jumble of disks, manuals and papers that cluttered her own desk.

She settled down in front of the computer and started on the files. The search soon became monotonous. Some people cluttered their house with junk; Jay Nesmith cluttered his disks with data, data and more data, most of which was as useful as Aunt Nellie's Mason jar collection. She found games, both children's and adult; she found the family budget, tax forms, even the Christmas lists from last year. Nothing, however, even remotely connected to Carmichael Shipyard.

Kathy poked her head into the doorway. "Do you want anything? A sandwich, maybe, or something to drink?"

"No, thanks," she said. "I see what you mean when you call Jay a fuddy-duddy."

"I warned you. I suppose I should be grateful he collects computer disks instead of, say, beer cans or matchbook covers. Sure you don't want anything?"

"Positive."

"Then I'll let you get back to it."

Lou turned back to the computer, vaguely registering Kathy's retreating footsteps. With an hour left before she had to get to work, she reached the last of Jay's files without finding anything that could help her.

Let it go, whispered a cynical voice in her mind. *You tried, and now it's time to walk away. It's only self-preservation.*

She'd never been able to listen to that voice before,

and this was no exception. With a sigh, she started in at the beginning of the disk file again. This time she compared each file with the corresponding one on the hard drive.

And found it. The anomaly. Trouble with a capital *T.*

Her recognition was more subliminal than conscious, her mind's automatic tag of something familiar. Jay had hidden it well, burying it in the middle of a file labeled "Savings Bonds, Children."

Lou sat back in her chair, staring at the screen. It was just a list of numbers, no other notations, no indication of what or who they belonged to. But if those weren't sequential numbers of past inspections, she'd eat that computer.

"Well, I'll be damned," she said. "I wonder what they're doing here, and why you hid them. And what do you want to bet these numbers are so recent that they're not going to show up on Deveraux's disk?"

She sat back in her chair, her gaze moving upward to the well-stocked shelf of computer books above the monitor. Jay had been much more than a simple dabbler; some of those books would be Greek to anyone without a sound working knowledge of computer systems.

The cynical voice popped up again, chiming crystal clear and hard in her mind. There was no better way of circumventing the inspection process than to have a QA inspector in one's pocket. Especially one who knew computers.

The time had come to talk to her absent boss. Even flat on his back, Harry Deveraux knew more about the shipyard than anyone.

She riffled through the desk, found a blank disk, and copied the Savings Bond disk onto it. Some heavy-duty work waited for her, she thought, slipping the disk into her pocket. Digging this stuff out of Central Files was going to be as easy as finding a contact lens in the ocean. Whistling under her breath, she switched off the computer and walked out to the kitchen.

Kathy stood at the sink, washing dishes. She turned the water off when Lou came in. "Finished?" she asked.

"Pretty much. I'd like to come back and look at the rest, if I may."

"Jay will be back by then. You'll have to ask him." Kathy twisted the dishtowel, an agitated gesture. "Do you think . . . Has he done something wrong?"

Lou hesitated. Lying would be easiest. But here, in this woman's kitchen with its buttery oak cabinets and warm copper colors, she couldn't. "Maybe," she said.

"He . . ." Kathy's voice broke. Taking a deep breath, she tried again. "He's never been in trouble before. If he hadn't run off like this, I'd never have believed it possible for him to *be* in trouble."

"Things happen, Kathy. Did he gamble? Drink?"

"No. Nothing like that. He'd seemed worried lately, but then we'd been arguing a lot, and I just figured . . ." She pressed the backs of her hands against her eyes. "Why doesn't he come back? Why doesn't he call? All I want to do is talk to him, ask him what he's done, and what he's going to do!"

You're not the only one, Lou added silently.

114

Nine

"What?"

Lou angled the receiver so Deveraux's shout passed over her ear instead of into it. "You heard me, Harry."

"You're sure about this?"

"Hell, no, I'm not sure. But there's an awful lot of funny business going on, and I can't believe one disgruntled employee is responsible for all of it."

"Damn," he growled. "I'm stuck here, flat on my back and doped to the gills with pain-killers—"

"It hasn't improved your disposition any."

"They'd have to give me a lobotomy to improve my disposition."

"Do you want me to call your doctor and request it?"

"My wife already has." He snorted, then gasped. "Ouch. Can't even grunt without hurting."

Pain leached the growl out of his voice, and Lou felt guilt settle like a stone on her shoulders. After all, the man had only been out of the hospital a few days. But he was the only one she could go to on this, the only one she could trust.

"Harry, I'm sorry. I shouldn't have bothered you—"

"Well, where the hell else would you have gone? Van Allen, maybe?"

"I thought about it."

"What are you going to tell him? You *think* something's going to happen to a weld that *maybe* isn't all that great? Remember, his ass is on the line, too."

"His money's on the line. The only people whose asses are on the line are those sailors in that boiler room."

He sighed. "I'll play devil's advocate, okay? Pretend I'm Van Allen. You've just told me what you suspect. My next question to you is how long do you think that weld will hold?"

"A while," she said, her stomach churning as she saw where he was heading. "Maybe a couple of years."

"Wow, Van Allen says. A couple of years. But I've got big money problems right now. The only hope I've got of pulling this shipyard through is to keep these Enterprise contracts going, no matter how shitty they are. If I tell those folks that one of their ships might have gone out of here with a faulty weld, they're gonna pull their business so fast it'll make your head spin. So you tell me about this, and I'm going to nod my head politely and ignore it in the hope that my situation will look better next year or the one after. You put proof in front of me, I might have to do something about it."

"That sucks, Harry," she said.

"Look . . ." His breath went out in a sigh. "Carmichael's not in the best financial health, okay? Something like this gets around, and that'll be the end. We'll all be looking for jobs."

"I can't worry about that, and neither can you. If they're passing bad welds, they've got to be stopped."

"Yeah, I know. But you listen to me, girl. You go charging into this thing with your usual full-speed-ahead-and-damn-the-torpedoes style, you're going to

116

end up hurting a lot of innocent people. You go soft on this thing, and you go quiet."

Lou thought about Tyrene and his six kids. There were a couple of thousand people just like him working at the shipyard, all depending on Carmichael paychecks.

"Okay," she said. "I'll go soft and quiet for now. But the minute I find something—"

"Then you kick their butts, and I'll help you."

She heaved a sigh. "Okay."

"Have you had a chance to check those numbers out yet?"

"Not yet. Without the QA database, it's going to take some time."

"Yeah, the database. Convenient little slip-up, wasn't it?"

"I thought so. Did they come by to get your copy?"

"Sure. But that stuff's a month old, and what do you want to bet what you need isn't going to be there?"

Lou pulled her antacids out and popped one into her mouth. "I'll just keep my fingers crossed so that I don't have to try to go through every purchase order in Central Files."

"Oo, that would be fun."

"It's better than surgery."

"Anything's better than surgery," he retorted. "Hey, have you heard anything more about the fire in the Quonset?"

"Whitaker hasn't said much about it. With this arsonist running around, he hasn't had time for small stuff."

"I detect a different note in your voice when you say his name. Is something going on there?"

Not enough. "I've met his dog."

"Wow. His dog. That's one hell of a hot relationship.

117

Now, if you . . ." His voice became muffled, as though he'd put his hand over the phone. "I *know* it's time for my pill. Damn it, Helen, the thing puts me to sleep. I don't want to go to sleep."

Lou heard a woman's voice in the background saying something about the doctor.

Deveraux's voice went up a notch. "You do that, I'll divorce you. Okay, okay, five minutes. *One* minute, goddamn it."

"Harry—" Lou began.

"Call me the minute you hear anything. Anything, understand?"

"Yes, Harry."

"I gotta go. Helen's threatening to administer that pill as a suppository."

"Tell her I think it's an excellent idea."

He hung up. Smiling, she set the receiver down and sat down beside the parrots' cage to work on the nesting box. Elihu clambered along the bars to watch her.

"What do you think?" she asked, holding the box up. "Maybe not my best attempt ever at woodworking—"

"Apple, apple!"

"No, it's not an apple. It's a nesting box."

He turned one eye to her, then the other.

"He doesn't get it, does he, Emily?" Lou asked. The female bobbed up and down comically. Lou's smile widened.

The doorbell rang, startling both her and the birds. Elihu let out a scream that made the fillings in her back teeth resonate.

"Easy," she said. "It's only the doorbell."

She peered out the peephole, her breath going out in surprise when she saw Whitaker standing on her porch. "What the . . ." she muttered, opening the door.

"If I hadn't known you had a parrot in there, that scream would have brought me right through this door," he said.

"You're not supposed to be here," she said, stepping back so he could come in.

"It's Saturday, isn't it?"

"It's five-fifteen on Saturday. You said six."

He smiled down at her, and she suddenly wanted to drop one wing and run in circles. Thank God she'd already showered and put her makeup on. He looked great; navy blue dress pants, white shirt, a paisley tie she wouldn't have believed him capable of wearing—a gift from one of his kids, no doubt—and a pale blue cotton sweater that turned his eyes the color of fine carbon steel.

"Blaire thought you might need some help with the nesting box," he said.

"Blaire thought I'd forget, is what she thought, and sent you over here to make sure I got it done. You can tell her for me that I built the thing this morning, and now the only thing I have left to do is attach it to the cage."

"Is that it?" Whitaker pointed to the rectangular wooden box that lay on the floor beside the cage. "I hate to say this, Lou, but it's never going to go through the door."

"It's going to be bolted to the *outside* of the cage. What do you think, parrots make little round nests like robins?"

He laughed. "After my first encounter with Elihu, I'd expect him to have a huge, eagle sort of nest way up in an aerie, where he can swoop down and carry off unsuspecting—"

"Ooooooh, baby!"

119

Whitaker's eyebrows went up. "Where did he learn that?"

"My son."

"Are you sure?"

She drew herself up. "I would never cavort with a man who said 'Ooh, baby.' "

His eyebrows went up another notch. "Cavort?"

They'd passed into uncharted territory, and Lou didn't know if she was under steam or sail. His eyes told her nothing; she saw laughter in them, the friendly warmth of companionship, but no trace of the sort of interest that went with "cavort."

"Come on," she said. "Let's get it on there so I can get dressed."

"Okay. I'll hold his legs while you do the bolting. Or maybe his neck would be better."

"Tempting, but no." Lou glanced at Elihu, saw the beginnings of agitation. "I'm not sure you should get anywhere near the cage. He's feeling kind of protective right now."

"Maybe he'll let me feed him."

"The way to a man's heart is through his stomach?"

He grinned. "Might work with birds. With men, the stomach thing is vastly overrated."

"Damn. And all these years, I've been going about it all wrong. No wonder . . ." Lou dropped that one, fast, and bent to dig a screwdriver out of the toolbox. "There are some peanuts in the canister beside the toaster. Peanuts are his absolute favorite food."

The bribe worked. Whitaker fed Elihu and Emily peanuts through the bars while Lou bolted the nesting box onto the side of the cage.

"There," she said, wiring the cage door open so the birds could access the box. "A few wood shavings, and you'll be all set."

Whitaker fed Elihu the last of the peanuts, then sat back on his heels. "Blaire's really excited about this."

"So am I."

"I hope you'll call her when the big event comes. She's got one more final this week, and then she'll be available day or night for parrot sitting."

"I'm not sure whether I should be reassured or terrified," Lou said.

Whitaker sighed. "She's just like her mother. Nola was an extremely organized and efficient woman. Nothing was ever out of place, nothing left undone."

Oh, brother, Lou thought. And here *I* am, wildly efficient when dealing with welds and ships and inspections, but a total screwup when it came to domesticity. Her mind conjured up Nola Whitaker in a Betty Crocker apron, dispensing love and cookies to her adoring husband. What would he get from Lou Malotti? Microwaved lasagna. And that was on the good nights.

"You loved your wife a lot, didn't you?" she asked.

"Yeah." He climbed to his feet, bending to brush sawdust off his knees. "When she died, I kind of lost it for a while. Blaire stepped in and took over, held things together. I probably let her take too much responsibility."

"Stop beating yourself over the head with it," she said, a bit more forcefully than she'd intended. "Blaire turned out just fine."

"Is something . . ." He glanced at his watch. "It's time for the news. Mind if I turn the TV on?"

"Be my guest. Are you keeping up on Fire Man news?"

"I can't seem to get away from it. He's really beginning to enjoy his notoriety."

He switched the channel to WAVY-10. Flames filled

121

the screen, a crackling orange and red inferno that looked as though it wanted to burst out into the room. Lou recoiled; the scene was so close to her dream that for a moment it seemed as though the television had picked her mind. A black wash of remembered terror flooded through her.

She flinched in surprise as Whitaker's hand grasped her elbow. "That's the building he burned Wednesday," he said, his calm voice bringing her back to reality with a jolt.

As though on cue, the camera panned backward. The building came into view, reducing the fire to its proper size. Lou let her breath out slowly.

The anchorman's head and shoulders came on the screen, superimposed on the image of the burning building. "This . . . Fire Man, as he wants to be called," said the anchorman, "struck again Wednesday night, setting a blaze that completely destroyed the Halberton Building. Losses are estimated to be several million dollars."

"Interesting effect," Lou said.

"Yeah."

"But the question," the reporter continued, "is not whether he'll strike again, but where. This afternoon he called this station and promised yet another blaze this coming Wednesday."

"Too bad they couldn't convince him to go for an interview," Lou said.

Whitaker didn't answer. She glanced at him, saw that his lips were moving in a soft but continuous string of profanities. His grip on her elbow tightened. Not enough to be painful, but enough to make her aware of the possibility.

"Take a breath, will you?" she said. "And watch the body parts; they're fragile."

"Huh? Oh," he muttered, letting her go. "Sorry."

"Thinking about wringing that firebug's neck, were you?"

"As a matter of fact, yes." He strode to the phone and punched savagely at the dial. "Gene, Whitaker here. Yeah, I saw it; that's why I'm calling." Then his face changed, going from grim to granite. "You're kidding. Jesus H. Christ! Yeah. Tell him to stay put, I'll be right there."

Lou watched him set the receiver back with a gentleness that was belied by the white-knuckled tension of his hands. Anger rolled from him in waves, an almost palpable force in the room. Lou shivered in the cold torrent of it, glad she wasn't the focus.

"What's the matter?" she asked. "What happened?"

He whirled, as though he'd forgotten she was there. She watched him pull his anger deep inside, tamping it down with an obvious effort of will. Interesting. Her ex-husband would have slammed out of the house, not to be seen again for hours.

"Remember that reporter MacLaren, the guy who was doing the articles on the arsonist?" Whitaker asked. "Well, he wrote a story on pyromania that ran in yesterday's paper, and it seems the goddamned firebug didn't like it. He told MacLaren to kiss off and went to WAVY-10 as his new sounding board. This afternoon MacLaren found a gallon can of gasoline in his garage, a big smiley-face drawn on the side. The Fire Man's farewell message."

"Holy cow!"

"Holy cow is right. MacLaren's scared shitless, of course, and is screaming for somebody to do *something*."

Lou shook her head. "Hold a lighted match for too long, and your fingers are going to get burned."

"Yeah."

Realization burst like fireworks in her mind, and she saw it dawn in Whitaker's eyes at the same time.

He doesn't like arson investigators, either.

"Goddamn it," he snarled. "Blaire's out tonight, and so's Mike. Keefe and Kelsey are there alone."

"Go to work," she said. "I'll run out to the house and stay with them until Blaire gets back."

"No. I'll get a squad car out."

"When?" she asked. "And for how long?"

He blew his breath out, a frustrated sound. "Long enough to check the place out."

"Fine. Have them check the place out. I'll stick with the kids, bring them over here if I have to."

He wanted her to; she could see it in his eyes. "I can't ask you—"

"Don't be primeval, Whitaker. I can take care of myself . . . and I'm bringing my .38 along for company."

"I didn't know you had a gun."

"First thing I bought when my ex walked out. Don't worry, I know what I'm doing, and I'm not the nervous type. Besides, you have an unlisted number, right? It's not like you advertise your address."

"Not in my line of work. But—"

"And you own the biggest dog on the East Coast. No arsonist is going to threaten *her* hamsters and get away with it."

He didn't laugh at her joke. "Shamu is the biggest chicken in the world. She's scared of the neighbor's cat, for God's sake."

"Well, I'm not."

He stared at her for a moment, then slipped a key off his ring and tossed it to her. "Thanks. I appreciate it."

Lou cringed inwardly, imagining the unsaid "good buddy" in his tone. She always seemed to do this with men; once she showed her self-reliance and general take-charge attitude, she passed from romantic interest to good friend. Well, to hell with it. She wasn't about to leave those kids alone tonight.

"You're welcome," she said.

"I hate Chinese checkers," Lou said after her third loss.

"I'm sure you do," Keefe replied, scribbling on a piece of scratch paper. "Let's see . . . You owe me two-twenty-five, and Kelsey one-fifty."

"Three-seventy-five?" Lou cried "You've got to be kidding!"

"You're the one who wanted to play for money," Kelsey pointed out.

"But I meant poker or backalley bridge, not Chinese checkers, for God's sake!" With a grunt of effort, Lou shifted her legs beneath the weight of Shamu's head and forepaws "Ouch! My feet have gone numb. What good are you, anyway, you, you . . . dog? You begged me to sit on the floor so you could sleep on me, promised me good luck. And what do I get? I'm out three-seventy-five, that's what."

Shamu's ears lifted briefly at the word *dog*, but her eyes stayed closed—and her head remained solidly in Lou's lap.

"Don't blame the dog for your lousy playing," Kelsey said. "Pay up."

"Hand me my purse. It's over there by the sofa—"

Shamu's head came up. Alertly. Tensely. Then she got to her feet with none of the elbow-thumping dog-clumsiness with which she'd lain down. She padded

125

toward the back door in deadly silence, head thrust forward, hackles raised. The family pet had turned guardian. Whitaker had branded her chicken; he ought to see her now.

"Shamu?" Kelsey asked.

"Shh," Lou hissed.

Ignoring the needle-stab of returning circulation, Lou climbed to her feet and retrieved her purse. The kids stared at her open-mouthed as she pulled out her gun.

"Stay here," she said.

Keefe started to get up. "But—"

"Stay here!" Lou glared at him over her shoulder until he sank back down.

She caught up with Shamu at the back door. The dog's nose was pressed to the crack between door and frame, and a low, threatening growl rumbled deep in her chest. Lou's heart banged hard against her ribs.

"Easy, girl," she whispered, opening the door an inch.

Shamu strained for her opening, her claws scrabbling on the linoleum. Lou grabbed her collar. "Wait for me," she said. "I've got the gun, remember?"

The dog looked up at her, dark eyes questioning.

"Stay with me," she said again. "No way are you going out there to get killed. Stay. We'll go together."

She waited until she could feel acquiescence in the wolfhound's body. Still keeping her hold on the collar, she eased the door open and stepped outside. The back yard seemed empty. A breeze stirred the trees, sending feathery leaf-shadows skittering across the grass.

The dog moved forward, as silent as she'd been in the house. Suddenly she stopped, her gaze snapping to the detached garage. Another long, low growl rolled out of her. Lou strained to see into the darkness behind the building, thought she saw movement. Shamu strained forward.

Beneath her hand, Lou could feel the power in the wolfhound's body. *Trust me,* she thought, knowing she'd never be able to hold on if the dog decided to charge.

"Easy, girl," she whispered, the barest breath of sound. "Stay."

Shamu's ears flicked toward her briefly, then angled forward again. She stayed. But not for long; a quiver had begun in those massive legs, and it was only a matter of time before she attacked whatever or whoever was behind the garage.

"Come out," Lou called. "Or I'll shoot."

Too late, she saw light glint off something metallic on the other side of the garage. *He's there, and he's armed!* Her field of vision narrowed to a tunnel, straight to that spot. A bass drumbeat of terror pounded in her ears.

Then Shamu lunged against the collar, emitting a sound that was more roar than bark. Lou dug her heels in, bracing herself against the dog's weight, and fought to swing her weapon around toward the other side of the garage.

"Police, drop the gun!" a man shouted.

Lou hesitated. Danger crackled like heat lightning in the air.

"Drop it!" the man shouted again.

No choice. Lou tossed the gun away and raised her free hand. The man stepped into view. Her breath went out in a sigh of relief when she saw his uniform. "He's for real," she whispered to Shamu. The wolfhound relaxed, responding either to her words or her emotions. Lou didn't care, as long as she stayed put.

"Get both hands up!" he called.

127

"You want me to let go of the dog?" she called back.

"Hold the dog," he said, coming forward to scoop her gun off the ground. "Who are you, and what are you doing here?"

"My name's Lou Malotti. I'm staying with the kids by Whitaker's invitation. We thought *you* were a burglar."

The door opened behind Lou, and she heard Keefe call, "Lou? Are you okay? What's going on out there?"

"Everything's fine, Keefe. It was a policeman come to check on us. Go on back into the house. I'll be in in a minute."

The cop put his gun away, relief plain in his eyes. "We almost had a situation here, Ms. Malotti. You shouldn't go running around with a gun like that."

"You shouldn't sneak into people's yards without identifying yourself," she retorted.

"Name's Greer. And actually, I just planned to drive past, make sure the back yard looked secure. Then I saw something moving around behind the garage and got out to check. Turned out to be a couple of cats." His gaze dropped to Shamu. "Speaking of animals, do you put a saddle on that thing, or what?"

"This is Shamu," Lou said. "Shamu, are you okay with the nice policeman?"

The dog wagged her tail. The cop put his hand out to be sniffed, then petted the animal's head. "I thought she was a puma or something when I first saw her. Scared the hell out of me. How much does she weigh?"

"One twenty-eight."

He whistled. "Whitaker said he had a big dog, but he should have said a *big* dog."

"He also said she was chicken."

"She was ready to come right into my gun."

"Yes," Lou said, letting her hand fall to the dog's head. "She was."

"Women and dogs—put their families at risk, and they're the most dangerous things on this earth. You got a permit for that weapon?"

"Of course." She held out her hand, and he put the gun in it.

"Okay, I'm out of here," he said. "Next time, I suggest you keep yourself and the dog inside. If you're not willing to let her go in ahead of you, which you obviously weren't, you'd just get both of you killed. Good night, Ms. Malotti. I'll wait until you're safely inside."

Lou obeyed, locking the door behind her carefully. Her hands didn't shake, although she was painfully aware of how near a miss it had been. Two frightened people pointing guns at each other . . . And Shamu, pure, selfless heroism. Humbled by the trust the dog had put in her, Lou knelt down and put her arms around the animal's neck.

"Good girl," she murmured. *"Good* girl."

The dog rested her big head on Lou's shoulder and heaved a sigh. Two friends who had just beaten the devil together, they stayed like that for a long, contented moment.

"Hey, Lou! Want to play another game?" Keefe called from the living room.

She smiled. "Sure," she called back, rising to her feet. "Come on, Shamu. I have the feeling my losing streak is over."

Ten

The Fire Man called the WAVY-TV anchorman at home. "Hello, Mr. Kursk."

"Who is this?"

"I'm the guy who's going to make you famous. We spoke last Wednesday, remember?"

The silence stretched long, and he smiled into it. Behind him, the sounds of the traffic blended into a sort of white noise that only underscored the lack of conversation.

"How did you get this number?" Kursk asked at last.

"I have your address, too." He smiled. "You don't like that very much, do you?"

"Let's just say I'm cautious after what happened to Kevin MacLaren."

"Nothing happened to him. It could have, but he wasn't worth my trouble. I have bigger fish to fry."

Kursk drew in his breath sharply. "That's an interesting analogy, considering your . . . profession."

"Isn't it?"

He knew the reporter was afraid. Good. That's why he'd called the guy at home. They were all afraid of him, those sheep out in TV land. This had gone on since the beginning of time: the frightened ones huddled in their homes, staring out into the untamed darkness where the wolves prowled. Afraid of the beast. Afraid of the ones who refused to live by the rules.

Afraid of him.

"Why did you turn against MacLaren?" Kursk asked.

"Why do you want to know?"

"Because I don't want to make the same mistake MacLaren did."

"That article on pyromania . . ." he took a deep breath, trying to control an upsurge of anger, ". . . was annoying. It wouldn't have been so bad if he'd gotten the facts right. Contrary to what he said, I am in perfect control over my impulses. *I* create the fire. And creation, Mr. Kursk, is true control."

"May I record this?"

"Yes. I am, of course, disguising my voice."

"Of course."

He chose to ignore the dryness of the reporter's tone. The man was just a tool; his opinion didn't matter, as long as he did what he was supposed to do. "You know what day this is, don't you?"

"It's Wednesday," Kursk said. "Are you planning to set another fire tonight?"

"I am."

"Where?"

"Somewhere." Triumph stung the back of his throat; he had Kursk hooked. The moment this interview hit the TV screen, he'd have the rest of Tidewater hooked as well. His audience. All wondering where the Fire Man was going to strike next.

"You've been setting your fires in untenanted structures. Is this a matter of your personal code?"

"I wouldn't take the lives of innocent people, Mr.

Kursk. That would be the act of a crazy man." He chuckled. "Actually, I bet there are a couple of owners who'd like to give me a medal for getting rid of their white elephants for them. Maybe I ought to start accepting orders." He swung his free hand in a grand arc. "Got a building you can't fix, swap or sell? The Fire Man can help. Just give him a call: Visa and Mastercard accepted."

Kursk didn't reply. Piqued, the arsonist pressed the phone closer to his ear. "You getting this, Kursk?"

"Of course I'm getting it."

"You didn't laugh."

"I didn't know it was a joke."

His eyes narrowed. "I want to hear this on the news tonight, *Mister* Kursk."

"You will. It's news, after all."

"I'm the news. The biggest news you've got in this goddamn place."

"Of course," Kursk agreed.

His voice was smooth and inflectionless, but the arsonist could feel the undercurrent of fear running through it. He basked in it. *I'm the wolf slipping through the darkness outside your door, the one who couldn't be tamed. I howl, and the only thing you can do is hide under the bedclothes and hope I can't find you.*

People. Sheep. All the same. Tonight they'd watch his fire on their television screens, each glad that the wolf had chosen somebody else this time.

A vision of flame bloomed at the back of his eyes. Bloomed, grew, rocked him with its power. It swept through the landscape of his mind. Hot. Beautiful. Behind it, the world had become empty, cleansed by the flames.

"Are you still there?" Kursk asked.

He opened his eyes, only now realizing that he'd closed them. His breathing had quickened, and a sheen of sweat covered his forehead and upper lip. He forced himself to relax.

"I'm here."

"When will you contact me again?" the reporter asked.

"Are you anxious for another story?"

"Yes, of course."

He smiled. "I'll be talking to you soon," he said, and hung up.

Hitching the tool belt higher on his hips, he turned away from the phone. He had a couple of loose ends to tie up before getting to the work he really enjoyed.

Fire Man. Touch me, and get burned.

Lou walked through the cargo bay of the Navy helicopter carrier, whistling to fill the echoing emptiness of the huge space. The doors were open, and she could see the flat, broad surface of the elevator that lifted the helicopters from here to the flight deck. The opening framed a wild, windy sky, where the moon hung like a pale jack-o'-lantern behind swiftly moving clouds. The predicted cold front was moving in.

The shipyard was unusually quiet tonight; with the wind kicking up like this, the sandblasting had been rescheduled for the next day. Most of the activity had moved to the shops, and only a faint clatter of sound drifted in through the bay doors.

She paused to look out over the yard, noting the bulky shape of the freighter that currently occupied the drydock. Her partially sandblasted hull gleamed dully in the moonlight. Another Enterprise vessel. Lou made a mental note to check if the ship was scheduled for a simple paint job or more complex repairs.

"If so, I'm going over you with a microscope," she muttered. "Permission or no permission."

With a sigh, she turned away. Tonight, she was getting paid to inspect *this* ship, and she'd better get to it before that IRA became her sole means of support. This vessel had come in for hydraulic pump and piping work. Routine stuff. She'd already inspected the pump parts back in the shop, and now had only one weld to check.

It had been a good night; she'd passed all three inspections she'd made tonight. She was well ahead of schedule. Hey, she might even get a chance to do some sleuthing before she went home. Her whistle changed to hopeful.

Squatting in front of the network of hydraulic piping, she scraped slag off the new weld and painted it with liquid penetrant.

"All right," she said as the purple dye sat on the metal without a change. "This must be my lucky night."

She'd feel luckier if Whitaker would show a little more interest. Heck, *any* interest would be nice. A guy with good taste in kids and dogs, and with those heart-stopping grey eyes . . . She might dredge up the courage to throw herself at him if she thought she had a chance.

He'd left a message on her machine here at work. It had been delivered in a rapid-fire monotone in which not even hope could find reflections of personal interest. "Whitaker here. Thanks for checking on the kids. Don't worry about them, we've got a regular swing-by arranged with the police, and Blaire and Mike are

134

sticking close by. I'm up to my eyeballs in work, will tag up when I get a chance."

Click. End of message. Now, *that* was a guy who was really interested. As Elihu would say, *Oooooh, baby!*

Ah, well. At least the dog liked her.

A faint scrape of metal on metal brought her swiveling around to face the doorway behind her. She held her breath, listening for its source. It didn't come again, so she shrugged and turned back to her tool case.

Scrape.

A small noise, surely not out of place in the metal world of the ship. She tried to ignore it.

Scrape.

Footsteps? Not likely; that had been metal on metal she'd heard. But one thing was certain: it had been closer the second time. She licked lips that had suddenly gone very dry. The Malottis had always run more to logic than intuition, but her imagination surged straight into high gear.

The lights flickered for a moment, then steadied. Her heart, however, did not. With her pulse stuttering in her ears, she slid a wrench out of her tool belt and hefted it. Then she headed for the door. No matter what might happen, she wasn't about to cower in here like a frightened rabbit. Run, maybe. But not cower.

The passageway was empty. She headed toward the cargo bay, the opposite direction from which the sound had come. Her footsteps echoed in the narrow space, almost seeming to cry "come get me!" Lou moved faster.

She stopped just inside the bay to listen for pursuit. The silence seemed to listen back. Her gaze darted from one doorway to the next, one shadow to the next.

Scrape.

"Lou?"

The man's voice came from behind her. She spun, swinging the wrench with the momentum of her body. Even as she swung, she registered him in a series of eye-blink pictures: blond hair, leathery skin, washed-out blue eyes that were just now wide with surprise and alarm. Recognition came too late for her to check the blow, however.

"Hey!" he yelped, flinging himself backward as the wrench whizzed past his face.

"Sorry, George," she said, dropping the wrench.

"Shit!" Overbalanced, he thumped down on his backside. His hardhat went rolling crazily along the deck.

Lou bent over him. "Are you okay?"

"Fine!" he snapped. "What the hell are you doing? You gone nuts?"

"I got a little spooked, is all," she said, weak-kneed from reaction. And feeling more than a little foolish. "I heard noises, and then the lights flickered—"

"Malotti, we're working on the frigging electrical system. I came up here to tell you we were gonna turn the lights off in this area for a half hour or so. Who the hell were you expecting, anyway? Freddy Krueger?"

He glared up at her, his hair sticking up in a wild mane around his head. Laughter bubbled up in Lou's chest. She tried to suppress it, but couldn't stop a smothered giggle from escaping. Fagan looked out-raged for a moment, then started to laugh. That set Lou off harder.

"Jesus Christ, Malotti, you're something else," he gasped.

She sank down to the deck beside him, fishing in

her overalls pocket for something to wipe her eyes with. "You should have seen your face."

"Man, this is my first time on this shift. Sure is more exciting than days."

"What *are* you doing on this shift, anyway?" she asked.

He shrugged. "Ronnie Waite pulled a tendon playing football with his kids. He'll be back in a couple of weeks, but there's no way he's gonna be able to climb around these ships. So it'll be desk work for him, while the rest of us juggle his assignments."

Lou whistled, a long, low note of dismay. "Just what we needed."

"Yeah. Anyway, we were left short-handed at night, and since I don't have a wife or kids to worry about, I volunteered to take Ronnie's shift until he got back on his feet." Besides," he leered at her, "it gave me a chance to be near you, my lovely Valkyrie."

"I think I'm going to puke." Lou got up, then reached down to help him to his feet.

"Thanks," he said. "But I should be the one helping you."

She laughed. "It's the least I can do. After all, not only do I outweigh you by at least twenty pounds, I also nearly took your head off with a wrench."

"You shouldn't make cracks about your weight. You've got everything right where it's supposed to be, and there are a hell of a lot of guys who like a woman with some padding on her bones."

"Tell that to Cindy Crawford."

He stepped close and kissed her—*kissed* her. Lou was too astonished to react, or even to register whether or not it felt good. Then she started analyzing her response. Or rather, lack of one. There was nothing

137

wrong with being kissed by George Fagan; in an objective sense, he was probably quite good at it.

There were a number of reasons why she couldn't become involved with this man, namely the argument against dating co-workers and conflict of interest between her job and his. But the most important reason of all was the fact that she just didn't get that roller-coaster feeling in her stomach—the one she got when Whitaker, damn his uninterested hide, only smiled at her.

After a moment, Fagan pulled back. "You're supposed to close your eyes," he said.

"You took me by surprise."

"Why? Can't a guy be attracted to you?"

"Not when he's known me nearly ten years without being attracted."

"I've *been* attracted. You just never noticed. You never notice. Besides, every guy who's ever tried has gone down in flames."

"I don't date people I work with," she said. "It's too complicated."

"Just arson investigators?"

"Who told you I was dating him?"

"Christ, Lou, it's common knowledge."

She frowned. Funny, she didn't remember telling anyone she'd gone out with Whitaker. "Who told you?" she asked.

"Who?" His eyebrows went up. "Jeez, Lou, I don't know. I just heard it somewhere. You know what this place is like; can't pass gas without everybody knowing when and how much." He checked his watch. "We'd better get going. They're going to be turning the lights off soon."

"You weren't worried about the lights a minute ago."

138

He grinned at her. "Hey, I thought we'd have our eyes closed and it wouldn't matter."

"Pervert."

"I know." Still grinning, he held his hand out. "So we'll forget the mad passion and still be friends, eh?"

She sighed in relief. "Friends it is. Let me get my tools and I'll be on my way."

He bent to retrieve his hardhat, sweeping it toward the door with a flourish. "After you."

Lou would rather have gone alone, but didn't protest as he accompanied her. He chatted amiably as they made their way through the ship. Maybe she was imagining things, but he didn't seem too terribly heartbroken. She suspected his kiss had been motivated by time and place (never pass up a chance for a roll in the hay!) rather than ten years of unrequited yearning.

As they reached the gangplank, he took her by the arm and swung her around to face him. For a moment, she was afraid he might try to kiss her again. Fortunately, he didn't.

"So, what does your investigator friend say about the fire we had here?" he asked.

"He isn't saying a whole lot about it, actually. I'm assuming he doesn't know yet."

"Everybody's saying it was Jay."

"How convenient."

"You don't think so?"

"I think it's pretty easy to blame it on somebody who isn't here to say he didn't."

"I guess so. But who else could it be?"

Anybody. "I don't know. But remember, if that fire was a grudge act, you can cross Jay off the list of suspects. He hadn't gotten fired yet."

"So much for that theory." He stuck his hands in

139

his pockets and walked beside her, head down. "You got a better one?"

A natural enough question. She glanced at him. His gaze was bland and uninformative, curious but not *too* interested.

"No," she said. "I don't have any theories."

"Maybe the fire and the rest of the stuff aren't connected at all."

"Maybe," Lou said. An interesting thought. "Weren't you ship supervisor on the *Gabriella?*"

He stared at her in obvious surprise. "Hell, no. I was on the LPH. Louis Delanski had the freighter, remember?"

"No, I don't remember. I never got to see him, with me on nights and him working days. And with the database screwed up, we can't go back and look things up."

"It's old age, Malotti, not the database."

She let herself be drawn into the old banter. "I was a lot younger upstairs, Fagan."

"So was my hope," he said.

"Is that what it's called these days?"

"When talking to a woman who swings a wrench the way you do, yes."

A waft of cool air whipped Lou's hair around her face as they reached the gangplank. Fagan stopped and turned toward her. The moonlight turned his eyes silver, as smooth and impenetrable as the man. Good old George, always so quick with a joke. She almost confided in him. No one except Harry Deveraux had his finger more firmly pressed to the pulse of the shipyard.

"I better go and make sure those yahoos of mine don't blow up the ship instead of repair it," he said. "Sure you don't want to meet me for a drink or something after work?"

140

The impulse to confide passed. Quickly. "I've got a ton of things to do, sorry."

He grinned at her, good-natured to the last. "Don't say I didn't give you a chance."

"Give it a rest, Fagan."

"Okay." His smile faded. "But you need anything, you call me, okay? We old-timers are the only ones who give a damn about what happens around here. We've got to stick together."

He strode back into the ship while she was still struggling with her surprise. Now, what had been the purpose of *that* speech? Did he have some inkling on what was going on? If so, he wasn't letting on.

So maybe he suspects you. An interesting thought.

Louis Delanski, however, was even more interesting. She'd never liked him much. And she couldn't shake the notion that the only thing better than owning a crooked QA inspector was owning an inspector *and* a crooked ship supervisor. Talk about greasing the chute!

Things were getting more complicated by the moment.

"Damn," she muttered. "I wish Deveraux were here."

Eleven

The phone started to ring the moment Lou walked in the house. She ran to catch it, shedding purse, jacket, briefcase and a bag of fast-food breakfast. Elihu jumped from bar to bar, tracking her from within the cage.

"Hello," she said, picking up on the sixth ring.

"Hi, Mom."

"Oh, it's you."

"It's flattering to be so missed."

"Oh, I miss you," she said. "I just thought you might be Mel Gibson calling for a date." Maybe not exactly Mel Gibson, she amended silently, but a certain arson investigator. Who, it seemed, had forgotten she existed.

Wade laughed, a deep, vibrant haw-haw-haw that was just like his father's. Too many years had passed for Lou to be bothered by the similarity, although she was grateful the laugh was all that Wade had inherited from Jake Malotti.

"Hey, Mom, if Mel Gibson *had* asked for a date, would you have accepted?"

"Gee, I dunno. He's married, you know."

"*I* know that it's been a hell of a long time since you had a date, any date. And it isn't because guys haven't asked."

142

"I'm picky."

"Picky! Don't you have hormones like the rest of mankind? And how long has it been since you kissed a man, anyway?"

Lou scowled, thinking that there was nothing worse than being patronized by her own child. "My hormones are perfectly normal, thank you. And I kissed a man last night, if you must know."

"No kidding?" His tone changed from teasing to protective. "Who?"

"None of your business." Not for the world was she going to admit that it was George Fagan she'd kissed, or that she'd been too surprised even to enjoy it.

"Well, well, well," her son said.

"Yeah, it's about time you realized your mother isn't over the hill quite yet." Levering one boot off, then the other, she propped her hip on the edge of the table. "Are you coming in this weekend?"

"Jeez, Louise!" Elihu shrieked.

"See what you've done?" Lou asked.

"Elihu, my man! Give him a peanut for me."

"I'm going to give him a cork, is what I'll give him. If you don't stop teaching him those corny songs, I promise I'll cut you off without a cent."

Wade laughed. "I love you, Mom. Will we have bird babies by this weekend?"

"We don't even have eggs yet," she said. "But Emily's been messing around in the nesting box the past couple of days, so I think it'll be soon. And speaking of bird babies, it's chilly in here. I'd better go make sure I turned the furnace back on."

"You know, all the other guys complain about how their mothers hover over them, sending them cookies and stuff, demanding to know every little detail of their lives—"

143

"I don't even *make* cookies," Lou retorted. "And if I did, I'd damn well eat them myself. If I haven't done my job raising you right, then it's too late to worry about it now."

"That's what I mean," he said. "Good old Mom. See you this weekend."

"Good old Mom, indeed," Lou muttered, hanging up. "How do you like that?" she asked Elihu. "Old!"

Elihu ignored her. He perched outside the nesting box, his head bobbing up and down in agitation. Emily, inside the box, made no sound at all, strange after the gnawing and scratching that had been going on the past couple of days.

"Oh, my God," Lou whispered. "Is it time?"

Rushing to the kitchen, she scrabbled through the drawer where she'd thrown the book the vet had given her. She thumbed through it frantically. Good Lord, she was more nervous about the parrot laying eggs than she'd been when she'd gone into labor with Wade.

"Let's see . . . three or four eggs . . . Oh, brother, it says the house has to be kept at eighty-five degrees."

She tucked the book under her arm and trotted to the thermostat in the dining room. Just as she'd thought, she'd forgotten to turn the furnace back on last night. The thermostat read sixty-eight degrees; it was going to take a while to get the house up to temp.

"Eighty-five degrees. Don't birds sit on their eggs any more?" she said; switching the heat to "on" and turning the thermostat up. The furnace hummed into operation.

She went back to the living room and squatted down beside the cage. Elihu had retreated to the top of the perch. He seemed bewildered by the soft, feather-ruffling sounds coming from the nesting box. Feeling reckless, Lou reached through the bars to stroke the iridescent feathers of his breast. He allowed the caress.

"Are you a little worried, fella?" she asked softly.

He arched his neck, offering his head. Lou stroked him gently. The light struck rainbow gleams in the blue feathers on his face. He chirped once, loudly, like a giant cricket. His sound of contentment.

"Don't worry about a thing," she said, opening the book with her free hand. "Look, Emily's a healthy lady, and before you know it, you're going to be a proud papa." She skipped the chapter titled "What Can Go Wrong," turning instead to the pictures of happy parrot parents with their fledglings. "See?"

He sidled away from her, toward the nesting box.

"This is going to take a while, sport," she said. "You might as well relax." He ignored her, of course.

With a sigh, she straightened and went to retrieve her now-cold breakfast. Grimacing, she dangled the sausage and egg biscuit between her thumb and forefinger. It seemed to have gone through some sort of chemical change in the past ten minutes, and had become sausage-scented rubber. One thing about fast food: it had to be eaten hot and salty to be considered edible at all.

She stood in the kitchen doorway, aimed carefully, and arced the biscuit into the sink. Her appetite went with it.

"Well, Ms. Malotti, now that you've been put off your feed, what's it going to be? Upstairs for a nice, hot bath, or a nice, long snooze down here on the sofa?"

The sofa beckoned, almost seeming to hold out its soft, upholstered arms to welcome her. She closed the curtains on the big picture window, then settled into the cushions. Something hard poked her in the back. Wriggling, she extracted the remote control.

"Looove me tender . . ."

"The soaps aren't on yet," she said, turning the TV on. "Besides, you're supposed to be assisting in childbirth, not watching the tube. Typical male," she added, *sotto voce.*

She flipped through the channels, finally settling on a talk show she had no intention of watching. But the voices blended nicely into a pleasant background of noise that sent her spiraling off toward sleep.

Lou ran through burning city streets, dodging the chunks of flame that hurtled down all around. She didn't dare turn and look, but she knew the Fire Man followed her, setting the world aflame as he walked.

Fire raced past on either side of her, leaping the spaces between the buildings. Even the street beneath her feet began to burn, the melting asphalt sucking at her feet like molasses.

Fire everywhere.

The street scene began to spin, faster and faster, until it became a flaming spiral galaxy, its stars glowing like coals in the indigo darkness of deep space. She lay face down upon it, pinned like a butterfly on a board. It spun at a dizzying pace. Whirling, sick and frightened, she had no choice but to spin with it.

A wild shout of canned TV excitement speared into her dream and dragged her back to reality. She opened her eyes to Bob Barker's elegant, white-maned head—and a steady tattoo of pain at the back of her brain.

Applause swelled and grew, and so did her headache. Nausea rolled upward from her stomach, spinning her body the opposite direction from her brain. She hadn't been this sick since the flu hit her a couple of years ago. Applause from the TV sent spurts of pain through her head.

Groaning, she fumbled for the remote, managed to switch the TV off. Ahh, quiet. Wrapped in the private misery of her body, she drifted off to sleep again.

And landed straight back into her dream of burning streets. The Fire Man waited for her, welcoming her back with open arms. She ran from him, crying out for help into the echoing, flame-filled abyss of the city.

Her footsteps pounded in her ears, counterpoint to her pulse as she ran. The buildings cast her voice back to her, their windows flickering with fire-lit laughter.

"Lou!" the Fire Man called. "Louuuuuuu!"

She ran faster. The pain in her head became a steady drumbeat, echoing the pounding rhythm of her feet and the rasp of her breath. The street narrowed. The buildings grew together, pressing close overhead. The fire reflected in blind, blank glass, dripping from roofs like gravy from a spoon.

And behind her, the Fire Man laughed. He sent fire out in a double arc, twin arms of flame to gather her in. She dropped, rolled beneath them, and scrambled to her feet again.

Run! Her breath sobbed in her throat. *Run!*

The street ended in an abrupt V, as though she'd been passing through a painted landscape and had simply run out of perspective.

A nearby wall groaned, a hurt-beast sound of overstressed wood and brick. She dodged toward the opposite side of the street, but was forced back by a gout of orange-red flame. Nowhere to go. Nowhere to run except into the Fire Man's arms. And that she wouldn't do. Couldn't.

The wall shivered and quaked, then fell toward her with a horrible, slow-motion grace. She flung her arms up, staring in terror at the hurtling mass of brick and burning debris coming straight down upon her.

The end of the world.

"Lou! *Louise!*"

Not the Fire Man's voice. Another voice. She clawed her way upward out of the dream. Gasping. Frantic.

The pain still beat at the back of her head, bringing jagged black flashes slashing across her vision. Her stomach bucked and heaved. Too sick to move, she flung her arm over her eyes and prayed for the nausea to subside.

"Lou!"

Realizing that some of the pounding was *outside* her head, she dropped her arm and tried to lift her head.

"Lou! Are you in there? Lou!"

The door. Someone was at the door. She tried to get up, but only managed to roll off onto the floor. Alarm speared through the agony in her head. *Open the door. Something's wrong, you've got to open the door.*

She tried to get to her feet. And failed. Black oblivion hovered at the edges of her mind. Seductive. Powerful. All she had to do was relax.

No! You'll never come out again!

Instinct made her defy that beckoning darkness, got her onto her hands and knees, drove her to crawl toward the door. Her vision narrowed to the bright brass circle of the doorknob. Foot by foot, inch by inch sometimes, she forced herself to move.

"Lou, open up!"

Whitaker's voice. She knew it now, knew she had

148

to get that door open. Thunderous dark wings beat around her, in her, trying to hold her back.

Almost there; she could feel the coolness of the tile floor under her hands now, see the door vibrate from the force of Whitaker's pounding. Her chest ached. She felt as though she were breathing through a straw that was getting smaller and smaller every moment.

She reached up, scrabbling along the wood toward the knob. Missed. Tried again. Her hands didn't seem to have any strength. Clenching her teeth, she forced her fingers to close around the knob. Forced them to turn it.

Sobbing, she felt the click of the lock, then a wash of cool air. Felt Whitaker's hands on her as he hauled her out into the patch of grass outside the door. She couldn't see his face; that was in the black beyond of her vision.

"Lou," he said, his voice low and urgent. "I'm going to leave you for a second to call an ambulance. Don't go to sleep on me, okay?"

"Can't . . . fight it."

He shook her. Gently, but it made her rattle around inside herself.

"Hang on," he snarled. "Don't go out on me. Lou! Do you hear me?"

"O . . . kay."

She managed to hang onto consciousness until he got back. After that, things got pretty fuzzy. The air felt thick, and she had to struggle to draw it in. Whitaker kept talking to her, his voice her only lifeline in a world that had suddenly turned into a whirling mess of lights and screaming sirens. Somebody fitted something over her mouth and nose. She fought it, terrified of the confinement.

Whitaker held her hands. "It's okay, Lou. It's oxygen."

She stopped struggling. The darkness swooped toward her, roaring. This time, she couldn't hold it back. With her mouth and nose covered, she could only wail silently as she fell into blackness.

Twelve

"Hello, Lou."

Whitaker's voice got her eyes open. Her vision swam dizzily for a moment, then focused on him. He looked as cool and calm as though he'd gone for a Sunday stroll, although his face seemed paler than usual. She glanced around, saw that she was lying in a hospital bed, with curtains all around to create an island of privacy. A hammer pounded steadily on the inside of her forehead.

"Where am I?" she croaked.

"Maryview emergency room," he said. "How are you feeling?"

"Lousy. What happened?"

"Carbon monoxide poisoning. We think it was your furnace; someone's checking it out now."

"I . . ." Thoughts snapped down like tiny, hot spears in her mind. "What happened to Elihu and Emily?"

He sat down on the edge of the bed and reached out to take her hand in both of his. "Birds are much more sensitive than humans. I'm sorry, Lou."

"She was laying her eggs."

"I know," he said softly. "We found her in the nesting box."

151

Lou closed her eyes against a sudden rush of tears. They leaked out anyway, running down her temples to soak her hair. She turned onto her side, not wanting Whitaker to see her cry.

His hand came down on her shoulder. She could feel its warmth through the flimsy hospital gown, but not its comfort. After a moment, he released her.

"You don't lean on anyone, do you?" he asked.

"Not if I can help it."

She wanted to look at him, to see his expression. But then he'd see hers, and that she was unwilling to allow. She felt naked, vulnerable, her defenses in tatters.

"Where are they?" she asked, the words burning upward in her throat.

"Elihu and Emily?" He let his breath out in a long sigh. "I called Blaire to come get them. I figured you'd be comfortable with that."

Lou nodded. More questions needed to be asked, but she was too tired to keep them straight in her mind. So she just lay there, her head drumming with pain, quiet tears slipping out to wet the pillowcase.

And in the midst of it all came the realization of just how close she'd come to dying with Elihu and Emily. A quiet death, one that crept up on her while she slept.

Strange. She'd always expected to go out fighting, kicking and scratching for every moment. But she hadn't. She'd lain down in the safety of her own house, unaware that the air she was breathing was about to steal her life away. If Whitaker hadn't come when he had . . .

"Thanks," she said.

"For what?"

"For being in the right place at the right time."

"Oh, that," he said. "No problem. Do you want me to call your son for you?"

She shook her head.

"What about your mother?"

"God, no! I wouldn't want her to worry."

"No," Whitaker snarled. "No one should ever *worry* about Lou Malotti."

Surprised by the savagery of his tone, she rolled over and looked at him. His expression hadn't changed, but something dark raged in the back of his eyes.

"What's wrong?" she asked.

"You almost died today," he said. "Doesn't that matter to you?"

"Of course it matters." She knew he wanted something from her, but God help her if she knew what it was. Her head hurt so bad . . . "Look, Whitaker. I'm sorry, but I'm really having trouble keeping up with this conversation."

He stood up abruptly, raking both hands through his hair. "They're going to keep you here overnight. The doctor said, and I quote, 'Ms. Malotti should get plenty of bed rest for the next couple of days.' Do you understand?"

"That's fine for him to say." Lou retorted. "I've got to get to work."

Whitaker crossed his arms over his chest. "Try. Go ahead."

She tried to sit up, she really tried. But her body ignored the dictates of her mind. Her vision betrayed her further, blurring every time she stopped concentrating.

"Damn," she muttered.

"Hah," Whitaker said, with far too much satisfaction in his voice. "I called Steggans and told him you wouldn't be in. Ah, you don't have to thank me now."

153

She tried to glare at him. His image tilted, however, and set her head to spinning as well as pounding. Instead of retorting, as she intended, she had to swallow against an upsurge of bile. "Payback," she said at last.

"Hah again. If you're smart, you'll stay home tomorrow night, too. You got a good dose of poison in your system, and it's going to take some time for your body to recover."

The room darkened, or maybe it was her mind. Either way, she started to drift off.

"Lou?"

Again, his voice brought her back. "Yeah?"

"Blaire asked if Saturday afternoon was all right for the funeral."

"Huh?"

Propping one arm on the bed, he leaned over her. "Not yours. Elihu's and Emily's."

"You're kidding."

"Sorry, no."

Lou thought about that empty cage, about the town house that would no longer ring with badly sung songs and Jeez, Louises. A funeral suddenly didn't seem as absurd as it had before.

"Saturday will be fine."

"Don't worry about preparations. Blaire will handle everything."

She couldn't stop her eyes from drifting closed. "I have no doubt."

The sun had just begun to set when Lou arrived at the shipyard Friday night. She probably shouldn't have come in; she felt like a shadow of herself, a bleached-out, leached-out remnant of a woman. But the town house had all the homeyness of a mausoleum, and she stayed only long enough to take a shower and change into fresh clothes.

Work was the answer, she thought as she rode the elevator up to the second floor; for twenty-odd years, she'd used the shipyard to keep the rest of the world at bay.

The doors slid open, and she walked out into the QA office. It seemed empty, although the reek of a recently smoked cigarette hung in the air.

"Hey, Malotti, you doing all right?" someone called from a nearby office.

"Who's that?"

Mason Bostwich stood up. Propping his elbows on the top of the partition, he grinned at her. "Only me."

"You started smoking again, didn't you?"

His cheeks reddened. "How did you know?"

"Cripes, Mase, it's a reasonable deduction. A) I can smell fresh cigarette smoke, and B) you seem to be the only one here besides me. Since I know I didn't smoke a cigarette, I have to assume you did."

"I'll have you know that Steggans is still here."

"He doesn't smoke," she said, dropping her purse and briefcase on her desk. "What are you going here so late, anyway? Did someone dump something nasty into the river?"

He grinned at her. "As a matter of fact, I was catching up on some of your inspections from yesterday."

"So, were you good at my job?"

"Lousy. You'll be fired for sure," he said. "Hey, I heard you were rushed to the hospital with carbon monoxide poisoning yesterday. Is that so, or is it only a wild rumor?"

"No rumor, Mase."

"Jeez." He ran one hand through his thinning hair. "How did it happen?"

She sat down, tilting her chair back so she could still keep him in sight. "It seems there was a problem with the connection to the heat exchanger. A bolt worked loose or some such. The furnace was pumping carbon monoxide into the house."

"Damn! You're supposed to have your furnace checked out every year."

"From now on, you can bet I will."

He straightened, pushing himself away from the partition. "Well, it's good to see you back. And now I think I'll head home to that steak dinner my wife promised me."

"See you."

She watched him shrug into his jacket and head toward the elevator. Dissatisfaction nagged at her. It wasn't Mase, or the conversation she'd had with him. He'd treated her exactly as he always treated her—as a co-worker, someone to crack jokes with or to complain about the management. Not a friend. That had always been fine with her.

So, Malotti, who are your friends?

Two days ago, that question wouldn't even have occurred to her. Today it was important. Something to do with nearly dying, she supposed.

She grimaced. Personal introspection was going to have to wait until she figured out what was going on around here.

She found Steggans's door closed. Light seeped out from beneath it, so she knew he was in. She knocked, got a "come in" in response. Surprise slackened his face as she walked into the room.

"What are you doing here?" he demanded.

"I work here, remember?"

"Your arson fellow said you wouldn't be in until Monday."

"Not only was he wrong, he isn't 'my' arson fellow."

"Oh, but I heard—"

"Yeah, I know. Who told you?"

His eyebrows went up. "Hell, I don't remember. By the way, what *does* the lieutenant think about our fire?"

"I don't know. He hasn't discussed it with me. And with that nut case running around the city, I doubt he's had much time to work on it."

"Nut case?" Steggans repeated. "Oh, you mean the Fire Man."

"Yeah, him," she said, echoes of her nightmare flaring through her mind. She glanced away toward the window. The sun had just touched the horizon, spilling ruddy light over the world below. For a moment, the city looked as though it was on fire.

"Beautiful, isn't it?" Steggans asked softly.

She looked at him, saw that he, too, was staring out the window. "What?"

"The sunset."

"Yeah," she lied.

His gaze shifted back to her face. "I imagine this Fire Man's got Lieutenant . . . What's his name?"

"Whitaker."

"Oh, right. I guess this guy's got Whitaker pretty fired up."

"That's not exactly the term I would have used," she said.

"I didn't think," he said. Red-orange light slanted through the miniblinds to lay knife-edged bars of brightness and shadow across his face and chest. Then he leaned forward, out of the sunlight. "I'm not going to make you go home, although I ought to. But you *will* be flying your desk tonight."

"But—"

157

"I didn't schedule any inspections for tonight. But don't worry, I've got something useful for you to do."

He waved her into one of the chairs in front of his desk. Propping his elbows on the desk, he regarded her over steepled fingers. Some women might have found that blue cracked-glass gaze attractive; some might have found it intimidating. Lou met it squarely.

"What have you got for me?" she asked.

"The computer tech has one last thing to check out, and that's whether the program might have been repartitioned."

Lou slid forward along the slick plastic seat. "That would explain why we couldn't access coherent information. But we'd have to go through a heck of a lot of old records to recreate the parameters."

"You *are* under orders to work a desk tonight."

"I'll need access to everyone's files. Especially Jay's."

"You think he changed the partitions?"

She spread her hands. "Everyone says he's the one who screwed up the program. Seems to me that he's the logical place to start."

"Lou," he said. "Is there something you're not telling me?"

This was the time to confide in him. He'd been helpful so far; with more information, he could be a lot more help. She opened her mouth to tell him. But the words changed somewhere in the passage from mind to mouth without her consciously willing it. "No," she said. "There's nothing."

The lie had come purely from instinct. Lou listened to that urging; logic—and trust—could come later, when she had a handle on who was involved in this funny business. So she let the lie remain, waiting to see if Steggans would trust *her*.

He leaned back in his chair, studying her. After a moment, he reached into his pocket and took out a key ring. He held it in his hand as though weighing it, then slid it across the desk to her.

"Thanks," she said. "Has Jay shown up yet?"

He shook his head. "I guess there's not a lot of incentive to come back when he knows there's nothing but trouble waiting for him."

"Has anyone heard from him?"

"Not that I know of," he said. "If his wife has talked to him, she isn't telling anyone."

Would Kathy Nesmith lie to protect her husband? Sure.

Lou stood up, feeling the warmth of the fading sunlight on her face and throat. "I'd better get started. Are you staying?"

"No. I've been here since seven this morning, and I'm beat. Besides, I have the feeling I'd be more of a hindrance than a help. Bet you wish you had Deveraux here."

"Of course not," she lied politely. She tossed the key ring into the air and caught it again. "I'll give you a call if I find anything."

She heard him leave as she ran water for a fresh pot of coffee. A few minutes later, steaming mug in hand, she headed for Jay Nesmith's office.

"Okay, let's see what you've got," she said.

Setting her cup on the four-drawer file beside the desk, she tried keys in the lock until she found the right one. Then she reached into her pocket and pulled out the paper on which she'd written the pilfered sequential numbers.

She started in the top drawer and worked her way down, checking every sequential number against the list in her hand. Nothing. Letting her breath out in a sigh of frustration, she went through her own files, then one by one, those of the rest of the department. Some almost matched; not the same jobs, of course, but inspections done in the same time frame.

She returned to Jay's office and went through the file cabinet again. And again found no match.

"Damn!" she muttered, flinging herself into the chair. "I ought to be able to find these *somewhere*. I was so sure . . ."

Her gaze fell on the open file drawers. They seemed to stare back at her mockingly, as though glad they'd wasted her time. Suddenly she leaned forward, eyes narrowing. Something bothered her about those two drawers, something so subtle she had a hard time . . . She exhaled sharply as realization came.

Jay was a methodical man; his computer files at home were clear evidence of that. So were his files here, at least the ones in the top three drawers. The tabs on the manila folders stretched from left to right in a perfect line, all labeled in his square, precise handwriting. Left to right, A to Z, January to December.

But in the bottom drawer, which held the most recent files, gaps yawned in the line of tabs. If she hadn't left the other drawers open, she wouldn't have noticed at all.

So she'd been right. But she'd also been too late.

Frustration burned in her chest. She got to her feet with a suddenness that sent the chair rolling backward to thump into the desk. Whoever had done this was very, very thorough.

"Hell," Lou muttered. "No way can I take any of this to Van Allen. He'll laugh me out the door."

Then let it go, whispered the voice of self-preservation in her mind. *Think of your mortgage, that too-thin IRA, the bills from Wade's education.* She had so much

160

to lose. Twenty years of hard work, of scratching her way up through the ranks. She'd fought for every raise, every promotion, every ounce of respect. None of it had been given; she'd *taken* it.

Pursuing this issue would be like carrying a stick of dynamite; finding proof would be like lighting it. No one would thank her.

Anyone with a shred of sense would walk away from this. But. *But*. Men worked in that boiler room. Men protected from eight-hundred-degree steam by a repair that might or might not hold. And if it failed . . . A very painful death. Ten men died that death on the *Iwo Jima* a few years ago in a boiler-room accident.

And the *Gabriella* was only one ship. Lou glanced down at the list of numbers in her hand. Seven. Seven ships, seven potential disasters.

"Damn you, Jay Nesmith," she murmured.

As the saying goes, the buck stops here. It was possible that Jay's list meant nothing. It was possible that the inspection report on the *Gabriella* was perfectly valid, and that the freighter had gone out of here a safe ship.

But she had to be sure. She couldn't walk away from this without knowing, and live with herself. Right and wrong, wrong and right . . . that same stiff-necked, black-and-white reasoning that made her a good QA inspector to start with. If she didn't find out the truth, the truth would die. And maybe a few men, too.

She slapped the file drawer closed. "It's hell to be the only one who gives a damn," she said.

The stars glittered coldly in the velvet sky, uncaring.

Thirteen

He tilted his head back to look up at the four-storey building beside him. The sign above the colonial (what else here in Williamsburg-imitation heaven) entryway read Euclid Retirement Community. A sign in the window read: An affordable senior housing community, convenient to shopping and medical facilities. In-house RN and dietician, private shuttle bus for residents.

A siren shrieked to life a few blocks away, where the long outline of Maryview Hospital showed how convenient the medical facilities really were. Bring 'em here to wait to die, then rush 'em to Maryview to prolong the waiting.

"Cripes," he muttered. "What a waste."

He sauntered past the bank of windows to the left of the entrance. This was the dining room. It was also dinnertime, and the place was crowded with people. Old people. White heads bent over their plates, peering at the food. Utensils quivered in gnarled, liver-spotted hands. Wrinkled faces, wrinkled mouths. Used-up bodies, used-up lives.

His gaze focused on one old man who ate with particular intensity. Revulsion swept through him, a screaming torrent of it that nearly sent him to his knees. It wasn't *him,* of course. Didn't even look like him, not really. But his eyes were set the same way, so close together that they looked as though they'd been hung like glasses on the bridge of his nose. And he had the same voracious enjoyment of food. The same greedy clutch of fingers on the fork, the same snapping gobble of his mouth.

Grandpa. His dad's father—a bigger bastard than his son, even. Lying in bed with his useless legs, eating their food, shouting at them incessantly. Day and night, night and day. Being the boy, being big and strong for his age to boot, he'd been assigned to take care of the old man. Christ. "Bring me something to eat, boy! Bring me the bedpan! Take it away! Turn me over, boy! Can't you move any faster, you little fucker?"

And that crap about the sins of the fathers . . . Well, Dad didn't have to pay. No, he'd passed it straight down to his wife and kids. Between him and Grandpa, they hadn't had a chance. Dad used his fists; Grandpa used his tongue and warped, evil mind, and had hurt far worse.

Suddenly the windows caught the rays of the dying sun in a blaze of orange, reflecting his memory of fire. Dazzled, he squinted into the bright glare. A creamy glow sprang to life in his guts, ran in tingling warmth through his veins. Power. A match, a moment in time, and he could make this all vanish.

It had always been this way. Even as a kid, he'd loved fire. Loved the leaping colors of the flame, the heat, the way it cleansed everything it touched. The power had crystallized in him the time the newspaper office in town had burned down. He'd watched it from beginning to end, trembling.

Dad thought he was scared. Called him a shaking little sissy. But it hadn't been fear, oh, no. It had been the power coursing through him, leaping wild and hot as the fire. He looked up at the man beside him, saw flames dancing in his pale eyes, flames dancing in every drop of sweat beading his face. In that moment, the boy knew he'd found his path.

"And then I was set free," he whispered.

He tilted his head back to survey the building. Of course, he knew the dangers of acting without a plan. But the power raged inside him more powerfully than it ever had before, and it couldn't be denied. *Feed a fire, and it only grows larger and hotter. Needing more and more to be satisfied . . .* He found himself breathing hard, his hands clenched so hard they hurt. *Easy. Don't get overanxious. It will come.*

He walked around to the back of the building. The rear door must open directly into the kitchen; he could hear the clank of pots and pans and smell the aroma of baked chicken. Grandpa's favorite. Moving down to another window, he peered in. This must be the director's office, judging by the nice desk and homey atmosphere. He broke out a pane of glass and reached in to unlock the window.

A moment later he hoisted himself inside. It was less of a risk than anyone might think; if someone stopped him, he'd just say he'd come to visit his . . . grandfather. And sure, he'd come unprepared, but there was bound to be something here he could use. There always was. He walked out into the hallway, going from door to door until he found the janitor's closet.

"Ahh," he whispered, hefting a metal can. "Acetone."

Returning to the office, he sloshed the acetone over the sofa and chairs and especially the rug near the duct. He crouched on the windowsill for a moment. Savoring it. Then he lit a match, shielding it from the breeze with his body, and tossed it onto the sofa.

Flame burst out in a sheet. He stared at it, as though to draw it straight into his soul. Heat licked at his face, and he held out his hands to warm them.

For a moment he lost himself. He became one with the fire, the Great Destroyer, consuming everything in his path. His father's face blackened and fell away, leaving nothing. Grandpa's face, his mouth open with either a curse or a scream. It didn't matter; in a moment, his face was gone. The Bitch, her red-brown hair ablaze, her skin peeling off in blackened sheets. Taken down. Other faces, other hurts, buildings, cities . . . All fell to the devouring flames. All were consumed.

He jolted back to reality, found himself covered with sweat, his chest heaving. Slipping off the windowsill, he ran off down the street. His coat flapped around his legs, billowed around him like the wings of a great bird. He felt as though he were flying on the back of the wind, flame-borne.

This was special. Too big to be contained. Too big to be kept to himself.

The world had to know. He wanted credit for this, his triumph, and he wanted it captured on film for all time. Tonight, he'd be the most important man in Tidewater; all the couch potatoes flipping through channels with their remote controls would find his work everywhere they looked.

Whistling, he fished in his pocket for a quarter.

Lou didn't know what to wear to a parrot funeral. She finally decided on a blouse and a denim skirt; the Whitakers had never impressed her as a formal crew.

Punctual, yes, she thought as a horn honked outside, but not formal.

She slipped her shoes on and trotted downstairs to open the door. The Whitakers, however, weren't there. But Shamu was, her long whip of a tail wagging. Lou scanned the parking lot, finally spotting the family just getting out of a station wagon a few doors down.

"Come on in, girl," she said, stroking the dog's massive head. "Want a drink of water or a ham sandwich?"

Shamu woofed.

"Ham it is," Lou said.

She headed for the kitchen, leaving the door open behind her. Shamu detoured briefly to sniff the empty cage. Lou didn't stop; that cage held ten years of memories for her. In a few days she'd work up the courage to clean it. It would take a few more days for her to decide what to do about it. She didn't think she'd want another parrot.

Opening the refrigerator, she pulled out the plateful of ham sandwiches she'd made earlier. The dog's claws clicked on the linoleum behind her.

"Here you are," Lou said, turning with half a sandwich in her hand. It disappeared, as did two more.

"You're spoiling her," Whitaker said from the doorway behind her.

Lou turned as he came in. The kids came in behind him: Mike—shovel in hand—Keefe and Kelsey. Blaire came last, carrying a box that had been covered with grey cloth. She gave it to Lou, then leaned forward and kissed her cheek.

"We're so sorry," she murmured.

It was corny as hell, but inexplicable tears stung the inside of Lou's eyelids. "Thanks," she said.

"Why don't you guys go outside and dig the grave," Whitaker said. "Blaire, go supervise."

"I'm gonna bury *her,*" Mike muttered.

The door banged shut. Lou stood, the box in both hands. It suddenly felt very heavy. And cold.

"This box is cold," she said.

"It's been in my freezer."

Apparently this represented normal Whitaker behavior, so Lou let it drop. Without looking away from her, he slid a sandwich off the top of the stack and tossed it into Shamu's open mouth. It didn't look as though it touched anything on the way down.

"Pig," he said fondly.

"Me or the dog?" Lou asked.

"The dog. Do you want to look at them?"

"No."

Her hands started to tremble noticeably, so she set the box on the counter and thrust them into her pockets. This funeral was turning out to be not such a great idea. She wasn't used to her emotions being so unruly. Or having people around to share them. The Whitakers seemed to take it as a matter of course . . . and their participation in it.

She felt as though someone had scraped fingernails across her soul. She felt stripped bare and inside out, her nerves strung taut as piano wires. And Whitaker, damn him, stood there taking it all in.

With an abrupt, awkward movement, she turned back to the refrigerator. Pulling out carrots and celery, she carried them to the sink and started running cold water over them.

Whitaker's long arm reached past her. He turned the water off, then grasped her by the shoulders and swung her around to face him. "What the hell are you doing?"

"I'm fixing some munchies," she said, clutching the vegetables in a grip that should have wilted them then and there. "Sustenance for the mourners."

"Christ, Lou." His eyes turned savage as he reached out to take them from her. "Give me those!"

She snatched them out of his grasp. "Mind your own business, will you?"

"Stop being so . . ." His mouth set in a grim line, he grabbed her by the wrist and hauled her closer, ". . . fucking prickly. I'll cut the goddamn carrots for you."

Lou tried to wrench out of his grasp, hurting herself. "They're my goddamn carrots. I'll cut them myself."

A small, rational part of her brain stood to one side, hooting at the ridiculousness of it. But something else had hold of her, something primal and powerful, and she had no choice but to obey it. Unfortunately, Whitaker seemed to be possessed by something equally primal and powerful, and he refused to be pushed away. Shamu, apparently thinking this was some kind of wonderful game, danced around them, barking, as they struggled for possession of the vegetables.

"Damn it, Lou—"

"Damn it, yourself," she hissed.

He finally got hold of the top of the vegetables. Lou pulled, he pulled back. Pieces of carrot and celery flew through the air, to land with meaty little thumps all over the floor.

"See what you did?" Lou cried.

His chest heaving with either exertion or anger, he looked at her, then down at the floor, then at her again. A sudden tide of mischief washed through his eyes and softened the grim line of his jaw. "At least you don't have to cut them up any more."

Lou drew a sharp breath. She started to laugh on

the exhale, although tears came, too. Whitaker held out his arms. Without hesitation, she stepped into his embrace.

Time sort of stood still then. Lou closed her eyes and let herself drift into a world where there were no demands, no need for speech or explanations, and comfort came from the solid, steady beat of his heart.

Then the back door swung open, and Blaire stuck her head into the room. "We're ready . . . Whoops. Excuse *me.*" She didn't ask about the vegetables, and no one explained them.

"Go away," Whitaker said.

She went. So did Lou's fantasy world, however, and she extricated herself from his embrace.

"I guess we'd better get it over with," she said.

"That's not the way to look at it." He reached out to brush away the hairs that stuck to her tear-wet cheeks. "Blaire says grief is an important part of the healing process."

"Where did she learn that?"

"She's minoring in psychology. If she can't minister to animals, then she's determined to work on humans."

Lou could only shake her head. Turning, she picked up Emily and Elihu's tiny coffin.

Whitaker touched the top lightly. "She made a little cushion for the inside. Satin."

"I'm supposed to look."

"Only if you want to."

Lou looked down at the box for a moment, hesitating. Then Shamu licked her hand in warm, wet dog-sympathy, and she found herself lifting the lid off the box.

Elihu and Emily lay together, their plumage gleaming like jewels on the bed of white satin. She drew in her breath sharply. Beautiful, yes, but something im-

169

portant was gone. A tear dropped onto Elihu's wing. For once, Lou wasn't embarrassed to have someone see her cry.

Almost fiercely, she looked up at Whitaker. "Do you think I'm stupid to feel this way about a couple of birds?"

"No." He reached down to stroke the wolfhound's ears.

Slowly, she fitted the lid back on. "I'm ready now."

Shamu led the way outside, where Mike, Keefe, Kelsey and Blaire stood solemnly around a freshly-dug hole in the flower bed. Lou leaned toward Whitaker. "If she starts in with 'dearly beloved,' I'm going to throw her over the fence."

"I'll help you," he whispered back.

Fortunately, no one spoke. Lou laid the box gently in the bottom of the hole, and then Mike shoveled the dirt back in and tamped it down. Kelsey bent and laid two obviously homemade paper flowers on the grave.

Lou swallowed hard, more moved by those flowers than she would have been by a dozen long-stemmed roses.

"They're your birds," Mike said. *"You* say something."

"What the hell is going on here?" Wade's deep voice shattered the moment, and everyone turned to look at him. He stood on the tiny back porch, fists jammed on his hips. "Elihu and Emily aren't anywhere in the house, and the kitchen floor's covered with pieces of carrot and celery!"

His gold-flecked hazel gaze shifted away from her, to Blaire, and locked on. Then he stepped off the porch and walked across the grass toward them. My son, Lou thought. Six-one, lean and athletic, his face with the clean, strong lines that youth and intelligence could

170

provide. He stepped through a beam of slanting afternoon light, and his hair flared into a bronze aureole around his head.

"Oooo," Kelsey breathed. "He's *cute.*"

Lou glanced at Blaire. The girl stood still, staring raptly at Wade. The breeze stirred her hair and molded her dress to the slim young curves of her body. Aphrodite and Apollo.

Holding out her arm, Lou beckoned Wade to her side. "This is my son, Wade." She introduced the Whitaker crew, saving Blaire for last. "And this is Blaire."

"Hi," Wade said.

"Hi," Blaire said.

Conversation lagged, but not communication. The two young people stared at each another, as unaware of their surroundings as the man in the moon.

"Cripes," Mike muttered.

Shamu broke the spell, rearing to plant her muddy forepaws on Wade's chest.

"Whoa," he said, propelled backward a step by the wolfhound's weight. "Who's this?"

"Shamu," Lou said.

He gently removed the dog's paws from his chest. "Well, hello, beautiful," he said, bending to scratch behind her ears. She licked his face. He laughed, getting another swipe across the cheek for his trouble.

"Oh, you like dogs?" Blaire asked.

"Sure. The bigger the better. You?"

She smiled. "Dogs, cats, horses, you name it. I'm going to be a vet."

They locked gazes again. Lou watched, waiting for the violin music to swell in the background.

Whitaker moved to stand beside his daughter, his gaze cool and just a bit challenging as he sized up the newcomer. Lou smiled. If Papa planned intimidation, he was in for a surprise; Wade had never been intimidated by anything or anyone. Not as a child, not as a man.

And as far as women went, Wade had always had things exactly his way. But, Lou thought, he'd never met anyone quite like Blaire. If anyone could handle Wade, she could.

"So," Wade said, straightening. "What's going on here?"

"It's a funeral," Kelsey said. "For the parrots."

"What?"

"Now, don't get upset—" Lou began.

"I'll tell it," Whitaker said.

Wade took it calmly enough, although a muscle jumped spasmodically in his jaw throughout the story. Afterward, he bent to touch the flowers Kelsey had laid on the grave.

"Oh, hell, Elihu," he said. "I'm sorry. And you, too, Emily." He looked up at Lou. "What about the eggs?"

She shook her head.

Straightening, he rounded on her. "Why didn't you call me? Dammit, Mom—"

"I knew you'd be in this weekend," she said. "What could you have done, anyway?"

"If I'd pulled the same thing on you, you'd probably kill me!"

"Perks of parenthood," she said.

He looked over at Whitaker, flinging his arms wide in an expressive you-see-what-I-have-to-put-up-with gesture. "You saved her life," he said. "You ever need anything from me, just ask."

Whitaker crossed his arms over his chest, his gaze unreadable as he studied the younger man. Then he nodded.

172

"I'm starved," Mike said. "Did someone say something about ham sandwiches?"

Lou put her arm around Kelsey's shoulders. "I think we could all use a snack."

Blaire started walking toward the house, and Wade fell into step beside her as though they'd been connected with a cord. Their voices dropped. Not from secrecy; it was just that their world didn't include others.

Lou glanced over his shoulder at Whitaker. He drew his finger across his throat in an expressive gesture. She nodded in agreement.

Wade's goose was cooked.

Did she mind? Nope. With his looks and undeniable charm, he'd had things his way for too long as far as women were concerned. Lou had the feeling that Blaire, no matter how starry-eyed, could handle him. She'd do it gently, with all the warmth and genuine loving spirit she possessed.

Lou sighed. Young as she was, Blaire was worlds ahead of the game. Wade would probably never know he was being managed. It must be a talent born in some women; Lou Malotti just didn't happen to be one of them.

"Did you like the flowers, Lou?" Kelsey asked.

"They're beautiful," Lou said. "Do you mind if I take them off the grave later? I'd like to keep them."

Pride glowed in the girl's face. Lou felt a pang of a loss she'd never let herself acknowledge before. Years ago, before her ex walked out, she'd wanted a little girl.

Not that she'd ever regretted Wade. He'd made her strong, kept her from folding, motivated her to make something out of herself so he wouldn't have to do without. She'd done it alone, and she was damn proud of it.

So why, at this advanced age, was she yearning for things she'd never let herself miss before?

Because you nearly died, stupid. And face it, because of this kid's grey eyes that are so much like her father's.

Inside, she found that the efficient Whitaker crew had already taken charge of her kitchen. Dishes, glasses, utensils—and most of the contents of her tiny pantry—were waiting on the table. No carrots or celery, however.

Between them, Mike and Keefe inhaled half a plateful of sandwiches and a couple of bags of potato chips. Kelsey ate with equal gusto and a tad more finesse. Wade and Blaire spent more time gazing into each others' eyes than they did eating.

Whitaker, who sat next to Lou, leaned close. "Do you pay his phone bills?" he whispered.

"I pay his everything."

"Well, better start working overtime."

"Blaire can dial a phone, too," she said.

He rolled his eyes. "I'm already working overtime—and not getting paid for it."

"Hey, Dad." Mike dropped a last corner of a sandwich into Shamu's waiting mouth, then pushed his chair back. "Can we go watch TV? *Terminator 2* is on at seven."

Surprised, Lou glanced at the clock. Five minutes to seven; somehow, three hours had gone by without her quite noticing it.

Realizing suddenly that the kids were waiting for her okay, she said, "Help yourself. The remote is probably on the sofa somewhere."

When Kelsey and the younger boys had disappeared

into the other room, Whitaker explained, "Before we came out here, they'd already decided to hog your set until you kicked us out. We don't have cable."

"They're welcome to it," Lou said.

"Thanks." Reaching across the table, he took her hand. "Are you feeling okay?"

"Yeah," she said, and meant it.

Wade looked away from Blaire, apparently drawn out of la-la land. "So," he said, "this is the guy you were kissing the other night."

Lou froze, inside and out. She saw Whitaker's eyes widen, then narrow. Then he leaned back in his chair and crossed his arms over his chest. He didn't have to speak; body language and a scowl that rivaled Hulk Hogan's said it all.

"Oops," Wade muttered. "Want to watch TV, Blaire?"

"Absolutely."

They escaped. *Cowards,* Lou thought. Although Whitaker's reaction was a good sign.

"So," Whitaker said. "Who was this guy you were kissing?"

This is the time to be coy. Get those womanly wiles in gear before you blow it, Malotti. But when she opened her mouth, instead of something feminine and wily, she said, "It's not really your business, is it?"

"I guess not." Shoving his chair back, he got up and headed for the door.

Another woman would call him back, she railed at herself. A few days ago she probably wouldn't have. Maybe it was almost dying; maybe it was the memory of his daughter's clear grey eyes, but she said, "Whitaker. Bob."

He stopped.

"It was a guy I've worked with for ten years. And

175

he kissed me, not the other way around. Curiosity, I guess. Or maybe just opportunity."

He took a couple of strides to reach her. Pulling her close with a jerk that made her gasp, he kissed her. Everything in her came alive in a soaring wave, and she realized that violins weren't only for the young.

¡Ay caramba! she thought, drifting in a haze of sensation.

His hands spread out over her back, pulled her in. He was hot and hard and all male. A sense of wonder swept over her, along with a lot of other things, and she drew in a short, sharp breath and moved even closer.

"Wow," he said, breaking for air. "God, I wish—"

"Shut up." She pulled him back.

Everything seemed to be one frantic heartbeat. She arched her back as his hands slid down to cup her buttocks. Cool air washed over her thighs as he lifted her skirt. His hands were hot, hot, hot against her skin, and moved with a leisure that was belied by the urgency of his mouth. He traced the line of lace that bordered the legs of her panties. First one, then the other, then again.

"This is good," he whispered against her mouth.

"This is good," she agreed. Wanting more. Wanting everything.

He bit softly at her lower lip, ran his tongue over the sensitive inner flesh. His hand drifted beneath her panties. Mindlessly, Lou shifted her legs to give him access. The world became one frantic heartbeat. Everything centered on him, his taste, his smell, his hands. Oh, his hands . . .

A loud beep speared through the fog. For a moment she thought it might be part of the violin serenade, but then Whitaker lifted his head and started cursing.

176

"What?" she gasped.

"It's my pager," he said, heading for the phone.

She watched his face change as he spoke to the person on the other end. All the grimness came back, settling his features into granite lines. An ache settled deep in her belly. It wasn't just unfulfilled desire; she'd dealt with that plenty in the past twenty years. Mind over matter. But now her mind had become involved. As she saw Whitaker slide away from her, that intense focus shifting from her to his job, she realized just how much.

"What kind of surprise?" he demanded. "Where did he call from? He called the TV station, too? They're out there already? Christ Almighty! Okay, I'll meet you there."

He hung up with a force that nearly took the phone off the wall.

"Him again?" Lou asked.

"Yeah."

"It's Saturday. I thought Wednesdays were his thing."

"Not exclusively, apparently."

She stared at him, unease twisting her stomach into a knot. For a moment, she almost thought she heard the crackling of fire in the distance. Or maybe it was just an echo in her mind. A frisson of dread ran up her spine.

"I've got to go," he said, raking his hand through his hair. "Will you see that the kids get home?"

She nodded. "Can they stay here for a while? I don't think Wade is ready to give Blaire up yet."

"Sure. I'm sorry, Lou."

"No more than I am. Be careful, will you?"

He nodded absently, obviously having moved on to other things. The lieutenant had returned. And the lieu-

177

tenant had a will-o'-the-wisp nut of an arsonist to catch.

She watched him stride out, then turned and started rinsing the dishes and loading them into the dishwasher. Shamu followed her from table to sink, sink to table.

"What do you think, girl?" Lou asked. "Is he going to be worth it?"

The dog woofed.

"Yeah, I know. But all men are a lot of trouble. The point is, some are worth it. You live with him; what's your opinion?"

"Mom."

She looked up to see Wade standing in the doorway. "What?"

"Come here."

Ordinarily, she didn't respond to such statements. But the look on his face alerted her to trouble, and she followed him into the living room.

One of the kids had switched from *Terminator 2* to channel 10, where a news update had supplanted regular programming. It wasn't much different from *Terminator*—destruction, debris, flashing lights and the shrill howl of sirens.

But this was real.

"What on God's green earth . . ." she began, but broke off when the camera's viewpoint switched.

A building filled the screen, smoke pouring out of every window. Firefighters played streams of water into the structure, keeping the fire at bay as other firemen carried people out.

"A fire broke out tonight in the Euclid Retirement Community here in Portsmouth," a reporter said. "Responsibility for the blaze was claimed by the self-named Fire Man. Firefighters think they have all the

178

residents out of the building. Most of the injuries have been due to smoke inhalation, although an eighty-one-year-old woman was taken to Maryview Hospital with chest pain, and one man is apparently suffering a broken hip from a fall."

"Oh, God," Lou gasped.

The arsonist had always picked uninhabited buildings before, almost as though he were trying to ensure that no one got hurt. Tonight he'd stepped over the line. *Way* over the line. An old-folks' home . . .

No wonder Whitaker had looked so grim. He was on the line, locked in a race to find this guy before he killed someone. Lou glanced at the kids. *They* knew. They knew. Mike's fists were clenched with white-knuckled force; Keefe and Kelsey just looked scared. Blaire's full lips were compressed into a tight line, and she sat straight and stiff in the circle of Wade's arm.

Lou's gaze went back to the TV. Flame crackled in the back of her mind, echoes of reality, echoes of her dream. The Fire Man wasn't going to stop. He couldn't stop. Her vision narrowed to a single, narrow tunnel. Flames licked high all around, consuming, leaving nothing but a black, roaring emptiness. No. Not her vision. His. The Fire Man's. She knew it, knew it as surely as if she'd touched his soul.

With a sharp, almost savage motion, Wade aimed the remote control and switched the TV back to *Terminator.*

The flames vanished. Lou let her breath out in a long, shuddering sigh, only then realizing how badly she'd been shaking. Shamu pressed close, and she laid her hand on the dog's brindled head, taking comfort from it.

Don't get carried away, Malotti. You're a practical person. You deal in realities, in facts and figures and the hard rules of the shipyard. You didn't touch this guy's soul, you didn't see his vision of fire. Get real.

"So," she said in her brightest, falsest voice. "Anyone for dessert?"

Fourteen

Jay Nesmith. Jay Nesmith. The name echoed in Lou's mind in time with her sit-ups. Breathe. Ouch. Jay Nesmith. She paused, curled around her burning abdominals. He had to be hiding. If he wasn't . . . Well, that opened up some really terrible possibilities. She had to get to him somehow, or at least find out if he was all right.

"What are you doing?" Wade asked from behind her, having come downstairs with his usual cat-footed silence.

"Sit-ups," she panted.

"They're called 'crunches' these days," he said.

She flopped back with a groan. "So what? I just did thirty of the things, and I think I'm gonna die."

"Romance is hell, isn't it?"

"How should I know?"

He came to stand over her, his face looming upside-down. "He was pretty upset about you kissing another guy. Besides," he added, "old people can't be expected to be as, ah . . . demonstrative as we young guys."

"Keep it up, and you'll *be* a homicide instead of investigating them."

"Mom, I've decided not to go to law school, at least right away."

Lou got to her feet faster than she would have believed possible. "You're kidding."

"No, I'm not."

"Then you're out of your mind."

"I'm not that, either. I just want to be a cop for a while. I want to get a feel for the job so that when I do go on to law school, I know what for."

All the usual parental arguments sprang into her mind. With an effort of will, she kept them inside. She'd never forced her opinions on Wade, and wasn't about to start now. Pushing her hair back from her forehead with the back of her hand, she said, "Let's get some coffee."

"I'll make us an omelette."

"Great."

She led the way to the kitchen. Wade poured her a cup of coffee, then waved her toward the table.

"Does this decision have anything to do with Blaire?" she asked.

He broke eggs into a bowl and started whipping them with a fork. "No. I've been tossing it around most of this year. College is an ivory tower, Mom. Law school, even more so. As you've said to me so many times, life beckons."

"Being a cop is a hard job."

"So's being a QA inspector. But that never stopped you, did it?"

Touché. "You'd be a damn good lawyer," she said.

"I'll be a better cop."

"You'll see the worst of this world. All the ugliness, the shame, the dregs of humanity."

He turned to look at her, apparently oblivious to the fact that egg was dripping from the tines of the fork. "I know. I'd like to do something about it, if I can."

"You're making a mess," she said.

"Oh, hell!"

She watched him move around the kitchen, this man who was her son. He'd grown up well. Karate and wrestling had honed his body, college had honed his mind. But there was a lot more to him than just fitness and intelligence. Wade possessed honor, something that was becoming more and more rare these days.

That finely tuned sense of right and wrong—she'd given him that. And his belief that he should act to change what was wrong. She'd given him that, too. He'd been born to be a cop; from the time he could talk, he'd always said he wanted to be a policeman when he grew up.

So now he'd grown up. And how could she feel anything but pride?

"I'll talk to Whitaker about it," she said at last. "He's bound to know someone in the police department who can help you."

The look in her son's eyes gave her all the thanks she'd ever wanted. "Is my old room available?"

"Well . . . I suppose." She tried to be gruff, even though she knew she'd never fool him into believing it. "When do you want it?"

"How about now? My rent's paid up at the apartment through the end of the month, so I can leave my stuff there for a couple of weeks. I'd like to stick around here for a while to be available for interviews or whatever."

"Does Blaire qualify under 'whatever'?"

"Blaire," he said, "qualifies under 'priority.' I like these Whitakers, Mom."

"Me, too." The ache had returned, her body's aware-

183

ness of Whitaker and what hadn't happened between them.

She sighed, concentrating instead on the smell of food as she watched Wade expertly turn the omelette. He'd inherited his cooking skills from somewhere other than his mother, and thank God for that. Lou watched him, enjoying the prospect of eating well again.

"I'm going to take the cage out for you today," he said.

Lou flinched from that. "I read in the paper that people were starting to use empty birdcages as part of their decorating scheme—"

"Not six-foot-tall ones."

"I can start a trend."

He snorted. "That's not a trend, that's a monstrosity. Let it go, Mom."

The inevitability of it settled on her shoulders, and she nodded. Sometimes you just had to let go. "All right," she said with a sigh.

"Good thing you built it in sections to be bolted together, or I'd never get it out of here."

She narrowed her eyes. "Wade, even a clam would know better than to build a three-hundred-pound birdcage in one piece."

"Man, I remember when you built that thing. My friends thought it was so cool. Nobody else had a mom who could weld."

"Did you tell them I couldn't cook?"

"Cooking was not cool." He slid her half of the omelette onto a plate and set it in front of her. "And that lack never bothered you before. Is this concern fostered by Bob Whitaker, maybe?"

Lou grimaced. Her son had always been able to read her much too easily, "Men like to be pampered."

184

"Gee, I dunno," he said with a grin. "It never happened to *me*."

"That's what I mean. I'm working under a handicap; I just don't know how to play the game, I guess."

He sat down opposite her. "You've developed a jaundiced view of men. I didn't get the impression that Whitaker was interested in playing any games."

To avoid that clear, too-perceptive gaze, Lou started to eat. The omelette smelled like heaven, but her taste buds seemed to have lost their enthusiasm. Wade had The Look. He had something in his teeth, and by God, Wade Malotti never let anything go until he worried it to shreds. Kind of like a bulldog with a slipper. She sighed; sometimes her jewel of a son could be a real pain in the neck.

"You know," he said, "you never told me much about my father."

"Come on, Wade. You know his profession, his background, everything I know about the guy."

"Yeah. But not about your relationship with him."

She stabbed at a piece of egg. "I was a kid. Head over heels in love with the man, and wanted to do nothing more than please him. For a while, it was great. But then he started in on me about my weight. I've always been a big girl—"

"Call it voluptuous."

"He called it fat. He fretted about every pound I gained, complained about my butt, my hips, my thighs. I felt like a toad. And I let him do a number on me. During that year of marriage, I didn't know whether I was coming or going unless he told me so. I was even dumb enough to let him browbeat me into growing my hair long just for him. The day after he walked out of my life, I had it cut. Kept the braid all these years as a reminder of my own stupidity."

185

Grimness thinned Wade's lips. "Did it ever occur to you that he was wrong?"

"Of course he was wrong," she said, surprised.

"Then why do you still believe him?"

"Huh?"

He shoved his plate away. "Don't you see it? You think a guy like Whitaker can't love you unless you're thin and handy at cleaning and cooking and doing the laundry. Jeez, Mom! You've done things most women wouldn't dare even consider. You've fought and scratched and managed to make your own way in the world, and that *matters*. And there are guys who want a woman, not a service."

Lou stared at her son in astonishment. "I—"

"All my life I've watched you push men away, but I didn't understand why. Now I do."

"Hey, a marriage that ended like mine did can make a person pretty damn cautious."

"Cautious, hell. The minute a guy shows interest in you, you run the other way. And don't tell me it's none of my business. You're too damned stiff-necked and bossy for anyone else to give you advice, but you don't scare me. I've got one thing to tell you, Mom." He leaned forward, aiming his fork at her like a gun. "You let a guy like Whitaker walk away because you're afraid of being hurt again, you're a fool. So your first marriage was a mistake. Twenty-three years of penance is enough."

Lou had had enough therapy for one morning. Shoving her chair back from the table, she got to her feet. "Thanks, Doctor Malotti. I'm so glad you pointed these things out to me."

"I'm right, and you know it."

Damn him. "If you'll excuse me, I've got to see a man about a horse."

186

* * *

The Fire Man spent Sunday morning cleaning his apartment. His version of religion; some people went to church, he tidied up his life. Now, surrounded by gleaming wood and clear, sparkling glass, he could relax.

It was a small apartment, just a living/dining area, kitchen, bedroom and bath. He didn't much like living in large places, anyway. And never a fireplace. He'd tried that once, thinking he might be able to indulge himself, but it was never enough. It was the *destruction* he craved, the knowing that he'd done it.

Dust rag and furniture polish in hand, he took one last tour through the apartment to make sure it was perfect. Furniture crammed the place comfortingly: a sofa, two recliners, end tables, bookshelves on every available inch of wall space. A large dining table more than filled the slot that served as a dining area, leaving barely enough room to squeeze by. The bedroom was even more crowded, with two dressers, a cedar chest and two nightstands to take up the space left by the twin bed.

But this . . . This was good. Comforting, with its grey walls and carpeting, and the buttery glow of polished wood. His nest, familiar things pressing close, order in the chaos of the outside world. Here he could sleep without hearing Grandpa's voice, without waking in a cold sweat at the stench of the old man's rotted teeth, the feel of his urine spreading from the other side of the bed they shared. Hot at first, then turning colder and colder until it was like a dead hand cupping him.

So, you took care of him. You took care of them all. With an effort, he pulled himself back to the present.

187

He'd thought more about the past in these recent few hours than he had in years. Brought on, no doubt, by his encounter with the old-folks' home.

He sprayed furniture polish on the already-shining top of the nearest dresser. Moving with slow, voluptuous strokes, he smoothed it onto the wood. Polished it. Polished it some more. The lemon scent of the spray surrounded him, buffering him from the voices of the past. Finishing, he moved on to the next dresser.

When he started to polish the bedside table, the one with the clock, he realized it was nearly twelve o'clock. Time for the news. Last night he'd dominated the local news, overshadowing even Saddam himself. But then, Saddam lived half a world away. The Fire Man, now, lived right here. Tidewater's own personal demon.

Whistling under his breath, he went into the living room and turned the TV on. WAVY-10, his chosen favorite. Light bloomed on the screen, resolving itself a moment later to a shot of the burning nursing home.

"Ahh," he said, settling into his favorite recliner. "Thanks. Just what the doctor ordered."

The camera pulled back, panning to the reporter, another of those pushy women he disliked so much. She had cornered Whitaker somehow, getting an interview out of him when it was obvious he'd rather be somewhere else.

"So, Lieutenant, what do you think about this latest blaze?" she asked.

"I just got here, Ms. Matuska."

"Then you didn't know that the Fire Man called the station to tell us he'd set it?"

His lips thinned. "No comment."

"Come on, Lieutenant. This is the first time he's set

fire to an inhabited building. Don't you think this is a rather disturbing development?"

"Disturbing in what way?"

The reporter looked a bit taken aback. "Well, he's always been careful to pick empty buildings before. Don't you think this latest fire shows a lessening in his concern for human life?"

"I never thought he had concern for human life," Whitaker said. "This is a very sick man, Ms. Matuska."

"Sick!" the arsonist hissed. "Wrong!"

The reporter pushed the mike closer to Whitaker. "You don't think he's going to stop, then?"

"I don't think he *can* stop."

"What is the Fire Department—and you in particular—doing about it?"

"We're following every lead we've got, but so far he hasn't been obliging enough to leave his driver's license at the scene, Ms. Matuska. And we simply can't be everywhere at once; the guy can pick and choose his targets, and we've got no choice but to clean up after him."

"I'm glad you understand that," the arsonist murmured.

"Lieutenant Whitaker, what does your department intend to do about this man?"

"This firebug," Whitaker stressed the last syllable, "isn't going to stop. He set this fire knowing that this building was full of elderly residents and that someone might not be able to get out. And he didn't care. Sooner or later, he'll kill someone. I want to catch him before that happens. So, people, I need your help. Keep your eyes open. If you see anyone hanging around, or anything at all suspicious, call us immediately. Call the police."

He walked away, so suddenly that the reporter didn't react in time to follow him. For a moment the camera caught his broad frame silhouetted against the pall of red-lit smoke.

Then Kursk's face appeared on the screen, the set behind him a sterile mockup after the chaos of the fire scene. "Firemen have brought the blaze under control, but twenty people have been hospitalized for smoke inhalation, and at least three for chest pain."

"A couple of geezers got overexcited," the arsonist said. "So what?"

"The self-named Fire Man has claimed responsibility for the blaze," Kursk continued. "Here is that taped telephone conversation. The call, incidentally, came from the 7-Eleven just down the street from the retirement home."

The Fire Man leaned forward as his disguised voice came through the speaker.

"Hello, Mr. Kursk." Worlds of emotion filled that whisper, and knowledge of things beyond the rest of mankind. "You've heard about the fire going on now at the Euclid Retirement Home."

"Yes, we have a crew at the scene."

"That's my fire."

"Why did you do it?"

"Because it was there."

A moment of silence. Then Kursk asked, "Are you saying that it was a spur of the moment thing?"

"Yes. And pass this on to Lieutenant Whitaker: I found some acetone in the janitor's closet, and used it to start the fire on the sofa and chair in the back office. Save him some time investigating so he can be ready for the next fire."

Sirens screamed in the background. The Fire Man's

breathing hissed in the speaker for a moment, then he said, "I've got to go. I'll be in touch."

The sirens cut off abruptly, to be replaced by a dial tone. As the camera cut once more to the fire scene, the arsonist threw his rag at the screen. It hit and slid downward, leaving a dull streak of polish on the glass.

"I am not sick," he said. *"I am not sick!"*

He'd found power beyond what most people could even imagine as they toiled through their vacant little lives. Even Whitaker was too blind to see it. The fool. If he had, he'd never have made that statement on TV.

The arsonist got up and retrieved the rag. The smell of furniture polish no longer gave him pleasure; his life had become complicated with too many loose ends.

The time had come to deal with them all.

Loose ends, loose ends.

Lou spotted the car as she strode up the sidewalk toward the Nesmith house. The black Taurus sat just around the corner of the intersection, where both the house and the street would be in view of the two men inside. Security people from the shipyard, no doubt; she wasn't the only one who'd like to have a heart-to-heart talk with Jay. Too bad they weren't a bit less conspicuous.

She whistled softly under her breath as she pushed the doorbell, and watched the Taurus in the polished brass face of the knocker.

No one answered. Lou rang again. "Kathy, it's me, Lou Malotti. I know you're in there. I need to talk to you."

After a moment, the door opened a crack. Kathy

peered out, her blond hair lank, her eyes swollen and red from crying. "This isn't a good time," she said.

"Please. It's very important."

Lou leaned closer, holding the other woman's gaze. Hoping the brief rapport they'd shared a few days ago would hold.

The suspicion faded from Kathy's eyes, to be replaced by fatigue and a grinding worry. "Okay, Lou." She swung the door open wider, turning to lead the way into the living room.

Motioning Lou to sit on the sofa, she perched on the edge of the loveseat opposite. "Did you see the black car at the corner?"

"Yeah."

"It's been there off and on for three days."

"They're looking for Jay, of course," Lou said.

Kathy clasped her hands over her knees. It looked as though she were trying to hold herself together. "I haven't seen him."

"But you've heard from him, haven't you?"

"No."

"Then why are you sitting there like you're ready to run out the door any second?"

Kathy looked down, letting her hair curtain her face.

"This is really important, Kathy," Lou said. "I wouldn't put you on the spot if it weren't."

"I haven't seen him." Dully.

She's a terrible liar. And scared to death. Scared of what he'd done, scared of what she doesn't know. "I just want to talk to him. A couple of minutes, a couple of answers only he knows. I give you my word that I won't tell anyone where he is."

Kathy shook her head.

"Listen," Lou said, keeping her voice calm despite the urgency clamoring inside her. "Jay's in trouble. Ig-

192

noring it isn't going to make it go away. If he comes forward and helps us reconstruct that database—"

"Are they going to write him a letter of recommendation?" Bitterness edged Kathy's voice. "Are they going to find him another job somewhere? Are they going to reinstate the benefits they took away?"

"I doubt it."

Kathy let her breath out sharply. "At least you're no liar."

"I didn't come here to lie to you. But I can promise you that Harry Deveraux and I will do everything in our power to help Jay. There's been some talk about filing a criminal complaint—"

"Criminal!"

"If Jay comes forward, Harry and I might be able to convince Van Allen to let Jay walk away from those."

The other woman shook her head. Slowly, as though trying to convince herself.

Lou leaned forward. "Look, we already know Jay queered the database. What does he have to lose?"

"Oh, God!" Kathy's face crumpled, and she covered it with her hands. Tears leaked out from beneath her fingers. "I don't know what to do!"

Lou went to sit beside her, putting her arm around the other woman's shoulders. Kathy cried quietly for a while. Then she took a tissue out of her pocket and dried her face.

"I don't know where Jay is," she said. "He got back in town a couple of days ago. Called to say he was all right and not to worry about him, that . . ." She took a deep, shuddering breath. "He wouldn't answer any of my questions. Just said he had to work some things out before coming home, warned me about the phone not being secure. And then he hung up. I haven't heard from him since. Maybe he's right about the phone; that car showed up a couple of hours after I talked to him."

"You don't know how to reach him?"

"No." Unfolding the tissue, Kathy pressed it to her eyes as if to hold the welling tears in. "I don't know what to do any more. I don't know what to believe. It's like he's been leading some secret second life, and I've only now found out about it. The kids are starting to ask questions, and I don't have any answers for them."

Lou studied her, wishing she could see what was behind those tear-reddened eyes. Was she telling the truth? Maybe. If it was an act, it was a hell of a convincing one. "Do you have family here in town?"

"No. My parents are dead, and my sister lives out in Seattle. With four kids of her own, she's hardly able to come out and hold my hand."

Lou sighed. If Kathy was telling the truth about Jay, then she was way too trusting for her own good. Somebody had to pull this woman up straight, and apparently there was only one candidate for the job. "What's Jay doing for money?"

"I don't know. Why?"

"He's not drawing a paycheck, is he? He's got to buy food and gas, and have a place to stay, doesn't he?"

"Well . . . I suppose so. What are you trying to say?"

Muttering a curse under her breath, Lou raked her hair back from her forehead. "Look, Kathy, I know I shouldn't push my nose into your business, but somebody's got to wake you up. Listen to me, and listen to me good. First thing in the morning, you go down to the bank and check every account you and Jay have.

Then transfer the funds to your own name." *If there's anything left.*

"But—"

"Do you have separate credit cards?"

"No, but—"

"Then you call each company and cancel the card."

"Why?"

Lou hesitated, trying to find a gentle way to say it. But there wasn't. And maybe this was better taken raw, anyway. "Because Jay is running from his responsibilities. And right now, I'm afraid you and your kids fall in that category."

"Jay would never do that to us."

"I said the same thing. And my ex-husband took every nickel we had, and ran every credit card up to the limit. It took me six years to dig myself out from under. Maybe Jay isn't like that. Maybe he's a good guy just having a hard time, and sooner or later he's going to wake up and face his problems. But you've got three kids who are depending on you. Can you take the chance?"

Kathy's expression became profoundly troubled, and her clasped hands whitened from pressure. "I don't know what to do," she whispered. "I just don't know."

Taking one of her business cards out of her purse, Lou wrote her home number on the back before handing it to the other woman. "If you hear from Jay, see if you can convince him to call me. Tell him I won't tell anyone where he is. I just want to ask him some questions." Kathy looked so lost, so completely vulnerable, that Lou had to look away. "And if *you* need anything, just pick up the phone, okay?"

"Okay."

Lou left in a hurry, driven not only by Kathy's problems, but by the ghosts of her own. She didn't like thinking about those first years after her ex left. They'd been too hard, too scary. Wade had been her lifeline then, her joy and her reason for fighting. It had taken her a long time to learn to fight just for herself.

Poor Kathy. With or without Jay, she had some tough times ahead.

Lou started her car and drove up beside the Taurus. She'd been right; they were both from Carmichael security. Al Bernard and Bill Davis. She leaned over and rolled down the passenger window, gesturing for them to do the same.

They obeyed, staring at her with identical expressions of innocence on their faces. It looked as though they were really enjoying their cloak-and-dagger assignment.

"Hi, Bernard," she called. "Having fun?"

"What do you want, Malotti?"

Lou smiled. "She's spotted you, you know. You can sit here until Doomsday and she wouldn't take you to her husband—even if she knew where he was."

Bernard rolled his window back up.

"Amateurs," Lou muttered. "Cripes."

She eased the Corolla into gear. As she moved past the Taurus, she caught movement out of the corner of her eye. She stopped, peering into the shrubbery that separated the Nesmith house from its next-door neighbor.

It had been an odd sort of movement. She squinted, hoping it would come again so she could identify it. Something prickled its way up her spine, a reaction much too powerful for the almost-seen presence that had triggered it. An image that didn't belong here in this place, at this time.

Glancing over her shoulder at the Taurus, she saw

Bernard and his partner facing straight ahead, obviously not alarmed.

"Come on, Lou," she muttered. "You're getting carried away, seeing shadows in broad daylight."

She peeled rubber when she left, a personal raspberry not only to Bernard and chum, but to her own disquiet.

Fifteen

Lou drove straight to Harry Deveraux's house in Hatton Point, not a half mile away. Harry lived well. He'd torn down the house that had once occupied this site and built a two-story modern structure with lots of angles and glass—his nose-thumbing of the area's love of Williamsburg architecture. The house sat stark and uncompromising amid its more conventional, azalea-shrouded neighbors. She could hear Harry's voice as he told her, "Piss on resale value. I'm gonna die in this house. Who the hell cares what happens after that?"

Helen Deveraux opened the door on the second ring. She was still striking at fifty-seven, helped by a gorgeous ash-blond dye job. A nice woman. "Why, hello, Lou. What brings you here?"

"I need to talk to Harry," she said. "Since I happened to be nearby, I took a chance that he might be awake."

The older woman swung the door open. "You're in luck, if you consider seeing the old grouch luck."

Lou stepped into the foyer, her running shoes squeaking slightly on the ceramic tile of the floor. Shards of multicolored light from a stained-glass window sprinkled the pale oak steps of the staircase. To Lou's right lay the vast stretch of the great-room area, done modern, like the house. To her left lay the formal dining room, done, to quote Helen, in eclectic. To quote Harry, done in expensive, mismatched junk.

"Who's that?" Harry called. "Helen?"

"It's Lou, Harry," she called back. "Get ready for company."

With a wink, the older woman led Lou upstairs.

"I don't know how you do it," Lou said.

"Thirty-eight years now," Helen murmured.

"Another woman would have poisoned him."

Helen laughed. "He's too mean to die. He'd spite me by merely becoming a vegetable, and then I'd have to take care of him for the rest of my life."

She ushered Lou into the master bedroom. This, Lou noted, was the house's only concession to colonial decorating. If Hinkel-Harris furniture could be called a concession. Lou had priced it once, and had given it up as hopeless. Sunlight streamed in through floor-to-ceiling windows, pooling golden on the hardwood floor.

Harry lay supine in bed, his head held at an uncomfortable-looking angle as he strained to see the doorway. "What's this about vegetables?" he demanded.

"Nothing, Harry." Helen bent over him solicitously. "Would you like something to drink?"

"Scotch."

"Sorry, not with your medication. Lou?"

"No, thanks. I'm only going to stay a couple of minutes."

Helen straightened, turning toward the door. "I'll leave you two alone. Call if you need anything."

Her husband watched her until she left the room,

then let his head fall back to the mattress. "She's enjoying this," he growled.

"I would, too, if I'd had to put up with you for thirty-eight years."

He snorted. Lou slid into the chair beside the bed, and studied the man who had been her boss and mentor for more than ten years. He looked shockingly old. Wrinkles she'd never noticed before lined his face, and even the curling salt-and-pepper hair seemed to have lost some of its vitality. But his black eyes were undimmed, by pain or age or anything else.

"So, what's been going on?" he asked. "Have they figured out what happened to the database program?"

"They think it might still exist, and that it's just been repartitioned."

"Repartitioned, hmm?" He rubbed his cheek. "There aren't many people who know enough to do that."

"Jay could, judging by what I saw of his computer books."

"Hell, *I* have tons of computer books and don't have any more idea of what they say than a chimpanzee."

Lou smiled. "Let's leave you out, then. But let's assume Jay knew what he was doing. Who else?"

"Hmm. Walter Hamilton, for sure; he's a whiz, does a lot of desktop publishing in his spare time. And Beth what's-her-name in Records—"

"Granger?"

"Uh-huh. And old Winesap—"

"You mean Mrs. Winstotter." The technical librarian, Lou noted.

"Yeah. And don't forget, most of the engineers are pretty computer literate, as is most everybody in our department. Now take you, for instance. You're no

200

computer whiz, but I haven't seen anything you couldn't learn if properly motivated."

Lou sighed. "Gee, Harry. The only people you left out are the shop people."

"Blue collar. Know machinery, not computers." He smiled a smile that Dracula would have envied. "But who knows what *they* do in their spare time? Plenty of intelligent people choose working with their hands over sitting on their ass in front of a desk."

"Fat lot of help you are."

"Hey, but don't forget access. There aren't but a few people who had that. There's Gage, head of Security. There's Van Allen." He ticked the names off on his fingers as he spoke. "There's me. And with me out, there's Dwayne Steggans. Although I doubt he has the interest or ability for something like this."

"Jay isn't on that list, I notice."

Harry grimaced. "He dropped by to see me a couple of nights before I went into the hospital. I had an unexpected problem with the guys who were drilling the new well, and I, ah, left Jay alone in my office for nearly twenty minutes. He could have gotten the code out of my file."

"You wrote it down?"

"I wrote everything down. Hell, Lou! I was going in for some heavy-duty surgery, and who knew what could happen? Do you think those guys have you sign those blanket release forms for nothing? I had to have everything down for Steggans if something went wrong."

"Jesus, Harry!" Lou leaned forward, propping her elbows on her knees. "Did you tell Security?"

"Sure. I didn't want to get Jay in any more trouble than he already was, but what could I do?"

With a sigh, Lou bent forward to rest her head in

her hands. Poor Jay. His fate seemed to be signed, sealed and all but delivered. She could almost hear the door of the cell clanging shut behind him.

"What's the matter?" Deveraux asked.

"He's gone to ground. Security's staked out his house, which his wife knows. She's scared to death."

"I can't do anything about it," he said. "This isn't my deal, it's Van Allen's. He's really on a tear about it."

"Yeah? Do you think he'd be interested in hearing about these inspection problems?"

"Not if they're a maybe. Look, he's barely treading water right now. Even Norshipco is hurting right now; you know how many people they've laid off recently. We're so small that something like this could pull us right under, and then we'd *all* be looking for jobs."

Lou sighed, not liking any of it. This thing was getting trickier by the moment. And she was holding a very hot potato alone. She opened her mouth to say something, but then took a good look at her boss, and closed it again.

Harry looked as though he'd aged ten years during their conversation. Deep lines bracketed his mouth, and those snapping black eyes seemed to have lost their luster. She realized he'd managed to hold the pain at bay for a few minutes, but the time of grace had ended.

"I'd better go," she said, getting up.

He nodded. "Sorry. I wish—"

"You'll be up and around in no time. Take care of yourself, Harry."

"What choice do I have?"

His eyes drifted closed. Lou walked quietly toward the door, intending to get out before he realized he was falling asleep.

"Lou?"

She stopped, turned. "Yes, Harry?"

"I liked Jay."

"He liked you, too."

She waited a moment, but he didn't say anything more. Silently, she pulled the door closed behind her and went downstairs. Good hostess that she always was, Helen came out of the dining room to meet her.

"How did he do?" she asked.

"Pretty well. I think he's paying now, though."

"Oh, dear." Helen glanced at her watch. "I can't give him any medication for at least an hour. Poor thing. This surgery has been much harder on him than he expected. Harry is so . . . obstreperous that you tend to forget he'll be sixty-one next month."

Lou put her hand on the other woman's shoulder. "He'll bounce back, don't worry."

"I hope so. But I have to tell you, he's mentioned retirement for the first time in his life."

Retire? Harry Deveraux? Lou recoiled from the thought. To her, Harry Deveraux *was* Carmichael Shipyard. He'd started with the yard nearly forty years ago, and had worked his way up through the ranks just as she had. He'd turned down a vice presidency a couple of years ago, preferring the hands-on involvement of the QA Department. And now he was talking about leaving all that to sit at home in his rocking chair? No. Not Harry.

"That's just the pain talking," Lou said. "He'll be singing a different tune once he's back on his feet."

"I expect you're right." Helen's smile looked brave, but tentative. "The prospect of having him home permanently is a truly frightening one."

"That, I can imagine." The light in the foyer sud-

203

denly seemed just a bit less cheerful. "Give me a call if you need anything, Helen."

"Thanks."

Lou stepped out onto the porch, stopping to take a deep lungful of the azalea-scented air. The cold front had passed through, leaving Tidewater in the embrace of a gorgeous sun-drenched spring. Birds cavorted overhead, their shadows racing across the ground in elegant precoital play.

That image led to memories she didn't want to deal with right now. She pushed them away as she'd done with a lot of other troublesome thoughts in her life, and headed toward her car.

"Where've you been?" Wade demanded when she walked into the town house.

"Out and about. Why do you want to know?"

"We're invited to the Whitakers' for a Sunday afternoon barbecue. Two o'clock, so hurry up and get dressed."

"What, is it black tie?"

Wade rolled his eyes. "No. But put something sexy on for God's sake. No, for Whitaker's sake. The guy's having a rough time right now—a little cleavage might cheer him considerably."

"Cleavage!" Lou couldn't help but laugh. "Did he say that?"

"Didn't mention it. I just thought I'd help things along a little."

"Well, forget it," she said, heading upstairs. "That place is crawling with hamsters. If you think for one minute that I'm going to expose tender portions of my anatomy around there, you're nuts."

"Coward!"

"Brat!" she snarled over her shoulder.

But he'd planted something in her mind—or maybe her id. Whichever, she stood in front of her closet considering clothes she hadn't worn in years.

She finally decided on a russet cotton jumpsuit that nearly matched her hair. She'd bought it a couple of years ago because it had not only flattered the generous volume of her figure, but was comfortable as well. This was the first time she'd worn it; somehow it had never seemed appropriate attire for cleaning out the parrot cage or tromping around the shipyard.

"God," she said, staring down at the deep V of the neckline. "Cleavage. I just hope one of those little fuzzy guys doesn't decide to go spelunking."

Now, if Whitaker decided to do a little exploring . . .

"Mom!" Wade yelled.

"Coming!" She hesitated in front of the mirror, wondering if a little lipstick or something might help. Then her focus shifted to the reflection of the room behind her. Piecemeal furniture, acquired over the years with little regard for continuity of style, the Southwestern print bedspread she'd bought more because it was on sale then because it went with the coffee-colored drapes that had come with the house— even if the room had been set to rights, it wouldn't have had much charm. She'd intended to get new curtains some day, but her schedule . . .

"Who're you kidding?" she asked, turning, arms akimbo, to survey the room. "Suzy Homemaker you're not. And you're not *ever* going to find the time to look for curtains while these have a shred of life in them."

"Mom!"

"Okay, okay." Taking pity on her son, she trotted downstairs.

Wade looked her over. "Wow. You look—"

205

"Like a reddish-brown blimp."

"Like a whole lot of luscious female," he corrected. "Shit, Mom, cut the blimp crap. You're a great-looking woman. Don't you know that I went through high school labeled the 'kid with the mom with the best-looking knockers'?"

Lou felt her mouth drop open. "You little perverts!"

"Yup. And now let's get to our barbecue so I can moon over Blaire all afternoon."

Still dazed from her son's revelation, she let herself be talked into letting him drive. By the time she regained her wits, they were in the Corolla and heading down High Street at twelve miles over the speed limit.

"You're going too fast," she said.

"It's okay, Mom. Trust me."

"If you wanted to speed, you should have taken your own car."

"It's not running right. I've got to work on it tomorrow."

Lou scowled. "Well, you should have taken the new highway—it cuts ten minutes off the trip."

"If you don't get off my back," he said in his most reasonable voice, "I'm going to tell Whitaker about the knockers."

A potent threat. Lou settled back in her seat and remained silent until they reached the Whitaker house. Spring was kind to the old home, wreathing it in pink azalea blossoms. The breeze tossed the branches of the small mimosa tree near the house, sending feathery shadows wheeling across the wide front porch.

"Hey, this is nice," Wade said. "Makes one wish for something besides a parking lot outside one's front door."

"One has forgotten the joys of lawn mowers, edgers and weed killer."

Wade winked at her, then got out and came around the car to open her door.

"Oooo," she said. "A gentleman."

"The lessons *did* sink in, once I passed those surly teen years."

He held out his arm, a courtly gesture. Smiling, Lou took it. Just then, Blaire opened the door and stepped out onto the porch. Although she was wearing jeans and a soft cotton sweater, her beauty, as the poets say, was undimmed. The breeze lifted her hair, spreading it so the sun could strike golden sparks amid the brown, and her skin almost seemed to glow.

Lou could feel the tension in Wade's arm. "You should have brought flowers," she whispered.

He looked down at her with eyes that had gone dark with emotion. "I'm going to lay my heart, raw and bleeding, at her feet. What do I need flowers for?"

"Holy cow," Lou breathed. "You're in love with her."

"Yeah."

They started walking toward the house. Wade gazed at Blaire, she gazed at him. Lou almost expected them to burst into flame right here in the yard. And old Mom might have been an alien from outer space for all they noticed.

"Hi," Blaire said.

"Hi," Wade said.

"Oh, cripes," Lou snarled, giving him a less-than-gentle shove toward the stairs. "Kiss her, will you?"

She stalked past Blaire and went into the house. The silence behind her told her that Wade had had the sense to follow his mother's advice for once.

"He's kissing her!" Kelsey's voice, high and excited, drifted in from the living room.

"Oh, man, if Dad could see this!" Keefe said. "He'd have a stroke."

Lou smiled. She thought Whitaker sort of approved of Wade. And vice versa. It said something about youth, however, that the daughter's relationship had progressed farther in one day than the father's had in weeks.

She walked quietly into the living room to find the two kids plastered to the window. "Hi, guys," she said.

They whipped around, identical expressions of guilt on their faces. "You sneaked up on us," Kelsey said.

"And you're fogging up the glass."

"Us!" Keefe jerked his thumb over his shoulder, toward the window. "What about them? The porch is starting to smoke."

"Better get used to it," Lou said. "I have a feeling you're going to see a lot of Wade. Now come on, let's go get something to drink."

"And leave them alone?" Keefe asked.

Ah, Lou thought, brotherly protectiveness. "Your sister is safe enough on the front porch," she said. Taking them each by the arm, she led them into the kitchen.

"*I* think it's cool," Kelsey said. "Did you see the way they looked at each other? I hope they get married."

Keefe looked at her, then at Lou. Finally he shrugged. "Things sure are getting complicated."

"Amen," Lou said.

She leaned against the counter while Keefe rummaged in the refrigerator. Something placid settled in her, maybe brought on by the birdsongs outside, maybe by the slanting lemon-yellow sunlight that poured in through the big old windows.

"By the way, Dad's at the station," Kelsey said. "He

said to tell you he's up to his eyeballs in work, but he'd try to make it later."

Some of the shine went off the day, and Lou heaved a sigh for the wasted cleavage. "Hand me the newspaper, will you? I haven't had time to sit down all morning."

The paper held no relaxation, however; a picture of the burning building occupied a good part of the front page. In color. The headline read: FIRE MAN STRIKES AGAIN! AUTHORITIES HELPLESS TO STOP HIM.

Poor Whitaker. Lou laid her hand over a smaller black-and-white photo of an elderly woman being carried on a stretcher, an oxygen mask over her mouth and nose.

She closed her eyes against the image, but the crackle of flames echoed through her memory. And the picture of *him* swooping toward her like a great black bird.

For a moment, she thought she heard him laughing. Her skin rippled with horror.

"What's the matter, Mom?" Wade asked from behind her.

Lou opened her eyes, surprised that she hadn't heard him and Blaire come in. "Why should anything be the matter?"

"You should see the look on your face. Like you came face to face with the bogeyman or something."

"Or something," she said softly.

He picked the paper up from the table. "Man, that guy is sure getting his share of media attention. It seems the more they give him, the more he wants."

"Dad's really upset about this," Blaire said. "For a while, the papers treated that nut like some kind of celebrity . . . sort of naughty, but harmless, like the

209

Mayflower Madam. But Dad said from the beginning that this guy was a real psycho and that he'd kill somebody some day. Well, he made a good try at it last night. It's a miracle they got all those people out in time."

"He's going to get worse," Lou said.

Wade turned to stare at her. "Intuition?"

"You know I'm not at all intuitive."

"Sure," he said. "Facts and figures, as you've always told me. But I remember getting lost on that camping trip in the mountains, and you finding me when the rest of the searchers had gone the wrong way. No one could believe it."

She shrugged. "It was nothing special, Wade. Mothers always know."

He looked skeptical, but let it drop. Relief flooded through her; she didn't want to acknowledge that intuitive part of her, even to herself. For it made her vulnerable to *him*. The Fire Man.

Shamu started barking out in the back yard, a sharp, imperative sound that got Lou up from her chair and Blaire to the back window.

"What's the matter?" Lou asked.

"I don't know. She's trying to get out the back gate." Blaire rose up on her tiptoes. "Mike's supposed to be out there changing the oil . . . Oh, my God, I think he's caught under the car!"

Sixteen

Wade reached the door first. Lou, a step behind him, shoved impatiently at his back as he yanked at the knob. She could feel Blaire and the kids pressing close behind her.

A moment later they made it outside, spreading out as they ran toward the alley—Wade in front, then Keefe, with Blaire a half step behind and Lou and Kelsey in a dead heat for last.

Lou could see Mike's legs sticking out from under the station wagon. They moved once, convulsively, and her heart skittered into high gear. Shamu, apparently unable to hear anything but her own barking, scratched furiously at the gate.

Wade hurdled the dog and the gate in one soaring, magnificent leap. While the rest of them dealt with Shamu and the latch, he grabbed hold of Mike's legs and pulled. The boy slid out from beneath the car as if he'd been oiled.

Lou and the kids reached the car a hair's breadth behind Shamu. The dog raced around the car, barking, as Blaire went down on her knees beside her brother and started to pat him down.

He stared up at her, eyes wide, then shouted, "What the fuck are you people doing?"

"We thought . . ." Blaire broke off. Sitting back on her heels, she regarded her brother with obvious astonishment. "The car didn't fall on you?"

"No!" He glared up at them, then shook his head and slid back under the car.

He squirmed out a moment later, cradling something in his arms. Lou could see nothing but stripes and a pair of furious golden eyes.

"It's a cat!" Kelsey said.

"Kitten," Blaire corrected, reaching for the tiny animal. "Oh, come here, sweetheart."

Shamu, realizing that her quarry was no longer under the car, came running toward Mike. The kitten squalled, lashing out with all four feet.

"Ow!" Mike yelped.

Lou pounced on Shamu as she went past, using her weight to slow the big dog down. Wade reached over Blaire and grabbed the kitten by the scruff of the neck. It dangled in his grasp, a tiny scrap of jutting bones and grey-tabby fur.

"Bring her in the house." Blaire got to her feet. "No one's going to hurt you, sweetheart. Shamu only wanted to help."

Lou looked at the cat, which hung from Wade's hand like a mad raccoon—back arched, eyes slitted, every claw it owned ready and waiting. "I don't think it's convinced."

Still keeping the kitten at arm's length, Wade swung it around toward him. "She, Mom."

"Whatever. Get it in the house while I've still got a grip on the dog."

Somehow, they got everyone sorted out. Not to Shamu's liking however; the kitten and the people in the house, the dog in the yard. The back door shook as the wolfhound hurled herself at it. Finally, however, she accepted the inevitable.

The kitten did not. It—she—backed under the coffee table, daring anyone to come get her.

"So what do we do now?" Lou asked.

"First," Blaire said, "Mike goes out for food, a litter box, litter and attendant goodies. Who's got some money?"

Lou sighed. "Somebody get my purse."

Mike took the twenty she held out. "My car's in the alley. If I open the back door, you-know-who is going to come in right over my face."

With another sigh, Lou dropped her keys into his outstretched palm. "One dent, one scratch, even, and you die."

She turned back to Blaire, who was trying to coax the kitten out from beneath the table.

"Try some food to lure her out," Wade suggested. "Poor thing's starving."

"I'll see what I can find." Blaire disappeared into the kitchen, returning a moment later with a dish of bread, ground beef and what looked like scrambled egg.

She put it on the floor beside the table, then pushed it under. The kitten, more famished than suspicious, began to eat.

"What are we going to call her?" Kelsey asked.

"Jaws," Keefe said.

"Claws," Mike said, rubbing his chest.

"Stripes," offered Wade.

"I like Fluffy," Kelsey said.

Lou looked down at the kitten, who growled as she ate. "She's not fluffy."

"Well, she will be when she fills out," Kelsey protested.

"I hate those cutesy names for animals," Mike said, making a gagging noise.

Kelsey started to bristle, and Blaire stepped into the breach. "Let's look at this logically," she said. "First, let's list what we know about her."

Lou snorted. "We found her in an alley. She's a cat. End of story."

"So call her Alley Cat," Wade said.

Blaire smiled. "Ali."

"Huh?"

"Ali," she repeated. "A. L. I. It's short for Alice, which means 'noble.'"

"Sounds good to me," Lou said, glancing again at the scrawny, ragged scrap of catdom. "I always like a name that fits so perfectly."

"Smartass," Blaire said. "Ali it is, for lack of a better one. Anyone got any objections?"

None were voiced. With an air of well-that's-been-taken-care-of, she said, "Come on, everyone. Let's leave her alone for a while. How about we get back to business and put the burgers on the grill?"

"Now *I'm* starved!" Keefe said.

The Whitakers headed for the door. Wade held Lou back a moment. "Is it always like this?" he whispered.

"Every time I've been here," she said. "And you haven't seen the hamster-herding yet."

"Do you think it's congenital?"

"I'm sure of it."

He sighed. "Well, I suppose there are worse things than a little family insanity."

"Take my word for it," Lou said.

* * *

Whitaker arrived at dusk, when the sunlight lay in bright orange bars across the yard. Lou, ensconced in a chaise after a surfeit of hamburgers, potato salad and fresh strawberries, scarcely looked up when the back door banged open.

"Why did I step in cat shit when I walked into my house?" he demanded.

"Because there's a cat in the house," Blaire said. "And close the door so she doesn't get out. She doesn't know us very well yet."

He closed the door, then picked up the nearest lawn chair and plunked it down beside Lou's chaise. Standing behind it for a moment, hands clenched on its back, he announced, "Hello, Wade, hello, my children. I have been awake for thirty-four hours, and I've worked like a donkey for every one of them. I do not want conversation. I do not want to hear requests for money or to borrow the car."

"Gee, Dad," Mike said. "Can we breathe?"

Lou opened one eye, saw Whitaker's hand tighten on the chair, and said, "Yes, you can breathe. But leave your father alone while you do it."

"Thanks." He sat down with a sigh, reaching to stroke the very large dog head that immediately appeared in his lap. "God, I'm beat!"

Lou closed her eyes again, wondering why she bothered with a man who was always too busy or too tired. But she knew the answer: he stirred things in her that hadn't been stirred in a long, long time. He made her feel reckless, to want the things she'd denied herself all these years.

"Lou?" His voice was soft, almost a whisper.

"Yeah?"

"He burned a retirement home."

Fire crackled to life again at the edges of her mind,

215

and she opened her eyes to keep the flames at bay. "I know." she took a deep breath to calm the instinctive rise of her pulse. "He's going to do it again. Something with people."

"Yeah. The next step up the ladder."

"Ladder to where?"

"The ladder from sociopath to monster."

"I think he's already there."

Whitaker touched her shoulder. "Tell me again what you saw that day when you followed him."

"He was just a shadow. With the coat flapping around him, he looked like some huge winged creature swooping at me."

"A very frightening image."

"Very."

He propped his elbows on the armrests and clasped his hands over his stomach. His eyes closed. For a moment, Lou thought he'd fallen asleep. Then he straightened.

"You're not a nervous woman," he said. "Why does this guy scare you so much?"

"Well . . ." She swallowed, feeling as though she were just about to step off a cliff. "I can feel him."

He didn't change position, but his body tightened visibly. "Explain."

"Remember when I told you I went to the scene of the fire in that office building downtown? Well . . . I knew he was there. I felt him watching me." She looked away, toward the beautiful pink cascade of a big azalea. "This is going to sound corny, but . . . I touched his hate, and I touched his sickness. And he scares the hell out of me."

"Come to the next fire. Wednesday."

She flinched inwardly. "How do you know there'll be one?"

"I know. And so do you."

"Look, I'm not going to do you any good. Do you think I'm going to be able to point him out in a crowd and say, 'Aha! There's your man!' "

"No. But I'm willing to try anything, Lou. Not only is this guy setting fires, but he's giving *other* nuts ideas; I've had seven copycat arsons in the past month."

"The one in the shipyard?"

"I've got no proof, but I think it was a copycat."

It made sense, considering the other things going on at the yard. She opened her mouth to tell him about the inspections. Then she closed it again; he had enough to worry about. She could handle it herself.

He continued, apparently unaware of her hesitation. "I'm not asking this frivolously; sometimes, in the right setting, even a shadow can be familiar. The way he moves, the way the light hits his hair—anything can trigger recognition."

"I'll be working."

"I'll square it with your boss. Steggans."

Instinct screamed at her to stick to the familiar and unfrightening: ships, welds, the orderly progression of mechanical things. Not the world of things that couldn't be pinned down, things that couldn't even be looked at by the light of day—only by firelight.

If anyone but Whitaker had asked, she might have said no. Somehow, without really trying, he'd touched the part of her she'd kept hidden and protected for so long. If she let him, he'd pull every last barrier down, leaving her standing unprotected against the chaos on the other side.

Leaving her unprotected, too, against the Fire Man. This was a primal sort of fear, born of the unknown, the uncontrolled, the uncontrollable.

Unbidden, her memory pulled up the image of the old woman in the newspaper photo. An oxygen mask had covered most of her face, but her eyes said it all. Her home gone, her possessions gone—her whole world turned upside down.

And only to make a man think, for one moment, that he just might be God.

You're going to have to face this one, Malotti. You're going to have to feel.

"I'll do it," she said. "For whatever it's worth."

"It's worth a lot." The dying light etched shadows in the creases bracketing Whitaker's mouth when he smiled. "By the way, I like the jumpsuit."

"Thanks."

"Why did you keep your ex-husband's name?"

The sudden change of subject didn't faze her; she must be getting used to Whitaker's revolving-door style of conversation. "I kept it because it's Wade's last name. Twenty-three years ago, people didn't get divorced as often as they do now, and different last names would have raised more questions than I wanted to deal with. Now I'm so used to Malotti that I doubt I'd answer to anything else."

"Some women would want to shed any reminder of their ex-husband, particularly one who left the way yours did."

She shrugged. "He doesn't matter. I learned the lesson, though, very well."

"Is that why you get so standoffish when we get onto personal subjects?"

"I thought you weren't interested in conversation."

"Not with kids. With you, I'll take it whenever I can get it," he said. "Why did you change the subject? Does it make you uncomfortable?"

"No. It's just the past. Long past." A mosquito

218

whined shrilly overhead, and she reached up to slap at it. "And it doesn't have anything to do with my present."

"Of course it does."

"Does not."

"How many relationships have you had in the past twenty-three years? Not dates, relationships."

"By what criteria do you call something a relationship?"

"You're stalling." He leaned his head back against the back of the chair and sighed. "Okay, a relationship is a long-term association between two people who share feelings of respect, liking, attraction, and maybe even love."

"Sex?"

"Usually, if they're breathing. Be honest, Lou."

God help her, she had to be. "One."

She could tell by his expression that he'd expected her to say none. It gave her a great deal of satisfaction.

"What happened?" he asked.

"It died of neglect."

"Yours or his?"

"Both, I guess." She shrugged. "Unfortunately, he worked at the shipyard, and the relationship was a favorite subject of the gossip chain. I learned *that* lesson, too."

"So why did you stop there? Did you swear off men?"

"Heck, no. But I was a single mom, and my son was important to me. After working a full shift, I went home to be with him. That doesn't give you many opportunities to meet men. And as I got older, even those few vanished, especially since I don't date married men."

"So you stayed alone."

"There are worse things than being alone," she said. "What about you?"

"Huh?"

"You made me spill my guts. It's your turn now."

"Your guts were pretty unexciting."

"Yours aren't?"

He ran his hand over his chin, and the rasp of new beard was loud on the quiet air. "Okay, fair's fair. I mourned Nola big time for a year. Fell apart in a lot of ways. Once I pulled myself together, I played the field. Nothing big. Nothing that mattered. The women were too . . . hungry, I guess. They wanted too much, and I guess I didn't want to become the be-all and end-all of another human being's life."

Suddenly he grinned. "Maybe that's why I like you so much. There's no chance of me becoming the be-all and end-all of *your* life, is there?"

"I doubt it."

"Why not?"

Lou rolled her eyes. "Because you're not rich enough to keep me in the style to which I'd like to become accustomed."

"You know," he said, "if there weren't so many people around, I might be tempted to test the weight tolerance of that chaise."

Before Lou could think of a response to *that,* Blaire walked up, balancing a plate piled high with food.

"May I speak, Sahib?" she asked.

Whitaker scowled. "As long as you're holding that plate, yes."

"I could hand this to you now. But the mosquitoes are starting to come out, and I suspect you'd rather eat instead of being eaten."

"You're right." With a groan, he heaved himself out of his chair. Then he leaned down to pull Lou up out of the chaise—fortunately, without another groan. He put his arm around her waist as they walked toward the house. Lou smiled; judging by the movement of his hand on her hip, he was fascinated by the texture of the smooth cotton fabric. She caught her breath sharply as he ran his hand up her side in a smooth, surreptitious caress, lingering for a moment on the outer curve of her breast. Heat pooled in her belly.

"That's not fair," she said.

"I'm torturing myself, too."

"Come on, you two!" Keefe called over his shoulder.

Lou shifted Whitaker's hand back to her waist. "There are always too damn many people around."

"And too damn many fires."

"You said it."

They joined the others, who stood in a semicircle around the dog. Shamu sat in front of the door, blocking it. Determination was clear on her furry, dog face.

"I can handle this," Keefe said. Taking a hamburger off the tray of leftover meat, he tossed it out into the yard.

The dog looked at him with obvious disdain, then turned back to the door.

Mike hooted. "Hey, you really handled *that.*"

"Oh, let the dog in," Whitaker said with no patience in his voice at all. "She won't hurt it."

"Her, Dad," Blaire said.

The wolfhound surged into the house the moment the door was opened. Her nails clicked on the linoleum as she cast about for a fresh scent.

"Come on!" Kelsey said, grabbing Lou by the hand and hauling her after the dog.

She glanced over her shoulder at Whitaker, who fol-

221

lowed more sedately, eating his hamburger as he walked. He winked at her.

The dog, nose to ground, trotted up the stairs to the master bedroom. And there, Lou came face-to-face with Nola Whitaker. Or her picture, rather. Enclosed in a silver frame, it sat on the nightstand beside the bed. Nola had been a pretty woman, thin and rather sharp-featured, with a determined chin and gentle eyes. She'd had gorgeous, curling red hair.

She's the last thing he sees at night, and the first thing he sees in the morning.

Lou turned away from it, uncomfortable with the image. Maybe Whitaker wasn't quite as healed as he thought he was.

She found her companions standing in front of the closet. The kitten had found a nice, cozy retreat way, way at the back of the top shelf.

"I'm not tall enough to reach," Blaire said. "But we're taking volunteers."

"Not me," Whitaker said.

Wade stepped forward. "I'll get her."

Lou looked at Blaire's shining eyes, and couldn't help but smile. Wade had had 'hero' pinned on his chest from the moment he'd sailed over that gate this afternoon. But heroism tended to be a heady thing, and apparently Wade wasn't ready to give it up yet.

He managed to extract the kitten from its hiding place with a minimum of damage to himself. Four parallel stripes up his forearm—his red badge of courage.

"We'd better get some medicine on that," Blaire said.

"Hey, nobody bothered with *my* scratches," Mike protested.

"Shut up," Whitaker said.

Blaire took the animal from Wade and passed it to

222

Lou, then led her brave swain toward the bathroom. Taken completely by surprise, Lou cradled the kitten against her chest. It dug claws into the jumpsuit, but gently enough, and Lou dared stroke the tiny, rough-furred body. Astonishingly, it began to purr.

"Look, she likes you," Kelsey said.

Realization—horrible, inevitable realization—burst in Lou's mind. "No!"

"Yes," the Whitakers said in chorus.

"You're the logical choice," Papa Whitaker pointed out. "After all, we've got hamsters. Hamsters and cats don't mix."

"And Emily and Elihu are gone," Kelsey said. "You need company."

"I've got Wade for company."

"Pets make a house a home," Mike said, grinning like the Devil himself. "Besides, you paid for the litter box and stuff. It's like, fate."

"It's like, being had," Lou snarled. Beneath her hand, the kitten vibrated with a purr that had grown much too loud for its size.

"Then why are you still petting her?" Kelsey asked.

"Because she's cute, damn it."

Mike's grin widened. "Like I said, fate."

Seventeen

Rain fell softly on the roof, blurring the division between sleep and wakefulness. Lou roused once at some indefinable rainy-day time, but, lulled by the warmth of the kitten lying on her stomach, drifted back to sleep again.

Her mind clicked relentlessly, if not always logically, through her dreams. Whitaker figured heavily in that clicking, as did the Fire Man. Deveraux made an appearance, as did Tyrene, who swept six little kids in his wake, and Wade, Blaire, Mike, Keefe, Kelsey and a whole herd of fuzzy little hamsters. Then came Fagan, his pale eyes full of contempt and laughter, his mouth pursed for a kiss. Shamu ran through the recesses of her dream, a giant ghost dog that herded the other spectres away from the fire that roared and gibbered like a live thing in its desire to consume them all.

But the wolfhound couldn't save Lou. Screaming, she plummeted into the searing heart of the fire. And discovered that it was not a heart at all, but a mouth. It sensed her. Knew her. As she plunged closer, it smiled. Opened wide. A vast, bright tongue moved, vast, bright lips formed a word.

Even in her terror, she strained to hear over the roar of the fire. Then the roar coalesced, becoming a voice, as vast and terrible and bright as the flames themselves.

"Lou," it called. "Lou. Come to me. Let me show you the way."

"No!" she shrieked.

She began to beat her arms. Frantically, hopelessly. Feathers sprouted from her flesh, bright, emerald green hope. They cupped air, gave substance to her flight.

The mouth roared. It launched into motion, ponderously at first, but soon moving faster and faster until it screamed along a swirling vortex of fire. Lou skimmed along the edges of the flames in terror—and almost-ecstasy at her own terrific speed. It couldn't catch her. She was free.

"Lou!" the mouth called.

The movement of her wings slowed. She strained against it, trying to regain the speed, the freedom, the safety. But they had all left her behind, soaring high above her head while something heavy seemed to drag at her wings. Her shoulders heaved as she tried to break free.

Her breath sobbing in her chest, she glanced over her shoulder. Fire billowed toward her, a monstrous, incandescent cloud that enveloped her in pain.

This is the place where people always wake up—the moment just before the monster catches them. She wanted to wake up, yearned for it, even as she still fought to escape.

The mouth opened eagerly as she spiraled down toward it. Vast laughter surrounded her, filled her, drew her in.

"No!" she cried, spread-eagled against the brightness.

Caught.

Consumed.

Her wings blackened, scorched, fell away. Then her skin, her flesh, her bones. And still she cried in agony, reaching out substanceless hands to try to catch the dusting of fine ash that had once been Lou Malotti.

With a gasp, she sat up, out of the dream. Sweat covered her body. Remembered terror jagged through her veins like hot acid, and she shook with the power of it. She drew in a shuddering breath, then another.

Logic told her it had been a dream. But she couldn't keep from raising her arms and examining them, nor from being surprised to find the skin unmarked.

"Oh, man," she breathed.

She glanced at the clock and was astonished to find that it was nearly one o'clock in the afternoon. Either the dream had gone on a lot longer than it had seemed, or she was finally getting used to working nights.

The bedspread shifted as something moved. Lou turned in time to see the kitten jump onto the bed and stalk toward her, then sit down Sphinx-like beside her, eyes narrowed to sleepy golden slits.

"Whatcha say, girl?" Lou asked. "Are you feeling a little better today?"

She reached out slowly, and was allowed to stroke the kitten's striped back. The vertebrae stuck out sharply beneath the fur. Lou continued the motion, and the kitten lifted her rear end to further enjoy the caress.

"You've had a hard life, haven't you?" Lou asked.

"Mrrrouw."

"I wasn't ready for you. I just lost two pets, you know. I've never had a cat before; and I'm not sure we'll get along. You slept on my stomach, for God's sake. And this thing with the litter box and the nifty little pooper scooper Mike bought . . ."

226

The kitten purred beneath her hand.

"So you're cute," Lou said. "Just learn to toe the line, okay? No sleeping on my bed. No pooping outside the box. No climbing the curtains. No sharpening your claws on the furniture. And no soap operas."

"Mrrrow?"

"Yeah, that's right." Lou swung her legs over the side of the bed. "I guess we'd better get you something to eat. Then I'll take you to the vet and get you some shots and things, hmm?"

The doorbell rang, scaring the kitten off the bed. Lou pulled the curtain aside and peered out the window, which had an oblique view of the tiny front porch. Her mouth dropped open when she saw her boss standing there.

"Steggans?" she muttered. "What the hell?"

The bell rang again, scaring the cat again just as she'd begun to emerge from her hiding place. Lou scrambled into a pair of jeans and a sweatshirt, then ran downstairs to open the door.

"Hi," Steggans said. "I bet you're wondering what I'm doing here at one o'clock on a Monday afternoon."

"The thought occurred to me."

"I had a dentist appointment nearby, and since I needed to talk to you anyway, decided to take a chance of catching you in."

"It must be important. And private."

"It is."

"Come on in," she said, stepping back out of the doorway to let him in. Belatedly, she ran her hands through her sleep-mussed hair. "Would you like a cup of coffee?"

"Sure. Thanks."

227

"Come back to the kitchen and we can talk while I get the coffee going."

As they passed the dining room, he asked, "What happened to your carpeting?"

"I . . ." Lou barely glanced at the square of compressed carpeting. Too many memories. "I had a birdcage there."

"Must have been a heck of a birdcage."

"Yeah."

"What happened to it?"

"The birds died." Her voice sounded too flat.

"Oh, right," he said. "The carbon monoxide. Sorry I brought it up."

He sat at the table while she moved around the kitchen. His gaze was so intense, so appraising, that Lou started to feel like a bug pinned to a board. She wished she'd worn a bra.

"So," she said. "What can I do for you?"

"The arson investigator called this morning to say he might have to pull you out of the shipyard Wednesday night. I said sure, but I don't think I had much choice; he was pretty official about it."

She nodded. "Is it a problem?"

"We can handle it. Thanks," he said, accepting the steaming cup. "No sugar, but if you've got some milk . . . Thanks. Now this thing Wednesday night. Are you helping him with the Fire Man investigation?"

"Not really," she said. "It's just that I saw the guy once—just his shadow, and a fast-moving one at that—but Whitaker thinks I might recognize him given the right setting."

"Like a fire."

"Yeah." An involuntary shudder rippled up her spine. She ignored it, occupying herself with pouring another cup of coffee for herself.

228

"It scares you, doesn't it?" he asked.

Startled by his perception, she glanced at him over her shoulder. He returned her gaze levelly, his cool blue eyes as clear and uncluttered as glass.

She turned back around. "Why do you ask?"

"I think most people would be. He's a very intimidating force."

"He's a nut."

Steggans got up, cup in hand, and came to lean on the counter beside her. "So, he's a nut," he said. "What if you come face-to-face with him? What will you do then?"

"Point him out, and then get back to work." Bravado, but it sounded good. Maybe she'd even come to believe it.

"Well, you've got more b— . . . guts than most people."

She shrugged, then grimaced inwardly as she realized the movement had set her breasts into sympathetic motion. Steggans didn't miss it, either; his gaze snapped to her chest and stayed there. After working in the shipyard as long as she had, she ought to be used to guys staring at her breasts. But this was her home, and by God, she didn't have to take it.

So she remained silent, intending to stay silent until he had the courtesy to look her in the eye.

She saw the realization of it come into his face. Some men might have flushed; he merely lifted his gaze and said, "I got a call from Mr. Van Allen this morning. Seems you went to Jay Nesmith's house yesterday."

"That's true."

"Why?"

"Because I wanted to talk to him about the database program."

229

"He's not living at home."

"I know that now," she said. "No one mentioned it to me before then."

"No one felt you had a need to know."

She sighed. Need to know. It was a euphemism for, I know stuff and I'll tell you only what I think is suitable. What a pain. When Harry ran the department, everyone knew what everyone else was doing. If someone called in sick, there were always several people familiar enough with his projects to pull his load.

"You can pass on a message to Van Allen for me: Bernard and that other guy are about as low-key as Howdy Doody. I spotted them, and so did Kathy Nesmith."

"You also went to see Harry Deveraux."

Lou studied him from beneath her lashes. She hadn't seen anyone following her, and she sure as hell would have noticed that Taurus. So, Van Allen and Co. had more than one set of folks watching the Nesmith house. Interesting.

"Harry's an old friend," she said. "I stopped by to see how he was doing."

"And how is he?"

"Okay."

He looked down into the depths of his coffee. "I bet everyone wishes he'd come back and straighten things out."

That was true. "Harry couldn't fix this one," she said, which was also true.

"Thanks," he said. "Harry's a tough act to follow." With a sigh, he passed his hand over his short hair. "Between him and you, I've had a hard time. I hear nothing but 'Harry would have done it this way,' or 'Why don't you ask Malotti? She knows this shipyard inside and out.' "

"So why don't you ask me?" A blunt question, yes, but he'd brought it up.

"Okay, I'll ask you. What do you think about the database?"

"I think trying to recreate the original partitions is going to be a waste of time and resources. Even if we do it, there's no guarantee the data is accurate, anyway."

"You mean Jay could have tampered with the data before repartitioning the program?"

"Heck, yeah."

"Shit." He pushed away from the counter and started pacing the floor. "Jay really diddled us on this one. What do you think about retrieving the data, but checking it against other records before accepting it as accurate?"

Lou shrugged. "Sure, why not?" She was sure of only one thing: the database entry was bound to match the report on the *Gabriella*. That's what the whole thing was about, anyway.

She watched Steggans pace. It was really too bad she couldn't trust him. Of all the people there, he was least likely to be the guilty party. He hadn't been at the shipyard long enough to learn his job, let alone form the kind of relationships that could pull something like this off.

But he was also second cousin twice removed or whatever to the shipyard's owner. If he told Van Allen what was going on, this thing might get buried so deep she'd never dig it up.

"What's next in the Enterprise lineup?" she asked.

Steggans stopped, just enough inside her space to make her uncomfortable. "A tanker, coming in tomorrow. Complete overhaul."

"Who's ship supervisor on her?"

"Louis Delanski."

Bingo. A match. The first one of this game. "Is this going to be my inspect?"

"I haven't assigned anyone. But I expect it'll go to one of the day people. Greg, probably."

"Slot me."

His eyes narrowed. "Why?"

"Because I want to."

"Why?"

"Greg's only been in the department a year," she said. "Everything associated with Enterprise is going to be a tricky job, and I want to make sure it gets done right."

His face remained impassive. "Is that the fabled Malotti nose for trouble that people keep telling me about?"

"The nose is only twenty years of experience. That's why you put me on nights, remember? Want another cup of coffee?" she asked, hoping to divert him.

"No, thanks."

His cracked-glass gaze slid from her face to her chest. She didn't like it. Turning, she slid the pot back onto the burner and moved away.

"Why are you so nervous all of a sudden?" he asked, moving with her.

"Who said I was nervous?" A lie, of course. She wasn't worried about handling him if he got frisky—twenty-odd years in the shipyard had taught her well—but he was also her boss.

You really should have worn a bra, Malotti. And then, *These guys! Don't they think about anything else?*

The front door opened noisily. "Mom, you up?" Wade called. "I smell coffee."

"I'm in the kitchen, Wade," she called back. Saved!

232

"I thought you lived alone," Steggans said.

"I did. But my son quit college, and I'm letting him stay with me until he gets a job."

Wade came into the room, his hair wet from the rain, his T-shirt and shorts soaked with sweat. "I ran three mi— Oh, I didn't know you had company." His gaze dropped to her arm, which Steggans was still holding.

"I'm not company," Steggans said, letting Lou go and reaching to shake hands with the younger man. "I'm the assistant shop foreman in QA. I just stopped by to talk shop; since your mother started working nights, I hardly ever get a chance to talk to her."

Tendons rippled in Wade's forearms as he put pressure into the handshake. Just enough, Lou thought, to establish territory. Men!

"Well, I'd better get back to work," Steggans said. "No, that's okay," he said as Wade started toward the front door, "I know my way out." Briefly, he turned back to Lou. "I'll put you on the tanker, as you requested."

"Thanks."

Turning, he strode out. A moment later Lou heard the front door close behind him.

"What was that all about?" Wade asked.

"Well, I'm not exactly sure. I *think* he came to tell me that the powers-that-be know I went to Jay Nesmith's house, and that Big Brother is watching."

"Yeah? Then why was he holding your arm?"

"I don't know."

"Bet next time he swings by to talk shop, you'll wear a bra."

Lou stuck her tongue out at him. "I'm going to see if I can coax Ali out from under the bed."

"She likes *you*," he said. "Doesn't seem to care too much for men."

233

"Wise kitty."

"Mom?"

Lou turned back. "What?"

"You'd better tell me about it, whatever it is."

"Are you detecting?"

"Spill it."

She sighed. He wore The Look again. Actually, there was no reason *not* to tell him; he might even give her a new perspective on it.

"Okay," she said. "But you can't tell anyone."

"Not even Blaire?"

"Not even Blaire. I . . . haven't told Whitaker yet."

Someone else might have asked why, but Wade had never been one to bother with minutiae; he'd get the facts, and ask why if he couldn't figure it out for himself.

She gave it to him straight and fast, from the fire in the storage shed to the present. Judging by the way his eyes darkened, she'd hooked him.

"Wow," he said.

"Wow is right."

"The fire in the storage shed doesn't jive with the rest of the stuff, you know. What does Whitaker think?"

"He thinks it was a copycat, someone using the Fire Man to cover up his own act. Other than that, he's been too busy with bigger fires. *You* saw him last night."

"He's letting it become personal."

"So would I."

Wade cocked his head to one side. "What do *you* think about the fire?"

"I think whoever set it was involved with this Enterprise scam. I'm pretty sure he took some records. Maybe he was just trying to get rid of them."

"So instead of using the company shredder, he blew them up and the Quonset hut with them. Verry sneaky."

"Smartass. Did it occur to you that if he used the shredder, then everyone would know records were missing? I figure he wanted everyone to concentrate on other things. To gain time."

Wade scrubbed at his chin, a fretful gesture. "To get other paperwork in place, you mean?"

"Give the man a cigar."

"So, why are they doing it?"

She smiled. "You've got a great future as a cop, my son. Human nature dictates there's something to be gained."

"Sure does. Money and power are usually primary candidates."

"Or avoiding consequences."

Wade nodded, accepting that. "Let's start with greed."

"Sure. Somebody looks at those two failed welds, looks at a big loss, and peels off a grand or so to buy off the inspector."

"Why the loss?"

"These aren't cost-plus jobs. They're bid too low, and the company's running too lean after that last round of layoffs. We've got to pull men off another ship for the redo, which puts us behind on two jobs, both of which are bid so we lose our butts, anyway."

"I get the picture. Redos ain't in the budget."

"Right. Not one, and certainly not two."

He sighed. "So who's doing it?"

"Best bet is two somebodies. A ship supervisor and QA inspector would be the likely candidates. *Which* two, I haven't figured out."

"Who do you think paid them off?"

She grimaced. "Whoever's got the most to gain by *not* fixing those welds."

"Somebody at Enterprise."

"I hope so," she said. "They're slick, I'll give them that. If I hadn't been assigned to both the *Santana* and the *Gabriella,* I doubt I'd even have tumbled to it. Now look . . . I think that weld will hold for a couple of years, maybe more. While I'm willing to take the time to look into this quietly, I'm not willing to let it go completely."

"Oh, man." He raked his hands through his hair. "Do you realize that this might have come straight from Van Allen—"

"That's why I've got to have proof. It's going to be tough going; I have the feeling they've buried this stuff so deep I'll have to dig down to the seventh level of hell to find it."

"I don't like it," Wade said. "You're hanging in the wind with no one covering your back."

"Carmichael's is barely treading water now," she said. "We get into an official investigation of something like this, and you can hang up the whole show. Two thousand people out of work, Wade. With every shipyard in the area laying off, where are they going to go?"

He sighed. "Cripes, Mom."

"Do you remember the accident on the *Iwo Jima* a couple of years ago?"

"I remember reading something about it in the paper, but didn't make special note of it."

"A Bahraini shipyard did some routine work on a boiler valve. They used brass nuts to fasten the valve bonnet . . ." She took a deep breath. "Those brass nuts failed, sending eight-hundred-plus-degree steam shooting out into that boiler room. Ten men died. Cooked alive, Wade. Not an easy way to go."

"And the repair on the *Gabriella* was, of course—"

"A boiler valve."

"Shit."

She nodded. "If I can find proof, I can force Van Allen to take care of this. Without proof, he's going to tell me to stick it in my ear."

"Nice."

"Hey, look at it from his perspective. He's sitting on a business that's been running in the red for a while, and has little prospect for doing better. He recalls that ship, he can kiss Enterprise goodbye. Say what you will, work is work, even lean jobs like this. In his mind, he'd be better off to hold tight and hope nothing happens to that weld. Then, when the ship comes back in here for something else, it gets fixed quietly and no one's the wiser."

"And if it doesn't come back in within that year or two?"

"Calculated risk. A maybe for the accident, a for sure if either Enterprise or the authorities get wind of it."

"That's fine if you don't consider the guys working in that boiler room."

"That's why I'm here," she said.

"You're in deep shit."

"And getting deeper every minute."

He took a carton of orange juice out of the refrigerator and swigged directly from the spout.

"I hope you realize that Blaire will never allow that in her kitchen," Lou said.

Wade smiled. "I'm willing to be tamed."

"At least I taught you to cook and clean and do your own laundry. I never wanted the guilt of raising a chauvinist and then foisting him off on some poor woman."

"Whitaker's going to be pissed when he finds out you didn't tell him about this."

"Whitaker's got his own problems. And the burning

237

of that little storage shed doesn't even hit his list right now. Besides, he has no jurisdiction here. This is mine. They've got me mad now, and I'm going to nail 'em."

"Jeez, Mom!" Wade flung his arms wide. "Whitaker's not going to care about the official crap; he's going to be pissed that you didn't confide in him. Don't you know *anything?*"

"I know I've got a tanker overhaul that's been brought in, and I've got to make sure she doesn't become another *Gabriella.*"

"I don't like you doing this."

Lou met her son's gaze squarely. "I have to," she said.

"But—"

"Hey, look at it this way: Whitaker's the one with the scary job. *He's* got to catch a real, live psychopath. I'm only trying to track down information. These are regular fellas taking a little cream on the side, using their pencils to erase one number and put in something else. They're as likely to break down in tears if somebody catches them as anything else."

He didn't like it, obviously. But he took it. "If you need anything, you come to me, hear? Anybody threatens you—"

"I know, I know. You'll karate-chop them into the next universe."

"Yeah," he agreed, without a hint of a smile. "You be careful."

"Of course," she said.

And she tried very hard not to think about Wednesday night and her date with the Fire Man.

Eighteen

The Fire Man parked beneath the overhanging branches of an oak tree and turned off the car. He'd "borrowed" it from a neighbor who'd gone on two weeks' vacation and had asked him to keep an eye on things. Sure. The blue Cavalier was perfect: not too plain, not too fancy, not too old, not too new. Nondescript. Some mud splashed onto the license plates, and he had anonymity.

He angled the rearview mirror so he could see the river behind him. Rain beaded the window, catching the streetlight and fracturing it into a million stars to replace what clouds had obscured. A magical scene. Even the chemical plant seemed beautiful, hazed as it was by distance and the softly falling rain. The West Norfolk bridge curved off to the left, a graceful ribbon of concrete.

He flipped the mirror back into place, turning his attention to the house. He couldn't tell if anyone was home or not; no figures moved in the backlit rectangle of the front window. Then he shrugged. It didn't matter whether anyone was home or not. He'd chosen his target—Whitaker's house.

He drummed his fingers on the steering wheel. It

239

was hard to wait. The urge rose high in him tonight, making his skin feel hot to the touch. He'd take payment for everything that had been said about him. Especially Whitaker's comment.

Sick. He glanced down at the newspaper lying in the passenger seat beside him. *Sick.* The papers had repeated it over and over, in bold, black print to make the lie seem true.

Sick. Sociopath. Pyromaniac. Firebug. They'd interviewed this psychiatrist and that psychiatrist, trying to put him in a category. As if to label him would make them less afraid.

His lips twisted in a snarl. They'd fucked with the wrong guy. *Look out there in the darkness, people. You can see the firelight reflected in the predator's eyes.*

A blue and white Portsmouth Police cruiser turned the corner behind him. Right on schedule. The arsonist started the Cavalier, leaning over to fumble with the glove compartment until the cop passed. Then he switched on his headlights, signaled like a dutiful citizen, and pulled out behind the patrol car. A proper distance back, of course.

The cop slowed as he passed Whitaker's house. The Fire Man slowed too, seeing what the other man saw. A nice, quiet house on a nice, quiet street, the porch light casting its radiance over the nice, well-kept lawn. Danger seemed very far away, no mad firebugs skulking in the bushes.

The Fire Man smiled.

He didn't follow the patrol car into the alley that ran behind the houses, but swung right onto Broad Street and right again to pick up the cop as he came out the other end of the alley.

"Nine o'clock and all's well," the arsonist said,

watching the patrol car's taillights disappear in the distance.

He'd staked out the house for two nights now, and it was always the same: a drive-by check between nine and nine-thirty, another one just after midnight, a third around 4:00 A.M. Cops were such creatures of habit. Most people were. But the predator had to adapt to survive.

Feeling safe now, he returned to his spot beneath the tree. He waited for another quarter of an hour. The street remained quiet, the only people out were a teenage couple more interested in playing grab-ass than in what was around them. They passed right by him, oblivious.

He folded the newspaper around a crowbar and tucked the package beneath his arm, then levered himself out of the car. After taking a last look around, he leaned in and retrieved a gallon can from the floor behind his seat. The gasoline sloshed gently as he strode down the sidewalk toward the house.

The porch light spilled a pool of light over the steps and front lawn, but left the sides of the house in darkness. The Fire Man walked past the house, then slid into the lee of the tall hedge separating Whitaker's from the next-door neighbor.

Speed was of the essence now. He ran along the hedge to the nearest side window, trusting the big azalea at the corner of the house to shield him from the street. With the house on one side, the hedge on another, and the privacy fence on the third, he found himself in a secluded little cul-de-sac. Perfect.

He peered in the window. This was the living room, well used, littered with books and games and the little girl's toys. The heart of the Whitaker household. Big area rug, two recliners, a sofa, skirted and overstuffed like a fat old matron—all nice, easy combustibles.

He looked up at the high ceiling, thinking of the dry, almost century-old wood behind the plaster. The place would probably go up like kindling. Nice. For once, however, destruction wasn't his point. Or his only point. This was his reply to Whitaker and the newspapers.

Taking the crowbar out from beneath his arm, he used it to break a pane out of the window. The dog started barking out in the back yard. The arsonist ignored it; he'd be out of here before anyone thought to investigate. He uncovered the can's spout. The smell of gasoline hung heavily in the rain-tinged air as he poured it through the broken window. The smell of power.

"Screw you, Whitaker," he muttered.

He emptied the can, watching the gasoline spread out over the floor and soak into the rug. Quickly, he rolled the newspaper lengthwise, then twisted it into a tight wand. Lit it. Tossed it through the window.

A sheet of flame burst into life, following the path the gasoline had taken. He stood transfixed, watching the rug turn black, watching the fire run up the arms and along the back of the sofa. Pleasure settled in the pit of his stomach, flickering higher and hotter with the flames.

He could feel the fire on his face and hands, in his soul. His eyes narrowed, and he drew a deep breath, pulling heat into his lungs. The world behind him faded; the only reality now was the fire. Figures formed there in the fire, ghosts of the past, spectres of the present. His father. Grandpa, toothless, crabbed, hateful. Whitaker. Agony made them dance there in the flames, agony made them scream with the fire's voice.

The figures shifted again, melting and reforming. Then the Bitch looked out at him through the flames. *She* didn't scream, didn't dance. Her hair spread out around her face, coiling, twisting, as though she'd become part of the fire itself. He felt his lips draw back into a snarl.

Suddenly the dog howled, wrenching him back to the present. Awareness flooded through him in a cold tide: he'd waited too long. He whirled away from the window, saw people run out of the house across the street, heard voices on the other side of the hedge.

He slid back against the fence. The dog hit the wood on the other side, its claws scratching, scratching as it tried to reach him. More neighbors, more voices, and now sirens wailing in the distance. The firelight seemed to come after him, eating away at his tiny pocket of concealment.

He had to go. Now.

With a grunt, he sprang upward and grasped the top of the fence, hung poised there for a moment as the dog reared against the wood below him. The animal was enormous, sharp white teeth flashing in a maw that looked like it could swallow him whole.

"Look over there!" a man shouted behind him. "Hey, you! Come back here!"

Nowhere to go but forward. The Fire Man leaped straight out over the dog's back and hit the ground running. In the heartbeat it took for the dog to drop down from the fence and come after him, he gained enough distance to make it through the back gate without getting caught.

Breath rasping, pulse driving like a triphammer in his brain, he cut through yards and ducked behind buildings until he'd put a good ten blocks between himself and the Whitaker house. A razor edge of pain lanced through his side, and he pressed the heel of his hand against his ribs and kept going. Finally, completely winded, he stumbled to a halt.

It took him several minutes to get his breathing under control. Then he straightened and took stock of his situation. He couldn't go back to the car; judging from the loudness of the sirens, the fire department had reached the house. But he could see the flickering glow of the fire, the blazing underbelly of a thick, black column of smoke.

"That's *my* fire," he said, trying to understand what had happened. He should have been able to watch that house go up, to feel that flooding pleasure his fires always gave him.

Until now. His fire had turned against him.

No, he thought. It had been taken from him. By her. She'd stepped into his fire and made it hers.

"Bitch," he gasped. "You've got no right. No *right!*"

He straightened slowly, drawing in a breath that sounded too much like a sob. "You're going to pay," he whispered. "Oh, man, you're going to pay."

Lou popped an antacid into her mouth, trying to counteract the chili she'd eaten at the snack bar. Night shift notwithstanding, her stomach wasn't up to chili at 9:30 P.M.

The rain beat softly on her hardhat as she made her way down the pier toward the tanker. The *Corinne* was fairly small as tankers went, or Carmichael's wouldn't have been able to handle her. Still, she looked big and squatty sitting there getting her bilges pumped out. Lou preferred the stiletto beauty of the navy vessels.

"Hey, Lou." a man called from behind her.

Lou glanced over her shoulder and saw George Fagan moving toward her. "Hey, George."

He came to stand beside her. Almost shoulder to shoulder, well within what she considered her personal space. Moving away would be to concede that he bothered her, so she just jammed her hands into her jeans pockets and waited for him to speak first.

"Fucking lousy night," he said.

She shrugged. "It could be raining *and* cold."

"You've got a point there," he said. "By the way, have you changed your mind?"

"About what?"

"Going out with me."

"Nope."

"I thought maybe since you almost bought the big one, you might be feeling a little alive and reckless."

"Nope."

He gave her a what-the-hell-it-was-worth-a-try grin, then thrust his thumb at the tanker. "She's a bitch," he said.

"Problems?"

"She should've been in here five years ago. Some of the work looks like it was done in a foreign yard from somewhere back in the stone age. If I had my druthers, I'd rip all that shit out and start over."

"Those druthers aren't in this job," she said.

"Don't I know it. I've seen that bid; it should have been eight, ten percent higher."

"Van Allen authorized it himself."

"Him? He don't know diddly about ship repair." Fagan scraped his boot heel over the asphalt, a grating sound that edged Lou's nerves like fingernails on a chalk board. "Louis says he'll do his best to stay under budget."

"But . . . ?"

"But if he can, he's a fucking miracle worker."

Why not? Somebody's been creating some very slick miracles around here. Dread settled in the pit of her stomach. This Enterprise deal looked worse and worse as time went on. Yes, the yard had gotten the work. But maybe at a price they couldn't afford.

"Eichmann's crazy if he thinks we can compete with those subsidized foreign shipyards," Fagan said, echoing her thoughts. "We can run at a loss for a while, but the well's gonna run dry eventually. Do I think military spending will go up again? Sure. And do I think Eichmann's got enough balls to carry through until times get better? Uh-uh. You mark my words, we're gonna see more layoffs soon."

"God, I hope not; we hardly have enough people to take care of what we're doing now."

"You know the drill. Work harder, work faster, and close your eyes to anything that doesn't hit you over the head."

She studied him out of the corner of her eye, wondering if that had been a toss-off phrase or a pointed suggestion. His face revealed nothing, and his tone was no different than it had been when he'd teasingly asked her if she'd changed her mind.

He cocked his head at her, and light hit the curve of his hardhat like the sun rising over the curve of the Earth. The sight triggered something in Lou, a visceral almost-memory that she scrabbled frantically to pull out into the open.

"If you ask me," he said, "they can get rid of your boss right now and save themselves some money."

Lou lost her fragile hold on the memory. "Steggans?" she asked. "What's wrong with him?"

"Nothing, if he was some clerk somewhere. But he's

running QA—and everything else he can get his hands on—and he doesn't know his ass from a hole in the ground."

"He's a fast learner."

"We don't need learners," Fagan said. "We need Harry. This place is going to slide right out from under us."

"I hope you're wrong."

"Me, too."

Lou looked over at the squat bulk of the tanker, glad she'd asked for this inspect. Call it logic, call it intuition, but she had the feeling that *Corinne* was the girl who'd give her what she needed to blow the whistle on the *Gabriella* repair.

"We've got another Enterprise tanker coming in tomorrow," Fagan said. "The *Whippoorwill.*"

Lou sifted through her memory, came up blank. "I don't remember us bidding on that one."

"We didn't. This is a straight repair. Sounds to me like propeller-shaft problems."

"Cost-plus?"

"Yeah."

"Hallelujah!"

He clasped his hands behind his back and rocked back and forth on the balls of his feet. "Maybe I ought to pull some strings. Get Delanski on the *Whippoorwill* and me on the *Corinne.*"

"Why?" Lou asked, turning to look squarely at him.

"Well . . . Louis is okay, don't get me wrong. But the *Corinne* is going to be a real beast. I'd like to make sure everything goes as smoothly as possible."

Lou studied him, trying to probe the thoughts behind those washed-out blue eyes. She didn't know what to think about Fagan's statement. Did he, too, suspect Louis of helping slip the *Gabriella* inspection?

"The inspect is mine," she said, dangling the bait.

His eyes didn't change. "Isn't it a little early for anyone to be slotted for it?"

"I asked Steggans to put me on her."

"Why?"

"Same reason you want her. I want to make sure everything goes well."

They stood, gazes locked, for a long moment of silence. Then Fagan laughed.

"Pretty conceited, aren't we?" he asked at last.

"What? Assuming no one but us can do a good job?"

"Yeah."

Lou realized he was no more willing to trust her than she was to trust him. Impasse.

"You'll get the *Corinne* if you ask," she said. "Sure you want a hot potato?"

"Sure. Especially now that I know you're on it. Everyone knows nothin' gets past Lou Malotti."

Compliment, or veiled warning? Lou couldn't tell. One thing was certain: the waters had just gotten a whole lot murkier. "Did I hear a 'Lucretia' in there somewhere?"

"No, ma'am."

He tipped his hardhat saucily. Then his gaze shifted, focusing on something above and behind her. "Holy shit," he said.

Lou turned, her heart stuttering when she saw a smoldering red glow against the Portsmouth sky. The Fire Man's mark.

"Look at that mother," Fagan said. "Must be that nut case again, out tryin' to burn the world. Man, that son of a bitch is spooky. I hope they catch him soon."

Unreasoning fear ran frost-fingers through Lou's veins, chilled the workings of her mind. An eerie certainty filled her—that this was going to be a bad one. She'd have to see it, whatever it was.

Come to the fire. Meet the Fire Man.

"Hey, is something wrong?" Fagan asked. "Lou! Malotti! Are you in there?"

His voice stirred her to movement, Turning, she headed for the nearest phone, which would be the security office. Fagan's voice faded out behind her.

The security guard looked up as she came in. "Hey, Malotti. What can I do for—"

"The phone," she panted.

"Now, look, why don't you tell me—"

"Give me the phone!"

Maybe it was her voice, or maybe the way her hands shook, but this time he handed the phone over without protest. She dialed Whitaker's work number, her breathing harsh against the emptiness of the line.

"Come on," she muttered. "Come on!"

"Arson," a man answered. "Lieutenant Whit—"

"I'm Malotti," she said.

His tone became urgent. "Whitaker wants you ASAP," he said, giving her an address.

Lou started to write it down. Then realization came like a good, hard punch in the gut, and she dropped the pencil. "Sweet Jesus!" she whispered. "That's his house!"

Nineteen

Mount Vernon was awash with flashing lights.

Lou brought the Corolla to a fish-tailing halt behind the police cruiser blocking the street. Abandoning the car, she went the rest of the way on foot. She couldn't see much from here, not with all the smoke and equipment blocking her path. A crowd of people, neighbors probably, milled around, making the confusion even worse.

She shoved her way through the mob and pelted up the street, her boots sliding on the wet, sooty asphalt. Smoke chuffed from every opening in Whitaker's house. The firemen seemed to be concentrating their efforts on the living room corner, aiming high-powered streams of water into the gaping holes that had once been windows.

"Oh, God," she said, her heart keeping time with her feet as she wound through the tangle of men and hoses.

A fireman caught her by the arm and dragged her to a halt. "Hey, lady! Get out of here. Can't you see we got—"

"The kids!" she panted. "Were the kids in there?"

"Come on, lady. Get back."

Adrenaline kicked in then, and she shoved him away. As she started for the house again, he and another fireman caught her arms and pulled her back.

"The kids might be in there!" she shouted. "Somebody's got to go in and check!"

A third fireman joined the two holding her. "We're looking for them right now," he said, putting his hand on her shoulder. "Are you Lou Malotti?"

She nodded.

"I'm Captain Johnson. Relax. Everything's being done that can be done. Come on, let's go over here and talk."

Lou stopped struggling, and after a moment the other two men let her go. She followed the captain a few dozen yards to one side.

"Where's Whitaker?" she asked.

His eyes turned bleak. "Inside. Looking for his kids."

Panic hit her then, the picture of four shrouded stretchers coming out of that house, the picture of Whitaker's face as he watched them. Her chest tightened.

"Were the kids home?" she asked.

"They were supposed to be."

"What can I do to help?"

"Pray," he said. "I've got to go. Can I trust you to stay put?"

She looked past him, at the house. "I love those kids," she said, laying it all on the line. To him, and to herself.

He nodded, the understanding in his eyes as stark and bare as her words. Then he turned, disappearing into the smoke and confusion.

She ignored the stinging smoke, the ash and bits of burning debris drifting down. In her mind, she walked through that house, down smoke-filled hallways and into charred rooms. *I'm not much of a prayer, Lord, as you know. But as they say, there ain't no atheists in foxholes.*

Something wet touched her hand. Gasping, she recoiled, then gasped again, this time in relief. "Shamu!" she cried, going down on one knee.

Leaves and debris matted the dog's coat. Lou brushed them away, reveling in the solid reality of the wolfhound's sturdy body. "Where are they, girl?" she asked. "Did you get them out? Oh, God, I wish you could talk!"

She started to cry then. Freely, openly, in a way she hadn't done for many years. Somehow, she found herself leaning against Shamu, her cheek pressed into the dog's taut, brindled fur.

The wolfhound's head went up with a suddenness that sent alarm shafting through Lou.

"What's the matter, girl?" she whispered.

Shamu stared off down the street, where smoke-wreathed darkness hung heavily beneath the trees. She didn't growl. Still, Lou felt the dog's hackles rise up beneath her hands, and felt her own nape hair lift in response.

"It's *him*," she whispered.

She felt him. His hate surrounded her, sank into her soul like an open wound. Yesterday, she might have been afraid. But tonight he'd gone too far.

The air felt cool on her wet cheeks. Slowly, she straightened and started walking toward the source of the hate. Shamu padded along beside her. Lou's awareness narrowed to this single, dark street and the even darker man hiding there. Reality tilted, and she knew she'd stepped into his world. Kill or be killed. Eat or be eaten.

Well, so be it.

No longer willing to hide from him, she strode down the center of the street. Accepting his hate. Accepting the rage that burned as hot as any fire he'd set. Her anger was cold, but no less consuming. It spread through her mind, numbed her to anything but one single, utterly clear thought.

"You bastard," she said. "If you've hurt those kids, I'm going to kill you."

She walked to the next intersection, stood in the center and turned slowly to take in the area. So many places to hide in this old neighborhood, shadows everywhere. She turned, turned again. He wasn't so crazy to hide here; almost everyone seemed to have deserted their own homes to watch the Fire Man's show down the street. If he'd wanted, he could have set a hundred fires.

Even as she thought that, she knew he was thinking it, too. For that was the source of his power—the knowledge that he could reach out any time, anywhere, and destroy something. Light a match, screw the world. He enjoyed it. And right now, he was enjoying the fact that Whitaker had to walk through his own home, searching from room to room to find out if his children were alive or dead.

Her eyes narrowed. Her rage flared higher, making her reckless. She stood exposed in the center of the intersection, arms akimbo. Daring him.

"You're a coward!" she shouted into the watching darkness. "Sneaking around behind people's backs, hiding in the shadows . . . Why don't you come out and try it face-to-face?"

"Mom?"

Wade's voice came from behind her. Lou spun, wrenched back to reality. Her gaze focused on her son, then shifted to the people standing behind and a little to one side of him.

Blaire. Mike. Keefe. Kelsey.

Shamu barked happily and ran to greet them. Lou felt the world tilt around her, not realizing that she'd swayed until Wade grabbed her.

"What the hell's going on here?" he demanded.

Lou couldn't look away from the Whitaker kids. Tears streaked Kelsey's face, and worlds of loss swam in the depths of Blaire's eyes. The boys bore a stark grimness far beyond their years. But it didn't matter. They were here, and safe.

"You're all right!" she cried in a high, breathless voice that didn't sound like Lou Malotti at all.

Relief flooded through her, then a stinging wash of joy. The Fire Man no longer mattered. Nothing mattered except those four kids who were staring at her as though she'd lost her mind. It didn't matter. She ran forward, caught them up in a hug—or at least as much of a hug as she could manage, considering that she was outnumbered.

"You're all right," she said, blinking against the sudden onrush of tears. "You're all right!"

"Well, yeah," Mike said.

"Does your dad know?"

"Yeah. They radioed him when we showed up."

Lou dropped her arms and took a step backward. "Where the hell were you?"

"Wade took us to a movie," Blaire said. "The Naro was playing—"

Heavy, rapid footsteps sounded nearby, and Lou turned to see Whitaker, looking bigger than ever in his fire gear, running toward them. Soot coated his face where the mask hadn't protected it. His eyes looked like chips of mica in that dark raccoon mask.

He swept his children into his arms, doing a better job of it than Lou had. His expression was so stark, so full of joy and the remembered terror of what-might-have-been, that Lou had to turn away from it.

After a moment, he let them go. "Where the hell were you?" he demanded.

"Wade took us to the movies," Blaire said again.

"We left a note for you," Mike added.

"Where?"

"In . . ." Mike's face changed. "Ah, in the house."

Kelsey buried her face against her father's coat and started to cry. "He burned our house!" she sobbed.

"Shh," Whitaker said. "It's only a house. Now that I know you're okay, nothing else matters."

"But our stuff, Dad," Mike said. "Everything we own—"

"Doesn't matter." Tears made pale streaks in the soot on Whitaker's face. He didn't bother to wipe them away.

"The hamsters were upstairs in my room," Kelsey said, her voice muffled against his coat. "Did they . . .?"

"Sorry, sweetheart," he said. "There was too much smoke."

Her shoulders shook with renewed sobs. Whitaker stroked her hair with a gentleness that brought renewed tears to Lou's eyes. Suddenly he glanced up at her. Their gazes locked, and it was like looking straight through into his soul. Lou saw the raw wounds of a man who'd just walked through his own personal hell. And anger. Rage to match her own. If the Fire Man had been standing here at this moment, she and Whitaker would have fought to be the one to rip his heart out.

It was savage, frightening, terrible. And in its own uncivilized way, glorious. She found herself smiling, matching the grin that showed startling white against

255

his soot-covered face. No humor prompted those smiles. No, it was the pure, unholy joy of knowing that someone else shared the rage, the savagery, the determination that no one was going to threaten these children again and live.

Lost in the power of what they shared, she walked forward. He reached out, drew her in. The kiss was fierce, almost violent, a primitive outpouring that matched their emotions. It tasted of smoke and tears and wildness. She felt his fingers clench in her hair, only realizing she'd forgotten to take her hardhat off when she heard it bounce on the street.

Coming out of that kiss was like swimming through a tidal wave. She wanted more. So did he; the need was as clear in his eyes as though it had been burned there.

"Whoa," Mike said.

Reality beckoned. Reluctantly, Lou returned to it. And found the kids standing in a ragged semicircle, their eyes wide with astonishment. And yes, awe. She couldn't help but smile; young people never seemed to think their parents capable of passion. Well, they'd certainly gotten a lesson tonight.

Wade cleared his throat. "Well, it seems as though we're all very happy to see one another."

"Yeah," Whitaker said. "We've all beat the hangman tonight, fellas."

"The Fire Man, you mean," Keefe said.

Whitaker's face turned grim. "I've got things to do here. Lou—?"

"Sure," she said, responding to the unspoken question. "Come on, guys. You're coming home with me. Wade, give Whitaker your key."

"But our stuff . . ." Mike broke off abruptly, his expression turning as grim as his father's.

Lou put her hand on his shoulder. "We'll stop at a store first thing in the morning," she said. "Pick up enough for the next couple of days, for a start. As for tonight, I think I have enough spare toothbrushes and T-shirts to go around."

"But what about our house?" Kelsey asked. "Is there anything left? Are we going to be able to move back in soon?"

Whitaker crouched, going down to her level. "Honey, I can't answer any of those questions right now. I'm just happy we're all okay. The rest I'll deal with when it comes up."

"But my hamsters—"

"We'll take care of them, too."

Another funeral, Lou thought, imagining tiny crosses in neat rows, a sort of animal-world Arlington. She might have found the thought kind of funny at another time. Not tonight.

"Who is Shamu riding with?" Wade asked, retrieving Lou's hardhat from the gutter. "I don't think she's going to fit in my Civic."

"The dog," Lou said, "is with me."

Lou woke to full daylight, and alone. "Blaire? Kelsey?"

No answer. She rose up on her elbow and glanced at the clock. Almost noon.

"Six whole hours of sleep," she muttered.

Ali bounced up onto the bed and settled in the dip between Lou's hip and ribs. Her purr vibrated through the covers. Lou stroked her, and the purr went up a notch. The kitten had settled down since last night, when Shamu's arrival had sent her straight to the top of the living room curtains.

"How's it cooking, little beast?" Lou murmured.

Then she saw the note lying on the nightstand. Only years of practice enabled her to decipher Wade's terrible scrawl. "Mom, I've taken Blaire and the kids to the mall to pick up some clothes and things. Shamu's out in the back yard. W."

Sleep beckoned. Actually, it was the thought of going the next twenty-one hours without sleep that beckoned. But the prospect of a nice quiet breakfast—alone—got her out of bed and into the shower.

It took seventeen minutes from start to a jeans-and-T-shirt finish. She padded downstairs barefoot to the kitchen to find coffee still hot on the stove.

"Thank you, God," she said.

She'd just cracked some eggs into a pan when she heard the front door open and close. "Wade, if you've . . ." Her voice trailed off as she saw Whitaker appear in the doorway.

His eyes were bloodshot and undershot with purple, and a half-day's growth of beard shadowed his jawline. The smell of smoke clung to his hair and clothes, and his eyes held echoes of last night's violence. Lou's internal temperature went up several degrees.

"You look like hell," she said.

"I feel like hell."

"Is there much left of the house?"

The violence became more than an echo. "More than I thought last night. I'll take you and the kids out there today. You can help me decide what can be salvaged."

"I'll put a couple more eggs on." She turned back to the stove.

He reached around her to turn the burner off. "I don't want any food," he murmured into her hair.

She leaned back against his chest as his hands slid

up under the T-shirt. His palms felt hot and gentle and urgent all at once, and her pulse stuttered into high gear.

"Ah, the kids are going to be back any time now," she said.

"I ran into them at the 7-Eleven," he said, his hands roaming further. "Gave them my Mastercard and told them to go to a movie afterward. We've got, oh, three or four hours alone."

Sudden panic set in. It was going to happen, and it was going to happen *now*. Forty-three years old, and she found herself shaking like a green kid at the prospect of making love to a man.

"Wade just . . . said go ahead, or what?" she asked.

"Looked me in the eye and told me to take good care of you. There was also an implied threat that he'd take my head off if I did anything to displease you. So," he ran his open mouth along the curve of her neck to the spot where her pulse beat frantically beneath the skin, "I intend to please you very much."

"I was planning on losing weight," she said. "I was planning on being a new me before—"

"You're babbling, Lou."

"I didn't expect this now. Today."

"It happens when it happens."

"There aren't any choices made?"

"No," he said. "Just rationalizations."

His hands drifted upward to rest on her ribs. Lou felt like one great big pulsebeat. Waiting for more. His thumbs moved up, brushing the undercurves of her breasts. She drew a deep, shattered breath, and still wanted more.

"I don't want you to lose weight," he said. "I don't want a new you."

He slid his hands upward, finally cupping her

breasts. Even with the bra between them it was like being dipped in fire. "I like the way you smell, the way you think, the way you fight for everything you want. And I especially like the way you feel."

She closed her eyes. It was too soon, he wanted too much, there was too much going on to complicate things. But her body pulsed in time to the stroking of his hands, and it didn't give a damn about either her reservations or her fears. She tried one last attempt at sanity. "Don't you think—"

"I want you *now,* Lou."

He did. The raw desire in his voice kicked her over the edge. The future didn't matter; nor did the past. There was only this moment. Almost savagely, she reached up and wound her fingers into his hair.

He unhooked her bra, slid his hands underneath to cup flesh that swelled to welcome him. Lou sighed, letting the sensations surge through her. God, she'd almost forgotten what it felt like. Heat shot through her in a long sweeping wave, pooled deep in her belly.

She let go of him long enough for him to rip the T-shirt up and over her head. The air was cool on her skin, his hands hot. He disposed of her bra—how and where she didn't know—and spun her around to face him.

"You're gorgeous," he said.

She felt gorgeous. Because of him, because he obviously thought so. Putting her palms flat against his chest, she held him away so she could look at him. He let her have this moment. But she knew it was his gift to her, not hers for the taking; his hands remained on her back, his fingers splayed with heavy possession. Desire, tenderness, the need for the comfort of a human touch—and a heavy load of pure male aggressiveness—filled his eyes. The warrior returned from battle.

"You look very fierce," she said.

"Does it excite you?"

She smiled. "Everything you do excites me."

"That?"

"Yes."

"That?"

"Uh-huh." *Oh, yes.*

Then he kissed her, and her world narrowed to the taste and scent and heat of him. She kissed him back, savagely. Their teeth grated as they shifted, seeking yet more heat.

She pulled his shirt up, a sharp, impatient motion that sent buttons bouncing over the floor. He stripped it off and tossed it away. Lou returned to him before he'd finished, winding her arms around his waist. Skin against skin was much better. Hotter. Nothing mattered but being close to him. Getting closer and closer until she lost herself, or gained him.

He groaned against her mouth. Reaching between them, he unzipped her jeans and pushed them down. She kicked them away, then echoed his groan when he lifted her, wrapping her legs around his hips. Mindless. Searching. Needing. She clung to him, rubbing herself against him, gasping as he sucked her tongue deep into his mouth.

The world tilted as he swung her around and laid her on the table, square in a spill of morning sunlight. It limned the hairs on his arms and chest, gilding him as he leaned over her.

"This is good," he said, echoing a previous conversation.

"This is good," she agreed.

Rational thought disappeared in a haze of sensation.

No doubts remained; her body knew exactly what to do, where to touch, how to bring that taut, shuttered look to his eyes. She lost herself in the power of it. Exploring, being explored; every inch of skin, every fold, every curve. The feel of his hands, his mouth, the surging liquid tide of desire.

She was aware of the passage of time, but measured it only by her impatience, the spiral of her emotions, the urgency of his hands. The sunlight moved away, creeping along the floor to the wall beside her to lay their shadows on the canvas of the wall. Hers, supine and shuddering, a wanton sprawl of limbs, curving breasts and hips; Whitaker kneeling, large and square and muscular, and there was nothing of submission in his position.

"Look," she whispered.

He laid his head on her thigh. His eyes were heavy-lidded, molten with things done and things yet to do. He looked at the shadow-pictures on the wall, then back at her.

"I need you now," she said.

He straightened. Sliding his hands beneath her hips, he pulled her forward and up. Their shadows merged. They gasped, clung and surged, and for one brief, glorious moment, became one. Became whole.

"Lou," he said, when the world steadied down again. "Lou."

She wrapped her legs around him, held him close. "Don't let go."

"Don't worry."

And she didn't.

Lou came downstairs, toweling her hair after her third shower of the day. Although the second could hardly be called a shower, not with Whitaker doing more loving than washing. Amazing that two people the size of her and Bob could fit in that little bitty town house stall. The triumph of lust over geometry. Lust over good, middle-aged sense.

"Whitaker?" she called.

No answer. She found him in the kitchen, his head on the table, a plate of untouched eggs near his elbow. He wore nothing but a pair of blue-jean shorts, and she thought he looked damn good lying over her table in a hairy male sprawl.

Smiling, she reached out to slide the plate away from him. His hand shot out, pinning her wrist.

"I thought you were asleep," she said.

"I smelled your perfume."

"Soap. I don't wear perfume."

"Whatever." He slid his hand up her arm. "I like it."

The front door opened noisily, and the sound of voices and rattling bags drifted in from the living room.

"Shit," Whitaker growled. "I need another couple of days alone with you."

"Wishful thinking."

"Maybe. But I'd damn well like to try."

"Dad?" Blaire called.

"Did you find my bra?" Lou whispered.

"Yeah. Behind the stove. I put it in the washer."

"Dad?"

He grinned at Lou before letting her go. "In the kitchen, honey."

Blaire appeared in the doorway a moment later, Wade following close enough behind to have been glued to her back. He looked over her shoulder, his gaze moving from Lou to Whitaker and back again.

"Get any sleep?" he asked.

"Of course," she replied, straight faced. "Let the dog in, will you? I've got a plateful of cold eggs for her."

Wade grinned, putting his hands on Blaire's shoulders to steer her toward the back door. The dog came in, the lovebirds went out, no doubt to snoozle out in the hammock.

"Can they get in trouble out there?" Whitaker asked.

"No more than we did in here." Lou set the plate on the floor and watched the dog move like a vacuum over it.

She went to look out the window, conscious of Whitaker moving with her. Blaire and Wade had managed to fit themselves in the hammock. The sun turned his hair to bronze and made her skin look as though it had been dusted with gold. She lay in the circle of his arm, her cheek resting against his chest, the netting of the hammock enclosing them like a hand. Lou could feel the heat from here.

"They look like they're going to spontaneously combust," she said.

"So am I." Whitaker slipped his arms around her waist. His hand started roaming.

"Stop it," she said, dragging his hand out from under her shirt. "We need to discuss sleeping arrangements."

"How about a motel?"

"Don't be ridiculous. With all the space I've got here, you want to share a motel room with four kids?"

"No, damn it," he said. "I want to leave the kids here, and share the motel room with *you.*"

"Tempting," she said, "and probably do-able. But not now. First order of business is making sure those kids are safe."

His breath went in sharply. She turned to face him,

bracing her hands on the counter behind her. Bleak grimness chilled his eyes, sharpened the planes of his face. He was reliving last night. Walking through his house, room by room, wondering if *this* room was the one in which he'd find his children's bodies.

She put her hand on his shoulder. "Don't."

"I can't forget it," he said. "I'll never forget it."

"Sure you will. When you catch him. Now let's get back to practicalities. You'll all stay here. I'll take days, Wade will take nights—"

"And what if he comes after them again?"

She smiled, knowing it was neither gentle nor pretty. "Well. I've got my trusty .38, and Wade a brown belt in karate and his very own .357 that I got him for Christmas last year."

"You bought him a . . ." He sighed. "I don't know about you Malottis. Guns for Christmas."

"You'll be free to do whatever you have to do to catch that SOB. And then none of us will have to worry about him."

"Is that the engineer in you? Step A, step B, then on to the conclusion?"

She met his gaze levelly. "Yeah. And here's my conclusion: He's trying to cripple you by blurring your mind with fear for your kids. If you let him do it, he'll win."

He let his breath out in a hiss. Lou could tell by the set of his shoulders that he'd accepted her judgment—and didn't like it. She put her arms around his waist, giving comfort and getting it. His heart beat fast and steady against her cheek.

"Dad, are you in there?" Kelsey called, her voice coming steadily closer.

Lou dropped her arms from around Whitaker's waist a moment before Kelsey came in. Ali lay like a baby in the girl's arms, her eyes half closed. She roused enough to hiss when Shamu sniffed her, but didn't move from her comfortable nest.

"Looks like you've made a friend," Whitaker said.

Kelsey nodded. "Are we going to be able to sleep in our house tonight?"

"No, honey, not for a while. We've got to get someone to come in and fix things up before we'll be able to live there. But as soon as I get some clothes on, we'll head over there and go through our things."

"Did you find the hamsters?"

His face tightened. "Yes."

"Were they dead?"

"Yes, honey."

The child reached down to touch Shamu. "I'd better make some flowers."

She turned to go. The wolfhound turned with her, maintaining contact with uncanny precision.

"I'm going to kill that bastard," Whitaker muttered. His eyes had turned violent again.

Lou licked her lips, tasted salt. "I'll flip you for him," she said.

Twenty

"Holy shit," Mike said. "I hope our insurance is paid up."

"It's not as bad as it looks." Whitaker's voice was too harsh to be comforting. "This section will have to be rebuilt, sure, but the rest of the house is okay."

Lou ran her hand along the wall, brought it away black. Puddles of sooty water still lay on the floor in places, and fire had gnawed at the doorway between the entryway and the living room, leaving a hole like an open wound. The television, blind witness to the destruction, had melted and run, falling in on itself. Blackened plaster sifted down from the ruined ceiling.

A few hours ago, this had been a living, breathing family home. Then the firebug had come. A single match. Cruelty, staggering in its casualness.

Kelsey began to cry quietly. That, and a few creakings as the walls shifted, were the only sounds. It seemed almost as though the house held its breath, appalled at what had been done to it.

"How did he start it?" Keefe asked. "Did he break into the house?"

"No," Whitaker said. "See the char there on the

floor and wall near the side window? He broke the glass and just poured the combustible inside."

Keefe, with the ability of the young to separate curiosity from the personal aspects of the scene, asked, "What did he use?"

"Gasoline, probably." Whitaker turned away, the movement sharp, almost savage. "Fast and easy. Just light a match and toss it in."

"We weren't going to go out," Blaire said. "Then Wade called and told us to be at the door in ten minutes if we wanted to see *Beauty and the Beast*. It was such craziness, running around getting dressed, that we forgot to bring Shamu inside. We always bring her inside when we're going somewhere. To . . . to keep her safe."

She ducked her head, a blind little gesture that made Wade's eyes flare as though someone had touched a match to them. He put his hands on her shoulders.

"It seems God *does* look down on this crazy world sometimes," he said.

Whitaker didn't turn around. "Kids, go upstairs and pack whatever of your clothes look salvageable."

"What about my books?" Kelsey asked.

"What about my baseball stuff?" Mike echoed.

"Later," Whitaker snarled.

Lou pointed toward the stairs. They obeyed, glancing over their shoulders at their father. All but Blaire and Wade.

"Spill it, Dad," she said.

"Spill what?"

"About the arsonist. And don't give me that don't-scare-the-women-and-children routine. I know he was here, watching what he'd done. It wasn't hard to figure. I mean, we found Lou standing in the middle of the

268

street, yelling for someone to come out and fight like a man."

"Jesus Christ, Lou." With a sigh, Whitaker raked his hand through his hair. "What were you going to do, wrestle him three falls out of five?"

"Whatever," she said, unembarrassed.

He flung his arms wide, capitulating. "Yeah, he stayed to watch. Some of the neighbors saw him jump over the fence. He got caught up in the beauty of his handiwork, apparently. Even left his gas can behind; we're getting it printed now. The bastard should have tossed the match in and gotten out, but he enjoys fires too much. Really gets his r— . . . jollies watching the buildings go up. This time it almost got him caught. And apparently even after that, he couldn't leave. He must have hidden somewhere down the street to catch the action."

"His methods are changing," Wade said. "Before, he set fires in places where people were unlikely to be. He's into something very different now. He's dangerous, and he's going to get more dangerous."

Lou nodded. There had been such hate, such smoldering anger rolling out of the darkness last night . . . The arsonist had meant to take Whitaker's children from him. Deliberately. Casually. *You spoiled my fun so I'm going to take something of yours.*

"You think he's going to try again," Blaire said.

"What better way to get back at your father?" Wade asked.

Lou watched emotions play across Blaire's face. Disbelief, fear, outrage—all finally jelled into determination.

"So what do we do?" she asked.

"You and the kids are going to stay at Lou's," Whitaker said. "You go nowhere without either me, Lou or

269

Wade. Baseball games, shopping, a stroll down the street—you go together, and you go with one of us."

"But what if he goes after you directly?" she asked.

Whitaker bared his teeth in something that was more snarl than smile. "He's welcome to it."

Blaire nodded. Reaching up, she rested her palm against her father's cheek for a moment, then turned and went upstairs. Wade swung around to Whitaker.

"I'm going to marry your daughter," he said.

Lou expected Whitaker to get possessive and fatherly. But he merely studied the younger man, then asked, "When?"

"As soon as she'll agree to it."

"You're both pretty young."

Wade's eyes matched the grimness of his jawline. "Not any more."

Without waiting for an answer, he turned on his heel and trotted upstairs.

"He doesn't give a shit whether I approve or not, does he?" Whitaker asked.

"In an abstract sense, he does," Lou said. "Wade's got a highly developed sense of honor, and on top of that I think he honestly wants you to like him. But in a practical sense, as to whether or not your objection would stop him from marrying Blaire, well, nothing has ever stopped Wade from going after something he wanted."

"Christ," Whitaker growled. "Just say no, Lou."

"Okay. No, he doesn't give a shit."

She moved farther into the living room. Bending, she picked up a melted videotape. The label had scorched, but she could barely make out the title, "Nola and kids, Christmas 1984." "I used to think words were the worst sort of attack," she said, turning the blob of plastic over and over in her hands. "I was a fool."

He took the tape from her and looked at the label. With a gesture that was rife with pain, he hurled it against the charred wall. Soot drifted on the quiet air, then settled to the floor with a finality that made the spirit ache.

Lou clenched her fists. She, who'd always seemed to lack the natural ability most women had to comfort their men, didn't know what to say or do. His rage and loss were an almost palpable force in this ruined room. It pressed on her, demanding something she wasn't sure she had to give.

"These are things," he said. "Objects. The kids are safe, and that's all that matters."

True. But it occurred to her that he'd been holding onto his memories of Nola pretty hard and close, and that it might take some time for him to realize just how much he'd lost last night.

"I don't know what to say," she said. "I'm no good at this relationship stuff. And I don't know where my boundaries are here."

"You mean because of Nola?" He looked down at his soot-stained hands, then wiped them on his thighs. "She's dead. I let her go a long time ago."

"Sure, you let her go. But if you think she's not still part of your life, you're kidding yourself. And there's nothing wrong with that. This house contained all you had of her, and that . . . freak took it all away."

"Yeah, he took it all away." His voice was tight and harsh. "You want to know what really hurts? I failed to protect my kids. He knew I wasn't here. He came here to kill my children, and if they'd been home, he might have done it. I underestimated him, Lou. And my kids almost paid the price for it."

271

"I . . ." She glanced away, feeling as though she'd been stripped bare, her soul exposed for him to see. At another time, with another person, she'd have pulled back. With him, she had no choice but to let it out. "Look," she said, "I know I'm not the ideal nurturing sort of woman—"

"Nola would have liked you," he said.

Lou's breath went out sharply. She went to him, put her hands flat on his shoulders. He slid his arms around her, pulling her close. Holding on. Letting her give the comfort she so badly wanted to give and didn't know how. She didn't say anything, and neither did he.

The Fire Man waited outside the Whitaker house. He'd retrieved the Cavalier last night after the fire trucks left and the neighbors went inside. The news crews had packed up hours before. He, patient hunter that he was, merely stepped out of his hiding place and drove away.

Tragedies came and went, but people always had to get up for work the next morning.

He glanced up at an upstairs window, saw someone moving around inside. In his mind, he saw the Whitakers walking through the wreckage of their home, saw the shock on their faces, felt their loss. And the Bitch with them, sunlight striking sparks in her hair.

His eyes slitted as his imagination went one step further: himself, pouring gasoline into every opening. Lighting the match. Watching it all go up in one magnificent burst of flame. And the screams. Her screams.

God, he wanted to do it. If he thought he had any chance at all . . . Common sense overrode impulse. Not now. It had to be done when he could walk away from it. Still fighting the need that ran in hot spurts through his brain, he started the car and headed back to Churchland.

He stopped to buy newspapers. The *Pilot,* the *Richmond Times-Dispatch, US News*—all featured his fire in color, front-page features. It pleased him. His smile faded, however, when he saw the headlines.

FIREBUG STALKS ARSON INVESTIGATOR'S FAMILY!

ARSONIST TORCHES INVESTIGATOR'S HOUSE, VENGEANCE A MOTIVE?

THE MONSTER IN OUR MIDST; WHERE WILL HE STRIKE NEXT?

In one night, he'd gone from madman to monster. He strode out to the car. Wrenching the door open, he slid into the driver's seat. Rage shook him, as he clamped his hands on the steering wheel. He opened himself to it, sucked it deep, waited for it to bring the power to him.

His power. It was there, right there. He could feel it, taste it, *almost* touch it. But it hovered just out of his grasp, taunting him.

His gaze fell to the newspapers that lay on the seat beside him. The photograph leaped with red-orange flames, the broken doorway of the house an open mouth screaming its pain at the world. His vision blurred as he saw *her* face in the fire again. Arrogant, hair rising above it in a ruddy billow, her eyes staring into his, laughing because she'd stolen his power.

Just like last night. He'd wanted to run. He'd wanted to get away. But she turned his own fire against him, trapping him in his own fascination until it was almost too late. No longer able to get to his car, he'd been forced to skulk in the darkness like an animal, blocked from the pleasure that was his by right.

And then *she* had come, the woman to match the

273

fire-vision. She'd walked straight toward him, as though she knew they'd been connected somehow. She'd stared directly at his hiding place and called him a coward. She'd shouted at him. Challenged him. A *woman.* He'd had no choice but to listen. To take it.

Bitch.

He took a deep breath, then another. When he'd calmed down enough, he drove to the gas station at the corner of 17 and Taylor Road, where Ma Bell had kindly installed a phone you could use right from your car. Dropping a quarter in, he dialed WAVY-10 and asked for Kursk. He disguised his voice, of course; attention to detail had always been one of his strengths. A moment later, the newsman came on the line.

"Hello, Kursk here."

"I don't like the way you're handling my story," he said. "And you can pass that on to your buddies at the newspaper."

"People tend to react emotionally when children's lives are threatened."

"Don't you think calling me a monster is going just a little too far?"

"Apparently *you* do."

He knew Kursk would like to hang up, and also knew that he wouldn't. Couldn't. The Fire Man was news, and you've got to keep those ratings up.

"Why did you do it?" Kursk asked.

"Whitaker stepped out of line in that TV interview. I just acted to make sure he stepped back."

"I see." Kursk's tone was very dry. "Did you know the children weren't home when you set that fire?"

"No," he said, surprised by the question. "What's that got to do with it?"

The newsman paused for a moment, then said,

274

"Nothing, I suppose. Does this mean you expect Whitaker to step down from the case?"

"Why would he do that?"

"To protect his children."

Realization dawned on the Fire Man, and it was a bright one. To him, the children didn't matter; didn't even register. Destruction had been his goal, and the message that arson investigators could be as vulnerable as anyone else.

Kursk simply didn't understand. He thought the *children* were the target.

And so did everyone else. Whitaker. The media. The police. Everyone figured he was still after the kids. That was why *she* had moved the Whitakers into her town house—to protect the kids.

Manna from Heaven.

"Are you still there?" Kursk asked. "I have more—"

He hung up. Triumph shafted through him, running like frostfire through his veins. Oh, it was beautiful! While everyone concentrated on protecting Whitaker's family, the Fire Man would strike hard, strike fast. He'd take his power back from her. Take it—the only way he could.

The car jerked as he slammed it into gear. "Bitch," he muttered. "Bitch."

Twenty-one

Lou ran into Louis Delanski at the grocery store. Literally. They, or rather their carts, met with a crash at the end of the pet food aisle.

"Whoa!" he said. "Oh, it's you, Malotti. How's it hanging?"

Lou studied him, thinking he was too skinny and too bald to be making that kind of remark outside the shipyard. She'd never cared for Louis much. Not only did he do only a so-so job, he'd made a few Lucretia remarks just loud enough for her to hear, but not loud enough for her to react and not be called for eaves-dropping. Just the kind of guy she could suspect of taking a handout to slip an inspection.

"Je-sus," he said, staring at the two twenty-five-pound bags of dog food in her cart, then back at her. His gaze didn't quite make it to her face, however, but stopped at her chest. "What are you feeding, Godzilla?"

"No. Just Shamu."

He laughed. A big hunk of a gold ring flashed as he smoothed his almost nonexistent hair. *Gabriella* blinked on and off in Lou's mind, bright as neon. And here, right in front of her, was the man who'd helped slide that failed weld past inspection. Her eyes narrowed. She had the strongest urge to take him by that scrawny neck and wring . . . Harry Deveraux's voice pinged at the edge of her hearing, pleading for discretion. *Take it easy, Lou. You go rushing into this like a bull in a china closet, you're gonna break things.*

"You know, you're looking especially good tonight," Louis said. "Did you lose weight or something?"

Her hands tightened on the cart's handle. Discretion, hell. All her aggressive instincts came to the fore. She'd be damned if she was going to stand here pussyfooting around while this jerk stared at her breasts. "Actually, Louis, I'm glad we ran into each other. I've been wanting to talk to you about something."

"What?"

"The *Gabriella.*"

His expression didn't change. "What about her?"

"You were ship supervisor on her, weren't you?"

"Yeah, so?" He bent and fiddled with the wheels of the carts, which had locked together somehow.

"Were you with Jay when he did the reinspect?"

"No," he said. "I wasn't at the shipyard that day."

"What?"

"I had two wisdom teeth pulled that day. Hurt like hell. They gave me something that knocked me shit-faced and I didn't wake up until nighttime. I thought they'd wait on the *Gabriella,* but I guess they were in a big hurry to get her out of there."

I guess they were. "Who took your place?"

He stood up, and this time his gaze reached her face. "I don't know. My boss told me it had been taken care of, so I went on to the next thing on my list. I didn't think any more about it. Why, is something wrong?"

"No," she lied. "Nothing's wrong. Well, I'd better get going—"

"Hey, too bad about Jay, isn't it? I knew he'd been

hitting the bars after work, but I figured it was women, not booze. Heard he was so stinking drunk that afternoon he puked all over the floor of the dry dock."

"I hadn't heard that."

"Everybody's saying he's hiding out somewhere so he won't get nailed for screwing up the QA database. I also heard his wife went out and took all the money out of the bank account, leaving him stranded. I heard he was shacking up with a girlfriend somewhere."

Lou pinned him with her coldest stare. "Why do you think it would be okay for you to go around saying that?"

"Ah . . . It's just . . . you know, a way of making conversation."

"Pick something else."

He looked so at a loss that she almost felt sorry for him. Almost. But he was the worst kind of gossip; just running his mouth without thought of the consequences for others.

"Look, I've got to go," she said, tugging on her cart.

"Hey, take it easy," Louis said, tugging back. "We're still hung up."

"Well, pull, will you?"

His smile warmed. "What's the rush?"

Lou had had enough of Louis Delanski. "Hold on," she snapped. With all her strength, she jerked her cart backward. Metal clashed, then the entwined wheels sprang free. Louis went sliding backward, his mouth and eyes making O's of surprise. He banged into the shelf behind him with enough force to make him grunt.

"Hey!" he said.

"Oops." With no sincerity at all, she added, "Sorry. And by the way, Louis, your fly is open."

She smiled at him as she sailed past, this time in genuine amusement. What a prick. And she didn't mean the sorry equipment he was trying frantically to cover.

The Fire Man parked at the far end of the lot that served the Bitch's section of town houses. He didn't like these places; too much glass. Too many people out and about, even at night. Not his sort of place at all.

He glanced at his watch. She should be arriving soon; he'd waited until she'd packed up her bags at the grocery store, then headed back here before her.

The Corolla turned into the parking lot a few minutes later, its headlights swinging in a bright platinum arc that didn't quite reach his car. Right on time. He drummed his fingertips on the steering wheel as he watched her park in front of the town house.

He glanced in his rearview mirror as an old lady came out of the house behind him, a pair of black Scotties on leash. She moved off to the left, her red tam-o'-shanter barely visible between the cars.

He stopped thinking about her when the door opened in the Malotti house. *She* came out, pausing in the doorway for a moment to talk to someone behind her. The light caught the highlights of her hair, turning it into a bronze halo around her head. He liked the warmth of the color. With that hair, and that chest, she wasn't bad looking. He'd always been partial to large women.

Too bad she was such a pushy bitch.

A sudden tap on the car window startled him. With a jerk, he turned to see the old woman in the tam-o'-shanter. The Scotties lunged at the end of the leashes like small ravening wolves, their fangs flashing white in their dark faces.

The old woman rapped on the glass again, imperatively. "Young man," she called, gesturing for him to roll down the window.

His heart kicked wildly. For a moment, he considered driving away. But the old woman was bound to take note of the license plate, and this car was registered to him. So he did the only thing he could, which was to roll down the window and try to think of a reasonable story.

"Hello," he said. "I was looking for—"

"Young man, you're parked in my husband's spot. Would you mind moving your car?"

Relief flooded through him. "Oh. Sorry. I didn't realize."

"Visitors' spaces are over there," she said, thrusting her thumb toward one side of the lot. "And if you're selling something, you should know that door-to-door sales are not allowed in this community."

"I'm not selling anything," he said.

She nodded, pulling the dogs back toward her house. He drove away, conscious that she was watching him.

"Old biddy probably committed the license number to memory," he muttered. Shit.

Lucky for him there was only the one way in or out of the town-house complex. He parked out on the street, out of the old woman's field of view, but in a spot where he could see the entrance. A moment later, the white Corolla pulled out past him. He gave her a few hundred yards lead, then followed.

Lou Malotti. His personal jinx. She'd begun to take over his life—waking or sleeping, he couldn't seem to stop thinking about her. What she'd cost him. There were times when he was sure she'd haunt him to the end of time.

He'd tried to rid himself of her. But all he'd gotten

out of jiggering her furnace had been a couple of dead birds. Again, she'd jinxed him.

Well, things were about to change.

Lou picked her way through the lines that snaked across the floor of the dry dock. A navy destroyer hung overhead, its sleek, stiletto shape as beautiful and deadly as a black widow spider. The *Corinne* would take her place there in a few days; trouble on the hoof.

"Hey, Lou."

Tyrene Bell's deep voice floated out from the lee of the wing wall to her right. She walked around to find him sitting on an overturned bucket, his feet propped on a second bucket.

"All you need is a television," she said.

"Hey, it's break time. I got five more minutes to relax until the whistle blows again, and I'm gonna rest my butt all five. I'm getting old, Lou. Got to take care of myself."

"How old are you?"

"Thirty-seven."

"Well, I'm older than you, so vacate one of those buckets."

He dropped his feet to the asphalt, then nudged the bucket closer to Lou. She sat down facing him.

"Today's my last day here," he said. "I got a job over at Norshipco."

"I thought they were laying off."

"They made room for me, I guess."

Lou nodded; there were a lot of good welders out there, but Tyrene was *good*. "Congratulations. But I'm sorry to see you go."

"I like the people here, but I can't say I'm sorry to be going. This place ain't been the same since old man

281

Carmichael died. I never thought I'd miss that old fucker, but I do."

"Amen," she said.

They sat in companionable silence, Tyrene with his head resting against the wing wall behind him, Lou with her hands clasped around her knees. She stared out over the Elizabeth River, watching coils of mist curl along the edges of the water.

And wondering why she didn't just chuck it all and get another job like Tyrene had.

Because you're scared, Malotti. Carmichael's was familiar. Safe. Twenty years of her life had been spent here, not all of them good, but then not all of them bad, either. And there were a lot more jobs for welders out there than there were for senior QA inspectors.

Someone else would have blown the whistle and then walked away. Or just plain walked away and saved themselves the hassle. But she couldn't. Fool that she was, she wanted to *fix* it.

"You find out anything about the *Gabriella?*" Tyrene asked, as though reading her thoughts.

She found her shoulders tightening, made a conscious effort to relax. "I'm working on it."

"If you were smart, you'd leave it alone."

"I know."

He shook his head. "You're a stubborn woman, Malotti."

"I know."

He didn't ask any more about it, and she didn't volunteer more. Tyrene was a wise man; he did his job, kept his mouth shut and didn't buck what couldn't be changed.

Voices drifted nearer, the sound of laughter as the work crew returned. Lou got to her feet.

"I wish you the best," she said, thrusting her hand out. "Stay in touch, will you?"

His big hand closed over hers. "You got it."

She turned away. It wasn't raining, quite, but moisture hung heavy in the air. Despite the bright lights overhead, the night seemed tight and close as she headed back to the office.

To her surprise, she found Steggans at work in his office, busily scribbling away at what looked like a stack of inspection reports. She leaned into the doorway. "What are you doing here at ten o'clock at night?" she asked.

He looked up, his pencil held suspended above the paper. "Oh, hi, Lou. I was just trying to get caught up. I've been spending so much of my time putting out fires lately that I haven't had time for the regular work."

"I'm glad you're here," she said. "I've been wanting to talk to you."

"Don't do it."

She blinked. "Huh? Do what?"

"Quit." He laid the pencil aside, and for a moment she thought she saw his hand tremble. "Look, I know things have been rough. I'll even admit I'm no Harry Deveraux; it's all I can do to keep afloat with all that's been going on. But I'm trying damn hard, Lou. This department is in danger of falling apart, and I need your help to keep it together."

Lou studied him. He usually had such cool self-assurance that he seemed immune to other people's insecurities. He wasn't such a bad fella, she thought, just pushed into a job he wasn't ready for. If Deveraux's back had held out a little longer, Steggans might have been able to run QA smoothly.

"I wasn't going to quit," she said.

"What?" It was his turn to blink. Then the tension went out of his shoulders. "Oh. I thought the I've-been-wanting-to-talk-to-you speech was the lead-in for a resignation."

"Nope. I was just going to ask to go back on days."

"Oh. Well . . ." He riffled the edges of the reports in front of him. "I can't do that. I need you at night to keep an eye on things for me."

"These hours are killing me. And now that I have a bunch of people staying with me, sleeping during the day is going to be tough."

"For a woman who lives alone, you have a lot of activity going on at your house."

Lou wasn't sure whether it was supposed to be a joke. His expression didn't offer a ghost of a clue.

"Are these permanent residents?" he asked.

"No, but they'll be staying with me indefinitely—"

"The arson investigator and his family?"

"Yeah," she said. "How did you know?"

"I'm only dense about shipyard stuff," he said. "I saw the headlines. Knowing you'd been seeing the lieutenant, I put two and two together."

Lou didn't know how to deal with the first part of his statement, so she moved on to the second. "I'm impressed. But you see my problem."

"And I sympathize. But I need you at night."

"How long?"

He spread his hands. Lou opened her mouth to protest, but the phone rang, loud in the quiet office. Steggans answered it. His expression darkened steadily as he listened to whoever was on the other end.

"I'll be there in a minute," he said, apparently cutting the other person off midword. He got up, reaching for his hardhat. "Sorry, Lou. We'll have to talk later."

He brushed past her, and a moment later she heard

the elevator doors open and close. And there she was, looking at the partially open drawers of his desk.

Her conscience bothered her for about thirty seconds. Then she sat down in his chair and started going through the desk.

"Please be there," she muttered.

She found the report in the left-hand file drawer, packed away with a stack of other papers. Her fingers shook a little as she flipped back to signatures on the last page.

The ship's supervisor had signed his name just below Jay's, the same loopy scrawl Lou had been seeing on reports for more than ten years. George Fagan.

"Shit," she whispered.

Her hands went numb. An ocean of implications crashed through her mind, too confusing to sort out now. She walked back to the copy machine, maneuvering through the maze of partitions more by memory than by design.

George Fagan.

Why couldn't it have been Louis Delanski? She didn't like Louis, didn't respect his work. But George . . . Maybe they weren't exactly friends, but she respected him. He did a tough job and did it well. In the end, that had always been her criteria for respect here at Carmichael's. And George qualified. Louis Delanski would have passed that bad weld for money; George would have done it for the yard, and for the two thousand men and women whose jobs depended on it.

Altruism. She closed her eyes, heaving a sigh that felt as though it came from her toes. Greed she could have handled. Now, she felt torn between loyalty to a man she liked and respected, and loyalty to a firm she wasn't sure deserved it.

So walk away.

Tempting. Very tempting. But even as she registered that thought, she ran into the same thing that had gotten her into this in the first place: that stubborn Malotti sense of honor. A lot of people might think this a special case, one that fell into the in-between of right and wrong. A shade of grey in a black-and-white world.

Her memory brought up an image of her father. He'd been dead fifteen years now, but she could still hear his voice as he'd told her about the affair he'd had with a woman in his office. "Lou," he said, "honor's the only thing in this life that's truly your own. You control it, you set its limits, and you're the only one who can make the decision to keep it or to set it aside. But remember, once you walk away from it, you can't go back. It's gone. You can find it again, even live it again, but you can never look in the mirror and know, really know, that you're not going to fall again."

Lou remembered watching the bleakness in his eyes as he talked. His wife had forgiven him the affair, and so had his daughter. But he couldn't. He'd lived six more years after that, and that look never quite left his eyes.

Lou made two copies of the report. One she tucked into her briefcase, the other she dropped into an envelope and addressed to Harry Deveraux.

The phone rang just as she slipped the original report back where she'd gotten it. She picked it up. "QA."

"Where the hell are you, Malotti?"

Well, speak of the devil. "What's up, George?"

"I'm at the *Corinne*. You were supposed to be down here twenty minutes ago, remember?"

"No, I don't remember."

"Well check the friggin' schedule."

"I did. There's nothing on the *Corinne* for me tonight."

He swore softly. "I called in a couple of hours ago and left a message."

"Who did you talk to?"

"Greg. Didn't he tell anyone?"

"Apparently not," she said.

"Christ," he growled. "Things are starting to slip up there, Malotti. You better keep a handle on them."

"What am I supposed to do, assassinate Steggans and take the place over? My own personal coup?"

"Hey, I don't care, as long as something gets done when I need it done. I got problems coming out my ass on this ship, and I want you to see them before Eichmann starts squawking about costs."

"You want me to get in hot water with you," she said, unable to keep from falling into the old repartee.

"Hell, yeah," he said. "Move your butt."

He hung up. She replaced the receiver gently, wishing she were someone else just now. The George Fagan she'd just spoken to had helped build this shipyard because he *cared*. He'd helped pass the *Gabriella* because he wanted to keep the yard going. And now he'd gotten himself put on another problem ship, one on which corners might have to be cut to have any hope of meeting costs. Oh, brother.

How did you go about telling a man you were going to take him down? Just look him in the eye and say, "Hey, George, it's been fun the past ten years, but you've been a very bad boy and now I'm going to make sure you never work as a ship supervisor again."

Yeah.

Twenty-two

The empty *Corinne* rode high in the water of the wet slip as Lou walked along her floodlit deck toward the bridge. At nearly five hundred feet long, the tanker hovered near the upper limit of the dry dock's capacity. Five hundred feet of trouble, Lou thought, noting the signs of neglect.

She followed a trail of lines down into the crew's quarters. It stank of sweat and old clothes, the effluvia that came from too many men in too little space. A cockroach scuttled out from beneath her feet.

"Give me navy every time," she muttered.

"Hey, Malotti!"

She turned, saw Tate Bucholtz, the electrical crew chief, step into the companionway behind her. "Hey, Tate."

"You're damn near a half hour late getting here."

"So sue me," she said. "I had to do my hair."

He laughed. "There's a rumor going around that you don't even *have* hair. That it's really glued around the edges of your hardhat."

"Tell 'em it's true," she said. "Tell me, what do you think of our big girl here?"

"Well . . . She's more seaworthy than some of those foreign scuttlebuckets that come in the port."

"In a couple of years, Enterprise will probably sell her to one of those companies and then she'll *be* one of those foreign scuttlebuckets. Where's Fagan?"

"He's in the forward tank. He came up a couple of minutes ago, bitching about a vent line problem and a buckled bulkhead."

"Oh, man!"

Tate nodded. "They didn't figure on this. It's gonna be a big cost overrun, and you know and I know there isn't room for it anywhere. Fagan looked madder'n Jack the Ripper."

"I guess I'd better go down and take a look. Forward tank, you said?"

"Yeah."

She turned away, wishing Fagan hadn't gotten himself assigned this ship, wishing he'd found another way to help the shipyard . . . wishing a lot of things.

She reached the tank, swung herself onto the metal ladder and started down. A cold, hard knot formed in her stomach, growing colder and harder with every rung she took. The tank had been flushed out, the air certified safe by an engineer. But it seemed thin and tainted to her, and her breathing accelerated.

It wasn't caused by the air, of course, but by fear. She'd never been claustrophobic, but she'd always found going into the tanks like walking into a big metal coffin—all anybody had to do was close the hatch.

Lights had been dropped down inside. The *Corinne* was a fairly old vessel. Her tanks were larger than most built today, about twenty feet deep, the other dimensions maybe forty by fifty. Lots of liquid, lots of pressure. T-beams added support to the walls, and interior bulkheads strengthened the large interior space. Oval holes pierced these interior bulkheads to allow passage of liquids and, in repair situations, people. A metal rim ran around each opening, again for strength. Lines snaked through the hole, indicating that someone had brought equipment down here.

Lou checked the lights, making sure all the bulbs were intact. Habit, and self-preservation; she'd gone down in tanks where bulbs had been broken when the lights had been dropped in, and she'd had to deal with open outlets against metal surfaces—and sometimes openings set several feet off the floor. But everything seemed to be in order, at least in this section.

A grinding noise began in the depths of the tank. It passed up through Lou's boots, shivered its way along her bones and set a resonance up in the center of her brain. Her pulse picked up even more. She knew someone must be working on that failed bulkhead, but logic had nothing to do with the reactions of her body.

She made her way through the tank, finally finding Fagan and another man in the far compartment. A section of bulkhead had buckled here, the thick metal crumpled by pressure. Fagan stood several feet away from the other man, who had just begun to cut away a twisted section of T-brace. Sparks skittered madly along the metal floor.

With that noise, Godzilla could have sneaked up on them, Fagan jumped a foot when Lou tapped him on the shoulder. He registered her, nodded, then indicated for the other man to stop cutting. For a moment, the silence seemed just as loud as the hissing had been.

"Take a break, Gary," Fagan said. "Five minutes."

The man nodded, slipping his safety goggles up onto his hardhat. Lou didn't recognize him. His footsteps echoed through the tank, the sound changing as he climbed the ladder.

"Is he new?" she asked.

Fagan nodded. "This is his first night. He's replacing Tyrene Bell."

"Nobody can replace Tyrene."

"So he's trying to replace Tyrene."

"They'd better hire two, maybe three."

"They'd better find some dimes deep in their change purse, that's what." Fagan swung around and pointed at the bulkhead. "Look at that bastard. They didn't figure anything like that in the frigging estimate, did they?"

"Nope," Lou said.

"Well, we're going to have to eat this one. No way can we let her out of here with that."

"Not on my watch," Lou said. She gauged the damage, then sighed. "That's Carmichael money you're looking at."

"Shit. I wish I'd never heard of goddamn Enterprise Shipping. We've had nothing but problems since we started with them. Give me the navy any day. I promise I'll never bitch about bureaucratic red tape again."

He looked as though he were going to say a lot more. Lou didn't give him the chance.

"I found your signature on the *Gabriella* report," she said.

His expression didn't change, but his eyes turned wary. A moment later he masked it, his pale irises opaque—mirrors that reflected the outside world, turning it away from what was behind them. "So?" he asked.

"You told me Louis Delanski had that one."

"He did."

She shook her head. "He had oral surgery the day that ship went out of here. *You* sent her out with Jay's reinspect."

"So I forgot."

291

Lou's hands twitched with the desire to shake him, to rattle that false indifference right out of him. "That weld was never redone," she said.

"Of course it was," he replied. Coolly. With complete confidence. "I wouldn't have signed that report otherwise."

"Who did the repair?"

He spread his hands. "I didn't ask. The weld was good by Jay, and it was good by me."

"George, that's a boiler valve we're talking about."

"It's still good by me."

"I found a list of sequential numbers in Jay's computer files. When I get down in Central Records and put those jobs together, do you think I'll find your name listed as ship supervisor on every vessel on that list?"

He smiled. "I don't know, and I don't fucking care."

His confidence shook her. Either he was innocent, or he thought himself very well protected. If he was protected, then she'd just jumped into some very hot water indeed.

Hot anger flashed through her. Screw him, and screw his protector. She took a step forward, almost close enough for the toes of their boots to touch. "I'm going to find out what happened if I have to tear this yard apart brick by brick," she said. "You'd better hope your ass is covered *good.*"

For the first time, she saw a crack in his mask. A little fear showed through that chink, and a whole lot of anger. She went after it, worrying at the opening. "Why did you do it, Fagan? Oh, I know you were just trying to help the shipyard, but surely you didn't think it could go on without somebody tumbling to it."

"I wouldn't pick my nose for this goddamn place," he said.

"Are you saying you did it for money?" she asked. "You're telling me you're just a thief?"

"I never said I did it at all!" he shouted.

"And I say you did."

His eyes narrowed. "Where's your proof? You don't have proof, you're just pissing up a rope."

"I'll get it," she said. "You said yourself that nothing gets past me."

"You're a bitch, Malotti."

"Yes," she said. "I am. And thank you."

His fists came up. Lou rose up onto the balls of her feet and leaned even further into his space. "Go ahead," she hissed. "But better make it a good one."

One moment passed, then another, and she realized he wasn't going to hit her. Didn't dare. She locked gazes with him one last time, putting all her contempt into it, then turned on her heel and stalked away. Her exit was marred somewhat when she had to duck through the bulkhead opening, but it was good enough. So much for loyalty and respect. Fagan had declared war, and by God, she was going to give it to him.

She encountered the new workman at the next bulkhead. He stepped aside, letting her come through first. His gaze was both curious and wary; he must have heard at least some of the argument. Tough.

"Hello, Miss . . . ah . . ."

Lou rescued him. Sort of. "Call me Lucretia," she said. "Or bitch."

"Yeah. Sure. Ah . . . nice to meet you."

He backed through the opening in the far bulkhead, as though afraid she'd run after her and bite his ankles. Maybe he wasn't so far off the mark; she was so damn mad right now, steam would probably rise off her skin if someone threw water on her.

She paused at the foot of the ladder to tighten the

lace of her right boot. No sense in making everybody happy by pitching off the ladder.

"You are so *stupid!*" she muttered. She wasn't sure if she meant Fagan or herself.

With a sigh, she straightened and started up the ladder. Twenty feet always seemed longer going up than coming down. She kept climbing. As she neared the top, fresh air swirled around her as though to welcome her back to the world. She drew it in gratefully.

The lights went out. Suddenly. Completely.

Disoriented by the sudden blackness, she clamped both hands on the rung and pressed her body against the ladder. A heartbeat later, something fell past her. She flinched away as it banged into the ladder just below her feet, then fell with a thud of metal on metal on the floor below.

She took a harsh breath, drew in the smell of gasoline. Her mind conjured a slow-motion terror of a thought: the workman slipping his safety goggles on, starting up the grinder and setting it against the metal, sparks everywhere . . .

"Fagan!" she shrieked. "Don't—"

The gasoline vapors flashed, a single, blinding strobe of incandescence. To Lou, clinging to her perch above, it seemed as though she hung suspended over the pit of hell.

And then the fire winked out, snuffed by lack of oxygen. Darkness reigned in the tank again. And silence.

Dead silence.

Lou's breath went out in a gasp of horror, and didn't come back. Sudden vertigo swept over her, pulling at her. Her stomach dropped as though she'd already begun plunging through the blackness to smash on the floor below. She fought it, clutching the ladder with desperate strength.

With an effort that brought sweat beading her forehead, she took a breath. Her chest closed around it greedily. Her brain started to clear. She took another, and another.

"Fagan!" she called, knowing she had to try, but also knowing it wouldn't work. "George, if you can hear me, make some kind of sound."

Nothing.

She pressed her forehead against the cool metal of the rung, fighting the instinct to climb down and help. But then she'd only die with them.

"Help!" she called, fear riding hard on her shoulders. Maybe she'd bring help, but maybe she'd bring back the man who'd done this. He'd probably object to survivors. She took a deep breath, shouted again. "Help! In the forward tank! Help!"

The sound of footsteps sounded above her. Black wings of terror beat in her brain, tightened her grip on the ladder.

Shoot me, stab me, strangle me, but don't shut the hatch, don't shut the hatch, please don't shut the hatch . . .

"Fagan? Malotti?" The voice belonged to Tate, and sounded like fear. "What the hell happened down there? Lou! George! Can you answer me? Hey, Rogers, Smith, Lawson, get over here and give me a hand!"

A flashlight sprang to life overhead, its beam spearing a sharp-edged path through the darkness. It played over the floor of the tank below the ladder, then crawled upward to Lou. Dazzled by the brightness, she turned her face away.

"Lou!" Tate called. "Oh, Christ! Hang on, we'll get you out of there."

It took her a couple of tries to get her voice going, but she did it. "Fagan's down there," she gasped. "And another man."

"Shit. Mike, get down there!"

"No!" She shook hair out of her face. "There was a fire . . . no air."

"Call Fire Control," Tate said, suddenly sounding very tired. "We need equipment. Go on, Lawson, get her out of there."

Lou hung pinned in the flashlight beam as someone started down toward her. Boots appeared on the rung above her head, and a moment later a man's hands gripped her own.

"Come on," he said. "I'll help you up."

She wanted to go. Badly. But for some reason, her body just wouldn't work.

"Let go," the man said.

"I can't."

He moved down farther, his body bracing hers against the ladder. Gently, he pried her hands loose. Freed from her strange paralysis, Lou hooked her elbows over the rung and flexed her aching fingers.

"Okay," she panted. "I can make it now."

"Go on. I'm right below you."

She kept her gaze fixed on the ladder as she climbed, much more slowly than she would have liked. If she could have sprouted wings, she'd have flown up; as it was, freedom came rung by rung. The flashlight beam moved with her. It felt warm on her hands, or maybe it was the heat of returning life. She reached the top at last, pausing half in and half out to catch her breath.

Tate leaned into her limited field of view. He grasped her wrists and pulled her forward, while the guy below planted a hand on her butt and heaved her upward. Once out, she lay supine, looking up at the stars overhead.

"They're dead," she said when Tate bent over her.

He nodded.

She raised herself up on one elbow. "Call Security, tell them to close down the gate *now*. And then call the police. We've got deep shit here."

"What happened?"

"Somebody threw a gas can down into that tank. And he had every intention of killing the people inside."

He drew his breath in with a hiss. "I'm gone," he said, suiting actions to words.

She lay back again, staring up at the stars. Suddenly their light didn't seem quite so warm or welcoming.

Twenty-three

Lou stood and watched as workers brought Fagan and the other man up from the tank. The lights had been restored; the blackout had been a simple disconnect, done for the sole purpose of staying out of sight while tossing the can.

"Are they dead?" someone whispered behind her.

"Sure," someone else whispered. "They look just like wax dummies. My grandma looked like that the day we found her dead in her kitchen."

"Who's that other guy?"

"His name's Gary. I don't know anything else; this was his first night here."

The other man whistled. "Christ. Talk about being in the wrong place at the wrong time!"

"Why are you whispering?" a third man asked. "It's not like they can fuckin' hear you."

Lou moved away from the conversation. She wrapped her arms around herself, trying to dispel the chill that had settled deep in her bones. It only got worse. Maybe she'd never feel really warm again, she thought as she watched a team begin CPR on the victims. She wished she could hope that it would work. But with George and the other man being without oxygen for more than fifteen minutes, maybe she should hope it *didn't* work.

"I'm sorry, George," she whispered. She'd rather have had her war.

Fagan's longish hair lay spread out around his head, and the breeze stirred it softly as the men worked on him. Lou whirled, unable to watch any longer.

"Lou, are you okay?"

The voice belonged to Steggans. She turned to look at him as he pushed toward her through the clot of men. For some reason, her voice just didn't want to work.

She must have looked as helpless as she felt, for he put his arm around her shoulders and started pushing his way back through the crowd. Once clear, he sat her down on a crate.

"Take a couple of deep breaths," he said. "What happened?"

"Somebody threw a can of gasoline down in the tank—"

"It exploded?"

She shook her head. "Not enough oxygen. But the vapors flashed as long as there was some. George and that other guy suffocated."

"Jeez. Not a nice way to go."

"No."

"How did you get out?" He scrubbed his hand over his chin. "I didn't mean that the way it sounded. I just don't know how to ask—"

"Why I didn't die down there with them?"

"I didn't plan to be quite *that* blunt."

She nodded. Propping her elbows on her knees, she rested her head in her hands and stared at the floor. The toes of her boots were singed. "I happened to be on my way out. When that can came down, I was near the top of the ladder where some fresh air came in from the hatch. Otherwise I'd be lying there with them."

"You were awful damn lucky," he said.

"Yeah."

She wished she *felt* lucky. Right now, however, she felt like a man who pulled back from a cliff while the guy he'd been walking with stepped off.

Good old Anglo-Saxon guilt for arguing with a guy a minute before he died.

Steggans let his breath out sharply. "You don't need to be here right now. Come on, I'll walk you up to the office. Better yet, get your stuff and I'll drive you home. You can pick up your car tomorrow."

His kindness brought tears to her eyes. She blinked to clear them. Wanting nothing more than to put this night behind her and never look back, she climbed to her feet.

"Miss Malotti?"

The new voice brought her swinging around to see two men whose manner labeled them cops as clearly as if they'd had signs painted on their foreheads. One was tall and lanky, with a fringe of brown hair around a bald head. The other was medium-sized, with a baby face he'd probably had to fight for all his life. He looked eighteen, probably came in somewhere over thirty.

Some people have all the luck. The inappropriateness of the thought cleared her brain somewhat. Maybe other people had strange thoughts like that after seeing violent death. If so, no one was going around admitting it. Neither was she.

"I'm Malotti," she said.

"Detective Obermann, Portsmouth Police Department," the tall one said, flashing a badge. "Homicide.

This is Detective Thomason. I understand you were in the tank with Mr. Fagan and Mr. Chiopinski."

She nodded.

"We'd like to ask you some questions," he said.

"Hey," Steggans protested, "she's pretty upset. Can't you do this tomorrow?"

Obermann looked him over. "Who are you?"

"Dwayne Steggans. I'm her boss."

"Well, Mr. Steggans, we like to talk to people in the heat of the moment. Time tends to blur the memory."

Steggans turned to Lou. "Want me to come with you?"

"I'm okay," she said. "But no thanks."

She led the policemen to her office. They glanced around at the partitions, then requested somewhere more private.

"You're more paranoid than I am," she said.

Obermann smiled. "Comes with the territory. You don't want something overheard, don't talk in open spaces."

"Does this come from dealing with spies and terrorists?"

"Hell, no," he said. "Journalists."

They both swung around as the elevator doors snicked open. "Finally," Obermann said. "Hey, Whitaker, what took you so long? Out eating donuts somewhere?"

"Screw you, Bert," Whitaker retorted.

He came around the corner, looking grimmer than Lou had ever seen him. His jaw looked like it had been cut out of granite, his eyes even harder. To her astonishment, he reached down, plucked her out of her chair, and squashed her hard against his chest.

"Hey, easy with the soft parts," she said, too damn glad to see him to be embarrassed.

"Oh, is this yours?" Thomason asked.

"It's squirming too much to be his," Obermann said.

"Screw you," Whitaker said again. He set Lou back on her feet. "Are you really okay?"

"I'm walking, talking and breathing," she said.

He nodded. "These two gentlemen are long-time friends and business associates. While I generally handle the investigations in homicide arsons, I interface with them all along the line. I thought it would save time all around if they were in at the beginning of this one."

"He's gonna make us do the work," Obermann said to Thomason, who nodded. "Well, let's get started." The elevator door snicked open again, and he sighed. "Is there someplace private we can talk?"

They ended up in Steggans's office, Lou in the big chair, the detectives in the armchairs, Whitaker leaning against the wall near the window. She gave them a rundown on what had happened. Her voice sounded inflectionless and flat—a mirror image of what she felt inside. Just the facts, ma'am. Okay, just the facts: two men had died tonight. Horribly. Snuffed out like . . . insects.

And face it, she felt responsible. If she'd blown the whistle on this thing in the beginning, if she'd chosen not to look at it at all, if, if, if. She'd told Wade these were just a couple of fellas taking a little money under the table. Tonight, the common thieves who'd set up the little scheme had become anything but common.

"It was my fault," she said.

All three men looked at her, their faces registering surprise.

"Would you care to elaborate on that?" Whitaker asked.

"I've been looking into some questionable repairs on certain ships George Fagan was responsible for."

302

She watched them assimilate it, tear it apart, and recognize the implications. And she saw Whitaker's jaw harden even more.

"Did you find anything concrete on that?" Thomason asked.

"No. Somebody screwed with the QA database, and I haven't been able to track down the records yet."

"Did you tell anyone about your suspicions?"

"My son." She looked at Whitaker, wishing they were alone, so she could soften this somehow. "And my boss, Harry Deveraux—"

"I thought Mr. Steggans was your boss."

"He's assistant shop foreman. Harry's foreman. He runs QA," she said. "I trust him implicitly." Her hands started to sweat as she realized how that must have sounded to Whitaker. Ah, well, too late to take it back now. "Harry's been out on medical leave for, oh, three weeks now. Back surgery—he's all but bedridden."

"Could he have told someone?"

"I doubt it. This was hot stuff, damaging to everybody if it got out." She raked her hair back with both hands. "Look, this thing is totally nuts. I mean, you've got a couple of guys taking some money under the table, not some kind of terrorists. Larceny is one thing. But murder? It just doesn't seem possible."

Obermann glanced at Whitaker briefly, as though expecting him to contribute something to the conversation. Whitaker merely stared at him, unresponsive.

"What did Mr. Deveraux say about the inspection situation?" the detective asked after a moment's hesitation.

"He said it sucked. And that I needed to go quiet and soft until I had proof. You can't crucify people over something like this unless you've got the nails."

"You're telling *us?*" Thomason snorted. "You said

303

the database was down. Can't you recreate the information from hard copies?"

"Not readily. I've got a list of sequential numbers to start with, but it's an enormous job. See, each department keeps records on the jobs they do, but each files it according to their own specific parameters. So cross referencing is all but impossible. We keep hard copies in Central Files, but those are filed according to specific purchase order, of which there might be several hundred for one vessel. Literally every purchase order will have to be looked at." A sudden thought popped into her mind, and she straightened. "Hey, it's evidence now. That means you guys can come in and do it all for me."

Obermann looked up again. "Everyone wants to be a comedian these days."

"Who was joking?" she asked.

He sighed. "Was Fagan working with someone?"

"Had to be." Lou looked at Whitaker. He returned her gaze levelly, his eyes as chill and dark as a cloudy winter sky. She could have dealt with open anger; this coldness left her helpless, unable to read him, unable to gauge what damage had been done.

His expression didn't change when she told the three men about Jay Nesmith, although the two policemen were perceptibly excited about it. Aha, she thought. A suspect. It didn't take much to please some people. Poor Jay. Always the fair-haired boy.

"Does Mr. Nesmith have access to the shipyard?" Thomason asked.

"Not through the gate. But you know and I know there are ways to get in anywhere. I suppose he could even swim in, although *I* wouldn't get in that water just to kill somebody."

After the words came out, she flinched from them.

Gallows humor—her way of keeping the guilt and horror at bay. Wiseass Malotti, always keeping the tough front going. But the detectives didn't seem to notice the inappropriateness of the remark; of all the people who'd understand, she realized, homicide detectives were probably at the top of the list.

"Where's Nesmith now?" Obermann asked.

"He's hiding out somewhere," she said. "I don't think his wife even knows where he is."

"We'll find him. Do you think anybody else might have been working this scam?"

"Probably. But there has to be a balance between having enough people to carry it off and having too many people to keep it quiet."

They nodded; she was talking their language. Suddenly, Whitaker's beeper went off. He waved at the detectives to continue, then stalked out of the office. Obermann watched him leave, then switched his too-perceptive gaze to Lou.

"Was Fagan taking bribes?" he asked.

She hesitated. "I . . . don't know."

He studied her from beneath his lashes. "Do you have an opinion on this? I'll even take a gut feel."

"I've known George more than ten years," she said, clasping her hands on the desk and staring down at them. "Or at least I thought I knew him. Maybe I've only been seeing the public George Fagan, not the man he really was. But I do know two things: he was a damn good ship supervisor, and he worked his butt off for this place."

"Plenty of good workers steal from their employers. Maybe he'd been doing it the whole ten years he'd been working here."

She lifted one shoulder, let it drop again. "Maybe. But remember, we've been doing exclusively Navy work until recently. Cost-plus. And where was the motivation for bribery? They were spending Uncle Sam's money."

"So you think this is a recent occurrence."

"Yeah." She sighed. "A couple of hours ago, I wouldn't have believed this if someone had told me. Fagan is . . . was . . . a pretty regular guy. Everybody liked him. He did a good job, he played fair with the guys who worked for him, and he stayed out of shipyard politics."

"Who would have bribed him?" Obermann asked.

"It could have been someone here at the shipyard, could have been the owner of whatever ship he was working on."

The detectives glanced at each other, and Lou could almost see the word "blackmail" hovering in the air over their heads. She sighed. They were obviously on track with this. Bribery plus blackmail equals murder. In their world, it probably happened all the time. Here, it didn't feel right.

"How many people knew Fagan was down in that tank?" Thomason asked.

"Most of the people on the ship," she said. "And anybody those people might have talked to. *I* wouldn't go down in one of those tanks without letting somebody trustworthy know. I mean, how'd you like to be inside and have some guy shut the hatch just to tidy up before leaving his shift?"

The thought lifted the hairs at the back of her neck, and she could see her feelings mirrored in the men's eyes.

"So," Thomason shifted in his chair, "did you talk to him about the inspection situation while you were down there?"

She met his gaze levelly. "I accused him outright."

"And?"

"And he denied it, of course. We almost came to blows over it. That's when I headed up."

Obermann scraped his thumbnail over his eyebrow. "Ah, you do that sort of thing often?"

"Nope. But I'm not about to let some guy get in my face. Besides, I'm bigger and meaner than George Fagan on his best day." She drew her breath in sharply. "And this sure wasn't his best day, was it?"

"How many people knew you were in the tank?"

"Me?" It was her turn to shift uneasily in her chair. "Ah, Tate Bucholtz was the only one, I guess. I wasn't officially scheduled for anything on the *Corinne* tonight. Why?"

She knew why he'd asked; she just wanted to be told she was wrong.

"We're just trying to get a picture of everything and everybody," Obermann said. He closed his notebook with a snap. "Thank you very much, Miss Malotti. You've been very helpful. Oh, we'll need that list of sequential numbers you told me about."

"It's at home. I can call you with it."

Thomason fished in an inside pocket, pulled a business card from its depths. "That'll be fine. And if you happen to think of anything else, no matter how unimportant it might seem, give us a call right away."

Lou got to her feet.

"I suggest you take some vacation time," Obermann said. "Stay away from the shipyard for a while."

"I can't do that, Detective," Lou said. "We're running short-staffed as it is. And after tonight," she added with a bitterness that surprised her, "we're down another two."

"Then I'll assign a man to you."

"What, I'm going to have a cop trailing me everywhere I go? Uh-uh. I won't get anything done, and neither will anyone else. Can I have one of my own security people?"

"You going to take one home with you?"

"At home I have a son who is a brown belt in karate, as well as his girlfriend, her brothers and sisters, and an overlarge Irish wolfhound. I also have my very own .38. If this guy wants to get me there, he'd better bring an army with him."

"I don't know—"

"Look, I wouldn't kick about this if I really thought I was in danger," she said. "Look, it was pitch dark down there. I couldn't have identified my own grandmother. *He* knows that."

Obermann glanced at Thomason, and got some message Lou missed. They must have been partners a long time. Then Thomason asked, "How thoroughly do you screen your security people?"

"We run a police check, DMV check, credit check, we send their fingerprints to the FBI. And they have to pass a lie detector test before they can be hired. Some of them might not be too bright, but I think they're honest."

Thomason snorted. "Pick the dumbest one then. It's the smart ones you've got to worry about."

She would have laughed in different circumstances. Reaching into her pocket, she pulled out her roll of antacids. They both took one when she offered it, and that, too, should have been funny and wasn't. And the fact that Whitaker hadn't come back didn't help at all.

"You know, fellas," she said. "I'd really appreciate it if this inspection thing stayed out of the newspapers. Something like that can close this shipyard down."

"We don't talk about the details of investigations with the media."

She let her breath out in a sigh. "Thanks."

"Are you heading home now?" Obermann asked.

Lou glanced at her watch. Twelve-eighteen. Astonishment shafted through her. It hadn't been quite two hours ago that she'd stepped aboard the *Corinne*. Such a short time for so much to happen.

"I've got almost seven hours left on my shift," she said.

"You had a real close call tonight," Thomason said. "I don't think anyone would hold it against you if you took the night off."

Lou shook her head. Maybe it was only bravado, but just now it was all she had. "I've got work to do."

"Famous last words," Obermann said cheerfully.

When Lou trudged wearily out to her car the next morning, she found Whitaker leaning against the driver's-side door, his arms crossed over his chest.

Obviously, he was feeling aggressive. And obviously, with his butt planted on her door, she wasn't going to get in the car without moving him. "I'm tired, and I had a bad night," she said. "If you want to fight, make an appointment for later."

"No wonder you haven't had any relationships."

She stared at him, dumfounded.

"A lot of women would have come out of that tank hysterical," he continued. "A lot of men, too. Ninety-nine percent of normal human beings would have called friends or family to tell them about almost being suffocated. But not Lou Malotti. *I'm* the one who called Wade and the kids and let them know what happened. They're ready to strangle you."

"I planned to tell everybody. After work."

"You didn't think they might be the teensiest bit worried?"

Fatigue and a hefty dose of guilt made her testy. And defensive. "What for?" she retorted. "If you told them the news, then you also told them I was okay, right?"

He reached out and plucked the keys out of her hand. "Get in the car."

"Hey, those are—"

"Get in the car."

Lou put her hands on her hips and glared back. For a moment she saw only his anger. Then she saw something else deep inside that got her moving toward the passenger-side of the car. He got in, slammed the door, and slid the key into the ignition.

"You didn't have to be rude," she said.

"Yes, I did."

Gravel sprayed out from under the wheels as he pulled out of the lot. Instead of heading toward Churchland, however, he turned toward downtown.

"Where are we going?" she asked.

"Somewhere. Now, tell me why you kept this inspection thing so tight and close."

She glanced at him from the corner of her eye. His face seemed calm, but he was grasping the steering wheel with white-knuckled force. "Don't you think we ought to wait to discuss this until emotions aren't running so high?"

"No." His knuckles got even paler. "Don't you think I should be worried that you almost died in that tank tonight? Jesus Christ, Lou! Don't you think I should *care?* Why couldn't you have trusted me half as much as you trusted Harry Deveraux?"

In a swift burst of realization, she knew that it was Whitaker the man, and not Whitaker the arson investigator talking. *Be honest. It's important—he's important.* "I should have told you. But I'm not used to . . . trusting anyone else."

"You trusted Harry Deveraux."

"Harry's my boss."

"So you don't trust men in general? Or is it only the ones you sleep with who are suspect?"

"Sex has nothing to do with it. I'm used to handling my own problems. And I'm used to being alone."

"No wonder," he muttered.

"I heard that." She swung around as far as the seat belt allowed. "This inspection thing is my problem. Mine. Do I interfere with your arson investigations? Do I expect you to tell me every little thing that goes on?"

"No," he said. "You don't fucking ask anything at all."

"Why are you so upset?"

"Pardon me for not being clearer about it," he snarled. "You see, I was operating under the assumption that we cared for each other—"

"I didn't say—"

"Let me finish, damn it. Here I was, thinking that we'd started some sort of relationship, maybe even the beginnings of a pretty good partnership." His voice rose. "Imagine my surprise when I found out I'd only been allowed to make love to you, not enter the holy of holies of your goddamned trust."

"Now, look—"

"If a guy's got to be your boss to be trusted, what does he have to be to get a piece of that prickly little heart of yours—the President of the United States?"

"Get out of my car!" she shouted.

"I'm not goddamned finished," he shouted back.

The car jounced roughly as he swung too fast into

a turn. Lou felt her jaw drop as she realized he'd pulled into the Holiday Inn parking lot.

"What the hell are you doing here?" she demanded.

"This is the only place where we're going to have privacy."

"What are you going to do, strangle me?"

"It's decision time, Lou."

Her pulse thundered in her ears as anger shifted to alarm. "What do you mean?"

"It's too late to play dumb. Last time we slept together it was a crazy, carried-away thing. This time I want to know that you mean it."

"What the hell do you want from me?"

"I want in. Today. Now. And tomorrow. I want us to have something together. Sharing, trust—in other words, a relationship."

"Gee, do I get to wear your class ring?"

His hands tightened on the wheel. "Is this what you do every time someone tries to get close to you? Drive him away with your damned stiff-necked independence and smartass attitude?"

That stung. Lou opened her mouth to hit back, but something closed it again. Maybe it was nearly dying, maybe it was simply the man himself. With an explosive sigh, she raked both hands through her hair.

"Look," she said at last. "I told you I was no good at this relationship stuff."

"It's time to learn, Lou. Or else stop looking at me the way you do. What do you say? Want to give it a shot?"

A simple yes or no, she thought. It didn't seem like much to ask for. But he wasn't asking for anything simple—or anything safe. He wanted it all. She hadn't been able to answer that kind of demand for many, many years. Maybe she never had.

She looked at the future with him. There were a hell of a lot of impediments. Five kids, a cat and a dog, and God knows, probably more hamsters. Two demanding jobs. College educations and mortgages, memories of ex-husbands and dead wives. It looked awful damn complicated.

Then she looked at her future without him. Without the kids, the jobs, the animals—the hassles. Peace and quiet. A home to herself, a life to herself. Alone.

And it was like that hatch banging closed over her head, sealing her in the confines of the tank. She might not be ready for everything Whitaker seemed to want from her, but taking this step could be a start.

She turned to look into his eyes. "You picked a hell of a time for this. I've been crawling around inside ships all night, my hair looks like crap, I'm sweaty and dirty and I've got grease under my fingernails—"

"They have bathrooms in there," he said, producing a room key and dangling it before her eyes. "And all those little bottles of shampoo and things. I'd like nothing better than to give you a hot, soapy shower."

She drew her breath in sharply, crowded by memories of the last shower they'd shared. "I don't understand what you want with a middle-aged, overweight—"

"Sumptuous. Ripe, bounteous. Now about that shower?"

"Did you say sumptuous?"

"Yeah," he said. "Sumptuous, succulent. And I want to taste every beautiful inch."

Something rich and sultry bloomed inside her, raced through her veins and nerves before settling deep in her body. Life—reckless and hot, tender and greedy all at once. "I'm too tired for a shower."

"A bath, then," he said, his eyelids dropping to half mast. "A long, slow, hot bath."

"Bubbles?"

"When I'm finished with you, you'll think you've been swimming in champagne."

She crossed her legs, uncrossed them again. "What about breakfast?"

"We'll call for room service. Later. Your nipples are hard. I can see them through your shirt."

"Talking about bubbles always does that to me."

"Me, too. What do you say, Malotti? Want to go inside?"

Slowly, languorously, she undid the seat belt and slid it into place. A deliberately provocative gesture. It was reflected in his eyes, the taut planes of his face. He enjoyed this game as much as she did. Smiling, she leaned back against the door, knowing it tightened the shirt over her breasts.

"Do you want me to touch you?" he asked.

"Do you want to touch me?"

"Immoderately. But if I do, I don't think I'll be able to stop."

"Impetuous, at your age?"

He smiled, a slow, lascivious smile that sent even more heat coursing through her. "Want to give it a try?"

"Here?"

"Here and now."

"What, and wind up having to get that gear shift surgically removed from something tender and important? I don't think so. Besides, that bath—"

"Get out of the car, Lou."

He had her shirt off and her jeans unzipped almost before the door closed behind them.

"You can't get the pants off without taking the work boots off first," she said as he tumbled her onto the bed.

"Goddamn laces," he growled. "Might as well be wearing a suit of armor."

"Let me get them." She pushed at him impatiently. "Go run the bath water."

"You want it hot?"

"Hot and long and soapy. Just like you promised."

He pulled her up, kissed her thoroughly and passionately, then dropped her back onto the bed. "Hurry," he said.

She did. And found him waiting in the water for her. Arms akimbo, she surveyed the expanse of male flesh that overfilled the tub.

"This wasn't what I had in mind," she said.

He sat up and smiled at her, his eyes almost luminescent in the harsh bathroom light. "Come here. There's plenty of room if you put your legs here, over mine."

Interesting. And definitely worth a try. She climbed in, letting him maneuver her into position. His skin seemed hotter than the water, and his hands trembled as he slid soap onto her shoulders. She ran her fingertips down his chest to his belly, then beyond, and he drew his breath in with a hiss.

"No," he said, taking her hand from him.

"But I want—"

"Shh. I almost lost you tonight. I need this, Lou."

Another time, she might have turned away from the intensity in his eyes. Now, however, she'd gone too far to turn back; his need matched an answering one in her.

He smiled, evidently reading capitulation in her eyes. "Lean back."

She couldn't have disobeyed if she'd wanted to; her skin was so sensitized now that she registered each separate hair on his thighs, felt the slide of every tiny soap bubble. When he raised her leg to kiss the full, wet curve of her calf, she felt her toes curl.

"Is it always going to be like this?" she asked.

"I hope so."

He washed her with long, sweeping strokes, finding nerve endings she didn't know she had. Even her feet. Toes, heel, the gentle curve of the arch. She shifted restlessly, reacting as his touch slid from one spot to another. Her body quivered in anticipation as his hand moved upward to the back of her knee, her thigh. Higher. Oh, God. Her mind drifted off on a tide of sensation.

There came a time when the slow sensuality wasn't enough. She sat up, put her arms around his neck and whispered, "Now."

He came into her then, and it was like riding a great ocean swell. The gentleness ended with the languor. Touching, kissing, biting—delight so sharp it almost felt like pain. She was as greedy as he, and as reckless.

Life. Precious, fleeting, yet cupped and held in this plain porcelain tub. Trapped by their passion and the sheer, vital power of sex. Lou gave herself up to it, letting it erase the taste of near death that had lingered in her soul.

Whitaker's eyes changed at the end, turning mindless and molten. Willing sacrifice, she fell into those depths. A surge. A cry, hers or his, maybe both.

For a moment, she really *did* feel as though she were swimming in champagne.

Twenty-four

The Fire Man spun the Cavalier's rear wheels as he pulled out of the Holiday Inn parking lot. He'd followed the Bitch from the shipyard, hoping she'd stop at a store or someplace he could pull her into his car. He hadn't figured on Whitaker, and he certainly hadn't figured on the two of them coming here to screw their brains out while he cooled his heels in the parking lot.

The old power hung at the edges of his soul where he could almost taste it. Almost touch it. Seductive, tantalizing, but no longer his. Damn her! Jinx, whore, bitch—everything she touched turned against him.

Rage burned in him, hot and powerful, too big to be contained. He had to let it out now, had to do something. Strike out. He didn't care that it was broad daylight, didn't care about anything except finding something on which to vent his anger. He drove down Crawford Street, casting right and left. But the office day seemed to be in full swing now, people in and around almost every entrance, so he turned onto High Street and headed west. Drizzle spattered the windshield. He liked the rain and lowering clouds; they enclosed him, made the world seem smaller and more secure.

Downtown, the area changed for the worse the farther he got from the water. Nice restaurants and civic buildings were replaced by pawn shops and dingy storefronts. Dirty glass and metal security screens—ripe for urban renewal.

He wished he could do it all himself; burn this block and the next, and the one after that. Flame burned in his mind, hot and bright and beautiful. He'd make it reality.

The colored neon signs in a furniture store window attracted his attention. He checked his watch. Not quite nine o'clock. The store wouldn't open until ten. Perfect. He turned left at the corner, then left again.

The rear of the store seemed deserted, the big delivery door closed. Another door, a regular-sized one, pierced the back wall. Employees Only had been stenciled across it in red. He continued down the road, finally parking the Cavalier near the intersection. Near enough for quick access, far enough away so that it might be noticed and identified.

He slipped his raincoat on. The weight of the flashlight in his pocket made it hang askew, and he took a moment to adjust it before leaning back into the car to retrieve the crowbar.

His luck held, and the street remained empty as he made his way to the employees' entrance. It held again when he discovered that the door was wood, not metal. A shiny new deadbolt gleamed brassily above the knob. Useless in any real terms.

"These old places are great," he murmured.

Jamming the end of the crowbar into the doorjamb beside the deadbolt, he heaved with all his strength. Wood groaned and began to splinter. He pulled back, jammed the crowbar in again. It took three more tries before he popped the door free. So much for security.

He slipped inside. The wet breeze slipped in with him, stirring the papers on the desk on the far wall. Mouse droppings lined the wall nearest the door, and the smell of mildew hung on the air. Nice place. As the sign said, a houseful of furniture for seven-ninety-nine; mouse droppings thrown in for free.

Softly, he eased the door shut behind him. Silence fell over the place, broken only by the soft sibilance of his own breathing. Quick and shallow, paced by anticipation. He felt the edge of the power courting him; maybe this would break the jinx.

He saw a kerosene heater beneath the desk, a half-full gallon can of kerosene in the storage closet at the far end of the room. His mouth twitched into a smile.

A doorway led into the warehouse beyond. He switched the flashlight off, preferring to navigate by the light seeping in around the perimeter of the delivery door. This was an arsonist's dream: furniture stacked high on sturdy shelving, pallets and stacks of broken-down boxes littering the floor. Tables, chairs, sofas, mattresses—everything combustible.

"Thank you very much," he said.

A door opened suddenly at the far end of the storage area. He dove into the lee of a pair of shelves just as a wedge of light spilled across the floor where he'd been standing. Bile rose in his throat, sour and sickening.

Jinxed. Nothing's going to go right until I take care of that bitch for good . . .

A man stepped into the doorway. His shadow, eerily elongated, bisected the light. "Calvin, is that you?" the voice had the reedy quality of age. "I heard you banging around out there; did you have trouble with the lock again?"

The Fire Man crouched, hardly breathing, his mind whirling frantically from one possibility to the next.

The man moved farther into the warehouse. "Calvin, are you in there?" he called again. Then, in an muttered undertone, "Where the hell is that light switch?"

All the possibilities coalesced into one absolute necessity. The arsonist set the kerosene can down carefully, then backed down the aisle and slid around the far end of the shelves. His rubber-soled shoes squeaked faintly on the concrete as he charged the shadowy figure.

He hit the man amidships, knocking him into the wall behind him. The fellow's breath went out with a whoosh. He folded up like a broken doll, his face cracking hard against the top of the arsonist's head. Then he went down, and stayed down.

The Fire Man leaned down and felt for a pulse. It was there, faint but fast. He reached up, felt along the wall for the switch. Found it, flipped it upward. Big fluorescent lights bloomed in the ceiling.

The man lay on his back, his eyes closed, arms and legs outflung. He didn't look at all like Grandpa, who'd been a big-boned, fleshy man. No, this fellow was small and wiry, mostly tendons strung on bones. Blood leaked from a nose that had gone askew, turning the lower part of his face into a crimson mask. Drops had spattered upward into his wiry grey eyebrows. His mouth gaped open, giving the arsonist a glimpse of stained smoker's teeth.

"You old shit," he said. "You sure were in the wrong place at the wrong time today."

He found some twine, used it to tie the old man's wrists and ankles. Then he went back to work.

It took only a couple of minutes to pull the flattened

boxes over to the shelves and stuff them underneath. Lifting a pallet overhead, he smashed it down on the concrete. The splintered wood went in with the cardboard.

He found a box full of excelsior near the door, used it to pack all around the cardboard. His hands started to shake. Anticipation, sweet and hot, coursed like wine along his veins.

He retrieved the kerosene, then went back and stood over the old man, who had begun to stir. This shriveled husk was a damn poor substitute for Lou Malotti, with her abundant flesh and even more abundant well of life. But that would come.

The old man's eyes opened. They wandered for a moment, then focused on the arsonist's face. Fear came into them. "Please," he gabbled. "Let me go. Take the money, take anything. I won't say a word to the police."

"I don't want your money," the Fire Man said.

"Don't hurt me, I won't say anything . . ."

The Fire Man didn't answer. Bending, he grasped the old man beneath the arms, and dragged him over to the shelves.

"What are you doing?" the man asked, a high note of terror in his voice.

"Just making you comfortable," the Fire Man said, propping the other man in a sitting position against one of the supports. "Just be quiet, and you won't be hurt."

With an almost tender movement, he took a tissue out of his pocket and wiped the blood from the old man's mouth and chin.

"What's your name?" the arsonist asked.

"A-Albert."

The Fire Man smiled. Raising his forefinger, he said,

"Now, remember, Albert. No noise, and you won't be hurt."

Albert nodded, his eyes stark with the need to believe what couldn't be believed.

The arsonist straightened. He walked the few yards to the spot he'd prepared, then poured most of the kerosene over the mass of packing.

"What's that smell?" Albert asked, his voice high with terror. His clothing rasped against the concrete as he shifted position with a convulsive movement. "Kerosene? Oh, my God!" he gasped. "Help! Somebody help me!"

The Fire Man lit a match, stood looking at the tiny flame for a moment. Then he tossed it on the fluid-soaked packing. Flame circled outward in a spreading wave. The excelsior caught, turned into black curls, then fell in on itself. But not before transferring the torch to the boxes. The fire had a heart now, cherry-red, layers of cardboard peeling away as it was consumed.

"Please," the old man wailed. "Please!"

The Fire Man went to stand in front of him. Smoke was already curling along the floor, wisps of it seeming to pluck hungrily at the man's pants.

"You've lived your life," the arsonist said. "It's time to make room for the young."

"No! You can't . . . Please, don't let this happen!"

The arsonist dribbled the rest of the kerosene over the man's legs and chest. He lit another match, held it steady while Albert whined like a frightened dog.

"This is out of my hands, old man," he said. "It's destiny, set the moment you walked into this room."

"No, please. Please, please . . ."

With a flick of his thumb and forefinger, he tossed the match. It landed on Albert's waist, flared above and below as the kerosene caught. A howl of agony came

322

from the old man's mouth, growing higher and more frenzied with every second.

The Fire Man watched.

Albert finished one scream, pulled air in for another, and sucked a gout of flame into his throat and lungs. His clothes wisped away with the smoke. He stared at the arsonist, begging to live, then begging to die.

The Fire Man watched.

Fascinated. Drawn by the pain, the destruction, the roast-pig smell of burning flesh and fat. The larger fire spread, reaching to claim the blackened thing that still writhed upon the floor.

Driven away at last by the heat, the Fire Man ran back to the office. He opened the door a crack to peer up and down the street. A car went by, then another. He waited for the street to clear, conscious of the crackle of flame behind him. Smoke wreathed around his head, swirled out the door.

"Go, go, go," he muttered.

It seemed to take forever for the cars to pass. But the street cleared finally, and he slipped out. As he walked to his car, he found his head spinning with the memory of the old man's screams. It blended with other voices, other times.

Grandpa had sounded like that. So had Pa. And so had Ma and Sissy. Fire—the great equalizer, bringing the bully and the bullied to the same level.

He'd never regretted that long-ago fire. Something in him had snapped that night, triggered by yet another spreading pool of urine in the bed. No more setting fires in corncribs and tractor sheds. He'd gone out to the barn, gotten a can of kerosene, and doused his sleeping grandfather. A single match, and he'd rid himself of grandfather, bed and urine all in one grand sweep. With that act, he set himself free.

He hadn't intended the whole family to die. But it had happened, and he'd always considered it a step in becoming the Fire Man. A necessary sacrifice.

Behind him, the fire leaped and roared.

He glanced over his shoulder at the furniture store, where smoke chuffed out around the big metal door. A powerful fire. Plenty of fuel, plenty of hate to sustain it. If left alone, it could take out this whole neighborhood.

He got in the car. Pressing his forehead against the steering wheel, he closed his eyes and waited for the sweet, exquisite rush of pleasure. And waited. There was only an aching emptiness, an awareness of what-might-have-been . . . if it weren't for *her*.

Fate had set Lou Malotti in his life to steal away the only precious thing he'd ever owned. He could feel the echo of the fire he'd created, feel its heat on his skin and in his soul, but it wasn't truly his.

Jinxed. From the moment her path had crossed his, he'd been jinxed. Well, mistakes could be rectified, jinxes fixed, failures turned into triumphs.

A single match was all it took.

The sound of sirens pulled him up. Somebody must have called the Fire Department. He thought of Malotti and Whitaker in the comfortable closeness of their hotel room. No doubt they'd chosen it as a nice little haven where nothing from the outside world could intrude.

"Well, get ready, Bitch," he muttered, putting the Cavalier into gear. "I'm coming in."

Now, *that* thought gave him a great deal of pleasure. He started the car and swung around the corner, not once glancing in the rearview mirror to see how the fire was coming along.

* * *

Lou rubbed her cheek against Whitaker's chest, feeling the solid thump-thump of his heartbeat. "So, what do we do now?" she asked.

He opened his eyes a crack. "What the hell's left?"

She laughed. "There's a whole world of things you and I haven't even heard of, let alone want to *do*. I was talking about the rest of the day."

"We could explore some of those limits."

"Tempting. But I'm too old to go without sleep, even for sex. More sex, I should say."

He rose up on one elbow. "That was not sex."

"No?" Lou looked down on the acres of bare flesh, hers and his, occupying the bed. "What was it, then?"

"Making love."

Her eyes drifted closed. "Mmm."

"Lou?"

"Uh,huh?"

"I heard Keefe and Kelsey making plans that you'll come back to our house with us when it's fixed, and Blaire and Wade can live in the town house."

Lou shot up to a sitting position. "What?" she yelped.

"Actually, it seemed like a pretty good idea to me. Of course, they figure we'd get married; I've never espoused cohabitation as a possible lifestyle for me or my children."

Suddenly, it seemed that all the air had sucked out of the room. Lou felt as though she'd opened a door to peer out into a mild spring morning only to find a hurricane outside. Panic beat hard in her chest.

"I can't do this right now." She had to fight to get the words out.

"This is the real thing, Lou," Whitaker said. "Real life."

"Yeah, but does it have to happen all in one day?"

"I love you, my kids love you, and I'm too old and too damned impatient to go slow."

"But *marriage!*"

"You make it sound like a disease."

"Look," she said. "I just got to the let's-trust-each-other part. You're way ahead of me."

He opened his mouth, but his beeper went off, stifling whatever he'd intended to say. With a sigh, he got up and started rummaging through the wild scatter of clothes on the floor. He'd gotten half dressed by the time he sat down on the bed again to use the phone, and buttoned his shirt with one hand while dialing with the other.

"James, this is . . ." he said. "Yeah. What's going . . . Goddamn it! Where? I'll be there in ten minutes. Make sure you find out who was first in, I want to talk . . . What? Christ Almighty!"

Lou slid off the bed and started getting dressed. By the time Whitaker had finished cursing, she'd laced her boots and fished her purse out from under the dresser.

"Where is it?" she asked.

"Downtown. A furniture store off High Street." He finished buttoning his shirt, ran his hands through his still-wet hair. "Let's go."

As soon as she stepped outside, Lou saw a broad, black pillar of smoke pouring up into the sky. Whitaker didn't give her a chance to gawk; grasping her arm in a grip that numbed her from wrist to elbow, he hustled her to the car and thrust her inside. A moment later he headed the Corolla out onto Crawford Street, weaving through the light midmorning traffic. Lou watched him out of the corner of her eye, saw a muscle jumping spasmodically in his cheek.

"Take it easy," she said. "You've got to keep perspective here."

"I'll give you perspective," he snarled. "Whoever called in the alarm said he heard screaming."

She swallowed hard against an uprush of bile. "Is it *him?* The Fire Man?"

"We don't know. We don't even know for sure it was arson. Can't get inside to look, can't get inside to see how many people were involved."

"Was the store open?"

"Wasn't supposed to be."

The muscle kept jumping, jumping in his cheek. Lou saw an edge to him she hadn't seen before, rage and fatigue and deep frustration all rolled together.

"You think he set it, don't you?" she asked.

"Yeah. We'll know for sure when the news at noon comes on, won't we?"

She put her hand on his arm. "If you let him get to you, he'll win."

"Looks like he's already winning."

He didn't look at her, and after a moment she removed her hand. His lack of response hurt more than she would have believed possible a couple of hours ago. The urge to talk left her. Folding her hands in her lap, she watched the pillar of smoke that seemed to broaden and darken as though to welcome her.

This had to be the Fire Man's doing; it looked like him, and felt like him.

As they neared the fire scene, Lou saw that the fire had been brought under control. Too late for the store, Lou thought, looking at the gaping holes that had once been the display windows, and certainly too late for whoever had been inside.

Whitaker pulled up behind the police cruiser that blocked this portion of High Street and put the car in park.

"What can I do to help?" Lou asked

He turned a cold, preoccupied gaze on her. "Go home. Go *straight* home."

"But—"

"For once, just do it the easy way, Lou."

She looked into his eyes, saw the stark bleakness there, and nodded. "Okay. Straight home."

He got out of the car and walked away. Lou watched him show his ID to the policeman and be let into the fire scene.

Her gaze returned to what had once been the furniture store. Someone had been in there. Her mind conjured an image of some poor soul running from window to window, door to door trying to find a way out. Choking in the smoke, pursued by the fire, finally cornered . . . She shook her head, dispelling the vision. But she couldn't stop the echoes of screaming in her mind.

Had the Fire Man watched this blaze, too? Had he stood out in the street somewhere, listening to those cries? How did it feel, she wondered, to hear such agony and know that you were at fault?

If he were anyone else, she would have wished him straight to hell. But that bastard would probably love it there; fire and brimstone, just his kind of place. And old Satan would have just the right kind of work for him.

Her watch caught a pulse of garish light from the whirl of emergency lights. Lou's gaze shifted, focused. Ten-twenty. Almost exactly twelve hours ago, George Fagan and his companion had been dying in the tank. *A new day, another death.*

She felt chilled, despite the heat and chaos. Sliding across the console to the driver's seat, she put the Corolla in reverse and backed away from the barricade.

Twenty-five

All hell broke loose the moment Lou walked into her town house. Amid the onslaught of questions, she tried to juggle her purse, briefcase and thoughts while trying to fend off an overenthusiastic Shamu. Finally she dropped it all and held up her arms to quell the babble.

"Pipe down!" she yelled, gaining a small bit of space in the din.

"Did you say yes?" Kelsey's question seemed to echo in the sudden quiet.

Lou felt as though someone had ripped the skin off her face; stripped bare and hurting. She wished Whitaker had let her know he was offering a group proposal. Right now, she couldn't deal with the kids' demands any more than Whitaker's. But, looking down into Kelsey's clear grey eyes, so much like her father's, and couldn't seem to find anger in her heart.

She cupped the child's chin in her hand, feeling the delicate bone structure beneath the flesh. "Honey, your dad and I have hardly had a chance to talk. Why don't we leave it for later?"

"But Dad said he was—"

Wade stepped into the breach, bless him. "Mom,

Kathy Nesmith happens to be sitting in the kitchen, waiting to talk to you."

"Kathy Nesmith?" Lou echoed.

"She's pretty upset." Blaire moved Kelsey aside gently, then put her hand on Lou's shoulder. "What about you? Are you okay?"

"Sure. I'm fine." *And feeling as transparent as glass—and as brittle.* It wouldn't have been so bad if she didn't care for these kids. With a sigh, she turned away. "I'd better go talk to Kathy."

Shamu came with her. Lou let her fingertips trail along the dog's grey-brindled back as they walked. The contact was comforting, and more important, undemanding.

"There are some fresh cinnamon buns in the oven," Blaire called after her.

Lou's mood brightened a bit. It brightened a bit more when Ali shot out from under the sofa and ran to meet her. She picked the kitten up, tucking the double handful of fur against the side of her neck. She could feel the purr down to her toes. Cats and dogs and cinnamon buns—there were some compensations in this life.

Kathy looked up as the trio walked into the kitchen, and it was obvious that she'd been crying. Lou might have tried to comfort her, but her crossed arms and hunched shoulders clearly stated a don't-touch-me-or-I'll-start-to-cry-again warning. Lou understood, having been there before. So, instead of a hug, she offered a glass of orange juice.

Kathy shook her head. Lou split a bun—very unevenly—between the kitten and Shamu, then took the plate of glistening, fragrant pastries to the table. She hadn't eaten since about eight the night before. Her whole being yearned toward those buns; if it had been possible to inhale the whole plateful along with the

330

aroma, she would have done it. But, conscious of Kathy's distress, she propped her elbows on the table and waited for the other woman to speak.

It took a visible effort, but Kathy managed it. "I know you had a rough night. I'm sorry to bother you—" she began.

"Don't apologize," Lou said. "I told you to come to me if you needed to."

"I know. That's why I'm here." Kathy's hands shook as she clasped them on the table in front of her. She drew in a deep, shuddering breath. "The police came to my house this morning."

"Ah."

"They told me about George Fagan and that other man being killed down in the tank. And they asked me a lot of questions about Jay. I didn't know what to think, who to . . . Lou, was it really murder?"

"Yeah," Lou said, remembering the sound the gas can made as it smashed onto the floor of the tank, the brief, bright incandescence that stole the lives of two men.

"They said Jay is suspected of helping George Fagan pass some bad repairs out of the yard. Is that true?"

"Yes."

Kathy bowed her head for a moment, then looked directly into Lou's eyes. "That's why you came out to look at Jay's files. You've been tracking this down, right?"

"Right."

"Why didn't you tell me?"

"How could I be sure you wouldn't tell him? Then he'd run again, and his cronies would bury the evidence so deep it would take me years to dig it all up."

Lou set the bun aside and licked the sugar off her fingers. "Look, if you know where he is—"

"I don't. The detectives didn't believe me, but I don't. Lou, is he . . . in trouble with the law?"

"Christ, Kathy, yes! Two men died last night because of what George and company were doing. And Jay's probably number one on those detectives' list."

"Jay? Murder?"

Seeing the incomprehension on Kathy's face, Lou gritted her teeth in frustration. "What are they supposed to think, Kathy? He's hiding out, not telling anyone anything, and all of a sudden his main partner gets killed."

Kathy shook her head. "Someone else must be involved."

"Maybe. But if so, Jay ought to run to the police and tell them everything he knows. That guy killed two people already, and I'm sure he wouldn't have any problem getting rid of the only person who could identify him."

Lou saw Kathy flinch from the brutality of it. But there it was: reality. And more was coming. "Even if he answers the cops' questions about last night, he's got plenty of other things to answer for."

"The inspections?"

"Yeah. He sent a ship out of here with a faulty boiler valve weld. You know as well as I do that the inspector is responsible for the repairs he or she passes, both morally and legally. If that weld goes and someone dies, it'll be Jay's fault. He'll go to prison."

"Do they think he took bribes?" Kathy asked.

"Yeah."

With a sudden movement, the blond woman got up from her chair and started to pace the room. Obviously, she needed time to think. Lou gave it to her, taking the opportunity to finish off two more cinnamon buns and a glass of orange juice.

As suddenly as she'd gotten up, Kathy slid back into her chair. "I'm trying to be objective about this," she said. "I'm trying to judge, not as Jay's wife, but as someone who's known him almost fifteen years. And I simply can't imagine him doing something like this for money."

"He was drinking, maybe doing a little gambling—"

"Not for money."

"Kathy—"

"Jay isn't perfect. Sure, we had some problems. He might have run around in bars a little, maybe even run to another woman there at the end. But he wouldn't have taken a bribe to pass a bad weld."

"Then why do *you* think he did it?" Lou asked.

"I don't know. Maybe they threatened him, maybe they held something else over his head. He's as capable of selling his soul as the next man—but not for money."

Lou felt sorry for her. Partly because of her pain, partly because she was too nice for this to be happening to her. She'd never learned to stand up and bark, and to realize that to be labeled a bitch was to be labeled a survivor.

"I know what you're thinking," Kathy said.

"Huh?"

"It's all over your face: Poor Kathy, she just doesn't see what's going on. She's just not tough enough. Well, you're wrong." She pushed her hair back with hands that shook just a little. "I'm not saying this about Jay because I'm a dutiful, long-suffering wife. I filed for divorce yesterday."

"You did *what?*" Lou asked, completely dumbfounded.

"I filed for divorce." With massive dignity, Kathy pushed her chair back and rose to her feet. "I could have forgiven the drinking. I could even have forgiven another woman. I would have stood by him through this thing, no matter why he did it. But he ran away. He left me and the kids to watch and wonder and cry because we couldn't understand why he didn't want us with him. And the one thing I can't stomach is cowardice."

"Are you sure that's what you want?" Lou asked.

"Of course I don't want it. But that's what it has to be, unless he does something to earn back the respect I once had for him."

Lou got to her feet and stood facing the other woman. "I take back what I thought about you being too nice to make it in this world," she said. "You know how to bark just fine."

"It took some doing, but I learned."

Impulsively, Lou held out her arms. Kathy stepped into them, hugged her hard, then pulled back.

"Thanks," she said.

Lou smiled, inordinately pleased. "Stay in touch?"

"You bet. I'd better get going; the kids are with a sitter and the meter's running. If I hear anything from Jay, I'll let you know. And remember what I told you. Not for money."

"I'll remember," Lou said. "Take a bun with you. They're delicious."

Kathy shook her head. "I'm on a diet. I want to be a size ten by Labor Day. I want the outside to match the new inside."

She marched out. Lou saluted the empty doorway, admiring the new Kathy. Maybe some day she'd discover a new Lou Malotti, turn her life around, get a new hairdo and a new outlook. Today, however, she was a forty-three-year-old woman who'd seen too much ugliness and too little sleep, and who badly needed another cinnamon bun.

The Fire Man sat in his car and watched the town house. A light went on upstairs, went out again a couple of minutes later. *Her* room. She'd be getting some sleep, then, after a night at the shipyard and a morning screwing Whitaker. Busy times for Lou Malotti.

Downstairs, the living-room curtains were open, and he could see the arson investigator's children. People everywhere, protecting one another, protecting *her.*

He'd thought he'd done the right thing in striking against Whitaker. But it had been a mistake, one he was paying for now. If he hadn't burned Whitaker's house, *she* would have been alone in there. He could have walked in and taken what he wanted from her. Now, all he had was the bitter, empty taste this morning's fire had left in his mouth, the coldness of dissatisfaction in his heart.

"What do I have to do to get rid of you?" he said, forcing the words through a throat gone tight with rage.

He felt the power hovering just out of reach. Taunting him. Daring him to reach out and take it back. Closing his eyes, he rested his forehead against the steering wheel and tried to pull it in.

Nothing.

He beat his fists on the steering wheel. *Damn her, damn her . . . She doesn't even understand what she's done.* He wanted that pleasure back. He wanted to feel that heady sense of owning the world as he watched a fire finish the destruction he'd begun. He'd take it back from her the only way he could.

The right way. He stared into the empty darkness of

his soul. It yawned hungrily, wanting to be filled. Needing the power, needing the destruction.

"Bitch," he muttered. "Bitch."

He'd strip her soul and cast her to the flames, and he'd take back what belonged to him. He wanted to do it now. Just walk in there and do it. He shook with anticipation, long, shuddering tremors that made his teeth chatter. Soon. It had to be soon.

A high-pitched bark brought his gaze up to his rearview mirror. "God damn it," he muttered, seeing the old lady with the Scotties come out of her town house and start across the parking lot toward him.

Shit. He hadn't parked in the visitors' spaces, and now the old biddy had come out to give him hell. He might not be driving the same car, but she'd recognize his face for sure.

It took some struggle to resist the urge to put the Cavalier in reverse and take the old woman out for good. Slamming the car into drive, he scooted out of the parking lot before she could get close enough to see his face. He could see her staring after him, forcibly restraining the Scotties as they lunged at the end of their tethers. God damn dogs.

"Malotti, you sure are a lot of trouble," he muttered.

Well, as the preachers liked to say, the time of reckoning was near.

Lou lay on her back in bed, exhausted but not able to sleep. It might be because of Shamu, who tended to hog the bed. Lou hadn't wanted company, but, facing the wolfhound's piteous expression and soulful brown eyes, she hadn't had the courage to say no. The dog had started out at the foot of the bed, but had managed to insinuate herself upward until her head occupied the pillow. She also snored. Not to be out-done, Ali had decided to make her bed on Lou's chest, which was fine until she got happy and started knead-ing her claws on the soft padding beneath her.

"Ouch," Lou said, gently disengaging the sharp little points.

Let's face it, Malotti. It's not them. You're just plain scared. Yes, she was. If she went to sleep, she might have to relive the accident in the tank, or face the flames that seemed to hover at the edges of her con-sciousness lately, waiting for her dreams like a bright, baleful vulture. The real and the imagined. Lou wasn't sure which would be worse.

Someone knocked softly at the door. "It's me," Whi-taker called. "Lou, I've got to talk to you."

"Come on in, it's unlocked."

She watched the door swing open, wondering what she was going to feel. Anger ought to be appropriate for a man who'd tried to use his kids to tie her down. But somehow, it just wasn't there. Maybe it was the fact that he looked as tired as she felt, and she realized it was as much spiritual as physical. He'd known the arsonist would kill some day, and had fought with all his resources to catch him before that happened. Being the kind of man he was, he'd consider himself person-ally responsible for that failure.

"Was it the Fire Man?" she asked, knowing the an-swer, dreading the confirmation.

"Yeah. He called in his accomplishment to Kursk at WAVY-10, as usual. Seemed downright proud of what he'd done."

"How bad was it?"

"We found the remains of one person," he said, clos-ing the door behind him and propping his back against it. "The owner of the store is missing, and we suspect

337

the body is his. Can't tell for sure yet; there isn't enough left of him for a visual ID. Judging from the position in which we found him, he'd been tied up."

"Tied . . . Oh, God." Lou couldn't control the involuntary shudder that ran up her spine. "I thought it was an accident, that the arsonist had set the fire without knowing anyone was in the building."

Whitaker's lips thinned. "We found the remains near the fire's point of origin."

"You mean . . . he was put there to burn."

"Put there to burn? Hell, he'd been doused and lit." His voice blurred, almost broke. "The owner was seventy years old. Had a bad heart, his wife said, and weighed a hundred and thirty pounds. He couldn't have put up much of a fight."

Lou shuddered again, imagining the Fire Man's dark figure silhouetted against the flames as he tossed a screaming man onto the pyre. Sacrifice. Seeing the haunted look in Whitaker's eyes, she knew he was looking at the same scene.

"He treated that old man like a side of beef at a backyard barbecue," he said, violence raging in his eyes, his voice. "He wanted him to burn."

"He wants everything to burn," Lou said.

That battleship-grey gaze snapped to her face. Looking into his eyes was like staring straight down into a volcano. She knew he'd seen his own children at that fire scene, imagined finding them as he'd found today's victim. Rage burned in his eyes. Implacable. Primitive. If he ever got his hands on the arsonist, there might not be anything left for the justice system to prosecute.

Someone else might have been afraid of such powerful hatred. Not Lou; it was only a reflection of her own. A powerful bond, that shared hate, perhaps as strong and blinding as love. Perhaps more so. But then,

338

extraordinary circumstances bred extraordinary feelings.

She pulled back from them. But not so far that she couldn't respond to the need for comfort in Whitaker's eyes. "It's not your fault, and you know it," she said.

He held out his hands. Big, square capable hands that shook just a bit. "It's my job to stop him. What's next? Will he go after a school, a hospital?"

Will he come after my children again?

The thought seemed to burn in the air between them, and Lou wasn't sure if it was his or hers. "You'll catch him," she said.

"I hope you're right." Some of the ugly emotion drained from his eyes. With a sigh, he raked his hand through his hair. "I've got mountains of data on every fire scene. I've got miles of videotape—every face in every crowd that gathered to watch his fires, and thousands of license-plate numbers. We can't find a single match-up. He's smart, and he knows what we're trying to do. If he drives in, he either parks some distance away or takes a different car each time. I thought we had him when he left the gas can at my house, but he'd wiped the thing clean, or else had worn gloves."

"He has to screw up sometime, somewhere." Needing comfort, she stroked the kitten's fur. Ali's purr went up a notch.

Whitaker's gaze dropped to her hands, and something new came into his eyes. "Have you gotten any sleep?"

"All I'm going to get. Why?"

"Because I want to crawl in that bed with you and snuggle up for a while."

"Where are the kids?" she asked.

"Downstairs."

"Ah, I don't think—"

"Take it easy, Malotti. I just need a little warming of my soul. Besides, I've got to leave for the station house in thirty minutes, and that ain't even enough to get started."

"I remember," Lou said, *her* soul warmed by the memory.

Her thoughts must have shown in her face, for he pushed away from the door and walked toward her.

"I ought to toss you out on your ear for letting those kids think—"

"Take it easy, Lou. They were the ones who brought up the subject of marriage. Came to me in a goddamn committee and asked if I was ever going work up the courage to ask you."

Lou sighed. "And was my son involved in this?"

"Do you think he's any less interfering than my crew? Not only that, he took me aside and gave me a lecture about safe sex."

Lou's jaw dropped in astonishment. "He didn't."

"He damn well did." Whitaker stopped at the foot of the bed and surveyed the territory. "Shamu, move your butt. You're in my spot."

Without lifting her head from the pillow, the wolf-hound sucked in air, let it out in a long, good-natured growl. Ali's ears went back.

"Hey, don't scare the cat," Lou said in some alarm.

Whitaker reached out and scooped Ali up off her chest. Tucking the kitten in the crook of his arm, he cocked his head to one side and regarded the wolf-hound.

"I think it's time to eat," he said.

The bed lurched as the big dog hopped off. Whitaker opened the door to let her out, and Ali jumped down to follow Shamu.

"That was sneaky," Lou said. "And mean—what are

340

they going to think when they get downstairs and find no food?"

"What makes you think they'll starve? Shamu trained those kids a long time ago; she wants to get fed, she'll get fed."

He settled on the bed, curling his arm around her. Lou found herself turned, pulled in and cupped into the curve of his body. His embrace wasn't sexual, didn't ask her for anything but comfort in a world that seemed too cold and uncontrolled to face alone.

A truce, setting aside the demands that had driven a barrier between them earlier today. It felt good. Damn good. And for now, it was enough for them both.

Twenty-six

Lou stopped at the main gate to collect her body-guard. Irwin Smith was one of those "average" people: average height, average build, a face you wouldn't remember ten minutes after leaving his company. He fell somewhere in the middle of the bright-and-not-so-bright range, which meant he'd probably keep her in sight and also have sense enough to let her get some work done.

"You look like hell," he said in greeting. "Didn't you get any sleep at all?"

"None to speak of."

"Where to first?"

"Up to the office to pick up my schedule. How are things going tonight?"

"Like shit," he said cheerfully. "Nobody wants to work."

"So, what's new?"

Since that was the entire stretch of common ground between them, the conversation lagged. Irwin walked beside her, arms swinging, lips pursed in a soundless whistle. He seemed to be pleased with his assignment—even pushed the elevator button for her.

"What did it feel like when that guy threw the can in?" he asked.

Ah, morbid curiosity, Lou thought. One of mankind's less attractive traits. "Like being one of those bugs in a Raid commercial."

"Scary, huh?"

"You could say that." *And probably will.*

"Man, I tell you, that was one ugly happening. People told me both guys looked like they'd seen the Devil himself. And their mouths were open, like they'd tried to scream. I wish I coulda seen it."

Fortunately, the elevator doors opened before she could reply. Irwin stepped back to let her go first, then cursed softly and caught her arm. "I'd better go first. Check things out."

"Yeah. Go catch that bullet for me, Irwin."

His stride checked abruptly. Just as alarm started to spread across his face, Steggans stepped into view.

"Don't tease the man, Lou," he said.

"I couldn't help it."

He shook his head. "Come on out, both of you. I promise there are no assassins lurking among the partitions."

Lou winked at him when she went past. "You're working late again?"

"Uh-huh. But I was just getting ready to head home. It's been a real bastard of a day."

"What's the problem?"

He blew his breath out with a hiss. "No one wants to work on the *Corinne.* I've been through hell trying to get something done on her."

"Sure, nobody wants to work her," Irwin said. "They figure she's jinxed now."

"I don't believe in jinxes," Lou said.

The words seemed to fall with a thump in the quiet

of the office. Both men turned to look at her, and she felt as though a trap had just clanged shut around her.

"Good," Steggans said. "Then you won't mind climbing down in that tank to inspect the repalr.

"Tonight?" Her voice sounded a bit hollow.

"They're not going to be finished for a couple of days, but I'd like you to check on how things are coming along. I don't want anyone rushing that job."

Both men watched her, speculation in their eyes. She knew what they were thinking: Is Malotti going to back down? Is she going to admit she's frightened and ask that someone else do the job?

Twenty-three years of fighting for respect stiffened her spine. Twenty-three years of knowing that to back down meant failure in men's eyes, and that she wasn't quite good enough.

You'd think I've already proven everything I need to prove.

"I don't mind," she lied.

She saw a different expression cross Irwin's face as he realized that he'd probably have to go down into that tank with her. It was some compensation, but not much.

"Well, I'm out of here," Steggans said. "I put the schedule on your desk. It's not that heavy tonight, so I expect you'll be able to get a report on the *Corinne* on my desk by morning."

Lou nodded. "I expect so."

"Keep your eyes open, Irwin," he said, turning toward the elevator. "QA inspectors are getting as scarce as hens' teeth around here."

"Famous last words," Lou muttered.

"What'd you say?" Irwin asked.

"Nothing. Just let me grab my messages and hardhat and then we can get the dirty deed done."

He looked as though he'd rather wait. Lou smiled a bit grimly as she punched her message code into the phone.

Beep. "This is Louis Delanski. You're scheduled to inspect the wiring on the *Whippoorwill.* I need to re-schedule for later. Get back with me."

Beep. "Malotti, this is Jeffries, down in the machine shop. I need to go over the specs they gave me on a fitting for the LPH. Before midnight, if you can."

"Yeah, yeah," she muttered. "Get in line."

Beep. "Lou, Whitaker. I've got to chase down a lead tonight, probably won't be able to pick you up in the morning like I promised. Wade said he'd wait for you at the front gate. Anything else breaks, I'll call you."

A lead. She let her breath out in a long sigh. God, she hoped something would come of it. Sometimes it seemed as though she'd have to live with that madman forever, afraid to sleep, afraid to dream lest he come in to haunt her.

You're letting your imagination run away with you, old girl. If you've got to worry about something, worry about climbing back down into that tank. That's reality.

"You coming, Malotti?" Irwin called impatiently.

"Yeah." She grabbed her hardhat off the top of the file cabinet and jammed it on, then collected her guardian and headed out into the yard.

A few minutes later, she and Irwin stood at the tank hatch and watched as a three-man crew climbed up the ladder. The last guy came up a lot faster than the rest. Didn't want to be left alone, Lou thought. At another time she might have said something about it, but not tonight.

"Creepy down there," one said.

"Maybe it's haunted," Irwin supplied.

The men turned and walked away. One muttered

345

something about giving him a hand down—and bypassing the ladder. Lou moved closer to the hatch and looked down. The tank looked exactly the same as it had last night when she'd first gone down. But it would never be the same; two men had died in there, and neither she nor anyone else was going to forget that.

"You sure you want to do this?" Irwin asked.

"It's part of the job," she said, while her insides slowly coiled into a cold, hard knot.

"I'll stay up here," he said, then added, "Hey, that crew just came up from there, so we can be sure no one's waiting to grab you. I'll do you more good keeping watch up here."

Lou stared at him. "Logic." *Of convenience,* she added silently. "Just make sure nobody slams that hatch while I'm down there, and you'll be my hero forever."

"Have a ball."

"Yeah."

She touched the powerful flashlight she'd picked up on the way over, shifting the tool belt so its weight hung against her hip, then swung onto the ladder. The knot in her insides became harder and colder.

"Hey," Irwin called, "don't forget we've got a break coming in a half hour."

"I'm not going to be down there that long, believe me."

She didn't want to go down. Her muscles tensed and jumped as the forced them to do what she wanted. Mind over body, she reminded herself. Her breath rasped, loudly enough that she worried about Irwin hearing it.

Why do you care? He didn't have the balls to come down with you.

Maybe not. But it mattered, to her and to the guys

she worked with. So she went down, one rung at a time, while her instincts screamed to go the other way. She made it to the bottom at last. Stepping away from the ladder took some effort.

Irwin's head and shoulders appeared in the opening above. "You okay?"

"I'm fine," she lied.

For all its size, the tank felt like a coffin. Her coffin. She forced herself into routine: Check the lights for open outlets, check the floor for obstacles, then step through the bulkhead into the next section. Do it again. And again. Her stomach muscles twitched and quivered, and fear clung with sharp little claws to the space between her shoulderblades.

She reached the last compartment. Her gaze lingered on the spot where George had stood. Over there was where the other guy—Lou couldn't remember his name—had begun working on the damaged section. Her imagination conjured up that last moment, when the new man had touched the grinder to the metal. That first spark . . .

Thrusting the image away, she forced herself to concentrate on the job at hand. She frowned, noting signs of hasty work. Not that she blamed the crew for feeling twitchy down here, but the job still had to be done right. Apparently she was going to have to ride herd. With a sigh, she reconciled herself to the fact that all those old Lucretia jokes were going to start circulating again.

And she was going to have to spend a good bit of time in this tank.

"Lovely," she muttered.

The lights went out. Her breath went with it, and for a moment she was sure she was suffocating. Then reflex kicked in, and she pulled in air with a gasp. She stood still, enclosed in darkness, while spots skittered across her vision. Her ears seemed hypersensitive, translating every tiny noise into the metal-on-metal crash of something falling into the tank.

She wanted to scream, run, fling herself against the hard metal walls and batter her way through. Her breath sobbed in her throat. Would she register the flash, or would she just drop into black airlessness?

Take it easy. Keep your head, or you'll have no chance at all. One step at a time.

Forcing herself to move slowly and carefully, she pulled the flashlight out of her tool belt and switched it on. Light speared through the darkness. Everything looked different now, knife-edged shadows outlining every brace and angle.

She slid a wrench out of her tool belt and hefted it before stepping through the bulkhead opening into the next compartment. Not that it would help her if someone decided to drop another gas can down here.

She started moving faster and faster, not caring if Jack the Ripper were waiting for her if he would just kill her up on deck. Time was measured in heartbeats, and those were going by awfully fast.

"Lou? Hey, Lou!"

Irwin's voice. It was the sweetest sound she'd ever heard. She could see light up ahead, radiance coming like the hand of God through the hatch above. As she stepped through the last bulkhead opening, she saw his head silhouetted against the light.

"I'm okay," she called. "What's going on up there?"

"Some fuckers were being funny," he said. "Thought they'd give you a scare. Pulled the plug to see if you'd howl."

"It was a joke?" Her voice rose as a red haze of fury clouded her vision. "A JOKE?" she screamed.

She didn't remember climbing the ladder. She only vaguely remembered swarming out onto the deck. But she did register the three men standing a few yards away, grinning like apes, and the fact that she was still holding the wrench.

"Hey, Malotti," one called. "Was it spooky? Are we gonna have to send a cleanup crew down there again?"

With a cry that came somewhere from the depths of primal memory, she went for them. They scattered. Behind her, Irwin yelled, "Get 'em, Malotti! Run, boys. Run before she gets you!"

They outran her, unfortunately—or fortunately, depending on point of view. She stopped, resting her hands on her bent knees as she tried to catch her breath. Out of the corner of her eye, she saw Irwin and Tate Bucholtz trotting to join her.

"You almost got 'em," Tate said. "Sorry bastards."

"Twenty years ago . . . ten years ago, I'd have caught them," she panted.

"We're all getting old, Malotti."

"Yeah. Too old to get the crap scared out of me like that."

"Sorry about that," he said. "I expected even twenty-year-old dickheads to have more sense than to pull something like that."

Lou straightened. "Just testing the lady QA inspector, I guess. They're not the first, and unfortunately, probably not the last. You know who they are?"

"Got 'em registered right here." He tapped his forehead. "I can get them fired, if you want. I don't think the brass is going to find their humor very amusing."

Tempting. But in twenty-three years, she'd never gone whining to management about anything personal, and she wasn't about to start now. Besides, there were worse things than being canned, and she wanted to give them the experience.

"No, I don't want them fired," she said. "I want them assigned to cleaning out bilges with Q-Tips for a month or so."

Grinning, Tate ripped off a salute. "Yes, ma'am, Lucretia, ma'am. It will be done."

Irwin handed Lou the hardhat that had fallen off during the chase. "The flashlight's down in the tank. I don't suppose you're interested in fetching it?"

"Not on your life." She fitted the hat on, then headed for the gangplank. "Come on, Irwin. We've got work to do."

The security guard remained silent for a while, but it was obvious that something was percolating. Finally he said, "I hope you don't think I had anything to do with it. I never left my post, never let anyone near the hatch."

"It's over, Irwin. Let's just forget it." She didn't necessarily believe in his innocence, but the issue wasn't worth pursuing. Her adrenaline rush had faded, leaving her feeling a hundred years old. She checked her watch. "Hey, it's time for a break. What say we brave the crowd and get something to eat?"

Relief washed over his face. "Sure."

Since he happened to be out of cash, Lou paid for his dinner. He chose the barbecue sandwich; she checked her pocket for her antacids, then ordered the same. She took a mouthful as they walked, savoring the taste that was hot and sweet and vinegary all at once. Too bad something that tasted so good seemed to spontaneously combust after contact with her digestive juices.

"Hey, what's going on with the investigation?" Irwin asked.

She swallowed. "How should I know?"

"Hell, ain't your boyfriend head of the whole she-bang?"

"Boyfriend?"

"You know, the arson investigator."

With a sigh, she put her sandwich down. "Where did you hear that?"

"Cripes, Malotti, I don't know."

Lou grimaced, amazed at how fast things got around. Why the hell would George, or anyone else, for that matter, be interested in her love life? Something scratched at the fringes of her consciousness, asking to be let in. She reached for it . . .

"So," Irwin said, shattering the moment, "Where do you want to go?"

"Let's head out to the dry dock. No one will be there at break time, and I want some peace and quiet with my supper. By the way, how *did* you hear the rumor about me and Whitaker?"

"Whit . . . Oh, the arson investigator." He crunched a potato chip while pondering that. "You really have a one-track mind, you know that?"

"Yeah. How?"

"Hell, I think it was George Fagan who told me." He crunched another chip. "Doesn't seem like much to gossip about, but then you don't give 'em much. I mean, if you'd been stealin' petty cash or having an affair with the boss, they might not have been inter-ested in the arson guy. But since nobody knows noth-ing about Lou Malotti's private life, this was news."

Lou fell silent. She and Whitaker hadn't exactly been *out* together. So, how had Fagan known?

"That's the last navy contract for a while, isn't it?" Irwin said, indicating the ship resting in the dry dock just ahead.

"Unfortunately."

"It's a damn good thing we've got these Enterprise jobs, or we'd all be walking the streets. Hey!" he said, snapping his fingers, "Speaking of gossip, do you want to hear something good? It's hot off the press."

"Not really," she said. All she wanted was a quiet spot and the chance to think. This guy talked so much that she couldn't string two thoughts together.

"You know that Ben Estermann and Cindy in Accounting have been an item for a couple of months, don't you?"

"No, and I—"

"Well, the other day they were in the office after hours, screwing up a storm on top of old Wolcott's desk. Knocked papers everywhere, broke his paperweight—"

"Look, Irwin, I don't—"

"Spilled grape juice all over his blotter."

"Grape juice?" Lou asked, startled.

He nodded. "Looked like somebody got killed in there. Lots of speculation going on as to what they were doing with it. Some people think they were drinking it and just happened to get carried away, but most votes go for something messy and kinky . . ."

He launched into a list of the possibilities. Desperation set in, and Lou started looking for an escape. Suddenly he broke off, and she almost gasped in relief.

"Let's stop here for a minute," he said, pointing to the line of shops to their left. "I gotta go to the can."

She held his plate for him while he ducked into the paint shop, silent and empty with everyone at break. Lou treasured the silence. A minute ticked by, then another. Glancing down at the plates, she saw that the barbecue had cooled enough for the grease to begin to congeal.

"Come on, Irwin!" she muttered.

Another minute went by. She poked her head into the doorway and called, "Hey, Irwin! What are you doing in there, reading a book?"

No answer. With a sigh, she stepped into the room. "Hey, Irwin!"

Again, no answer. She set the plates on a nearby work table, intending to go knock on the bathroom door and roust him out. But then she stopped, instinct shrieking at her that something wasn't right. The bathroom door hung open.

She held her breath, straining to hear. Hoping for anything. There was only silence. But a part of her that had nothing to do with sight or hearing caught something in that room, a malevolence that seemed to roll toward her like a dark sea. It enveloped her, submerged her. Terror beat frantic wings in her chest.

He was here. The Fire Man.

Insane as it seemed, he was here. She didn't know how he'd gotten in, didn't care.

Without looking away from the bathroom doorway, she moved toward the foreman's desk, and the phone. She picked it up, sure that *he* would come charging out to stop her. He didn't, and something cold and hard dropped in her stomach. Of course. She stood for a moment with the dead receiver to her ear, her body refusing to believe her mind.

Then she dropped it and ran.

Twenty-seven

Lou caught the doorjamb to swing herself around the corner. Footsteps sounded behind her, quick and urgent. Faster than hers. Her breath came in fear-driven rasps. She turned a corner, turned one again, then ducked into cover behind a couple of fifty-gallon drums.

The footsteps faded. But the taste of his hate lay strong all around her, and her danger sense howled a warning in her brain. She looked down the line of shops. Pipe shop, boiler shop, rigger . . . all quiet and empty. And she'd bet he'd taken care of the phones in every one. He'd picked his time well; she could scream her head off and he would be the only one to hear.

She peered around one of the barrels toward the long, cinderblock rectangle of the machine shop a few dozen yards away. The door was closed, but she could hear a radio inside, the solid thump-thump of rock music audible even here.

Help. If she could just get there, she'd be safe. A few dozen yards of open space, a few seconds of exposure. It didn't sound like much. But just now it looked like miles.

He'll see me. He'll come after me.

The Fire Man. How had he gotten into the shipyard? And why had he come? Lou Malotti was no threat to him, never had been. Or was it some crazy way of getting back at Whitaker? In the end, it didn't matter; he'd come for her. Right in the middle of the yard, with all its lights and people, he'd come. And despite the lights and people, he'd managed to isolate her.

She didn't think he had good things planned.

Fire crackled in her mind, for a moment so real that she thought she could feel its heat. It brought terror with it, bright and powerful. Something bubbled up in her throat that sounded suspiciously like a sob. She pressed the heel of her hand against her teeth, bit down hard. The pain steadied her. The terror retreated—not gone, but held at bay for the moment.

She pressed the knob to light the dial of her watch. Nearly twenty minutes until break was up and those lights and people came back. She didn't think she had that long.

Where is he? She could feel him somewhere close, knew he was waiting. If she made a run for it, he might catch her before she could get to the machine shop. But if she stayed . . .

"Like a rat in a trap," she muttered. "Not me!"

Careful not to jingle, she slid her tool belt off and laid it aside. She hefted the wrench, wishing it were her .38, damning the rule that banned firearms from the shipyard. The wrench lay cold in her palm—not much of a weapon against a madman.

It's all you've got, Malotti. Use it, and use your head.

With a sudden burst of motion, she sprang out from the shelter of the barrels and pelted toward the machine shop. Her hardhat slid off her head and bounced on the asphalt behind her. The back of her neck twitched with the anticipation of footsteps, of a hand grabbing her. But she made it. Made it!

She pressed her back against the cinderblock wall and surveyed the area around her. The scene came in bits and pieces like snapshots: the line of shops against the backdrop of the dry dock, the navy cruiser hovering above like an avenging angel, the water of the nearby wet slip gleaming black and oily beneath the lights. There was no sign of movement. No dark, swooping form leaping out to catch her.

Lou swallowed hard. She couldn't see him, but she could feel him. She could almost taste his emotions. Her chest rose and fell as she tried to control her breathing. Hate, as hot and deadly as flame, as twisted as the man himself. The why of it didn't matter; the hate existed, and she had to somehow find a way to save herself from it.

She slid along the wall, feeling her way with her hands so she wouldn't have to stop watching for movement. The blocks rough and comforting against her palms. Comforting in a world gone askew. She kept moving, her lips moving in unconscious prayer. *Just a few feet, and please, God, let the door be unlocked.*

Feeling the change of surface as she reached the door, she groped behind her for the knob. A moment later she made it inside, closed the door behind her. Locked it. Took a deep breath, tasted safety.

This shop consisted of a large, L-shaped space that wrapped around the paint storage warehouse. It was filled with equipment, from grinders and saws to huge lathes. The music came from the far end of the L, out of her field of view. The foreman's desk was back there, too. And the phone.

Grit rasped beneath her boots as she walked toward the far end of the room. Three windows pierced the longest wall of the L, and each held the possibility of danger. She watched those rectangles of dirty glass for any sign of movement.

She rounded the corner of the L. "Hey, I need—" she broke off abruptly, disbelief shafting through her as she found the room empty.

The boom box sat atop a tool cabinet, blaring away with something Wade would have liked. Its owner must have left it playing when he went on break.

Or someone else had turned it on.

Her heart revved. She ran to the back door and wrenched it open. As she darted through, someone grabbed her by the arms.

"Hold it," he said.

Steggans. Relief brought her breath rushing out in a gasp. "Oh, man, am I glad to see you!"

"What's the matter?" he asked.

"Someone's ch—" She broke off as the light caught his hardhat, glinting like a small sun off a sticker that bore his initials.

And then she had it. It had nagged at her, this fugitive memory, but now it burst on her in a flood of realization and terror: during the Quonset hut fire, she'd caught a brief glimpse of something curved and smooth reflecting the flames. And on its lower curve sat a small rectangle, just turning brown from the head. A tiny fact, one her conscious mind had discarded. No one but Steggans marked their hardhat. Another memory, another tiny fact—a day after the fire, Steggans scooping a hardhat off Jay's file cabinet and putting it on.

She sucked air in for a scream, but he clamped his hand over her mouth and dragged her back inside.

No! Not like this!

He slammed her back against a metal cabinet with

enough force to knock her breathless. She slid down into a crouch, gulping for air. Bending, he plucked the wrench from her lax fingers and tossed it away. Then he slapped her wrists together behind her and tied them.

With frightening gentleness, he put his palm on the center of her chest and overbalanced her so that she landed on her rear. He hunkered down in front of her.

"Hello, Bitch," he said.

She opened her mouth, fully intending to scream. But then she saw him smile. No one was going to hear her; she knew it, and so did he. Slowly, she closed her mouth again.

He nodded. "You've always been quick on the up-take, haven't you?"

"You're him. The Fire Man."

"In the flesh."

"Why?"

He leaned closer. "Why am I the Fire Man, or why am I here with you?"

"Both."

"I just like fires," he said. "Always have. And I came after you because I'm tired of you meddling in my life."

Lou shook her head. With a movement that was terrifying in its swift brutality, he grabbed her by the hair and jerked her head backward.

"It was bad enough here with you busting my balls every time I turned around. People kept saying 'ask Lou Malotti, she knows what's going on; get Malotti to do it, she'll see it gets done right; have Malotti call the subcontractors, they know better than to jerk her around.' The great Lou Malotti. Everyone knew you should have had my job, and a day didn't go by when someone made it plain they thought you'd be better at it than me."

"But—"

"And then you started pushing your way into my fires. That's where you made your big mistake, Bitch. That's sacred ground, and I'm not about to share it with anybody. Everything you touched, you ruined."

Lou shook her head, denying his words, denying what she knew was about to happen to her. "I had nothing to do with your fires."

"Yes, you did." His irises had shrunk to thin, blue rings around enormously dilated pupils. She read death in those eyes. Her death. "Every time I turned around, I saw your face. You interfered. It took me a while, but I finally realized you were my own personal jinx. Don't shake your head at me," he said, raising his hand to strike. "Don't. And don't try to deny it. We're bound, Lou. Fate tapped us both as players in this, and now it's time for the game to be brought to an end."

"This isn't a game," she said. "None of it is a game. You killed a man the other day."

He nodded. "That was a waste. I thought I could get it back from him, but now I realize only the one who took it can give it back."

Time. Just buy yourself some time. Fifteen minutes. Five minutes. Anything. "Get what back?" she asked.

"The power."

This guy was *way* over the edge. Lou bit down on the inside of her lip, fighting panic. "What power?"

"Fire, Lou. The power to destroy. The power of sweeping it all away in a glorious burst of flame. They have to dance to my tune then, don't they? They have to play my game."

"How did you get away with this in the navy?"

He smiled. "The Navy was great. Nice and ordered.

359

I never set fires on ships, only when I could get away with it in ports of call. But the power was building in me all that time, and once I hit civilian life, I could set it free."

Lou watched his eyes change. Satisfaction gleamed in them, and a hot anticipation that sent terror rocketing through her chest. Flame hissed in the recesses of her mind. She'd slipped into her nightmare, and this time there was no waking up.

"You're crazy," she whispered.

"No, I'm not. I just happen to like fires. And I don't like being called names." He cupped her cheek in his hand, an almost tender gesture. Then he hit her.

Pain exploded in her face, a second blast going off as the back of her head slammed into the metal cabinet behind her. For a moment, the world reeled around her. She tasted blood, sharp and metallic and sickening.

"You're not much of a woman," he said. "Too damn pushy. You've got no right doing a man's job, and you had no right to shove your way into my personal business. You followed me that day on Effingham Street, when even a man might have thought twice about it. And that night at Whitaker's, you walked down that street, bold as brass, and *challenged* me! Did you think I was going to sit still and take it?"

Lou drew her breath in sharply. *"You* threw that gas can down into the tank!"

"Who the hell else?"

Her breath went out sharply, as though she'd been sucker-punched. Maybe she had been. *She'd* been the target, not Fagan. It hadn't had anything to do with the inspection scam at all. Two separate situations, two different kinds of danger—Steggans, all unknowing, had muddied the waters so that she couldn't trust her own instincts. The wild card. Everything clicked into place.

Fagan and Jay Nesmith became the men she'd thought them to be all along. Men she could judge, men whose motivations she understood.

And now the truth stood out, sharp and clear. She should have seen it before.

"Are you surprised that I tried to kill you?" Steggans asked.

Her attention shifted back. "Nothing you do surprises me any longer."

He got to his feet and stood looking down at her. His pupils dilated even more, and she could almost imagine flames leaping in those black depths. "You've been a real problem for me, Lou. Nothing's gone right since you touched my life. And every time I tried to do something about you, I failed."

Every time. *Every time.* Her mind scrabbled for purchase. "You tried before?"

"Maybe you're not as quick as I thought," he said, baring his teeth in something that didn't remotely resemble a smile. "Remember the carbon monoxide? I jiggered your furnace."

"You killed my parrots." A bright spark of anger bloomed amid the fear. She hugged it close, fanning it, warming her spirit. "Don't you care that you've taken innocent lives?"

"They've got nothing to do with it," he said. "I was after you."

"You went after Whitaker's kids. You can't imagine *they* had anything to do with this mess."

"The lieutenant annoyed me. I was just delivering a message to back off. I expect he got it."

"They're *kids.*"

He spread his hands wide. "It was the message that was important."

She realized that the kids' lives didn't matter to this

man, nor did the rest of the lives he'd taken. Steggans simply wasn't plugged into the same circuit as the rest of humanity.

"Are you afraid of me?" he asked, his voice soft and deadly.

Yes. Oh, yes. "No."

He slapped her again, hard enough to knock her sideways onto the floor. Her shoulder took the brunt of the impact. Jagged flashes of agony ran through her back and arms.

"You bastard!" she gasped.

With an abrupt, angry movement, he turned away, disappearing around the corner of the L. She struggled to lift herself back to a sitting position, but lacked the leverage. Panting, she lay on her throbbing shoulder and listened to the grit rasp under his feet as he walked.

He stopped. Her pulse throbbed frantically as she imagined him pouring gasoline around, lighting a match . . . No. It wasn't going to be that way. This time, he was going to make sure of her. Up close and personal.

Rasp. He'd started walking again. Coming back. *Rasp, rasp.* Purposeful, swift. Her heart settled into the same rhythm, and so did her breath. Terror dried her mouth, constricted her throat.

He came around the corner. Her gaze fastened on the can he carried, registered the faint tremble of his gloved hands. His eyes had gone heavy-lidded and hot, as though he were about to make love to her. The Fire Man's brand of love. Terror closed around her in a choking blanket.

"I want what you took from me," he said.

"Okay," she said, desperate enough to try anything. "I give it back."

He blinked, obviously taken by surprise. Then he

smiled, a real smile this time, and it was much worse than the snarl. "It's not that easy, Lou. It took me a long time to understand my mistakes. I went after you for all the right reasons, but went about it all wrong. That's why I failed. There's only one way I can free myself of you, and that's by fire."

With agonizing slowness, he unscrewed the cap. She smelled kerosene. Her skin twitched, anticipating pain.

There has to be a way out of this. I want to live. I want to walk out of here in the morning, I want to see the sunrise . . . Please, God, help me. Make someone come in, make the phone ring, anything.

The old man at the furniture store must have wished for the same thing, prayed the same prayer as the fire consumed him. So had Fagan and the other man in the brief moment before their death. Wishes hadn't helped them, nor had prayers.

You're on your own, Malotti.

He tilted the can and poured kerosene over the desk. The liquid dripped down over the side and pooled on the floor, reaching out toward her. Lou pulled her feet up reflexively.

"What do you think?" he asked, moving the can closer. "Are you afraid yet?"

Her gaze focused on the opening of the can. It seemed to swell to enormous proportions—encompassing the remainder of her life. Kerosene dribbled out, splashed on her boots, made oily, fan designs on the legs of her jeans. Adrenaline pumped through her, a sweep of mingled terror and outrage that made her chest feel about to explode.

"I asked you a question," he said.

"What?" she gasped.

"What do you think?" He moved closer, holding the

can over her so that kerosene sloshed out onto her torso. "Are you afraid yet?"

"If I said yes, would you let me go?"

"No."

"Then go to hell!" With all her strength, she kicked out with both feet, straight at his groin. And missed; the blow caught him in the lower stomach, sending him staggering backward but not incapacitating him at all.

He straightened, wiping at the kerosene that had splashed down the front of his clothing. His face twisted. "You bitch," he said. "You bitch."

Frantically, Lou hitched herself backward. He leaped forward, skidding on his knees through the pool of kerosene, and grabbed her by the ankle. She felt bones grate beneath his grip.

"You're going to pay," he snarled.

She didn't want to scream. But as he pulled her toward him, she found one rising up into her throat, irresistible.

And then his fist connected with her temple, and she fell into a roaring blackness.

Twenty-eight

Light filtered in through Lou's eyelashes. It took a moment for her to realize she was still alive, a moment more to realize Steggans still stood nearby. She'd only been out a second or two, then. Her legs lay in the pool of kerosene, and the oily liquid seemed to creep along her skin like a live thing.

Instinct cried for her to do something, anything. Panic welled in her, ran in tittering streams through her brain. She fought them both, conquered them, and lay still, watching the Fire Man from beneath her lashes.

His breath coming in rasps, he stripped off his soaked gloves and dropped them on the floor. He retrieved a towel from a nearby workbench and used it to wipe his hands. Then, with a movement rife with anger, he tossed it down on Lou's feet.

Is that it, God? Is that all you've given me to work with?

It would have to do. Her heart felt as though it were about to beat its way out of her chest. But she ignored it, concentrating on keeping her breathing slow and regular.

He turned back to her, a pack of matches in his hand. Up close and, personal, she thought. He had to do it himself, and he had to watch. She didn't know how he'd become so twisted, and didn't care. She just wanted to live.

His eyes looked completely black now, twin pools of dark delight. "Goodbye, Bitch," he said, holding the matchbook well away from his body.

The sound of the match striking echoed through her brain. Scratch! Lou's world narrowed to that tiny point, that insignificant stick of cardboard that held agonizing death for her. It flared.

With a single, galvanic effort, Lou kicked both feet, hurling the towel up and forward. Time seemed to stand still as the towel flew toward him. Lou watched it hit his hands, watched it flare as the match came into contact with kerosene-soaked fabric. Fire burst up his arms toward his chest. Shrieking, he staggered backward.

Move, Malotti, break the connection! If he hits that pool on the floor, you go up, too!

She started moving before the thought was complete. Adrenaline pulled her to her feet, got her leaping to the top of the nearest workbench. Her bound arms pulled her off balance, but she managed to straighten, then jump across to another work table. She teetered there, blindly scraping the cords binding her wrists against a saw blade. Her arms were free!

Steggans reeled, flailing his burning arms as though trying to take off. Then he staggered forward and fell against the desk. The spilled kerosene burst into flame, seeming to reach up fiery arms to embrace him. He started to run, flame trailing behind him like an incandescent coat. His skin crisped away in sheets. And still he burned. Howling, he hurled himself through the window.

The fire was between Lou and the back door, so she

launched herself off the workbench and pelted toward the front of the shop. She spotted a tarp on the way and grabbed it.

"I ought to let you burn," she said, knowing she couldn't. She wasn't like him. Wouldn't be like him.

She hit the door with her shoulder, flung it open. The night air hit her like a cool fist as she ran around the side of the building.

Steggans had fallen midway between the shop and the wet slip. His screams were continuous now, a high-pitched, almost inhuman sound of pure agony.

Sobbing in horror, she shook out the tarp and ran toward him. Something hit her, knocking her aside, then snatched her up and hurled her into the wet slip. She caught a crazy, topsy-turvy glimpse of Whitaker as she spun through the air. Then she hit the water, swallowing a bellyful of foul, oily stuff as she went down amid a torrent of bubbles.

She flailed wildly for the surface. Breaking through, she sucked air in, coughed it out again. Then she started dog paddling toward the ladder at the end of the slip.

"Lou?" Whitaker's head and shoulders came into view above her. "Come on," he said, holding his hand out to her.

Nothing had ever looked so good. Her breath went in sharply, and she swam faster. Water sluiced from her as she climbed the ladder toward him. She reached out, touched his hand. His fingers closed around her wrist.

"You *idiot,*" he snarled. "Your clothes are soaked with kerosene. If you'd touched him, you'd have gone up, too."

"Well, shit, Whitaker. Did you have to drown me to save me?"

"Just diluting the kerosene, darlin'."

Lou opened her mouth to retort. But then he hauled her upward and pulled her against him, wrapping her so close and tight that she thought her ribs were about to give way.

"You scared me," he said. "You scared me good."

She clung to him, feeling the beat of his heart against her cheek. Somehow, she'd cheated old Death. She'd cheated the Fire Man.

After a moment, she straightened, and Whitaker let her go. The machine shop swarmed with uniforms. Smoke still oozed from the broken window, but the fire appeared to be out. Lou's gaze shifted to the group of men who stood around something on the asphalt.

"Is that him?" Lou asked.

"Yeah."

The Fire Man. She started toward him, but Whitaker held her back. "You don't want to see, Lou. Trust me on this."

"I have to."

His forehead creased as he studied her. Then he nodded and led her to the cluster of men. "Let us through," he said.

They stepped aside, giving Lou her first good look at . . . him. It. The blackened hulk on the asphalt didn't look much like a man. And then a thin, mewling sound came from it, pain and protest mingled.

"Oh, God, he's still alive!" she whispered.

"Not for long," someone said. "Christ."

Lou couldn't look away. She wanted to, but she couldn't. He had no face. In fact, until he moved his arms, Lou couldn't tell whether he was lying on his front or back. Bone showed in spots. She took a deep breath, fighting the bile that rose into her throat.

This was no longer Dwayne Steggans, no longer the

Fire Man. He'd passed beyond the hate and fear and whatever twist of mind had driven him. Whimpering, he raised charred stumps of hands toward the sky. Lou closed her eyes; he'd passed beyond mercy, too.

Whitaker's arm came around her, and she realized she'd started to shake.

"Can we do anything for him?" she asked.

"No," Whitaker said. "I called for an ambulance, but I don't think anyone or anything can help him now."

She turned to look at him. No, no one could help Steggans. But Whitaker had tried. It had been an act of humanity toward a man he hated, a man who'd tried to kill his children. If anything could mark the distinction between mad and sane, this was it.

"There's a guy in the rigger shop——" she began.

"Your intrepid bodyguard. We found him. He's okay, just a knock on the head."

Steggans whimpered. Lou took a deep breath, wondering how much pain he could take and not give up. "How . . ." Her voice was a harsh rasp. She cleared her throat and tried again. "How did you know to come here?"

"Plain old grunt work," Whitaker said. "Someone spotted a blue Cavalier parked down the street from my house the night of the fire. Nothing unusual about it, but we put it on the list with everything else. Then some lady who lives in your complex called in a report of a suspicious man hanging around, driving a blue Cavalier. She took down the license plate, we checked the owner and tracked him down to a Las Vegas hotel. He said he asked a neighbor of his to take care of things for him——"

"Dwayne Steggans."

"Right. The minute I heard, I marshaled the troops and came on out."

"You got here first."

"I had more to lose than anyone else."

The look in his eyes brought feeling rushing back through her limbs. Life. She welcomed it. The Fire Man had burned all the fear from her, gave her the recklessness to take whatever life had to offer.

A crowd of shipyard workers gathered, growing larger every moment. The noise level went up dramatically. In the distance, Lou could hear sirens. Somehow, she didn't lose Steggans's whimpering amid the din.

"It's going to be a zoo," Whitaker muttered. "I'd better go help with crowd control. Coming?"

She opened her mouth to say yes, then closed it and shook her head. He stroked the back of his hand down her cheek before moving away.

Leaving her alone with the Fire Man. She didn't want to watch him die, didn't want his pain. But something tied her here, keeping a deathbed vigil for her enemy.

It wasn't easy. But, like so many things that passed before, this was between her and the Fire Man. Up front and personal. And somehow, she felt he knew she was there. Would he consider it kindness or punishment? She didn't know herself; she just had to do it.

Steggans drew breath in harshly, let it out with that mewling sound that seemed to wring her soul. Again. In, out. Lou found herself breathing with him, forced herself to change rhythm. His movements slowed. Those pitiful, upraised hands drifted downward.

The whimpers stopped. Lou felt a great weight lift off her shoulders, and imagined it flapping off into the night sky. The Fire Man had gone.

She drew a deep breath. The air flowed in, tasting sweet and cool despite the tinge of smoke. Whitaker's hands came down on her shoulders, and she let herself feel the offered comfort.

"Is it over?" he asked.

"Yeah."

He'd conjured a blanket from somewhere. Slipping it around her shoulders, he turned her toward the gate. "Come on. Looks like I'm going to have to give you another bath."

Lou didn't ask where or how or when. She just went with him, willing to take a shot at anything he had in mind.

Epilogue

It rained the day of George Fagan's funeral.

A canopy had been erected over the grave site, but the crowd overflowed it. Lou stood at the far edge of the gathering, listening to the raindrops fall upon the forest of umbrellas overhead.

In death, as in life, George was a popular man. A lot of people had come to say good-bye: George's parents, his kids, a couple of old girlfriends, his boating buddies and a slew of people from the shipyard. Even Harry Deveraux had come, with Helen to shield his wheelchair with a golf umbrella.

George's mother started to cry during the ceremony. Lou felt those tears somewhere deep inside, that small, burning place where guilt began.

The Fire Man. Madman, arsonist, wild card. Logic told her it wasn't her fault that he'd tried to kill her and got George and that other man instead. It had been a classic case of being in the wrong place at the wrong time. They'd died for it. And she couldn't shake the feeling that she'd dodged that proverbial bullet with her name on it, only to let it take the guy behind her.

A touch on her shoulder brought her swinging around. Too swiftly; it would take her time to get used to surprises again. But it was Whitaker, looking tired and drawn after nearly twenty-four hours' work. She lifted the umbrella higher to allow him in.

"Hi," she said. "I thought you weren't going to be able to make it."

"I thought you might need some moral support."

"You were right." Funny, the admission didn't hurt much, just a slight ache that might only be unfamiliarity.

It started to rain harder, drowning out the pastor's words and churning the ground into a muddy mess. The noise seemed to isolate the mourners, cutting them off in umbrella-sized pockets of privacy.

"What have you found so far?" Lou asked.

"Steggans's navy record was okay, nothing stellar, but nothing untoward, either. His CO had been surprised when he opted out at twenty. Said the guy had no close family to speak of, no home outside the navy."

"Steggans told me the 'power' took him out of the navy. He just felt the urge to set fires, I guess."

Whitaker took the umbrella from her and angled it more into the wind. "We found out that his family died in a fire when he was thirteen. Mother, father, grandfather, younger sister. There were rumors around that little farming community about how that fire started, but no one looked into it. It must have been a relief for everyone when Steggans was sent to live in a religious-run home for kids, where he'd be kept on the straight and narrow. They turned him loose at eighteen, and he joined the navy a few days later."

"More straight and narrow."

"Yeah. We traced back a few years and found a few arsons in his ports of call, so apparently he'd been indulging himself from time to time. But I guess it finally got too imperative to ignore."

"He kept talking about 'the power.' He liked the feeling of destroying something, and watching everyone running around trying to stop it."

Whitaker's eyes chilled. "You should have seen his apartment. Crammed to the teeth. Furniture, books, gewgaws, anything you could think of. He'd painted his bedroom grey—a little memento of his service days, maybe—and there was hardly enough room to walk. Like he'd needed everything pressing around him to keep himself from escaping."

Lou stared down at her feet, which were encased in unaccustomed high heels. Mud had begun to lap above the soles. Warm as it was, a chill ran through her. She'd never be able to understand the Fire Man; maybe no one who could remotely claim sanity could. At least she'd stopped dreaming about him.

"Are you okay?" Whitaker asked.

"Maybe this," she indicated the mourners around them, "wouldn't be so hard to take if George had been killed because of that inspection scam. But that . . . nut didn't even know about it. It just seems so unfair."

"Fair would have been Steggans's mother miscarrying him."

She drew in her breath sharply. Harsh as it was, Whitaker's statement was true. Maybe the only truth she was going to find in this. The wind tore water from the edge of the umbrella and slung it into her face. Whitaker wiped it away as though it were tears.

The ceremony ended, and the crowd dispersed quickly. Lou stepped out from under the umbrella to meet Harry Deveraux as his wife wheeled him down the sidewalk.

"Hi, Harry," she said.

"Hey, Lou. So you beat the Grim Reaper one more time, eh?"

"I'm trying to make a habit of it." Lou glanced at Helen. "Why don't you let me take that umbrella? I'd like to talk to Harry alone."

Whitaker came forward. "Come on, Mrs. Deveraux. I'll walk you to your car."

"Well, all right. Harry, don't let yourself get agitated, now. You know what the doctor said."

"Yeah, yeah." He waved her off. Turning back to Lou, he asked, "What's the scoop? Did they get everything straightened out with Steggans?"

"He's dead, if that's what you mean."

He shook his head. "Man, that was weird. The cops said they thought George and that other man were killed by someone else involved in the inspection scam. And then it turns out to be the mad arsonist, who was trying to kill *you*. My daughter would call it a cosmic error."

"She might be right."

"Christ, I never would have thought it of Steggans. I mean, he didn't have the experience for his job, but he wasn't stupid, and he certainly didn't look like some mad arsonist. Goes to show that you can never tell."

"No," Lou said. "You never can tell."

She looked down at this man she'd admired for more than twenty years. He'd brought her into his department and taught her everything he knew. He fought for her raises and promotions, gave her room to work but backed her when necessary. In a way, he'd been almost a father to her. Now, he'd aged to fit the part. Deep creases etched his cheeks and forehead, and a wattle of skin hung down from his chin.

"Jay turned himself in last night," she said.

His eyebrows went up. "No kidding. What did he have to say?"

"He went in with me to Van Allen today and took

full responsibility for sending the *Gabriella* out with a faulty weld."

The creases in his forehead deepened. "What did Van Allen say?"

"He wanted to keep it quiet, of course. I told him either he got that repair fixed in whatever shipyard is handy, or Jay and I go public with it."

"No shit! Would Jay do it?"

"He wants his wife to take him back. She won't consider it unless he makes things right." Noticing that the rain had all but stopped, Lou closed the big umbrella and tucked it under her arm. "He's willing to spill his guts about the inspections, Fagan and almost anything else. But there's one thing he's keeping to himself, isn't there, Harry?"

"Huh?"

"He's not willing to admit that he and George were *told* which inspections to slip."

"Told? By whom?"

"By you, Harry."

Color bloomed in his cheeks. "Now, just a minute—"

"Shut up and let me finish," she said. "Everyone told me they had to be taking bribes. But I just couldn't buy it, not with George Fagan. I knew that man ten years, Harry, and I know it would take something other than money to get him to do what he did. And what would it take? Loyalty. And who was the one person who could command that kind of loyalty? Only you."

"Bullshit."

She crossed her arms over her chest. "Okay, let's forget loyalty for a moment. George Fagan didn't have the brains for this, and Jay didn't have the guts. They didn't even like each other much. Somebody else set it up, and somebody else orchestrated the cover-up. And that same somebody told Jay to hide out and gave him the money to do it. The whole time he was hiding out, he never touched the money in his own accounts."

Harry's mouth clamped into a thin line. He grasped the wheels of his chair, gave them a spin. Lou grabbed the armrests and stopped him, leaning over to stare directly into his eyes.

"I know why you did it," she said. "You saw the yard slipping away, and did whatever you could to hold things together. But it was wrong, Harry. And it didn't work. Van Allen had already decided to lay off seven hundred people—planned it for months. The slips went out yesterday. What do you want to bet it's only the beginning? He's not going to be able to hold things together, Enterprise or no Enterprise."

"Damn." Harry's shoulders slumped, and he aged visibly. "All right, Lou. I did wrong. I didn't think there was a choice. Those Enterprise jobs represented a last-ditch stand for us; without them, there is no shipyard."

"Not a boiler-valve weld," she said. "You knew better."

"I knew it was better than the alternative." He closed his eyes. When he opened them again, she saw the sheen of tears. "I had to do it," he said. "Van Allen is a poop. He doesn't know ships or shipyards, and I knew he didn't have the guts for the tough times ahead."

"I know," she said softly.

"What are you going to do? About me, I mean."

She slid her hands off the chair arms, wiping them dry on the front of her dress. "I told Van Allen you were planning to retire."

"What?"

"All you have to do is confirm it. Say something like the surgery has given you a good, stiff jolt of awareness of your own mortality. You want to take time to enjoy your wife, travel, do all those things you haven't had time for."

"And if I don't?"

"Then I'll tell the police about you. How long do you think Jay will hold out if they lean on him?"

He grimaced. "Jay was always the weak link. Smart as hell, but he didn't have the balls for something like this. I would rather have had you," he said. "But you've got that damned, stiff-necked honesty."

"You always said you admired it."

"I do. But it's still a pain in the ass."

She sighed. "I'm sorry that I have to do this. But you don't belong in QA any more. You stepped over the line, and you can't be trusted not to do it again."

He clasped his hands together. Lou had to look away from the shame on his face; she'd prepared herself for defiance, cussing, all the typical Harry Deveraux reactions. But not this. He seemed to shrink before her eyes. It might be justice, this thing she'd done to him, but it didn't feel like it.

"Are you going to step into my shoes?" he asked.

At another time, in another tone of voice, the statement might have been a challenge. But not today. "Actually, Van Allen said something about promoting Bostwick," she said. "He even asked my opinion about it. I told him Mason would do an excellent job."

"Bostwick? He's only been there six years. By rights, that job should be—" He broke off, a stricken look in his eyes.

Gently, Lou reached and laid her hand on his shoulder. "That's why I love you, Harry."

"I'm sorry, Lou. Sorry for everything."

"So am I." With a sigh, she walked around to the back of the wheelchair and started pushing him toward

378

the car where Helen and Whitaker waited. "I quit to-day."

"What?" Harry's voice went up in surprise.

"I've accepted an offer from Meclaren's over in Norfolk. They've just landed a government grant to study construction of double-hulled tankers. It's the future, and I'm going to be in on it."

"You've got more than twenty years at Carmichael's. You can probably get Steggans's position—"

"Van Allen already offered that. I turned him down."

"Jeez, girl, it's such a risk!"

She glanced over at Whitaker. Beside Helen's sophisticated perfection, he looked like a bum after a hard week. "A little risk is good for a person," she said. "Under the right circumstances."

Reaching the street, she handed Harry over to his wife. Whitaker helped lift the older man into the car, then closed the door and took Lou by the arm.

"Did he agree to do it?" he asked.

"What choice did he have?"

"None, I guess." He slid his arm around her waist. "Are you okay?"

"Right as rain." And to her surprise, she found it to be true. "What's on the agenda today?"

"Mmm, Blaire's going over to the house to supervise the reconstruction. Your son, of course, will be bird-dogging her trail."

"If you were him, would you let someone who looked like her spend the day with a bunch of construction guys?"

"Never. Now, back to the agenda. Kelsey wants to go to the pet store—"

"Not hamsters," Lou said.

"Blaire says Shamu is grieving for her babies."

"Cats and hamsters don't mix."

"Everything mixes in the Whitaker household. Somehow."

Too true. "And after the pet store?"

"I'm taking the day off. We can argue this marriage thing for a while, and then . . ." he grinned, that slow, lascivious smile that did all kinds of interesting things to her insides, "what do you say we take another shot at the Holiday Inn?"

"Compromises go both ways," she said. "I'll go for the hamsters and the arguing . . . *if* we hit the hotel first."

"Done!"

As she'd said so many times before, life beckoned. Only this time, it was true.